Roger Su[dden]
by
Thomas H. Raddall

INTRODUCTION: J. R. Leitold
GENERAL EDITOR: Malcolm Ross
NEW CANADIAN LIBRARY NO. 85

McClelland and Stewart Limited
Toronto/Montreal

The Canadian Publishers
McClelland and Stewart Limited,
25 Hollinger Road, Toronto 374

Printed and bound in Canada by
T. H. Best Printing Company Limited

Contents

Introduction

Having "lived and played and worked almost his whole life as a Bluenose amongst Bluenoses," Thomas Raddall has been able to perceive the visible rhythm of life on the Atlantic coast, and has experienced the sense of continuity and permanence which the Canadian Maritimes exudes. Along with this personal familiarity with the region, he has diligently acquired a wide knowledge of Nova Scotian history, which has given him not only recognition as a competent historian but also a sensitive understanding of, and a close sympathy with, the Maritime character, shaped as it has been by the uncompromising demands of the sea and the self-inflicted pressures of political, social and cultural forces. Indeed, although born in Kent, Raddall insists that he *is* a Bluenose. And because he has this certainty about where his roots are, he has not been plagued by an "identity" neurosis, unlike many of our Canadian writers in the past.

But the sense of place that infuses Raddall's historical novels is not self-consciously cultivated. On the contrary, it is the happy product of merely telling "tales"; his preference for writing historical fiction, Raddall says, was motivated simply by a desire to make a living as a writer and to write about a subject that he knew best – eighteenth-century Nova Scotia. Yet this apparently casual approach to his writing disguises an intense passion for history and a strong conviction that the historical novel is an ideal form with which to probe cultural roots, a belief implied in this angry response, delivered in a public lecture several years ago, to criticism persistent in Canada and elsewhere that the historical novel is "escapist" or at least fails to deal seriously with its subject:

"Many critics . . . utter the contemptuous phrase 'escapist literature,' as if the historical novelist and his readers had fled into a cave to dream of some golden Elysium while heroes outside manfully faced the storm. Escape! Escape into what? Is the atomic bomb a greater reality or a more frightful one than the plague of the Black Death in the fourteenth century, which killed a quarter of the population of Europe, and in some countries as many as three-quarters? Is the present war in Vietnam any worse or even as bad as at least a hundred wars in the past?"

Critics of the historical novel have perhaps been persuaded to see it as escapist because the standard line of action in the romance is the motif of flight. The hero is compelled to flee in the face of real dangers, and hence swift movement within the novel is guaranteed. Although Raddall certainly employs this convention in his novels, along with coincidence and the introduction of historical figures and incidents, his purpose is not merely to link episodes and to facilitate movement within the novel, but rather to structure his work and to promote larger aims.

Nowhere is this better illustrated than in *Roger Sudden*. A characteristic feature of Raddall's historical fiction is a focus upon growth, whether it is the maturation of an individual character or the birth of a frontier commmunity. Thus, in the novel, Sudden undergoes a *rite de passage* which forces him to adapt to several cultures, exposes him to physical suffering and mental anguish, and prolongs an agonizing self-deception. "Like Theseus entering the labyrinth," Sudden is confronted with his most severe physical ordeals after being carried off by the MicMacs, and his Ariadne offers no aid to ease his suffering. From his initial feelings of astonishment and fear at the cruelty of the Indians, particularly the women, he comes to admire their endurance and patience, to understand their innocence and to envy a freedom circumscribed only by the seasons. He finally sees them as Raddall has portrayed them, not a group of noble savages or a nineteenth-century literary convention but, like the Acadiens, an exploited and oppressed race caught up in a dynamic struggle in which they have no stake, and who, like the white man, experience pride, hunger, lovesickness, anger and superstition, and possess an "overmastering resolve to find and kill." And Raddall invites his reader to share in the cyclic rhythm of MicMac life, poignantly expressed in terms of Indian legend:

"Winter was a bitter thing. Life was a thread, no more, quivering in the north wind, never far from breaking. . . . The Frost Giants screamed and smote them furious blows, besieged them with white armies and tree-cracking frost artillery, and paused with a silence that made the ears ache. . . .

"In the vast silences, the least sound carried far. From the forest, now near, now far, came those mysterious knockings which the savages knew only as *keaskunoogwejit* – "the ghostly woodcutters." And on the nights of intense frost came the steady woomp-woomp-woomp of pressure cracks ripping the thick ice of lakes upstream and echoing down the wooded glen like thunder. . . .

"Spring was a joy that came slowly, with fits and starts, with sunshine at hide-and-seek with snows and rains and fogs. . . .

"Summer was the time of ease, of warmth, of indolence."

But Sudden's long absence in captivity and his return to Halifax serve to emphasize the slow growth of the garrison, viewed earlier by Sudden as "a brown sword cut in the green flank of Citadel Hill, festering under the heat and flies, erupting sores of canvas and brush-wood, and swarming with human maggots," and now still only "a palisaded almshouse." He immediately compares this pitiful sight with the well-defended fortress at Louisbourg, knowledge of which he has gained through the beneficence of the coincidental character, Mme. Ducudrai. Yet Sudden senses a certain vitality, a permanence about Halifax that remains unarticulated and has no connection with its appearance, but which Raddall wishes his reader to see as sympto-matic of the popular spirit that finally defeats the French.

It is these intangible qualities which Raddall is able to communicate so vividly. He is adept at distilling the essence of historical character (Sudden is drawn from the lives of real Nova Scotians, Michael Francklyn and Joshua Mauger) and using it effectively for his own purposes; diligent about ensuring the accuracy of the facts that he uses (Wolfe did not land at Coromandière as commonly believed, but some distance round the point at the east end of Colonel St. Julien's battery); and skilful at introducing history through dialogue, as well as by direct narration. But his particular forte is his uncanny ability to penetrate history and permit his readers to share in the imaginative experience of a past reality, to recreate scenes so ac-curately and vividly that the reader can himself possess the sense of place and time. Raddall's descriptions of Halifax's "Drury Lane," of the festivities at the Great Pontack, of the "curious tumult" of emi-grants and soldiers ashore at Point Pleasant eager to lay out the town properties, and of the clearing of the forest so that construction of the garrison may begin, are superb. He captures perfectly the energy and dynamism of a people enduring tremendous hardship as they try to ensure a foothold in an overwhelming wilderness:

"The summer marched — and its footsteps burned. . . . But it was the immigrants who truly suffered. They came ashore from the transports, the 'husbandmen,' the 'artisans,' their women and their noisy broods, pale from the London streets and the confinement of the ocean passage, twenty-five hundred of them swarming between the hilltop and the shore. The sun blistered them. The black flies tor-tured them by day and the mosquitoes by night. They rubbed the sunburns and scratched the bites, and broke out in sores and blamed it on the food. They chafed their hands on the ax handles and cut themselves with the blades. They felled trees on each other and suffered the crushing consequences. Children scorched themselves in the slash fires and were lost in the woods and fell off the makeshift wharves. The 'reputed surgeons' of the Whitehall advertisement went from overwork to indifference and at last to disrepute. But the clear-ing grew. . . . And the town began."

And, with a few deft strokes, Raddall contrasts this scene nicely with the static and secure life at Louisbourg, as Sudden makes his night escape from the fortress:

"Dusk at last, and the sea creeping in gray wisps between the warehouses; and the scrape of a fiddle somewhere down the Quai, and Breton voices raised in song. A woman's laugh in the alley, a slap and a man's voice urgent in the dialect of St. Jean de Luz. A roll of drums from the ramparts beating the retreat. The gray of the dusty windows black at last. A scurry of rats in the silent Magasin de Rodrigues."

In the same way that Sudden's education and the growth of Halifax mutually emphasize each other, ambient themes reinforce one another in *Roger Sudden*. The motif of flight again serves to integrate these themes. Indeed, early in the novel, Sudden romantically describes himself to Mary Foy as a "wanderer," a man without king or country. Thus, dismayed by the lack of support in England for the Jacobite cause, for which he has endured several years of exile on the continent, Sudden chooses to go to America in search of his fortune, symbolically perceived in terms of prosperity as the Golden Woman. And though he is convinced that his method of wooing her will be more effective than that of the seamen of Wapping, he is as fascinated as they "by the notion of those golden breasts beyond the seas." But Sudden is cast adrift in more subtle ways. Deprived of the lodestone that had given him an identity as a supporter of Bonnie Prince Charlie, Sudden discovers that he is lost – just as the Stuart cause was an *ignis fatuus,* so England itself assumes an illusory dimension, a quality hauntingly described by Raddall as the ship carrying Sudden sets out on its perilous voyage to America:

"Like a fire of cannel coal at the water's edge, the sun flared yellow behind black bars of cloud, touching the Isle of Wight with long pale rays that gilded the headlands and hilltops for a few moments and then were gone. The shadow of the heart of the land crept out, and now it was all a mystery, an illusion in the twilight, now near, now far, now part of the solid darkness in the east. A few lights pricked out of the dusk. Somewhere a sea bird cried, like a wail from the heart."

Raddall has thus adroitly introduced a second theme – the distinction between illusion and reality – and has linked it to Sudden's unconscious search for himself, again metaphorically described, in his conversation with Old Hux, as a challenge cast by an inarticulate foe, " 'a riddle to be solved, a game of chance with strange cards.' " This theme is sustained throughout, even during his brutally real baptism into the New World by the Indians when, to save Sudden's life, Gautier advises him to *pretend* that Wapke is " 'a beautiful virgin under the spell of a sorceress, like the old hag in the tale.' " And this theme serves to illuminate the phases of Sudden's progression from footloose rake and adventurer through cynical and opportunistic merchant to self-sacrificing hero. These several themes climax with Sudden's recognition that the Golden Woman, too, is a self-deception, a delusion that is finally pricked and "made human by some alchemy that had to do with himself." Ironically, too, it is the seemingly impregnable fortress of Louisbourg that succumbs to "a rush of ignorant redcoats under a madman" and is blown away, while it is the tattered collection of English huts at Halifax, vulnerable and apparently transient, "a cluster of lonely fires in the darkness of a continent," that endures and fills Sudden with "a strange impression of permanence." This feeling remains a puzzle for him until, stirred by the sight of the emblem on the caps of the English grenadiers, he aids the British attack on Louisbourg and the source of his unease becomes clear. And, like David Strang's decision in *His Majesty's Yankees,* Sudden's is also more personal than patriotic: " 'I tell you simply there must come a time when the soil of his birthplace means more to a man than all the world.' "

All these psychological conflicts occur against the background of the French-English struggle for supremacy in Canada, a contest into which Sudden is thrust involuntarily by the nature of the role of exploitative merchant that he has cast for himself. As a result, he becomes familiar with the positions of all three combatants – French, English, and Indian – and thus his resolve to ally himself with the British is much more substantive. But most significantly, Sudden discovers that identity is not simply an image that one creates of and for oneself, but rather an individuality fashioned in relation to others or, more appropriately in his case, out of an attachment to place.

J. R. Leitold,
Dalhousie University

PART ONE

England

CHAPTER I

Warrior's Return

IT WAS NOT the home-coming of his dreams; but then so many dreams had come to nothing in the past three years. And he had grown used to furtive journeys. Only details differed enough to mark one from another—details and destination.

This time it was England after all the wandering. A small and frowzy lugger had carried him across the Channel and set him afoot by Romney Marsh in the early winter dark. The crew had pointed the way to New Romney and gone about their business, which had to do with fifty ankers of right Nantz brandy in the hold and a number of shadowy men and ponies at the head of the beach.

At New Romney the last of his money got him a horse, a poor galled beast, worn out, he suspected, in the brandy trade, and a saddle that a gypsy would have spat upon; but he was in no position to bargain and no mood to walk. The horse coper gave him a dram for good measure, and with the nag between his knees and the brandy glowing under his belt he jogged along the dark home road, whistling *"Auprès de ma blonde"* and thinking of the look on his brother's face.

There would be no father to give him a prodigal's welcome, for the merry drunken squire had died last year. This he had learned from a wandering man of Kent abroad. His mother had died of childbed fever when he was born. Brother Charles had inherited Suddenholt together with his father's debts, his father's thirst, and his father's younger son—liabilities all. He grinned when he thought of that.

Earth and sky were one bowl of ink, with a keen wind across the marshes from the east, and presently it began to rain, a few hard-flung drops at first and then a torrent slanting on the wind. His cloak whipped about him for another mile or two and then became too sodden to flap any more. Water seeped into his big jack boots and bubbled between his toes at every wriggle of his chilled feet in the stirrups. He took off his hat to unbutton its high French cocks and let the rain run out of its gutters, and rode on with the great brims hanging and flapping like an old wife's bonnet come untied. A wild night. But he had lived too close to the weather for too many months to care very much about it now. What mattered was that it was English rain, aye, Kentish rain, with a wind over the Downs that smelled of Kentish sea and Kentish earth. The mud that splattered the poor hack's legs was Kent itself, the good brown flesh of it.

It was something to be a man of Kent. He had decided that early in his Oxford days when one of the exquisites who lorded it in those halls of learning twitted him with a smell of hops. He had given the fop a bloody nose and told him to be careful how he sniffed a Sudden and a man of Kent. Thereafter he was known as "Sudden" Sudden. He had lived up to it so far. He smiled a little in the rain. Fore-thought had never been one of his virtues. Even this journey home had been undertaken on the spur of the moment, the outcome of a fit of melancholy in a small Italian town. The girl Simonetta had wept and implored in the dramatic Italian manner, and he had kissed her firmly and taken one of her new green silk garters to bind his queue and gone. She would find other lovers, as she had before.

For himself, the world was full of women, none of whom mattered very much. He was a little appalled when he thought how many there had been. He could not even remember all their names. Tall girls in the little Highland villages with worship for Prince Charlie in their blue eyes—and open arms for those who followed him; laughing girls with fine white breasts in Donegal and Connaught and the merry town of Cork; elegant patch-and-powder Parisiennes who took their amours as their husbands took wine, as often as possible and with a keen taste for a new flavor; sly-eyed and moist-lipped daughters and wives and servant girls in far-scattered billets in France and the Rhine towns and Spain and Italy. Yet he had never

gone out of his way to chuck a chin. They had come to him in lonely
bothies in the Scottish hills, in drawing rooms and inns and billets on
the continent, murmuring commonplaces for the world's ear but
breathing a little too fast, lingering a little too long, avoiding his
eyes, and gazing over his shoulder with a sheen in their eyes that was
nothing but the sun on Eden's apple tree.

He had taken what they offered, pleasantly, and gone his way. Not
without adventure. There had been jealous husbands and other in-
conveniences. There had been blows and swordplay, stones flung and
cudgels wielded in the darkness of foreign streets, and once an absurd
affair of pistols at fifteen paces on the riverbank outside a French
garrison town. These matters, like the women, he had taken carelessly. His heart was his own and his mind was always on the
Chevalier, for like many another Jacobite in exile he had found King
James too cold a man for worship. Three years he had followed
Prince Charlie's one bright star. And now he was going home.

At Boulogne he had picked his day and his passage carefully,
lolling on the quays, sipping brandy with luggermen in the cabarets
of La Beurrière. The chosen day was January thirtieth, when in
Jacobite clubs the length and breadth of England men would be
gathering to drink the memory of Charles the Martyr—and the health
of the king "over the water." Such a club had been founded by his
father on the lines of the famous Cycle, meeting in rotation at the
homes of its members in a compass of fifteen miles; and so he had
reckoned on a landing just after sundown, a decent piece of horseflesh, and a frosty road to put him in Suddenholt not later than ten
of the clock.

These nice calculations had gone amiss. The lugger lost time in
dodging a revenue cutter off Dungeness; the horse was fit for the
crows and the weather not fit for a dog. The road was at its wintry
worst. It would be midnight at the very earliest, and, short of a
miracle, the club would be far too drunk for his business. Fortune of
war! He shrugged his wet shoulders and spurred the melancholy nag.
Slowly they drew out of the flatlands into the woods and pastures of
the Weald. An eternity passed before he rode out of the wood above
the village and saw a few late candles pricking the dusk in the
hollow. But his mind's eye could see the place as if it were daylight:

the cobbled street, the old half-timbered houses and shops clustered about the small market place, and the tall church tower rising grandly out of the huddle. As a boy the church had fascinated him. He remembered the mounting stone with its five steps for portly horsemen like his father, the massive oak door, the queer carven woman-faces that ornamented the ends of the chancel arch, the great oak pulpit with its marvelous carving done in the time of Queen Bess, the painting of St. Michael weighing souls and the evil spirits trying to pull down the little mannikin in the scales, the altar rail carved like a twist of rope twelve inches round, the heavy oaken pews and choir benches—all wood from the Weald, all the work of village craftsmen going back through centuries.

When he thought of it now, with his new-found cynicism, he wondered what sort of men were able to put pleasure behind them for so long a time and for so little reward.

But now he saw the dark bulk of Suddenholt aloof in its hundred acres, with the avenue of oaks and beeches tossing a wild tangle of naked branches across the lit panes of the lower chambers. The big wrought-iron gates were closed.

He rode up to them and drew the handle of his riding crop sharply across the bars and hailed the porter's lodge inside: "Crockham! Crockham! I say, Crockham! Crock! Open up!"

Silence. Another rattle and another shout. The lodge door opened and an old man came, wrapped against the rain in a moth-eaten watch coat that might have served him soldiering in Queen Anne's Wars. One lean hand clutched the faded cloth about his skinny throat and the other held a lanthorn before him. The lanthorn's bottom kept his legs in darkness and his torso seemed to move on invisible wheels toward the gate, an uncanny spectacle. He held the fluttering light up to the gate and peered. The delicate ironwork of the gate was a thing of beauty then, wet and glistening in the candle flicker, and Roger felt a warmth within. Good Kentish iron, dug out of the earth and smelted over furnace fires of charcoal from the Weald itself—there was an old furnace pond behind the house—and hammered and wrought by stout-armed and cunning-handed smiths in the forest forges generations ago. Or was it centuries? He had never been much good at history. It was enough to be part of it, a

Sudden, a man of Kent (for "Kentish men" were another breed), a son of the great White Horse— *Invicta!*

"Who are you?" he cried, and then, "I know. You're old Kittle from the village!"

The old soldier blinked and muttered, dazzled by the lanthorn's fuzzy radiance in the rainy dark.

"Why, Kittle," the horseman said, "you're drunk!"

"Like master, like servant," returned Kittle, intelligently enough.

"Damn your impudence, Kittle, let me in and get back to your bottle."

"Not without the word, I don't. Nunno! Gentlemen's meetin' and I got me orders."

"Umph! Well, unless it's changed since I last tipped a bottle with the gentlemen the word is *Fiat. Fiat,* Kittle, then. *Fiat,* ye drunken fool!"

The toper set the lanthorn down with care, fumbled, brought forth the big key at the end of a belt chain. The lock clicked, the bolts were drawn, and the gates swung slowly wide. Roger rode through and pulled up the horse, looking down at the fuddled wretch fastening the gates. The old man turned and held up his light.

"You're young Roger! Home from your jackanapesing. And none the better for it, I'll warrant. Face brown as a carter's, ecod! Where've ye bin?"

Roger grinned and chanted in the singsong of the nursery rhyme, "Been to London to see the Queen."

Kittle spat. "No queen in Lunnon but that High Dutch woman. Don't doubt there was a woman in it, though."

Roger nodded toward the house, and the wet brim of his hat flapped wetly.

"Is it . . . ah . . . the usual?"

"Ay, too dam' usual for the good o' Sud'n'olt." And, vindictively, "And them that works for Sud'n'olt. Parson's there, and Sir Jeremy and Mr. Frampold and that feller Cheveril as I never did like and——"

"Where's Cousin Penny?"

"Off to stay the night wi' Miss Boyce at Den'urst. She's allus sent away when there's to be an evenin's drinkin'. Or hev ye fergot, young Roger?"

Kittle chuckled. "Never did see a young gen'leman drink like you, from time ye was seventeen. And I've seen fair drinkin' in me day, what wi' your father diggin' his own grave wi' the bottle screw, and your brother and the rest——"

"Never mind that! My brother's well, I take it?"

The porter leered. "Oh, he's well, is Charles. Holds his wine well, Charlie does. Allus had a stiffer head than yourn. Experience . . . him ten year older and all. Ye sat a better saddle, Roger, I'll say that."

"Get indoors," Roger said curtly, "before you catch your death."

He put spur to the Romney hostler's nag and sprang away toward the house lights under the heavy drip of the trees.

The stables were deaf to his shouts. He swung a cramped leg to the ground and groped his way inside. The stalls were filled with the horses of his brother's guests. He walked carefully past the row of tail-twitching rumps in the dark, whistling softly for Anne and Colonel and Gloss and Dainty without the ghost of a whicker in reply. He had an alien feeling, as if he had walked into a room full of strangers. A dozen leaks in the ancient roof were pattering on the flags. The crazy doors and shutters rattled and thumped in the gusts. The wind thrust cold fingers into the warm, horse-reeking gloom. The place was a ruin. The stables had needed repair as long as he could remember, but never so much as now.

He went out and tethered the Romney nag to the old iron hook by the door. He was tempted to walk down to the kennels to see if the dogs would know him in the dark, but he put that aside. The dogs could wait.

He set his face toward the house, his heavy boots splashing in the rain pools on the worn stone flags. He went in by the servants' door, his favorite approach to the stables in the old days. In the kitchen he found an old woman he had never seen before, sitting over a gin bottle by the hearth.

"Who are you?" he demanded. She was a filthy thing.

"Faggott," she announced after a long stare.

"Where's Bramshaw?"

The hag chuckled. "Gone a twelvemonth. Dunno as I blame un, neither. No wages for a matter o' five year. Same wi' the Marden man and his 'ooman. More kicks than ha'pence to Sud'n'olt nowadays."

"Where's the stableboy?"

"Where?" She leered, and gestured with the bottle toward the front of the house. "Ye'll find stableboy in there, pretty man. Ye mayn't see un right off, like, but ye'll find un, ye'll find un!" Her voice trailed off in a long, tipsy giggle that went on and on behind him as he swung away.

A single candle guttered at the end of the drafty hall. In the east drawing room he found three common tallow dips burned down to their butts in a brass candelabra gone green for want of polishing. The long-untrimmed wicks drooped like shepherds' crooks. In such a light all things must look unkempt, but there was something frowzy and unclean here, as if a succession of slatterns had swept dirt into the corners for months on end and gone their ways. The west-drawing-room door was closed, with a low buzz of voices on the other side.

He rapped on the panel and stepped inside. The wet folds of the cloak muffled him still, and the drooping cocks of the big French hat concealed his face.

The scene within was comfortable and familiar. Here, at least, nothing had been changed. The shades of poverty and neglect which in his father's time had begun to creep on Suddenholt like a winter mist out of the woods had never darkened this chamber, and there was no sign of them now.

Silver gleamed on the whiteness of good linen and gave back the glow of the great six-branched candelabra on the table. The dishes of the dinner, doubtless begun at the fashionable hour of four, had been cleared away, and a pretty array of his father's wineglasses marched in file about the great round board. Each of those fine-drawn glasses, with their lovely air-twisted stems, was engraved with the royal Stuart cipher and a verse of "God Save Great James Our King."

In the midst of it all sat the mighty silver bowl, filled with water for the rite of the supreme toast. Over such bowls tonight, in meetings such as this, the Jacobites of all England were clinking glasses of smuggled French wine and crying, "The King!"

Roger wondered cynically what would happen if they could see "over the water" to that royal refugee in Rome. These convivial scenes were as far removed from the austere and gloomy exile in the Palazzo Muti as earth from heaven.

The tall case clock in the hall struck one. The club had been drinking long. The chamber was thick with tobacco fumes, fresh and blue in the light of the candles or hanging in stale gray wreaths about the seated figures like a ground mist on an autumn morning. Some of the long clays were cold and laid aside, the owners probably under the table. He could see a pair of stout legs protruding in wrinkled silk stockings and silver-buckled shoes. A snuffbox had scattered its contents over the carpet, and there was a litter of pale fragments where a pipe had fallen.

On the long mahogany sideboard against the old dark wainscoting stood his father's fine flint-glass decanters, each with its ivory ticket hung on a silver chain about the neck to announce the wine within. All were empty now, and the table was cluttered with dusty bottles straight from the cellar, some standing, others scattered like ninepins among the pipes and corks and bottle screws.

A dozen guests had sat down to dine, apparently, and three had succumbed. He could hear them snoring under the board. Others would soon be there. He surveyed them all with a dark contempt: Parson Balleter, with his round red face and his sober black surtout and waistcoat; Gilbert Royce of Amblemere; lean Barcombe Tarver in his great full-bottomed wig; Sir John Harroll, sitting drunk and solemn as he sat so often in Parliament; the young fop Harry Storer, in a blue frock coat with gold buttons, a watered silk waistcoat trimmed with silver, red velvet breeches, and silk stockings; Barry Cheveril in a Spencer tiewig; round, purple-faced Charles Frampold; pale, moonfaced Baxter Rivers in a white coat with plate buttons, gold brocade waistcoat, and white satin breeches, all stained with claret; old Sir Jeremy Waystrode, with his periwig's forelock brushed three inches high in the fashion of King Charles the Second.

They stared at him stupidly, Sir Jeremy with mouth agape and his queer false teeth of carven ivory grinning together like the teeth of a skull. But Roger's brother rose and faced him, frowning and defiant.

Three years had not changed Charles very much. Indeed a lifetime's self-indulgence had left surprisingly few marks upon him, though his handsome face was flushed and swollen with this night's drinking. His eyes were bloodshot but steady. The suspicion of a paunch spoiled the cut of his pink silk coat and gold-embroidered waistcoat, but he carried his shapely bagwigged head in the Sudden manner, poised and sure, and he had a huntsman's shoulders.

The others looked like a parcel of schoolboys caught at some guilty game. It occurred to Roger that they did not know him in the cloak and the drooping and shapeless hat. He tossed them off.

"God's blood!" Charles cried. "It's our Roger!"

CHAPTER 2

God Save King James

THERE NEVER HAD BEEN MUCH LOVE between the brothers. They were too much alike, though Charles was ten years older. Both had the bold black Sudden eyes and the paradoxical family nose, curved and sharp yet small and shapely, that had in it all the Sudden history—robber Norman at the root, with privileges won in the train of the Conqueror, a hard temper softened a little by marriage with the pleasant Kentish women and polished by centuries of ease at the cost of their tenants' sweat, but not too far refined for rude enjoyments—and the strong, thick-fingered Sudden hands, the plowman's hands that went so oddly with their small neat heads and narrow feet.

"Have you supped?" Charles said easily.

Roger was amused. He might have been gone for an afternoon's ride.

"On the road, after a fashion. I could do with a dram, though. Where's the stableboy?"

"Here, sir!" said a muffled voice. A freckled and shock-haired head appeared from beneath the board, thrusting up the hanging tablecloth in a sort of cowl that gave him the ludicrous look of a monk.

"What's he doing there?" Roger demanded.

Charles shrugged. His voice was cool and even, his tongue a little thick. "To loosen the gentlemen's neckcloths when they fall out of their chairs. Done in the best Cycles nowadays, I assure you. Brann, go and put up my brother's horse."

The boy scrambled forth.

"What'll you have to drink, Roger?" Charles went on. "We're

sticking to claret, of course, in the fashion of the club. But there's some good Mountain in the sideboard and a very fair Madeira."

"Madeira, thanks."

There was an empty chair by Charles's own, and Roger sat and poured himself a glass. A stupid silence hung over the guests. They were far gone.

Roger murmured, "I should have come earlier."

"Don't you think," Charles snapped, "you've played your little mystery long enough, Roger? After all, it's been three years or more. You owe an explanation, I think. But perhaps"—he ran a glance about the board—"perhaps we could talk a bit in private. My guests will excuse us, I think."

He led the way into the library, where a sea-coal fire had sunk to gray ash and the candles were at their last.

"Now, my lad, stop posing like a play actor and let's have it all— why you decamped from the university, where you've been, and why you've come back now like a thief in the night."

"I've a few questions of my own to be answered first. What's happened to Suddenholt? How did Father die? Where are the horses? The old servants?"

"Ha! Well, Father died in a drunken fit, if ye must know, young Roger. Under his own table. Wore a fine cambric neckcloth that night and choked to death for want of someone to loosen it. That's why I keep a boy under the board when there's to be serious drinking. Don't look at me like that. What d'ye expect when a dozen full-blooded men sit down to thirty or forty bottles of Margaux?"

"A number of things. For one, when the heir of Suddenholt provides forty Margaux at a sitting he must sell his horses to pay for 'em, and let repairs go hang and——"

"My dear Roger, the heir of Suddenholt inherited nothing but debts. As a fact, Father sold the horses. I merely sold the dogs."

"Ah!"

"The old servants left because they couldn't get their wages, and the new ones are insolent because they know they won't get theirs. Now d'ye understand? I tell you, Roger, the moneylenders begin to hover over Suddenholt like crows about a corpse. The only thing that keeps 'em off is Cousin Penny's money."

"I see. And what'll Cousin Penny live on when you've poured the last of her money down your throat?"

Charles's black eyes glittered. "Don't take that tone with me, Roger. Who are you to criticize? The money you had at Oxford was Cousin Penny's, if ye come to the fine point—Father was borrowing from her funds with one hand and paying your bills with the other. And for what value? You quit the university—with some woman, I don't doubt—the price of an education flung away on tapsters and a trollop!"

Roger laughed. His teeth showed white and even. "We'll be at each other's throats in a moment, and I think I should warn you that I've learned the art of slitting throats since I left home. You see, Charles, I quit the university for Prince Charlie's army."

"Eh!"

"Why so astonished? A good Jacobite should fight for his rightful king, shouldn't he? Or should he? You were too busy drinking King James' health to join the fight for his son's. You and the others . . ." Roger waved a disdainful hand toward the other chamber.

"Suppose," Charles said coldly, "you tell me your adventures. I'm sure they must be interesting."

"That's handsome of you, Charles. The word is misadventures. I joined the Manchester Regiment, the only Jacks in all England willing to put their sentiments to the test of the sword."

"And the hang rope, surely? I seem to remember Prince Charlie left his Englishmen in the lurch."

"He asked 'em to guard his retreat and they did. After their capture the Manchester officers were hanged and the men flung into jail and transported to the colonies. I escaped from Carlisle the night before the surrender and made my way through Scotland to the prince's army. I stood with him at Culloden and wandered through the Highlands with him for a time afterward. When he went to Skye I remained in the north—I spent a year in the heather altogether, an education in itself, Charles. The Highlanders drink a cordial they call usquebaugh, not a bit like Margaux; and they drink the king's health with a foot on the table, standing up like men, you understand, and not down on one knee like you old-fashioned cavaliers. A remarkable people, not without their points. I made my way at last through the Isles to Derry, and then southward afoot the length of Ireland. From Cork I took ship——there was some formality about scrubbing decks and hoisting sails, and I was a long time getting the tar off my hands—and got to France, and so to the prince's side again. It's not much to talk about, really."

"I see. And now England's patched up a peace with France, and by the terms of it France agrees to expel the Stuarts and all their works, and so you've come home."

"Try not to sound so smug about it, Charles. The game's not over yet. The Chevalier was arrested and thrust out of France like a leper, true. And, true, there was sanctuary for him at his father's house in Rome. But Prince Charlie's not the man to sit and moon in Italy with swords to be drawn and his father's throne to win. When I left him a fortnight ago he contemplated a return to Paris in disguise. More—he intends a visit to London."

"You're not serious!"

"This year or next."

"For God's sake, why?"

"For the reason I've come myself. To meet some of the Jacobites of England, to find out where they stand and how much they mean. To be or not to be, that is the question. Will you and your friends cry 'Fiat' then, Charles?"

He could not keep the malice from his voice.

"The thing's impossible!" Charles uttered harshly. "Has he learned nothing from the '45?"

"Nothing."

"And you want an answer to take back to him, is that it?"

"I want an answer. Whether I take it to the Chevalier or not depends on the nature of it. If it's no—there's an end to everything, for I've no mind to wander up and down the continent watching him drift from drink to women and from women to perdition. I'd rather remember him as I knew him first. If you could have seen him then, Charles! On the road to London at the head of his little army, wearing a short tartan coat and kilt, and the order and emblem of the thistle, and with the white rose of the Stuarts in his bonnet—by heaven, there was a man!" Roger's dark face glowed under the brown. "He looked like a prince out of a book, and had the manner. Yet he'd be first to ford a stream in the frosty Highland mornings, and he lay down in his plaid at nightfall like any rough ghillie on the hillside."

"And yet," Charles said, "he fled when all was lost and left the Scotch to hang and bleed for their faith in him."

A hot blaze sprang in Roger's eyes. "That remark would cut your throat today, Charles, anywhere between Clyde and Moray Firth, for all the hanging and the bleeding. But that's your answer, is it? You won't lift a finger, much less a sword, if the Chevalier should come to England? Is that the mind of all the Jacks you know?"

His brother answered in a chilled voice, "My good Roger, our allegiance is to King James . . ."

"Who sits in Rome and counts his beads!"

"Precisely. He don't want the throne. So why should we put our necks into the noose for some wild whim of his son's?"

"And all this"—Roger waved a hand toward the far chamber—"all this huggermuggery—this drinking to a king over the water?"

"A sentiment. Toward something that was charming and is dead."

Roger stood up and put aside his glass half tasted.

"Where are you going?" Charles said indifferently.

"To bed and to sleep, if those guests of yours don't howl too loudly."

"And in the morning?"

"I leave England for good."

Charles was silent a moment. A nerve twitched in his cheek.

"Why, Roger?"

Roger paused, feet planted apart in the heavy riding boots, his old blue frock coat opened carelessly, his hands rammed deep in the waistcoat pockets.

"Because," he said deliberately.

"A woman's reason. What shall I tell my friends?"

"I could give 'em a dozen man reasons. None would afford 'em any satisfaction. Say I've no wish to live in an England that suffers a German king and hasn't the spine to fight for her own."

"Too heroic, Roger. A line from a bad play."

"Then say the prodigal found the parable askew—the swine at home and the welcome abroad."

"And that's insulting."

Roger sauntered to the door. Over his shoulder he said carelessly, "Why not tell 'em the truth?"

"And what is that?"

"That all honest men in England and Scotland have been hanged or transported to the colonies, that I didn't care to be hanged, that I've gone to join the others."

The door slammed at his spurred heels.

Charles sat long in the chair, regarding his blue Morocco shoes with their high red heels, his left hand playing with the silver chain about the Madeira decanter's neck. He felt that he had kept his temper admirably. Now the heat of the wine had somehow gone out of him and he felt cold and empty and . . . and old.

The rain beat on the panes; the wind howled in the great chimney. From within doors came a chorus of drunken voices lifted in song—a Jacobite song.

He shivered—and went back to them.

CHAPTER 3

Promise to a Lady

THE HAG IN THE KITCHEN got Roger a breakfast of sorts. There was no sign of the other servants or of Charles. The sun was barely over the edge of the Weald, a wintry sun that poured a pale yellow light over the east slates of the roof and struck fire from the raindrops hanging from the eave spouts. The weather was clearing, with a great hurry of dark clouds across the sky, and the air gave a hint of frost by nightfall.

He had slept well in the few hours left of the night. He had a vague recollection of doors opening and banging, a scatter of drunken footsteps, and much shouting in the stables toward morning. He found his hat and cloak in the west chamber, where he had flung them off, keeping silent company with the stained cloth and the litter of bottles and shattered glass. A cork floated impudently on the symbolic water of the great silver bowl. He lifted the cloth and peered with a whimsical curiosity under the table, half expecting to see the recumbent forms of the club, or at least the stableboy waiting still. All were gone. The chamber reeked of stale tobacco and spilled wine. He buttoned the cocks of the old French hat and swept it against his chest in an ironical bow to the empty room and went out with his head up, a hand grasping the hilt of his hanger and its scabbard lifting the skirt of his cloak behind like the tail of a jaunty dog. His heels rang on the flags outside, and the silver spurs—gift of a naughty lady in Milan (or was that in Verona?)—jingled the merry tune that had followed his heels through Italy and France.

The stables were empty save for the New Romney horse. The poor screw looked in place in that ruin by daylight, a rack of bones wrapped in a galled hide and fitted with head and tail. It gave him a whicker of welcome and accepted the old wooden saddle with resignation. Outside he mounted and paused for a last look at the house, searching the casements for one glimpse of a friendly face. Only Faggott looked out at him from the kitchen panes, blinking in the sunrays from the east, a dissolute ghost. He shrugged and rode away. The porter's lodge was as dead as the house. The trees still dripped with the last of the rain. But the gates stood wide, and as he passed outside he called an ironical *"Fiat!"* at the drunkard's door. There was no reply.

Three miles along the road he heard a clatter of hoofs ahead and saw the apparition of a coach and pair coming toward him along a lower level where the morning mist hung thick. Only the coachman and the dew-wet top of the coach and the tips of the horses' ears were visible, swimming in the vapor.

Roger pulled up at the roadside, and as the horses strained up the hill into sight he recognized the venerable equipage of Sir Miles Boyce of Denhurst. He swept off his hat, chiefly to allay the suspicions of the wary coachman, and held up his open hand. The fellow pulled up with a tremendous "Whoa! Whoa-hoa!"

The panel of the door flew open, and out popped Cousin Penelope's head, each eye a large round inquiry. Roger swung to the ground and went over to her, smiling.

"Roger?" Cousin Penny said. "Roger! Oh, my dear!"

She was not changed. Her cheeks were as thin, as sallow as he remembered them, the lips as tremulous, the eyes as sad and enormous. She wore a cloak against the morning cold with the hood thrown back, exposing the fine Valenciennes fichu drawn about her head. She put out a hand, and Roger stooped over it gallantly, hat under elbow. Three years ago he would have condemned such behavior as "foreign." It came very easily now. He straightened, and Cousin Penny regarded him with her liquid black eyes. "Oh, Roger, how *nice* to see you! It's years since I saw you, but of course it can't be, for you only went up to *Oxford,* didn't you? How handsome you've grown! Did you come with the gentlemen last night?"

"Yes," Roger said. It was simpler than explanations.

"And now you're out for a ride before breakfast. What it is to be a *young man!* A night over the wine and then into the saddle for the morning *air.* So like your dear father. No weariness! No weariness! Dear me! I shall be seeing you at dinner, Roger, shan't I? There's so *much* you must tell me. Are you *very* wise with all your learning, Roger? And *where* did you learn to kiss a lady's fingers?"

All this in a light, sweet voice that had the tinkle of a thin silver bell. That was how he always thought of Cousin Penny, somehow—as a small, thin bell, quite empty except for the little clapper running on and on. He hesitated. It would have been easy to pass on his way with some remark light and disarming and trust that she would forget all about him by the time she reached Suddenholt. The devil of it was that she would probably remember; she would question Charles, and Charles would be brutal in his careless, contemptuous way. Cousin Penny's mind was so easily bruised. He said carefully, "Cousin Penny, I'm going away for a time. Probably a long time. I'm going to the colonies."

She gave a start, fingers at mouth in her poor silly way. "So far, Roger?"

"Every young man must seek his fortune now that the wars have come to an end."

"Must you seek your fortune, Roger? I have money."

"Not enough for me!" he cried gaily. "I want the wealth of the Indies, no less. I shall come home and drive you about in a coach and six, with a little black boy to hold your fan in summer and your muff the rest of the year."

She said one of those shrewd things that came out of her confused mind at times, disconcerting because of their very unexpectedness.

"Shall you bring home money enough to make Suddenholt what it was when you were young, Roger?"

He was a little startled that she should have seen his dream so nakedly.

He said gravely, "I shan't come with less, I promise you."

"And you're going to the colonies? Which one, Roger? There are so many, and I'm told the weather is very hot in all of them. *Do* keep your hat on there."

"There are two ways to go, Cousin Penny—east and west. I'll toss a sixpence when I get to Rochester. What's it matter? East or west, the fortune's the thing."

Her big eyes roved over him, and he was acutely aware of his hat with its frayed silver lace, the weather-stained blue cloak, the battered leather of his jack boots, the travesty of horseflesh at the end of the reins. A sad equipment for the road to fortune. The Boyce coachman, blowing his fleshy nose in a large red handkerchief, inspected him from the depths of it with undisguised contempt.

"Are you sure you've told me everything?" Cousin Penny said plaintively.

"Everything except that you're very beautiful this morning and I can't keep a lovely lady sitting in the cold."

A blush spread over her cheeks and her eyes sparkled.

"You talk like your dear father—such a charming man. And you'll come back, Roger? Say you'll come back to Suddenholt again!"

"I swear!"—hat against heart. He caught her fingers again, kissed them, and swung into the old wooden saddle with a cavalier's grace.

"Hup!" cried the coachman, and snapped his whip over the steaming bays. Away they went with Cousin Penny's handkerchief fluttering forlornly from the panel.

Roger rode across the heart of Kent, drinking it in like a beast of the desert before leaving an oasis, wishing it could be summer for this one day but seeing beauty nevertheless in the bare trees and thorny hedgerows, the night's rain lying like silver in the brown field furrows, the smocked men and red-cheeked women moving placidly at tasks about the ancient farms. Absence had sharpened his sight, somehow; there were details he had never noticed before, like the wisps of vapor rising from each sodden thatch where the south slope caught the sun.

At Maidstone he halted for mutton and ale and gave his sad-eyed steed a rest. Here he had first gone to school. He remembered the day his father took him there and how he had pointed out the home of the Astleys, once the palace of the archbishops, reflected then, as now, in the bright still waters of the Medway with its tall chimneys and its great square tower. "There," his father had said, "lived Sir Jacob Astley, who fought for his true king at Newbury against that sour fellow Cromwell, and made a prayer for soldiers that all young men should remember:

> *"Lord, I shall be very busy this day;*
> *I may forget thee.*
> *Do not thou forget me."*

In Rochester at dusk he put up at a small inn by the waterside and, to pay for his night's lodging, sold his faithful hanger (still nicked in the blade from Culloden fight) to a naval lieutenant from the Chatham docks for ten shillings. He wondered why he had come this way, seeing that Rochester had no trade with the colonies. But of course he had come by the instinct of a man of Kent—following Medway water to the sea. *Invicta!*

He discussed his prospects cautiously with the lieutenant over a pot of purl and learned that instinct is a poor guide in such matters.

"The colonies!" cried the lieutenant, a hook-nosed man with a stiff knee got at Belle Isle with Admiral Hawke—or so he said. "London's the place to find your way to the colonies, lad, and Bristol's better. Waste no time here. O' course ye might go down to Deal for a chance with an Indiaman in the Downs." He added shrewdly, "Ye haven't the look of a sailor, nor a farmer—and God knows there's more farmers than sailors goes to sea—I'd say ye were a gentleman down on your luck. Now a colony's no place for a gentleman unless he's got a guinea or two in his breeches, aye, and a good few more sewed away in his waistcoat somewhere. Business, d'ye see? It don't matter what kind so long as ye can read and write and know the sum o' two twos.

India—that's the place for a gentleman! 'Struth! The niggers'll let a sahib have for sixpence what they'd charge any other man a guinea for, aye, and wait on him hand and foot for nothing. It's got to be seen to be believed. In a few years ye'll have a fine house, full o' servants, a business that runs itself, money from nowhere, your pick o' pretty Hindu women to while away the time, and a boy to pop curried meat in your mouth to save ye the trouble of eating. Why, I know Calcutta pilots that live like nabobs, and they ain't even gentlemen!"

"That's a long way from home, the other side of the world," Roger said restlessly. "I had a notion of Jamaica, myself."

"Ah! Well, mind this, young feller, the farther ye go the better the pickings. Jamaica, says you. Well, that's old ground for white men. There's creole whites in the islands who can count five generations back, all soaked in rum and lime juice. They've got a grip on trade in those parts that ye couldn't pry loose with a handspike. Best a young gentleman like you can hope for is a post as factor or writer, maybe, on one o' the sugar estates, where ye'll be worked like one o' the niggers and get precious small pay for it. No good, I tell ye! Them that ain't carried off by yellow jack take to rum and black women and go to the devil at a jog trot. Now in India——"

"What about America? Have you been there?"

"America?" The lieutenant made a mouth. "All wild savages, outside a strip along the coast. Not like the Indians of India, mind, that's got jewels and mohurs and such stuff to come by in the way o' trade. A lot o' naked heathen with nought but a feather, a fur, and a clay pot to bless 'emselves. I've only seen the ports, myself. *They're* full o' Yankee traders, a sharp lot—skin a louse for its pelt—bless the Lord through their noses—look upon a man from England as a foreigner. Find yourself swinging a hoe in the tobacco fields. Or piling stockfish in a Boston warehouse. Lucky to get it. No place for a gentleman. Take my advice—India or stay at home."

With which advice the lieutenant strapped on the hanger over his striped flannel waistcoat, drew a tarry blue surtout over both, tossed a shilling on the board to pay the reckoning, tipped a wink to the barmaid and a hand to Roger, and went off to Chatham.

A day along the quays, talking to bargemen and seamen, was discouraging. The end of the wars had smitten their trade like a blight. Ships and men were idle in every port between the Needles and the Kyle of Tongue. Even the press gangs had vanished—a phenomenon. The navy was actually discharging men by the thousand. Add to these another multitude discharged by the army, and the crews of privateers out of a trade with the peace and you had a pretty kettle of fish.

Roger's mouth grew longer as the tale unfolded. Rochester was overrun with men paid off at Chatham, money gone, and begging now at every tavern door and about the cathedral steps. Roger gave away the proceeds of his precious hanger before he realized the folly of it. The innkeeper was rather impressed with his manner but doubtful of his clothes, and demanded a daily payment of the reckoning.

Roger searched his worn saddlebag for something else to sell. The little looking glass was not worth sixpence. He could not part with his razor or his spare shirt and stockings, and wild horses could not have dragged from him the great cairngorm brooch Prince Charles had given him when they parted in the Highlands.

The silver spurs, then. He hated the thought. It had been wrench enough to part with his faithful hanger—like parting with a good right hand; but the cheerful music of the spurs at his worn boot heels had been a stay and comfort all these weary months. He pawned them for a guinea and was rich for a week, telling himself that he would redeem them at the first turn of his luck and knowing dismally that luck lay somewhere beyond the sea.

What troubled him most was his own uncertainty. His restless mind had always given him a quick decision in the past, to be followed for good or ill. Now he was lost. He had thrown away the loadstone of the Stuart cause which had led him into such strange and perilous scenes. Suddenholt was impossible. Oxford had given him a smattering of learning, no more. His impatient Sudden mind had hated the drudgery of study and leaped too eagerly at the university's devout faith in the Stuarts. He wanted passionately to get away. But where? Where? There was no answer—not in Rochester, at any rate.

CHAPTER 4

On the King's Highway

HE TOOK THE LONDON ROAD on a bleak February morning with a purse as empty as his mind. The way was deep in mud, but the Romney nag stepped blithely after his long rest, snuffing the salty air as if he smelled in the offing the brandy luggers of home. Along the road they passed little knots of seamen tramping hopefully for London. Men were tramping to London from all the ports, from all the garrison towns, as if London were some kind of Mecca in this hardest of hard times.

They cadged for money as he passed and cursed him foully when he said he had none to give. He was tempted once or twice to get down and teach them better manners, but swallowed the notion and kicked the nag to a trot.

A sea mist drifted across the Thames marshes, cold as charity. Parts of a flat and dreary landscape emerged and vanished in the uneasy white swathes. The few yards of highway before and behind was always the same, and he had a whimsy that the horse had led him upon some sort of treadmill that revolved and got him nowhere.

Houses were few and far apart and had no life about them to the passing eye, looming as dark square shapes in the vapor to right or left and sliding behind without a word, without a footfall, without the sight of a face. A dog barked once, that was all. He had passed long since the last of the ragged pilgrims who had set out afoot from Rochester that morning, and when he came upon a gibbet the illusion of a dead world was complete. The horse gave a great snort and shied at the thing. Roger brought him down with a savage jerk on the bit.

"That's your bad conscience, my old smuggler. Steady now!"

He looked for a crossroad, but there was none. The gibbet stood against the high road in the midst of the waste. Its outstretched wooden arm dangled a corpse in chains. The dead man had hung there many weeks, since autumn, probably. A paper setting forth his crime had been fastened to the post but had rotted and blown away, its outline marked with a pattern of rusty nailheads. The flesh of the corpse had rotted and gone too, except for his face, which was tarred to preserve it for the purposes of the law; and that black mask had shrunk against the skull, eyeless, with lips gone thin and wrinkled like old glove leather snarling away from a set of very good teeth. Rags of clothing hung loosely on the bones—a round blue jacket and a pair of wide, short-legged slops such as seamen wore. Someone had stolen his shoes. A bight of rusty chain drooped between the anklebones and another fastened his wrists before him, and the whole lamentable ruin hung from the gibbet by another rusty chain fastened to an iron collar about the neck.

The hanged man carried his head slightly to one side, which gave him a quizzical look, and the wet breeze from the Thames turned him slowly from side to side, so that he had a horrible air of watching for someone to come along and take him down.

Roger inspected these details with a cool eye. He had seen a good many dead men in the past three years. He speculated on the hanged man's crime, and while he meditated, with the uneasy horse wincing under him, a harsh voice cried, "Money or your life!" It seemed to come from the thing on the gibbet, but now Roger saw a grassy bank behind it, rising steeply from the roadside, and on the top of it, vague but menacing in the mist, the figure of a man very much alive.

The man came nearer rapidly. He wore a jacket and trousers of the sort that clothed the corpse, and a small blue hat thrice cocked, and had a large red Barcelona handkerchief tied about the lower half of his face. This much Roger saw distinctly—and something else. All the menace in the man's voice and attitude was concentrated in the object in his hand, a large horse pistol pointed straight at Roger's stomach.

"You offer a beggarly choice," said Roger, sitting very still.

"I know no better," said the man, coming down the bank. His hair was gathered in a short pigtail stiffened with tar. A pair of yellow metal rings dangled at his ears.

"The trade cry of a footpad," Roger said. "You look more like a sailor—and a damned unhandsome one at that."

"Handsome is as handsome does. Get down."

Roger got down. "I have no money," he said.

"That's what they all say."

"Would I be riding this bag of bones if I'd a guinea for coach fare?"

The fellow looked him up and down and ran a hard gray eye over the horse.

"Turn out your pockets—and no tricks, mind! Off wi' the cloak, fust!"

Roger unfastened the great brass button at his throat and gave the cloak a twirl as if to throw it off. For a moment the flying cloth hung widespread in air between him and the highwayman, and in that moment he dived swiftly at the fellow's legs. Down they went together in the mud, Roger smiting a hard fist into the other's belly. The highwayman uttered a gasp of anguish and struck at Roger's head with the heavy pistol barrel. The blow fell on Roger's shoulder; he caught at the wrist thus exposed to him and wrenched shrewdly, drawing his knees under him and throwing himself forward. They struggled together in silence while the horse looked on and the dead man on the gibbet kept his endless watch upon the road. Five minutes passed. They rolled over several times in the mud. In one of these convulsive movements Roger found his chance, slipping his right arm under the other man's, forcing it back, turning himself away and working his hand and wrist under the fellow's chin. He tautened his arm sharply then and the man uttered a terrible cry.

"Ahhhhh, God! Don't break my neck!"

"The hangman will do that. Have ye had enough?"

The fellow made a desperate effort to free himself, but now Roger had a firm grip with his legs as well. He set his muscles again, and again the fellow screamed.

"Give me the pistol," Roger said. He felt for it with his left hand. The highwayman opened his fingers and let the weapon go.

Roger jumped to his feet. The man remained in the mud, groaning, feeling his jaw, and twisting his head from side to side. The red kerchief had slipped from his face in the struggle and revealed a nose like a potato, a wide mouth grimacing with pain, a set of strong jaws badly in need of a razor.

"Where'd ye learn that trick?" he gasped, without looking up.

"In Lancashire."

"Ye talk like a Kentish man."

"I'm a man of Kent," said Roger, with the pointed pride of those born east of Medway. "Where did you learn the highway trade?"

"Here," said the fellow ruefully. "And little good it's done me. Four shillin' off a sluice man from the marshes and a brass ticker that don't keep time." He went on feeling his jaw. "You're a cool un," he observed in the process. "That there pistol's loaded and well primed. I might ha' shot ye dead."

"Not this morning, my friend. A pistol held abroad in a drizzle like this would miss fire every time. If you'd held it under your jacket I'd have given you more respect. What's your name?"

"Tom Fuller."

"Seaman?"

"Yes." He added an oath for emphasis.

Roger nodded toward the gibbet. "So was that pretty piece of fruit up there, by the cut of his slops."

"Jemmie Calter, that was. I knowed him well. Shipmets with Jemmie, I was. As good a pair o' seamen as Old England ever fed poor vittles. The things we seen! Last Michaelmas we was paid off at Chatham. Cursed small pay it was, too. Jemmie drunk his up inside a fortnight. Then he was for Lunnon, straight off. But I had a sweetheart, Gillingham way, and stayed there buying her ribbons and such. All for nought, mind. Fortnight ago I was down to me last farden and she ups and offs with a half-pay lootenant as was old enough to be her father. So I lifted a pistol off o' the gentleman she kep' house for and took arter 'em. 'Tweren't no use. Diddled me, they did, somewhere atween Faversham and Canterb'ry. So I offs for Lunnon, and what do I see by the road here? Why, old Jemmie hisself, tucked up like a bloody mutineer for liftin' of a farmer's purse, and a bit o' paper nailed to the mast a-settin' out his crime. Knowed him by the shoes, I did—which same I'm wearin' now—and my old brass button on his sleeve that I give him for a keepsake in Jamaiky."

"Some thief that lifted Jemmie's clothes," suggested Roger for the sake of argument.

"Besides which," said Tom Fuller, sitting up, "there's Jemmie's teeth as clean as a hound's and his big toe a-missin' as he lost under

a carronade in a blow off Gibberaltar. That's him all right. And now"
—with a dreary eye on the gibbet—"you're a-goin' to turn me in and
do the same for me that's just a poor seaman down on his luck and
never got a penny off ye. Waitin' for the tidecoach from Gravesend,
I was."

"What for?"

The seaman shrugged. "Them that can afford the coach can afford
a bit o' road tax."

Roger considered. "That's the most sensible thing you've said this
morning. Get up out of the mud."

Tom Fuller got up slowly. "Goin' to turn me over to the coach
guard, I s'pose?"

"Not so fast. A toll for the king's highway intrigues me, Tom
Fuller. I've an empty purse myself."

"God's blood! I thought ye was a gentleman."

"I am a gentleman—short of cash. Now what's it to be—a share of
the dibs or hang at next Rochester assizes?"

"I'm with ye," said the seaman promptly.

"Good! Now about the guards . . ."

"Two outriders—about two lengths astern as a rule—and a feller
on the box beside the coachman with a blunderbuss."

"I see. This calls for a horse and high stratagems. Follow me."

He rode on slowly to the next milestone, Tom Fuller trotting at
his stirrup. The mist was thicker toward the Thames, and the smell
of the marshes was overlaid with a gust of salt, of old fish, of the
tide-borne filth of London.

"Wait here, off the road a bit," Roger said. "I'll bring the coach to
a stand by the milestone. You're to run out and catch the horses'
heads."

"Hark!" snapped the seaman.

From the fog toward Gravesend came a crack of whip and the
splash of hoofs and wheels. Roger galloped his nag two hundred
yards along the road, turned off, and rode a little way into the mist.
The coach was nearer than he thought. It appeared almost at once,
four big black horses dragging a fat yellow vehicle through the deep
mud at four hard miles an hour. Two dim figures sat on the box,
huddled in cloaks against the cold and wet. The coach was splattered

with mire and the glass door panel was obscured by the breath of the passengers. It lurched past and out of his view. An enormous wait. Then the outriders, ambling along the roadsides for the better footing there. He rode into the highway behind them, wondering how soon they would hear the splash of hoofs at their backs. They seemed absorbed in their own discomfort, two shivering fellows in battered cocked hats and thin, round jackets. One lagged a length or two behind the other, and Roger was up to him before he sensed new company. He turned sharply and found the pistol muzzle at his side.

"Get down," said Roger in a whisper, "and do it quietly or you'll never drink another pint of porter."

The fellow slipped out of the saddle without a word. Roger caught his bridle and trotted up to the other horseman. This one heard the double splash of hoofs and turned his head idly.

"What——" he began, and saw the pistol.

"Off with you!" Roger said. The man slid off into the mire, mouth agape.

Holding both captured reins in his left hand, Roger now kicked his steed into a shambling gallop. He drew abreast of the dripping hind wheels, then the spattered door and its gray-vapored glass. Just ahead to the left the milestone gleamed white in the fog. His hat was level with the coach box.

He shouted, "Stand! Stand and deliver!"—pointing the pistol at the man with the blunderbuss. The man turned a pair of popping eyes and at once cast the gun into the road as if the thing were hot.

The coachman bellowed, "Stand be damned!" and raised his whip for a lash at the horses, but now Tom Fuller ran out of the mist and caught the reins of the front black on the nigh side, jerking its head back savagely. The horses reared at this apparition. The coach stopped with a jerk.

"Get down," Roger said. They scrambled to the road, the coachman swearing.

"Tom!"

"Sir?"

"Mount one of the outriders' horses and hold the other. You'll find pistols in the saddle holsters."

"What about these 'ere coach horses?"

"They'll stand."

Tom swung himself up and drew a pistol. Roger abandoned the New Romney nag for the other outrider's horse. He rode up to the coach door, which was opening to make way for a strong voice demanding, "Coachman! What the devil d'ye mean by——" The voice ceased abruptly. Its owner was a man in the forties with large light eyes very wide apart, a pointed nose, and a short mouth with little irascible folds at the corners. A thick traveling cloak was draped about his broad shoulders, but Roger could see a rich red velvet frock coat embroidered with gold lace, a glimpse of blue satin waistcoat, a ruffled shirt with a good deal of fine Flemish lace at the throat, and a pair of black velvet breeches. There ought to be a fat purse in such breeches. On the seat beside him sprawled a most ungainly young man of twenty-one or -two. Everything about him was long and meager: his body, his legs, his nose, which turned up sharply at the end, his neck, his face—his face was like a reflection in a too-cheap mirror. His upper lip sloped away to the mouth, and his lower lip sloped in to the throat with little or no chin between. He was wigged and curled like the other and, like him, wore a gold laced hat with high military cocks, but his heavy cloak was muffled about him, leaving nothing to the eye but the lean, silk-stockinged shanks. There was no one else in the coach. Evidently the martial pair had engaged the whole accommodation to be sure of their own company.

They looked at the pistol and then at Roger's face, trying to outstare him. The older man's expression was a quaint mixture of anger and amusement, but it was resigned, it accepted the situation. Not so the long young man's. His large eyes were balls of blue fire under the knitted carroty eyebrows.

Said Roger quickly, "Keep your hands away from your sword hilt, if you please, Major Wolfe—it *is* Major Wolfe, isn't it?"

The blue eyes blazed higher. "Who the devil are you?"

"Never mind, sir. Your hand—don't tempt me, I beg, for I could kill you with a great deal of pleasure, I assure you."

"Why?" barked the older man.

"And you too, Colonel—it's Colonel Belcher of the Twentieth, isn't it? I have the advantage of you both, I see."

"You talk like a gentleman," said the young officer stiffly. "Are you gentleman enough to own your name?"

"I'm not fool enough, Major. Besides, it wouldn't mean anything to you. You've never seen me before, except at a distance, amongst a great many others, and in much tumult and bad weather. You see, I was at Culloden—on the Stuart side of the field."

"Ah!" said Colonel Belcher, nodding.

"He's trying to frighten us," snapped young Major Wolfe. "Tell me, Sir Highwayman, what you saw of me at Culloden."

"Not much, I admit," Roger answered promptly, resting the heavy pistol barrel across his left forearm and watching them warily. "You were on old Hangman Hawley's staff, safely removed from the broadswords. I remember you best before the battle, about Aberdeen, robbing the Highland gentlefolk in the name of King George."

"Name one instance!"

"Mrs. Gordon, for one instance. Why, you even stole a picture of her son because old Hawley wanted the frame. Everyone in the Highlands knows that."

"Pish!" said the young man irritably. "Why should I defend myself to a thief?"

"The pot calls the kettle black. As for you, Colonel Belcher, I remember how your regiment slaughtered the wounded on the battlefield and the fugitives along the road. Their hands were as red as their jackets when they got to Inverness. That butcher Cumberland must have been proud of you and them. Do you sleep well o' nights, even now? But don't answer—it's your money I want, and the devil with your conscience. Your purses, please!"

"You'll be happy to know," Belcher said, drawing out a heavy silk purse and flinging it out into the mud, "that I'm giving up command of the Twentieth to Major Wolfe here—and it's still stationed in the Highlands, where you come from, I suspect."

"Your purse!" demanded Roger of the major.

"Shoot away!" said the young man defiantly.

"Tut! He would," Belcher said. "Don't be such a rash young fool, Wolfe. One of the first things a soldier has to learn is to recognize superior force and yield the field."

"There," cried Roger, "speaks a man who has seen Fontenoy and Prestonpans!"

Belcher twisted his lips as if those memories were sour indeed. "You seem to know a great deal about me, Jacobite. I wish I knew half as much about you."

"I don't doubt that," Roger said, deftly catching with his left hand the purse which the young major tossed toward the open door. "I may be able to tell you, someday when King James comes into his own. Tom, my boy, cut the traces of the coach horses and give 'em a lick down the road. You"—motioning with the pistol to the crestfallen guard—"pick that purse out of the mud and hand it up to me. I hope your fare has better manners when he comes to pay his coach hire."

"Hup!" cried Tom Fuller to the horses, and away they went toward Rochester.

The coachman and guard watched them disappear into the mist with doleful eyes. A little way behind the coach stood the discomfited outriders, mud to the calves. The New Romney horse had wandered off into the mist, cropping the poor winter grass.

Roger swept off his hat gracefully to the officers and rode away toward London whistling "Hey, Johnnie Cope, Are Ye Waukin' Yet?" for their pleasure, while Tom Fuller rode at his side.

As the derelict coach and its forlorn group faded into the vapor behind, Tom slipped the handkerchief off his face and exclaimed, "Ecod, sir, you're a game un!"

"How so?"

"Standin' up the tidecoach—three armed men, more for aught ye knew—with that there pistol o' mine as got its primin' soaked in the fog this mornin'!"

Idly Roger pointed the pistol at the road ahead and pulled the trigger. The flint snapped down in a torrent of sparks, the priming flared, the long muzzle jumped and spat a stream of fire between the horse's ears. The report was like a thunderclap.

The horse reared and plunged indignantly and Tom Fuller said, "Well I'm damned!"

"So am I," said Roger Sudden thoughtfully.

CHAPTER 5

Tooley Street

FOR CAUTION'S SAKE they left the London road, with its hazards at both ends—the horses were sure to be recognized at the Gravesend post inn, and there would be a lively hunt from Rochester when the stranded coach was found—and struck westward across the fields. Tom Fuller steered by the sun, a pale white coin in the fog, and with this guide, and by a maze of paths and lanes which they used as it suited their purpose, and by no small amount of luck, they turned toward London at last by the Epsom road. It was nightfall then, with the horses badly blown and Tom complaining that "all the skin was off his transom," so they abandoned the foundered beasts in a field and walked stiffly into the village ahead for a bite and a sup at the inn. Tom was for sleeping there, but Roger said no. "The horses will be found in the morning, and those postriders' saddles are a dead giveaway. We must leave 'em far behind tonight, my friend. In London we can disappear and none the wiser."

So they pushed on afoot and saw the first lights of the city from the crest of Streatham Hill. They were weaponless, for Roger had flung away Tom Fuller's empty pistol as they left the Rochester road, and the postriders' heavy weapons were too awkward to carry concealed and too easily identified in the open.

There would be a fine hue and cry. The young major of foot would not count for much, but the Honorable Edward Belcher was another matter. Roger thought whimsically that life would be very difficult for wandering sailors on the Rochester road in the next few weeks.

Walking was difficult in the mud and darkness, especially for Roger in his jack boots.

A light breeze blew down the Thames, and the air was crisp and clear, with a cold fire of stars overhead. It was very late when at last they trudged through the empty waste of St. George's Fields into Southwark. Most of the houses were dark, and they had a mean look in the starlight. Roger halted.

"I don't know London very well, Tom, but I've a feeling we should go over the Thames by boat. There's only London Bridge to cross afoot, and the watch there will give a sharp eye to such vagabonds as you and me."

"Ye won't get a wherryman this time o' night," Tom said.

"Then we must find lodgings this side the river. Do you know these parts?"

"Well enough. South'ark's a thieves' rookery, sir—Dirty Lane, Foul Lane, Blackman Road, Stony Street, Dead Man's Place, Bandy Leg Walk, Love Lane, Maid Lane—and that's a joke, I tell ye, for there ain't a virgin in the borough. Them buildin's yonder in the edge o' the fields is the Surrey Bridewell and the King's Bench Prison. Over there to starboard is hospitals—Guy's and St. Thomas—and another jail. No place for a gentleman like you."

"On the contrary," quoth Roger, "it's the very place for gentlemen of the road like both of us. Lead on, my Tom. None of your Love Lanes and Thieves' Walks, either. There's a thoroughfare down the right bank of the Thames. I see a church; there must be Christians in those parts."

"That's St. Olave's, in Tooley Street."

"And could we get a wherry, think you, nigh Tooley Street in the morning?"

"There's Tooley Stairs, right below London Bridge, sir."

"Ah! Now I seem to recall a rhyme concerning nine poor tailors of Tooley Street that called 'emselves 'We, the people of England.' A tailor that squats on his bench all day must have a place to stretch at night. Lead on! A lodging in Tooley Street!"

Tom knocked at three doors before he got an answer. A nightcapped head was thrust from a window overhead, a sharp male voice demanded their business, and a hoarse female voice within suggested loudly that it could be no good at this hour of the night.

"Lodgin' for the night," said Tom promptly. "We're two cold sober sailormen that has good money to pay."

The window closed, footsteps came, and the street door opened on a stout though rusty chain. The face that regarded them by the light of a farthing dip was incredibly evil, an old thin man, hook-nosed and snag-toothed, with a straggle of dirty white hair under a red flannel nightcap.

"See their money fust!" urged the female voice. "A shillin', mind!"

Roger thrust one of Major Wolfe's florins into the light. The door opened magically.

They stepped inside and found themselves in the presence of a huge woman whose vast red face was so hairy as to be well-nigh bearded. She was wrapped in a large shawl over a greasy nightgown, and she held in one mighty fist a cudgel of stout blackthorn.

"You're no sailor!" she said to Roger at once.

"This florin says I am," he returned. She took it, bit it, closed an eye, pursed her hairy lips, and grunted, "It's the garret, mind! Sal's bed, but she ain't 'ome tonight. Ye'll 'ave to be out before breakfast, though. Sal's pertickerler, 'specially when she's 'ad a good night of it."

"This way," the old man said. They followed his lean shanks up three flights of rickety stairs and stepped into a low chamber containing a flock bed, a broken chair, a looking glass, a box draped with a piece of muslin and apparently used for a dressing table, and some odd-ments of female clothing hung on nails along the wall. The old man put the dip on the box, announced in an oily voice, "Stay longer, if ye like. Sixpence a day each, mind, and sixpence, say, for Sal. Sal's obligin'. Seafarin' men like Sal, they do." His thin giggle trailed away down the stair well in the dark.

Tom looked at the bed. "Poor 'commodations for a gentleman like you, sir—a strump's pallet in a South'ark slum."

"I'll sleep on the floor," said Roger. "And so will you if you're wise."

Tom prowled about the garret with the light. "Everything's clean, sir. No bugs, that's a comfort. This 'ere corner's still wet where the floor was swabbed 'smornin'. Why, I've see worse quarters in a public inn. I'll take the bed if ye don't want it."

"First," Roger said briskly, drawing the purses from his pockets, "we'll divide the spoils." He emptied the coins upon Sal's dressing box and counted them off in two exact portions. The purse of Major Wolfe contained six guineas and some silver. Colonel Belcher was the richer man by far—by eighteen guineas to be exact.

"Look 'ere, sir," Tom said, wide-eyed, "you're a-splittin' 'em even!"

"D'ye want more?" Roger said.

" 'Struth, sir, ye know what I mean. You did it all—bold a piece o' work as ever I see, and I've see some bold lads in me time. . . ."

"I say half."

Tom said urgently, "Beggin' your pardon, sir. You're a gentleman and I'm jest a poor seaman on the beach, but—but d'ye think, sir—I mean to say would ye mind if—if we was to sail in company? I'd be your servant, like. I wouldn't be in your way, sir. I could do things for ye, sir. . . . I'd do anything for a man like you. There ain't many like you in England nowadays."

"There'll be one less in a week or two," Roger answered brusquely. "For I'm off to the colonies the first chance I get. And gentleman be damned! I'm out for my fortune, any way I can get it, anywhere! I'm putting home behind me . . . and all that goes with it. You—you're just home from years abroad in the King's ships. Take the money and find yourself a good healthy girl, that's my advice, and buy yourself a dramseller's license Bristol way, where the seamen come."

"Girls and drams! I want to go along o' you, sir, that's what I want. Look 'ere, sir, ye can't afford to go without me. Fortin! I can show ye where fortin is. In the West Indies—in the seas about Jamaica for choice. I know a crick in the Cuba coast, with good huntin' in the Windward Passage a couple o' gunshot away, and I know where ye could get a good fast sloop and pick up some stout lads . . ."

"It smells like piracy. What! A sea highwayman?"

"Why not, sir? There's more'n one gentleman like you made a fortin at it and settled down respectable in Jamaica with a creole wife and a carriage-and-four and a summer house in the mountains. Long as ye leave the English ships alone, the admiral on the Kingston station won't trouble his head about ye. There's good pickin' amongst the French and Spanish as ever was, and there's the fat Dutch traders out o' Curry-sow."

"How did you learn all this?"

Tom grinned. "I jumped the *Burton* frigate off o' Tiberoon along o' three other lads, in the summer o' '45, and took over the mountains to the French plantations about Gonaives. Afore long we fell in wi' some buccaneers—English, French, niggers, all kinds—as was workin' the Windward Passage trade. God rot me, there was a time! Jem

Calter was with me—him that's on the gibbet now by the Rochester road. Lived like blessed emperors, we did, every man Jack with a mulatto woman in a hut ashore and all the tafia he could drink. Piracy? Ye could call it that. None o' them high old games ye hear tales about in Kingston, mind. Just canoes and row galleys, huntin' close under the land."

"And the emperors came home with scarce a penny to their names!"

A sheepish grimace. "Got a hankerin' for Englishwomen and a sup o' Kentish ale. Worked our way to Kingston, me and Jemmie, and signed aboard the old *Stratford* as was flyin' the homebound pennant in the Roads."

"And that's your notion of a fortune in the colonies?"

"Ah, sir, we was just young fools and drunkards that had no eddication—not a scratch o' pen amongst the lot of us. But a gentleman like you—why, sir, I could point to many a gentleman in Kingston or Spanish Town that got his fortin quick and easy in the 'Red Sea trade,' as some calls it, and nobody thinkin' a mite the worse. And there's them as lives quiet on their money for a time, till things blows over, like, and then comes home to old England, takes a fine house in the country, marries a lady, takes up fox huntin' for to shake the rum lees out o' their liver, and goes to church a-Sundays in a coach the same as a lord."

"Umph!" grunted Roger. "Fortune's where you find it, and where I find mine depends on any sort of passage to any sort of colony."

With a sudden gesture Tom swept the little piles of coins together. "This 'ere money's yourn, sir. You keep it. Let me have a shillin' from time to time and I'm your man. I've got a feelin' about ye, sir. You're a-goin' to make your fortin right enough, and ye'll need that there to give ye a start, like."

"All right," Roger said abruptly. "I'd prefer to go alone, mind. I've plowed my own furrow the past three years and found it to my liking."

"I'm jest your shadder, see?" the seaman said. "You go along the same as ye always did, and I'll foller ye to hell itself."

"I've a better destination," murmured Roger piously, "I hope."

CHAPTER 6

"We, the People of England . . ."

THE HOUSE SLEPT LATE, for it was Saturday night, a fact of which the wayfarers were not aware until well into Sunday morning, when the bells of St. Olave's broke the peace of Tooley Street with a thunderous clang.

The house woke with a scurry that had nothing to do with morning devotions, however, for at that moment the old man's voice was heard crying up the stair well, "Here's our Sal come home in a chair!" and there was a great patter of feet in that warren of poor rooms and windows flung open and voices crying down.

Roger lay wrapped in the big riding cloak with his boots for pillow, a bed he had slept in more times than he cared to count. He jumped up and was amused to see Tom Fuller crawling sheepishly out of the flock bed. The single window, three of whose small panes were broken and stuffed with rags, presented some difficulty, but it opened after an effort, and they peered down in time to see a young woman emerge from a sedan chair, pay the chairmen with a flourish, and stand for a moment, hands on hips, receiving a shower of ribald congratulations from what seemed all of Tooley Street. Then she came indoors, and all the windows closed together against the chill of the February morning, and in the house below doors flew open and voices shouted greetings down the stair well. Roger and Tom stepped out upon the landing, not wishing to be found in the lady's chamber, and nonplused to find their retreat cut off by the lady herself. She came up the stairs greeting the inmates cheerfully at each landing, with the old man at her heels babbling in his oily voice that he allus knowed she would get orf well, and making unintelligible signs to Roger and Tom behind her back.

Sally wore a dress of flowered stuff with the skirt looped up in front to show a quilted petticoat finely sprinkled with embroidery. Her shoes were old and broken, but that did not seem to matter in view of her well-turned ankles, which were clad in white silk. But it was her face that took the eye—a fresh skin, a slender nose, a wide red mouth, a pair of lively blue eyes, all framed in the lace frills of her cap.

She saw Tom Fuller as she neared the stair top and cried at once, "A bloody tarpaulin!"

She turned to demand of Old Evil what a' devil he meant by letting her garret to a pair o' tarry sailors as soon as her back was turned.

"Let me explain," suggested Roger pleasantly.

She gave him a hot blue stare. His boots were crusted with the dried mud of yesterday's roads; so were his plain blue breeches; his shirt was soiled; his waistcoat flung on askew; there was a wide tear in the front skirt of his coat, and all looked slept in. His hair was unpowdered and still tied with Simonetta's garter ribbon, and his dark jaws needed a razor. As her eyes met his own steady black gaze he saw a change in them, the blue softening like a spring sky after rain, and then a too-familiar succession—curiosity, unease, and finally the strange leaping eagerness that had in it a quality forlorn and surrendered and lost. Other women in other places had told him that the mere look of him turned the blood in their veins to wine—or possessed them of devils. An observant Paris physician had once told him it was "animal magnetism," whatever that meant, and warned him (the physician had a pretty wife) that he would die in a ditch of debauchery if he did not enter a monastery as soon as possible and give his embrace to Heaven. He had parried with some quip from a French poet about an ardent soul enclosed within cold walls of flesh and passed on to the crowded salon where Prince Charlie was dispensing his own particular magic.

All this flickered through his mind while the girl Sally inspected him, and he was filled with self-contempt that this weird gift should put him, even for a moment, on speaking terms with a common trollop.

"Who are you?" she cried.

"My name's my own," he replied curtly. "My friend and I were hard put for lodgings last night, and your landlord suggested that we sleep in your garret and pay you in the morning. I assure you it is none the worse."

"I didn't mean to be so sharp," she said meekly. "Did you pay Old Trope? You did?"

She turned on Old Evil in a fury. He was sidling down the stairs at a great rate, seeing the turn of events. "Give the gentleman back his money, you hear?"

"Never mind," Roger said.

"You can have the garret anyhow," quoth Sally. "I've only come to get my bits o' things. Had a stroke o' luck, I have"—with a challenging smile. And in a sudden scream, for Old Trope's benefit, "Got a nice chamber in Charing Cross, I have, and no more draggin' my legs up three pair o' stairs to a five-shillin' garret in South'ark!"

She stepped into her chamber under the slates, leaving the door open, looking at Roger over her shoulder as she untied the lappets of her cap, and humming "Why Should We Quarrel for Riches?" in an inviting sort of voice.

Tom Fuller turned and spat down the stair well. Roger caught her sidelong eye and shook his head coldly. She tossed her brown head and set about gathering her "bits o' things." It did not take her long. She came out with a flounce and a sniff and went running down the stairs singing, "Me name is Sally Madigan, kiss-me-quick and come ag'in," in a little scornful chant.

"Let's get out o' here," Tom Fuller growled.

"Where away?"

"A wherry to Wappin' Stairs and take a lodgin' thereabouts, where the ships come."

Roger thrust his hands in his breeches pockets and sauntered into the garret. By daylight it looked clean, as it had by candlelight.

"I think we'll stay here a bit. It's cheap and we're well hidden. Wapping—they'll be turning Wapping and Gravesend upside down. Those men in the coach must have spotted you for a seaman, and remember we rode off toward the Thames."

"Wappin's the place for ships," Tom insisted. "We'll never find a berth to the colonies layin' high and dry in South'ark."

"We can look for ships without living where they come. We can take a wherry from Tooley Street Stairs to Wapping any time we choose and come back by the river as we went. If you'd ever hunted foxes, Tom, you'd know that water's the stuff to hide a scent."

"Must we live in a vixen's nest?"

"There's worse in Wapping, I venture."

They bought an extra pallet and cheap bedding, and so began a strange existence among the denizens of Tooley Street, whose narrow houses tottered together as if for mutual warmth and support and looked as if one stiff breath of wind along the Thames would blow them all together like a heap of cards.

The lodging house of Isaac Trope leaned in the perpetual twilight of the shadow of St. Olave's, whose tall square tower supported a small and ridiculous pinnacle on the side facing the lane, a gray hand pointing a withered and foreshortened finger to Heaven. When the sun was in the west the great stone gate of London Bridge cast a long shadow across the housetops to the edge of Tooley Stairs Lane.

It was a turbid little backwater on the edge of the great traffic which poured from Kent and Surrey along the Borough Highway to the bridge and the marts and courts and countinghouses of the city. The Borough Highway formed a dividing line through Southwark, and Roger was amused to find that Tooley Street looked with a sense of superior worth and even virtue on the people of the other side. There, in spite of the noble bulk and tall tower of St. Mary Overy, lived the inferior tribes of Foul Lane, Stony Street, Dead Man's Place, and other queer places, the resort, said Tooley Street, of thieves and rogues and murderers. Tooley Street prided itself on working for its living.

Within its three narrow floors the Trope house contained four-and-twenty men, women, and children. The housekeeper was the hairy woman Lumley, who passed for Trope's widowed daughter and was whispered to be no such thing. With them on the ground floor lived Bob, the hackney coachman, and his wife and two children; also Ned and Jack, a pair of chairmen, and a furtive person named Little Bob (to distinguish him from the hackney coachman), who spent his days and half his nights across the bridge in the city and was said to be a pickpocket.

On the second floor were Maggs, a chimney sweep, with his wife and four youngsters; a journeyman barber named Vace, with a wife and three; a waterman named Killick, who kept a boat at Tooley Lane Stairs, and his wife, an oysterwoman.

Each morning Killick ferried his wife across the river to Billingsgate, where she loaded her tray with Whitstable oysters and cried them through the streets. When her stout woolen ankles had vanished up the greasy steps of Billingsgate wharf Killick dropped down the river to set Tom Fuller and Roger in Wapping for the day.

Roger's first purchases provided him with a check shirt, a frieze jacket, a pair of wide-legged seamen's slops cut off just below the knee, and a pair of coarse stockings and shoes. These, topped with a blue hat whose brim was fastened close against the low crown in three tight little cocks like an apple tart, a style much favored by man-o'-war's-men, enabled him to stroll the narrow streets and lanes of Wapping without exciting comment, although, as Tom Fuller said, he talked too much like a gent to be proper mistook.

Tom did most of the talking and all of the tobacco chewing and spitting which marked the seamen of Wapping quite as much as their trousers and hats; and he knew not only the taverns and ordinaries of the tarry community between Ratcliff Highway and the Thames but the snug back-room dramshops and upstairs drinking dens where all the talk was of ships and foreign parts. Here they heard queer things of the world, seen through the eyes of Jack Tar: tales of shipwreck and pestilence, of barratry, piracy, slavery, and knavery of astonishing kinds, the seamy side of the traffic of the seas. None of this was very strange to Tom Fuller, who spun some notable yarns himself. But Roger drank it in.

These seamen out of London River seemed a race apart, a tribe of wandering Gentiles cursed with a knowledge of the sea, and any Wapping dramshop was the crossroads of the world. The earth was a great golden woman, many-breasted like one of those heathen Hindu goddesses, and about her all these brutal and thirsty children swarmed to suck, to explore, and to suck again. Yet all their sucking and exploring brought them little nourishment, for along their hard road waited a many-handed god to wring them dry—merchants, shipowners, tidewaiters, crimps, and whores. The moral seemed to be that it was better to wring than to suck, and Roger made good note of it. Nevertheless he was fascinated by the notion of those golden breasts beyond the seas.

The difficulty was to get there. Somehow, because the wars had ended, the trade winds had ceased to blow about the world. Ships and men were idle all along the river. The shrewd gentlemen of the countinghouses had fastened their moneybags and were waiting for something to happen. Some declared that the peace could not last long, a patched-up thing, a giving back of conquests that left neither king with value to show for the money spent. Others whispered that penny-pinching George cared nothing for colonies or foreign trade, was interested only in his mistresses and his beloved Hanover, like the first George, his father.

Wapping growled. All London growled. And the Lord Mayor was disturbed, for the city was full of discharged soldiers and seamen, tradesmen out of work, a growing army of beggars and vagabonds.

CHAPTER 7

"All Persons Desirous to Engage . . ."

As an occasional change from Tooley Street and Wapping, Roger sought out a tavern off the Strand where a Jacobite group met once a week to toast the king over the water. Their dinners were held in a chamber at the rear, and none but the chosen few were admitted, but the taproom was a sort of meeting place for Jacobites in that part of the city, and they smoked and talked with surprising freedom over their wine. The tavernkeeper was a Scot, like so many of the men who came there. London was full of Scots, most of them merchants in diligent pursuit of bawbees. There was even a Scotch Walk on 'Change. It was amusing to think they had invaded England successfully after all.

For these visits Roger wore what Tom Fuller called his "gentleman's rig." The French cut of the coat was a passport in itself, and the note of shabby gentility in his whole appearance bore out his story more faithfully than documents.

It was at once a relief and a pleasure to be able to talk of the '45 to men who understood. France and Italy had been full of men with tales of battle, important battles and tremendous tales. When you mentioned the Highlands a glaze of indifference came into their eyes; they had never heard of Scotland, and the queer ramifications of English politics—Whigs, Tories, Jacobites, and two complete sets

of royalty—made all you said incomprehensible. You learned to shut
your mouth and save your breath. What were Falkirk and Culloden
to such famous names as Belgrade, Fontenoy, Dettingen? Could you
mention Lord George Murray in the same breath with Marshal Saxe?
You could not mention him at all.

Yet here, from the very men who heard his tales so eagerly, he
learned again the truth that Charles had told him so cynically at
Suddenholt. Jacobitism as a force in Britain was dead. Only the
sentiment survived. A Jacobite officer in the Guards presented it
brutally: "My dear fellow, England's full of Jacobites who love the
mystery and romance of the pledge over the water, the notion that
they belong to something older and more genteel than these German
upstarts and their court of boors—and wouldn't lift a finger for the
Stuarts if it meant one drop of blood."

"And the army?" Roger hinted.

A shrug. "I am an officer in His Majesty's Foot Guards, sworn to
fight the King's enemies—and they don't let you take *that* pledge
over water, my friend. I bought my commission with good coin of
the realm. Not a few of my guineas bore the head of Charles Stuart,
such as you'd find in any stout Whig's coffers, such as you'll see in
any shopkeeper's till in London at this moment. But—a pretty para-
dox, wasn't it? And d'ye see the point? The value's in the coin regardless of the head it bears. Just so, the army fights for England
regardless of who's king. If only those poor fools plotting in Paris
and Rome could see that!"

Roger returned to the Trope house a little sour about the mouth.
It was gall to think that for three years he had been merely a poor
fool plotting. He climbed the stairs glumly and on the second landing
found a cluster of his fellow lodgers, and in their midst Killick, the
waterman, waving a soiled newspaper.

"Here!" cried Killick. "Here's a gentleman as can read as good's a
parson—maybe better. Mr. Sudden, sir!"

"What is it, Killick?"

"This 'ere paper, sir. You read it to 'em. I tried to tell 'em, and
they won't believe me!"

Maggs, the sweep, declared tipsily, "I says it's gammon, paper or no paper, eddication or no eddication." A strong reek of raw gin hung over the landing, not all of it from Maggs.

" 'Ear! 'Ear!" cried the chairman, Jack.

"If Trope hadn't broke his spettacles he could read as well as any gentleman," announced the great creature Lumley with a defiant look at Roger.

"Ow, give the feller a charnce," pleaded Vace, the journeyman barber.

"Is it true, Mr. Sudden, sir?" thrust in Trope. "All that about a free passage, I mean, and free vittles for a year?"

"Some other time," said Roger curtly, and set a foot on the stair. But several hands caught at him, and the hackney coachman said earnestly, "It means a lot to the like of us, sir, if it's true. A chance to get my woman and the young'uns away from this starvin' town. A chance to make my fortin, maybe."

"Fetch a glim, someone," demanded Mrs. Maggs. "It's too dark 'ere for the gentleman to see which end o' the paper's which."

This was a hint for the barber's wife. No one else on that landing could afford such a luxury. Mrs. Vace gave a sniff, but she went into her chamber with her lean, long-legged stride and came forth with a tallow dip.

"Now!" cried Maggs, snatching it from her and spattering himself with hot grease. "Now let's 'ave it, sir."

Resignedly Roger held the paper to the light, a London *Gazette*, old and soiled. The object of their interest, an advertisement, was framed in grimy thumbprints. He began to read aloud:

Whitehall, March 7th, 1749.
"A proposal having been presented to His Majesty for establishing a civil government in the province of Nova Scotia, in North America, as also for the better peopling and settling the said Province, and extending and improving the fishery thereof, by granting lands within the same, and giving other encouragement . . ."

He looked up, protesting, "The thing's as long as my arm!"

"Give us the main bits, then," Killick entreated. "Go on, sir . . . all them bits about free land and such."

"Very well. Where was I?"

" 'Encouragement,' " declared the vigilant Trope.

"Ah! '. . . encouragement to officers and men lately dismissed His Majesty's land and sea service, and artificers necessary to building or husbandry . . .' This doesn't apply to any of you!"

"Oh yes, it do!" insisted Killick. "It's all over the town—they'll take anybody, 'specially if he's got a wife and fambly. Read on, sir!"

"Um. 'Settlers will be granted passage, and subsistence during their passage, as also for twelve months after their arrival . . . arms and ammunition for their defense . . . proper utensils for husbandry, fishery, erecting habitations and other necessary purposes . . . civil government to be established, with all the privileges of His Majesty's other colonies in America, and proper measures taken for their security and protection . . . lands . . .' "

"Ah!" they cried together.

" '. . . lands granted shall be in fee simple, free from quit rent or taxes for ten years, not more than one shilling per annum per fifty acres after that. Fifty acres to every private soldier or seaman, and ten acres over and above to every person (including women and children) of which his family shall consist . . .' "

" 'Struth!" cried Vace. "That means, lemme see, fifty, sixty . . . ninety acres for me and the missus and the kids. How big's an acre?"

" '. . . eighty acres to every officer under the rank of ensign in the land service and that of lieutenant in the sea service . . . two hundred acres to an ensign . . . three hundred to a lieutenant . . . four hundred to a captain'—the colony will be owned outright by half-pay colonels at this rate, my friends!—'. . . reputed surgeons whether they have been in His Majesty's service or not . . .' "

"Never mind all that," protested Killick. "How do we go about gettin' our names on the list?"

"Are you sure you want to go?" Roger asked. "I mean, you don't even know what the country's like. And it's a long way from Tooley Street if you can't abide it when you get there."

"We'll charnce that," Vace said confidently.

"But . . . 'husbandry' . . . you've never seen a farm!"

The barber winked and smiled. "Right you are, sir! Could ye see me pushin' a plow? I aim to sell my ninety blessed acres arter I get there and set up in me old trade. There'll be gentlemen in the colony and chins to scrape and wigs to comb."

"And chimbleys to sweep," said Maggs.

"And oysters? Be there oysters in that country?" demanded Mrs. Killick with professional interest.

"There's everything," the hackney coachman said.

"Read on, sir," Killick urged. "Can we get our names on the list now? It ain't too late? That there paper's old, sir, ain't it?"

Roger hitched the *Gazette* a little nearer to the candle. "It says, 'All persons desirous to engage are to enter their names on or before the seventh of April, 1749, at the Trade and Plantations Office, or with the Commissioners of the Navy residing at Portsmouth and Plymouth. Transports shall be ready to receive such persons on board on the tenth April and be ready to sail on the twentieth.' And now, friends, if you'll allow me . . ." He passed the sheet to Killick and started up the stairs.

"This 'ere Novia Scosher," Killick called after him. "Where is it?"

" 'North America,' it says. That's half across the world by sea, I think, and a choice of climate from the tropics to the pole. More I couldn't tell you."

He entered the garret blithely and found Tom Fuller sitting in the dusk on the bed that had been Sally Madigan's, with his head in his hands.

"What's the matter?" he demanded at once.

"Matter enough," Tom growled.

"Well?" Roger sat on his own pallet and faced the man.

"I'm done for, sir. I'm as good as took and tried and tucked up on a gibbet. In a fortnight's time they'll have my carcass by the Rochester road along o' Jemmie Calter's. But it's you I'm worrit for, sir."

"What's happened? It can't be as bad as all that."

" 'Slike this, sir. I'm down in Wappin', see? Speakin' strict, I'm down by Shadwell Dock, mindin' me own business and sober as a Methody parson. There's a young woman . . ."

"Ah!"

". . . as keeps bar in the Sun tavern and is partial to sailormen, 'specially me. So she's got the arternoon off and we're walkin' up the Ratcliff Highway for to sit a while in the fields at the end o' Cannon

Street, when up comes a cove as she knowed in Kent where she comes from. 'Hillo, Polly!' says the cove, and, 'Hillo, Jack!' says me lady, and they fall to jabberin' about the folk in Dartford nineteen to the dozen. As for me, I'm flabbergasted, for this cove is one o' them outriders behind the tidecoach that day. And he keeps dartin' a queer look at me. Course he never seed much o' me face, wi' the hankitcher slung across me mug that day, but he keeps lookin' and lookin', and I starts edgin' away, till Polly sings out, 'Come back, Tom, ye jealous creatur. This is on'y an old friend from Dartford.' And, 'Jack,' she says, 'this is me friend Tom from South'ark.' 'South'ark!' says the cove. 'Whereabouts in South'ark, now?' By that time I see what he's a-squintin' at—this starboard claw o' mine that I got a bullet through at Cartagena. There ain't two hands like that in England. 'What part o' South'ark?' says the cove. 'The hind part—to you!' says I, and I'm off, makin' all sail down Old Gravel Lane for the river, wi' the sharp cove close astern bawlin', 'Stop, thief!' at the top o' his pipe. Afore long it strikes me I'm makin' straight for Execution Dock, which is the last place I want to see, so I make a sharp tack into one o' them alleys that twist atween Old Gravel and New Gravel. There I lose him. He can't run anyhow—one o' them coves that's got hisself bowly-legged livin' aboard a horse—but he knows whereabouts I make my landfall, and I hear him bawl there's fifty guineas reward for me. That means they've got a hundred up for you, sir."

"How much have you told this Polly woman?" demanded Roger.

"No more'n a man tells a woman as he wants a kiss and a squeeze off."

"That might be a lot, if I know women."

The sailor shook his head sullenly. "All she knows is I'm Tom from South'ark, a seaman out of a berth as promised her a shillin' for ribbons."

Roger nursed his knee and whistled the air of "The Black Joke."

"By this time they're watchin' all the roads out o' town," Tom went on gloomily. "Caught, sir, caught like a rat in a cask!"

"Southwark's a big cask, Tom."

"There ain't a soul in it wouldn't cut me throat for a guinea, let alone fifty."

"Nobody knows you by sight except a few people in Tooley Street."

Tom Fuller held up the scarred hand. "Here's what they'll be lookin' for, sir. I can't cut off me blessed claw. They'll have that all over Lunnon by mornin'—broadsheets on the tavern doors and a crier ringin' his bell and howlin' it out on every corner in the Borough. Somebody's sure to blow the gaff. You get away, sir, while there's time."

Roger shook his head. "We'll both stay where we are."

"Humph! We can't stay here another week, sir! Trope's fell to loo'ard with his rent, and the landlord was here yesterday, a fat man in a chaise. Said it was pay up or get out. Dressed like a lord, he was, and kep' dabbin' at his nose with a scented hankitcher to drown the smell o' Tooley Street. Went off shoutin', 'I'll evict, damme, I'll evict!' and a-shakin' of his stick."

"Trope will pay up, never fear."

"Trope ain't got it to pay, sir. We're the on'y lodgers in the house that's reg'lar pay. Times is mortal hard, sir. Them two chairmen and Bob can't hardly get enough fares in the run of a day to buy vittles, let alone clo'es and rent and such. Vace says people's took to shavin' 'emselves to save a penny. Maggs says everyone's dodgin' the chimbley law and he can't get a flue to sweep. Killick vows people walks for miles to cross the river by London Bridge to save 'emselves the price of a wherry. And his wife says nobody's eatin' oysters any more. Why, sir, even that bloody pickpocket can't make a livin'. It's desperation times, sir, that's what it is."

"What did Trope say?"

"Went down on his knees and cadged for a bit more time. No good. 'I'll evict!' says Fatty in the chaise, and off he goes. That's why Trope's afire like all the rest of 'em over this yarn about a new colony in Ameriky. 'Tain't the free voyage nor the land that tempts 'em, sir, it's the notion o' free vittles for a twelvemonth. Nothin' in the world to worry about, a whole blessed year!"

They lay on their beds and talked in the dark of the warm April night. A light breeze down the Thames valley seemed to carry into the open window of the garret a smell of trees and hedges and green grass. A smell of fields in Tooley Street! Roger thought of the rich earth of Kent, the green land of England, and this hungry swarm upon the edge of it, oblivious of it, catching at such fancies as free pork and biscuit on the wild shores of America. A mad world, surely.

"They'll never get on the list," he said. "The advertisement said 'discharged soldiers and sailors,' and 'artisans,' and 'husbandmen.' None of these people——"

"Ah!" Tom grunted. "But 'discharged sogers and sailors' ain't a-goin' to Ameriky. They know them parts too well. They know what His Majesty's 'subsistence' means, too. So Gov'ment's takin' anyone that's fool enough. I heard the talk in Wappin'. Knowin' ones down that way say the whole thing's a plot o' the Lord Mayor's to ship a couple o' thousand Lunnon poor across the Western Ocean where they can't come back. It's to take the edge off o' the city mob afore there's any trouble over the hard times."

"And a man's trade is no matter?"

"Not a hap'orth!"

"Not even an amateur highwayman?"

Tom Fuller sat straight up on the flock bed and uttered an astonished oath.

"You're coddin', sir!"

"I was never so serious in my life."

CHAPTER 8

Exodus

IT WAS A QUAINT PILGRIMAGE. Upon the day appointed by the Lords of Trade and Plantations the Tropes and their lodgers left Tooley Street in a body and were joined by other migrants from Pickle Herring Street, Shad Thames, and as far down-river as Rotherhithe. Roger wore his seaman's clothing. The "gentleman's rig"—jack boots and all—was in a small and old portmanteau bought of a pawnbroker in the Borough road and now carried between Tom and himself by a stick thrust under the straps. The short way to Whitehall lay across the great bend of the Thames, so they turned their backs on London Bridge and journeyed along the Borough Highway and Blackman Street, where they were joined by groups from Mint Street and Dirty Lane, from Love Lane, from Chalk Street and White Cross Street and Dead Man's Place and Bandy Leg Walk, from all the queer congeries of Southwark. All carried their belongings in small bundles. Here and there Roger noticed a sea bag or the knapsack of an old soldier, but they were very few. The men sang and whistled as if going to a fair, women and older children chattered in shrill cockney voices, and the babies squalled. A pack of lean dogs crept humbly and hopefully after them all the way through Southwark, across the upper reach of St. George's Fields and down to the Thames bank at King's Arms Stairs.

There the straggling procession halted and drew together, and discovered itself to be several hundred strong. Those who had a few pence to spare refreshed themselves with pints of flip at the Arms. There was much haggling with the watermen at the stairs, but at last the ferrying began.

Watching the crowded wherries cross to Whitehall Stairs, Roger was reminded of another river and another passage. The date rang in his mind like a trumpet. It was just three years to the day since he and a party of Highland scouts had watched the English army cross the high spring waters of the Spey. He remembered the band's tune as the troops splashed over the ford:

> *Will ye play me fair,*
> *Bonnie laddie, Highland laddie?*

—and heard again the harsh Gaelic curses of his men and the sort of play they promised. That was six days before Culloden. He had crossed a good many rivers and some salt water since, and every passage had marked a little epoch. He wondered what sort of Rubicon he was crossing now.

As they straggled up from Whitehall Stairs the pilgrimage from Southwark found itself merged in a greater stream pouring toward the Cockpit from the city itself. The Cockpit was a solid mass of humanity. Among them stood little knots of discharged soldiers in their shabby red coats, or seamen in tarry slops and check shirts and the apple-tart naval cock to their hats; a few—a very few—countrymen gazing openmouthed at the throng about them, with their wives and children clinging close. From these could be heard the accents of all England—the border country. Yorkshire, Lancashire, the odd tongue of the Fens, the slow drawl of Kent, the singsong of the Cotswold country. Only the west-country tongues were missing; they were awaiting the ships at Portsmouth. But through and above the hubbub rose and triumphed the sharp voices of London town. It was largely a cockney mob that chattered and milled and made its slow way to the Whitehall office of the Lords of Trade and Plantations.

Few had thought to bring food, and none was willing to leave his place in the crawling procession to seek it at a tavern. They dared not put their bundles down in that tide of doubtful honesty, nor let their urchins stray out of reach. They clung to their sorry chattels and each other through the weary, shuffling hours. The hungry group from Tooley Street finally edged its way indoors and along the halls, kept in line by bawling soldiers of the Whitehall guard, until at last it faced a battery of perspiring and short-tempered clerks in charge of a gentleman in a pink coat and an elegant three-tailed wig who was, no doubt, the "John Pownell Esquire" of the advertisement. The day was far spent, and so was Pownell's staff. Voices that had been sharp and exacting with the head of the ragged procession in the morning were listless and perfunctory about its tail. The cunning cockneys, listening to the questions asked and answered in the line ahead, had soon discovered what was expected of them. Each man in turn answered glibly "carpenter," "shipwright," "smith," "mason," "joiner," "brickmaker," or "husbandman"—and passed on his way rejoicing.

A smell of unwashed flesh pervaded Whitehall's sedate halls and chambers in spite of open windows and the light breeze from the Thames; and the clack of their tongues, outside and in, added uproar to outrage. The mind of England's empire was down-river at Westminster, but here in Whitehall's offices beat its heart, the machine that moved half the world—all gripped and possessed for the space of a day by London's canaille. What would happen if instead of lying about their trades they all started breaking windows? To be sure there were blue-clad cavalry across the way; but half the Horse Guards had been disbanded after Culloden, and quite possibly some of their old troopers were in this fetid throng.

Roger was aroused from these whimsies by an irritated voice repeating, "Name? Name?" and found himself facing a bilious young man in a small tiewig.

"Roger Sudden," he answered boldly.

The quill raced and splattered.

"Are you registered in the book?"

"I'm afraid not."

The fellow broke into a peevish tirade. Did he realize, had he the faintest notion what a demned nuisance he was—he and the others who'd failed to register? It was distinctly stated—*distinctly* stated—in the *Gazette* that all persons must register by letter or in person by the seventh. It was a demned outrage. Serve him demned well right if the ticket was refused.

He called behind him to another tiewig, "Another of 'em, Lorimer. Name, Sudden—Roger."

"Occupation?"

"Husbandman."

"Ha!"—quill racing—"If a close acquaintance with dirt means anything, the whole demned mob are husbandmen. Family?"

"None."

"No wife?"

"None."

"Fifty acres! Age?"

"Twenty-four."

"Transport?"—this to a third tiewig at the left.

Third Wig examined his register carefully and announced in a sour voice, "Demned if I know where to put him. *Charlton's* full. *Winchelsea's* full. *Everly, Merry Jacks, Beaufort*—they'll have to arrange more transports, demme, or close the list. Wait! There's room for a man or two in the *Fair Lady,* snow. Put him down for *Fair Lady.*"

Again the quill. "Here you are!"

The ticket in his hand.

"Next! Name?"

"Tom Fuller—and I want to sail along o' Mr. Sudden, there."

"Are you registered in the book?"

"No sir, sorry, sir."

"Do you realize——"

"Beg your pardon, sir. But is it cold-like in that country? I can't abide cold, never could."

The clerk pointed with his quill to a framed plaque on the wall, a weary gesture, as if he had done it many times this day. "There's the coat of arms of Nova Scotia. Observe the savage man. Observe his garments. Would you say the air was cold?"

The savage in the frame wore nothing but a kilt of flimsy feathers and a cap of similar feathers standing on end about his head. He looked brown and well nourished in this airy costume.

Tom was impressed. "Proof enough," he said. "And there's a unicorn, too. I thought they on'y had them beasts in Afriky."

The line shuffled on. Behind the clerks, watchful, bored, the gentleman in the pink coat and three-tailed wig kept a vinegar-soaked handkerchief close to his face. What a rabble! Reeking of jail fever. Lucky if we don't all come down with it. How many more? It's an exodus, Good Ged! Nothing like it since the Gadarene swine! Not enough transports. Have to make up another fleet later in the summer. And the next summer, probably. Well, a good riddance. The savages of America would find a new tribe in their midst. His Majesty's colonists! Ah well!

What if the urchins watching them pass along the London streets were gibing, "Tinker-tailor-soldier-sailor-poor man-beggarman-thief"? Let His Majesty's ink transform this multitude of sinners with a flourish of the quill! Write 'em down and ship 'em off; the husbandmen of Knaves' Acre and the joiners of Saint Giles, the artificers of Tooley Street, the dairy maids of Drury Lane, the carpenters of Dead Man's Place, the bricklayers of Wapping.

Shuffle-shuffle of broken shoes. Drone of voices. Scratch of pens. "Next! Next! Next!"

CHAPTER 9

The Fair Lady

"What's a snow?" Roger asked.

Tom Fuller spat into the muddy Thames. "Nothin' but a brig with a bit of a trys'l mast rigged close abaft the mainmast. A Dutch rig, I reckon. Most of 'em's small. I'd as soon cross the Western Ocean in this hoy."

They were passing down-river in the Greenwich tilt boat, and most of the passengers were, like themselves, bound for the transports in the lower Thames. The tilt-boat fare had been too much for the artisans of Tooley Street, now part of the rabble tramping Thames Street and the Ratcliff Highway toward the distant ships at Tilbury. The boat was passing Wapping in the sunset, and the Pool was glorious, a sea of golden fire on which the squat black river barges swam unharmed like wooden salamanders. Even Wapping was beautiful in this light, all the squalor hidden in the haze that softened its ragged outlines and wrapped its rooftops in a half-luminous veil of chimney smoke. A Londoner bound for the world's end might well have wept at such a sight.

There seemed to be no tears in the hoy. The little group of passengers seemed to be half-pay officers of the Army with their wives and families and baggage, a great assortment of trunks, chests, boxes, portmanteaus, and bundles, all clearly marked in new white paint with the owner's name, the name of his transport, and the magic words "Nova Scotia."

Roger regarded the grownups with some curiosity. A mixed lot, none very young, none very handsome, none very prosperous if appearances meant anything. The dress of the women spoke of garrison towns in the country rather than London, and the boys in cocked hats and smallclothes and little girls in hoops and small sack gowns looked so exactly like their papas and mammas, and ran about the decks and laughed and chattered in a manner so very unlike them, that the contrast was amusing. The men scarcely looked at the passing shores of Thames. No doubt going abroad was an old story to most of them. They were busy talking of old campaigns, addressing each other by their service titles. None seemed to have held a rank higher than captain. Roger wondered how many parties like this were going to Nova Scotia. Enough to leaven that crapulous cockney mass?

"Ah! There's our snow!" Tom Fuller said with satisfaction. "Good thing she hadn't dropped down to Gravesend like that quill driver thought she might."

"Why?"

"We board her here at Greenhithe, nice and proper, and drop down the river to join t'other transports innocent as lambs. The water bailiffs won't trouble to search the transports; everyone aboard's s'posed to be a proper-examined settler for Ameriky. But if we had to go on down to Tilbury in the tilt boat we'd be overhauled proper. They'll be watchin' all the hoys and such that goes by Tilbury like a cat at a mousehole. Fifty guineas reward. 'Struth!"

The master of the tilt boat swung his ponderous tiller, roaring to his two-man crew to "Watch them sheets!" and to his passengers, "Heads, there! Mind the boom!" He laid his craft alongside the moored snow by a neat calculation of wind and tide, one of those offhand miracles which Thames-men perform as if by instinct. The snow was not impressed. A harsh voice on the deck above objected loudly, "God's wounds! Who are ye and what's your license to lay me aboard in this fashion?"

"This is the Gravesend tilt boat——" began the master of the hoy.

The voice of the *Fair Lady* became manifest in a dark, rough-bearded face leaning over the bulwark in the dusk.

"Damn and blast your tilt boat—and you too, ye bloody——"

"You, sir!" snapped one of the half-pay officers. "Mind your language in the presence of these ladies, or hell confound me I'll swarm aboard and put a yard of steel through your drunken belly!"

The *Fair Lady* declared promptly that, 'Od rot and damn it, that was a game two could play; whereupon several of the half-pay officers snatched out their hangers and, amid shrieks of alarm from wives and offspring, leaped to the deck of the snow.

At once the bearded man set up a bellow. "Boarded, by God! All hands repel boarders!"

He whipped out a cutlass and flourished it in a drunken but determined fashion, while from the forecastle ran half a dozen seamen looking astonished but warlike enough with cutlasses, handspikes, and belaying pins. From the boarding party, from the master of the tilt boat crying encouragement from his poop, from his two men striving to hold fast to the snow in the surge of the outgoing tide, from the belligerent master of the *Fair Lady* and his loyal and strong-lunged crew, there rose upon the evening air such a chorus of oaths that it seemed the fair cheeks of all England must blanch, let alone those of the gentlewomen in the hoy.

At this point Roger and Tom swung the old portmanteau aboard the snow and followed themselves. Cried Roger, stepping forward, "One moment, gentlemen! There's some misunderstanding, surely?"

The *Fair Lady's* master looked him up and down. "Who are you?" he demanded.

The half-pay officers looked astonished. A common tarpaulin thrusting himself into their righteous quarrel and talking like a gentleman!

"My name is Roger Sudden, and this is my companion, Thomas Fuller. We are accredited passengers in your good ship to Nova Scotia, if you'll do me the honor of examining these papers." He proffered the tickets of admission.

The master took them suspiciously, called for a lanthorn, and stared at the papers and Roger and Tom with a most owlish gravity for several minutes without saying anything.

"And now, if you're satisfied, sir," Roger pursued smoothly, "the tilt boat can proceed with these gentlemen and their families down the river."

The officers took the hint, a little sheepish now, but slapping their swords into the sheaths and vowing that, by Gad, if Sudden hadn't spoken when he did there'd have been no master nor crew to take him to America, not by a damned sight. They were officers and gentlemen, damme, and on His Majesty's half-pay list, by God!— and were not to be insulted by any Billingsgate rascal that . . . The voice faded over the side and down the river.

"Very neatly done, sir," said a voice in the dusk. Roger turned and saw for the first time a tall, elderly man in a blue cloak and a silver laced hat with the immense cocks favored in Marlborough's time, and at his side a young woman in a riding cloak with the hood thrown back. In the light of the master's lanthorn they looked to be father and daughter. The girl's face was in shadow, but Roger noted that her hair had reddish glints.

"I feared a bloodletting," the elderly gentleman went on, "until you stepped into the thick of the blades and settled matters. Not many men would have tried it."

"Not every man is so anxious to board a ship, find a berth and something to eat," returned Roger lightly.

" 'Ods heart!" exclaimed Black Beard. "Berth, he says! Eat, he says! My gay cock, I'll give ye a hammock to sling for'ard and my leave to bite your fingernails till breakfast time. We make two meals a day in the *Fair Lady,* no more if ye was a royal duke in disguise—and will someone tell me what a gentleman's doin' in them cloes?"

"Going to Nova Scotia, I hope," said Roger, and picked up the portmanteau.

"Ha!" coughed the tall gentleman. "Perhaps you will give us the pleasure of your company at supper, sir. We too are for Nova Scotia."

Roger's eyes went to Tom Fuller.

"And your companion, of course," added the tall gentleman quickly.

"That's very kindly of ye, sir, and you too, ma'am," spoke up Tom.

"Perhaps Captain Huxley will join us?" suggested the young woman.

But the *Fair Lady's* master was in no mood for company or supper. He reeled away to his cabin, calling loudly for his steward and a bottle of gin, and was seen no more until morning.

In a small cabin under the poop, and by the light of a pair of candles, Roger gained a clear look at his host. He must have stood well over six feet in youth, but his shoulders had the stoop which comes to tall men after fifty, and the stoop was a positive crouch here under the low deck beams. His large wig fell in a mass of well-powdered curls about his shoulders, with two tresses hanging forward, one each side of his lean neck. His eyebrows were black and bushy. A pair of eyes of a blue so pale as to be well-nigh colorless twinkled beneath them. He had a long, pointed nose and a thin mouth, and his cheek was marred with an old sword cut on the right side which gave a whimsical twist to his smile. He had thrown off the cloak and appeared in a red surtout of a military cut with immense cuffs and silver buttons which, like his hat, had a flavor of Duke Marlborough's time.

Roger's glance flicked carelessly over the young woman—and came back again. She was not beautiful. She had red hair, for one thing, a sad blemish, and an independent spirit, for another, since she scorned to disguise it with powder as most red-haired ladies would have done. The color of her eyes was a matter of doubt in the light of the cheap chandler's dips. Gray? Blue? He was not sure. They were large, at any rate, and clear and steady. Her nose was neither good nor bad, an ordinary nose. In the candlelight the shadow it cast on her cheek was small. Her mouth was too large to be fashionable and too small to be generous, yet the lower lip was full and red, and both were firm. A puzzling mouth. It might be indulgent and it might be rather cruel. If a woman's mouth were the key to her soul (and Roger had found them so), this one's soul was an enigma. The rest of her was slim in a green gown, as tall as himself, perhaps a shade taller.

This inspection he accomplished swiftly and exactly, from old habit, as he would have inspected her in passing in the street or anywhere. He guessed her age at seventeen, but her poise and assurance were those of an older woman. He was not prepared for what followed.

"I am John Foy, late captain of His Majesty's Dragoons," said the white-wigged man, "and this is madam my wife."

"Charmed!" uttered Roger, astonished, and, recovering quickly, "My name's Sudden—Roger Sudden—late of Kilnhurst, Kent, and Oxford University. And this is Tom Fuller, late of His Majesty's Navy." There was a trace of irony in this, and the girl looked at him sharply; but his smile was disarming, his smile implied only a sense of comradeship in the great adventure of leaving England.

She rapped on the bulkhead, calling, "Jenny!" and a womanservant appeared from the adjoining cabin. Tom, with the prompt handiness of a sailor, showed Jenny how to sling the table board from its hooks overhead and helped her set out the plates and provisions. She accepted his help in silence and with a rather comical mixture of wonder and disapproval. Plainly she was not used to such guests at her mistress's board.

"You're going out as a gentleman volunteer, I take it?" John Foy murmured, passing the wine.

"Something like that," Roger said.

"What are you going to do in Nova Scotia?" asked cool young Mrs. Foy.

He shrugged. "Make my fortune, like everyone else, I suppose. Just how, I don't know."

Mrs. Foy addressed herself to Tom. "And you?"

"A-follerin' of Mr. Sudden, ma'am."

"I see."

From a hamper against the bulkhead Jenny had conjured bread, some excellent Cheshire cheese, a cold roast fowl, a gallipot of good Sussex butter, a bottle of brandy, and four bottles of red Lisbon.

John Foy ate little, complaining whimsically that as a man became worn in the teeth he could no longer take his stomach for granted. But he addressed himself vigorously to the Lisbon and later the brandy. Mrs. Foy ate with a healthy appetite, and Roger felt encouraged to do the same. Tom needed no encouragement from anyone.

"I feel guilty," Roger said at last, surveying the wreck of the fowl and the cheese and three empty bottles.

"Please don't," said Mrs. Foy. "We've private supply enough in the hold to last us a year."

"One can't be sure in a new colony," Foy explained gravely, and added, "There was not enough room in the other transports for our supplies and furniture, nor could they warrant a separate cabin for my wife and her maid. That's why we're in the *Fair Lady.*"

"Are there any other passengers?" Roger asked.

"No more cabin room. Captain Huxley said he'd take six or seven more men in the forecastle, that's all."

"He seems a swine."

The eyes of the Foys went large and round. Mrs. Foy gestured. Foy said softly, "These bulkheads are very thin, my friend."

Roger changed the subject. "If the snow can't take more than ten passengers, why is she making the voyage?"

"I'm told she's to carry some special supplies and will act as some sort of dispatch boat in Nova Scotia. There will be plenty for her to do."

"Such as . . . ?"

Foy gave him a shrewd glance. "How much do you know about the expedition, Mr. Sudden?"

"Only that the Lord Mayor's found a convenient way to ship his poor across the sea."

"Ah, you mistake an effect for a cause! His Majesty's Government hasn't voted forty thousand pounds merely to build an almshouse on the shores of Nova Scotia, my friend. This is a matter of high politics. Do you know anything of the war against the French in America?"

"Nothing."

Foy's long fingers played with his brandy glass. "Do you know anything of America at all?"

"Only that we've ten or a dozen colonies scattered along the Atlantic seaboard and the French have everything else."

"Humph! The French have Canada, which lies along the north, and they've followed the great lakes and rivers into the heart of the continent, which gives 'em a claim to the whole hinterland—or so they say. That's by the way, of course. The point is, the French and English are forever at war in America, regardless of what the diplomats may be saying in Europe at the moment. At present there is a lull—but never peace. There will never be peace in America until one people have it all. The strategy of the French is to pin the English colonies to the coast, to throttle them by shutting off their trade with the interior. The English plan is more simple. They aim to seize Canada by the throat"—he drew a finger among the crumbs on the board—"which is the estuary of the St. Lawrence River. With that in their hands they can choke the life out of the French Empire in America."

"And what has that to do with us?" Roger asked politely.

Again the finger scrabbling on the board. "Suppose you want to choke a man and you discover he wears a sharp pin in his stock?"

Foy's tongue was a little thick—the brandy on top of the Lisbon, no doubt—but this pot-serious talk of his filled the time. Roger flicked a glance at Mrs. Foy, expecting to see boredom in her eyes, or amusement at most, and was startled to see her leaning forward with a pair of shapely elbows on the board, eyes brilliant and lips parted avidly. He was a little shocked. A woman should not look like that except when one is making love.

He recalled himself. "I'd try to remove the pin first, I suppose."

"Yes," she said, with that eager intentness, "but how? You couldn't just make a snatch at it."

Foy seized the subject again with tipsy gravity. "No, my dear Sudden, the thing must be done with care. The pin must be plucked swiftly when the time comes, but first one must contrive to get one's hand in position—close to the pin, d'you see?—and one must know exactly where to seize the pin, and how much force to apply, and in what direction. In short, sir—*hup!*—to abandon all these play words, England must build a fortress and naval station near the mouth of the St. Lawrence."

"And what is the—ah—pin, sir?"

"A fortress called Louisbourg, in the island of Cape Breton. From it the French can guard the St. Lawrence or descend upon the Atlantic seaboard as they choose."

"Louisbourg!" Tom Fuller said. "Why, sir, the colonists captured that place back in '45. I knowed some lads as was there wi' the fleet."

"So they did, Fuller, so they did! Amazing! A rabble of farmers and fishermen and townsmen against the strongest fortress outside Europe. They deserved something for their hardihood, so Fortune smiled upon them—the French had too small a garrison and too little powder. The English colonies were jubilant, I tell you. For with the fall of Louisbourg all Canada was doomed. And then, sir, then came the peace last year, when England handed Louisbourg back to France—for what? For the expulsion of Charles Stuart from French soil! The colonists in America were furious. They're furious still. They've raised such a rumpus that His Majesty's Government feels it must do something toward restoring the position. And so, my friends, this expedition of ours is to create an English fortress within striking distance of Louisbourg, aimed at Louisbourg, designed for nothing else but a blow at French power in Canada."

"I see," Roger said. But he did not see and did not care. It was rather involved, and he suspected the man was drunk. He murmured diffidently, "Why is His Majesty's Government sending out a rabble of poor Londoners? Not one in twenty knows one end of a musket from the other!"

"Partly they're to offset the *Acadiens,* the native French in Nova Scotia—which has been under the English flag nigh forty years without an English settlement. But chiefly they're to clear the forest, till the land and fish the sea, they're to build sawmills and gristmills—in short they're to create a handy source of supplies for the army and fleet which someday will move against Canada."

"But that will take years!"

A shrug. "Ten years, twenty years, what does it matter? His Majesty's Government is laying long plans."

"And where shall we get a garrison for this fortress of ours?"

"From Louisbourg! The English garrison there is about to hand it back to the French, under the terms of the peace, with all its stores and cannon. When we arrive on the coast the English troops will simply move down the coast to our new town. Like a game of chess, isn't it?"

"And how do you like being a pawn?" asked Roger of Mrs. Foy. Her eyes shone. "What a game!"

CHAPTER 10

"If 'Ee Stay, Lackaday!"

Job huxley of the *Fair Lady* was, he was fond of saying, a man who had traveled far and lived rough, and these pursuits had given him, among other things, a vast thirst and a stock of oaths which were the awe and admiration of his crew. There were four seamen, a cook, a steward, a boatswain, and a master's mate, all of whom lived in the forecastle, although the master's mate, a morose man named Cheeny, had the privacy of a canvas partition in a corner. The men were the common run of Wapping, with the marks of old service about them. One and all they had traveled as far and lived as rough as their master, but they went in great fear of him and told Roger that Old Hux was a holy terror, no mistake.

Old Hux confirmed this himself the day after that snug supper in the Foy cabin. When the Foys came in to breakfast with him in the small stern compartment called by ship custom the "great" cabin, he informed them bluntly that he would have no more of this "coddling common sailors and steerage people" in their quarters.

"Mr. Sudden is a gentleman," began Foy stiffly.

"He wears a damned ungentlemanly rig," retorted Old Hux.

"Do you swear in front of my wife?" demanded Foy in a passion.

"I swear in the presence of Almighty God every time I open my mouth, and who is your wife to God or me? I am the master of this vessel, damme! If ye don't like it, change your berth."

"You're not in a good humor this morning, Captain," suggested Mary Foy placidly.

"I am not in a good humor any morning," said the master of the *Fair Lady,* but he laughed, and looked younger. A man of five-and-forty, perhaps, with piercing blue eyes set in a broad frame of bronze skin and black beard. His black hair was pigtailed like any seaman's. He had worked aft from the hawse and boasted that all the soap in the lazaret could not take the tar from his hands; but now that he was aft he knew his privileges and he dared anyone to abuse them.

Having put the cabin passengers in their place, he stalked out on deck in an old long-skirted coat, cut very square, with tarnished brass buttons, and a round hat cocked at the back with a single leather button, a pair of white breeches badly in need of a laundress, and wrinkled black stockings and stout shoes with enormous pinchbeck buckles. Roger and Tom were leaning against the foremast shrouds enjoying the sunshine and the view along the Thames. Old Hux crooked a thick finger and they came to him, Roger with some reluctance—it was too much like being whistled up, dog-fashion. Old Hux wasted no words.

"I've just told them people in the cabin that I'll have no more o' this winin' and dinin' my steerage passengers. Stay where ye belong. I'm a rough dog and can bite."

"Yes sir," Tom said, with a respectful pull at his forelock.

Roger was not inclined to be so docile, but at this moment there was a diversion, a boat hailing alongside, and Tom running to catch a painter heaved over the bulwark.

"What d'ye want?" snapped Old Hux over the side.

Four men sat in the boat at the oars, and a fat man in a round blue jacket and cocked hat at the tiller.

"A good look at your passengers and crew," said the fat man importantly.

"Blast your eyes," said Old Hux, "my people suit *me* well enough. What's your business?"

The fat man pulled a paper from his jacket pocket. "A seaman wanted for highway robbery, gray eyes, rings in his ears, large scar on the right hand, age about five-and-thirty. Reward offered by two officers of His Majesty's Twentieth Foot——"

"Avast! You and His Majesty's foot! He's not aboard. I've a man with a timber leg and a bosun with a deadlight over his larboard eye——"

"I'll come aboard."

"Come aboard and ye'll find yourself in the Thames next minute! 'Od rot your impudence! Rings in his ears! Half the men on the river's got rings in their ears—and you'd have one in your snout if I'd my way. Damme, what next!"

The fat man drew another paper from his pocket. "Wanted for highway robbery, suspected of high treason, slim man, black eyes, blue surtout, jack boots, comes from Kent, looks like a gentleman——"

"More than I can say for you, Blubbergut! Shove off!"

"In the name of the King——"

"In the name o' hell's whole kingdom, shove off, or I'll souse ye in Thames water, and that crew of ugly rascals with ye! Cast off that painter, there!"

Tom dropped the painter's end as if it were hot. The Thames swept the boat away at once, the fat man yelling and shaking his fist, his men snatching up oars in too great a hurry and fouling all together, the crew of the *Fair Lady* jeering at them for a lot of lubbers, and crews of other craft moored below running to their bulwarks to join in the fun.

Huxley turned and favored Roger and Tom with a long, slow wink.

"Thank you," Roger said.

"Keep your thanks," growled Old Hux. "I ask no favors and I grant none. D'ye think I'd stand by and let that fat fool take two pair o' hands out o' my ship? I'm short o' men—all along o' them thick-headed Lords o' Trade. Where's the seaman willin' to hand, reef, and steer on the Western Ocean when he can idle his passage over in the hold of a transport? Eh? Settlers! Ye'll bear a hand this voyage, my brave boys, and so'll them others that's to come aboard tomorrow. Oh, I'll work ye, never fear! Job Huxley's the boy to eddicate a seaman— or a gentleman, come to that! But mind this—bear a hand and he'll treat ye well. Bear a hand and Job's a lamb—ask any o' them scoundrels for'ard."

He stalked away and left them to their thoughts.

Next morning the rest of the *Fair Lady's* passengers came off in a wherry from Greenhithe, half-a-dozen hangdog fellows, deserters from the King's ships, by the look of them, and tempted out of hiding now by the disappearance of the press gangs and the prospect of free victuals in America. None had more baggage than a bundled handkerchief.

With his passenger list complete, Old Hux stirred this curiously gathered crew and dropped down the river to Tilbury. There lay the transports for Nova Scotia, and as the snow slid past one after another in a search for moorings her crew called off the names—*Charlton, Winchelsea, Wilmington, Merry Jacks, Alexander, Beaufort, Rockhampton, Cannon, Everley, London, Brotherhood, Baltimore.* The ships were of four or five hundred tons each. Two were old navy frigates. Every deck was aswarm with men, women, and children; each hull, with its wide tumble home, seemed to bulge with the press of humanity inside, and against each curved wooden flank clustered the bumboats of Tilbury. Ports were open and black with heads chaffering with the raucous bumboat women for gin and cheese and other cheap items of the river trade, passed up to them through the nettings. The weather-beaten hulls, the nudging swarm of boats, were like nothing so much as a herd of sows each suckling a greedy litter on the broad water of the Thames.

The *Fair Lady* rounded to at a mooring below the fleet, and there she lay, and there the fleet lay, for days that grew into weeks. Mr. Foy, after a few days, took his lady ashore to stay at an inn. The transport captains spent their time in visits to taverns ashore or visiting each other in their gigs, when sounds of song came drifting from stern cabins on the evening air and bottles on the tide.

The bumboat trade went slack as the meager coins of the emigrants were spent, and the boats disappeared except for one or two making a hopeful daily round of the ships. Once there was a burst of activity aboard the transports. Sounds of carpentry drifted down to the *Fair Lady* from morn to night, and the Thames wore a drifting wig of shavings. From the deck of each moored ship sprouted a number of queer wood-and-canvas structures that set the whole river front agog. The things looked like fat little chimneys. Were they planning to stay off Tilbury forever? Rumors flew.

Someone remarked a curious resemblance between these transports and the prison hulks moored off the Thames marshes lower down. Was it all a scheme to lock up London's poor?

Job Huxley solved the mystery for his crew one evening late in April, returning in the twilight from a visit to the *Wilmington*. He seemed in a jovial mood, and Tom Fuller made bold to ask, "Them new things rigged aboard the transports, sir—might they be chimbleys, now?"

Old Hux paused with a heavy hand gripping each side of the gangway. He laughed, and the teeth flashed white in his black beard.

"Chimneys? Ay, they might be. They might be pigeon cotes, or kennels for such hounds as you! They might be sentry boxes for to watch the tribe o' thieves they've shipped. But they ain't! They're air pipes, begod! 'Ventilators'—that's the word. A new invention o' the Lords o' Trade. Whether it's to let in fresh air or to pass off the stink o' the passengers I couldn't say—not bein' eddicated like the Lords o' Trade. But it's for to 'prevent sickness amongst the emigrants'—them's the words. D'ye ever hear such nonsense? Eh? Why, too much clean air'll kill that dunghill spawn o' London like a pox. They ain't used to it and can't stand it. 'Slike keelhaulin' a man that's never even had his face washed afore. Stands to reason." Away he reeled to his cabin.

"Ventilators!" muttered lugubrious Mr. Cheeny.

"What'll happen in a seaway, with the decks awash, say?" demanded the boatswain.

"All them openin's in the ship!"

"Drownded," a seaman said. "Like rats."

"Lords o' Trade!" snorted Tom Fuller.

"How's the crew to bowse and haul with all that clutter about the deck?" the boatswain said. Nobody seemed to know. Aboard the transports nobody seemed to care.

May Day came, with the ships still idle in the river and their ragged population wandering about the decks like penned cattle or standing at the bulwarks in long rows for hours on end, staring emptily at the green Kent shore.

The fleet had become a joke in the river. Crazy little wherries manned by urchins begging pennies from the ships had long since given up the transports for poor business, but they thumbed their dirty noses as the wherries drifted past and cried a doggerel up to the glum faces at the rails.

> "Goin' to Ameriky?
> Bring me back a parakeel
> If 'ee stay,
> Lackaday,
> Lord save Amerikyl"

The emigrants answered always with a broadside of Billingsgate, to the intense delight of the urchins, and "Ameriky" became a by-word of the traffic on the river. Bargemen cried it up to the ships as they passed; the little coasters, the Holland hookers, the fishermen, the watermen, all shouted, "Amerikyl"

The emigrants were sick of the word and of all the things it meant. They wished themselves out of the ships, yes, and out of the clutches of the Lords of Trade.

But suddenly things began to move. Barges came down-Thames from the city and moored alongside in half-dozens, in dozens, laden with cargoes that silenced all the gibing tongues: boxes of blankets, of woolens, of shoes, of lines and nets for the fishery, of stationery, surveyors' instruments, seeds, medicines. Thousands of brick, barrels of rum, beef and pork, barrels of ship biscuit and flour and peas, a full equipment for a hospital. Many chests of arms, of axes, of hatchets, of knives. Casks of sugar, of vinegar, of powder and shot. Coils of rope and cases of tools. Artillery—mostly fieldpieces and swivel guns. Furniture. Live cattle and pigs and poultry.

Astonishing! Somewhere behind the distant smoke of London was a will and a purpose. Someone in that warren of Whitehall offices had an eye fixed on America.

The last lighter slid away empty, the last bale was whisked into the hold. The transports unshipped their cargo booms and bent their sails. An air of expectancy hung over the fleet where there had been nothing but despair.

John and Mary Foy came off to the *Fair Lady* in a galley piled high with new purchases. Job Huxley greeted them curtly and let fall a growl about the space below being cluttered with private stores. Most of it was wine in casks—Madeira, Lisbon, and port, some claret, several cases of brandy, and a butt of ale. Mr. Foy seemed prepared for a long sojourn in a desert.

His lady wore a light gown of some flowered stuff and a milkmaid hat tied with a white ribbon under her chin. Roger saw for the first time the true color of her eyes, a strange hue, a clear sea green with faint gold specks. She gave him a swift smile and vanished into the cabin with her maid.

Said Old Hux, "Well, sir, you're in the know, it seems. When do we sail?"

Foy shrugged. "I was simply told to get aboard, Captain. I'm told that all's ready bar the naming of a commander for the expedition."

"Zounds! That'll take Whitehall a twelvemonth! What ship's he to sail in?"

"In none of these. There's a sloop of war awaiting him and his suite at Spithead."

"Her name?"

"*Sphinx.* 'The Sphinx with her enigma.' "

Old Hux slapped a disgusted hand on the rail. "Who said that?"

"Sophocles."

"Damme, there's a new lord on the Board o' Trade and Plantations every day!"

CHAPTER II

All in the Downs

THE WORD HAD COME. The new captain general had sailed for his distant province from Spithead, and the transports were to follow at once. The fleet awoke with a cheer that passed from ship to ship, and the emigrants crowded the rails with wild, rapt faces, shouting over the water. Their tumult brought the shore folk out of their houses and bargemen from their cabins.

"Ye'd think they was goin' to a fair," Tom said soberly.

"So they are—a damned rum fair," the boatswain said, and spat. "They'll be playin' at cockshies with the Indians afore the summer's out—at the wrong end o' the pitch."

"Hands there! Man the capstan!" roared Old Hux. "D'ye think I want to be the last ship out o' the river? Mr. Cheeny, get the head-sails on her!"

Roger and Tom were standing with some of the Greenhithe passengers near the forehatch.

"Come on, you idlers!" snapped the boatswain. "Rouse out them capstan bars and walk the anchor up."

If there were any doubt about the history of the *Fair Lady's* male passengers, it vanished in a moment, for they sprang at the word of command and knew exactly what to do. Roger found himself beside Tom at one of the bars, trudging slowly about the capstan to the mournful chant of "Spanish Ladies."

"Anchor's apeak, sir!"

"Vast heaving, then! Mr. Cheeny, get your boat away and slip the mooring aft!"

Old Hux was in fine voice this day. With the after mooring slipped and the boat in, "Now walk that anchor up! Stamp and go, ye Wappin' water rats! A tune, there!"

Stamp of feet and clack of pawls, flog of headsails in the river breeze, "Farewell and adieu to ye, Spanish ladies . . ."

"Anchor's aweigh, sir!"

"Walk it up, then! Helm, there!"

The snow swung neatly under the thrust of her headsails, and the river current did the rest. Away she went on the yellow ebb tide, with hands swarming aloft to shake out canvas and the flat shores of Thames-mouth sliding past.

The Essex shore withdrew mysteriously into the offing. The Kent shore held, low and green, with a rim of black mud as the tide ebbed. Tom Fuller gave Roger a nudge and a jerk of his head, grinning. Over there somewhere, beyond the marshes, Jemmie Calter's lonely bones were swinging in the breeze, keeping that endless watch upon the Rochester road. The adventurers had cheated him of company.

But it had been a long wait and a hard strain there in Thames-mouth, constantly expecting a reappearance of the fat man with his descriptions and his warrants. The fleet had lain there five-and-thirty days, and it seemed as many months.

Behind the *Fair Lady,* as she passed the Nore, the white canvas pyramids of the transports filled and shone in the sunny May morning. Distance lent them grace and beauty and erased all their smudges and patches, and the sight of that thronging canvas was stirring even to Roger's landsman blood. In such a fashion fleets of Englishmen had gone out, through and through the long years, to seek and woo the golden woman of the world.

It was pleasant enough bowling along the Kent coast under the westerly wind, but when the *Fair Lady* rounded North Foreland toward evening and fetched the wind ahead there was a sorry change, with short tacks and hard labor at the braces, all hands scrambling continually to the roar of Old Hux and the shrill voice of Mr. Cheeny while the snow crept slowly into the Downs.

There she anchored in the last of the light. She had outpaced the transports, which came in during the night with a great flogging of spilled canvas and splashing of anchors and bellowing of orders.

Job Huxley went off in his gig toward the twinkling lights of Deal. Roger stood at the main chains watching the boat lanthorn dance away. The deck was deserted except for himself and a seaman at anchor watch beside the forebitts; he could see the fellow's pipe glow in the dark, a forbidden luxury on deck but safe enough now with Cheeny turned in and Old Hux off for a carouse in Deal.

Mrs. Foy's voice startled him. "A penny for your thoughts, Mr. Sudden!"

She had come like a ghost in her silken shoes, and the pale stuff of her gown made a ghostly blur in the dark. "But wait," she added quickly. "I wager sixpence it's a woman!"

"You win and you lose, ma'am. I was thinking of *The Fair Quaker of Deal.*"

She stepped to the rail beside him. "The play? I saw it. Mr. Foy thought it shocking to take me to the theater, but I'm a headstrong creature, and why should men have all the pleasure?"

"Why indeed?" he murmured politely.

"I think I've seen Garrick in all his parts. Did you know he'd given up that pretty creature Woffington for a demure little dancer from Vienna? Mam'selle Violette. They say he's going to marry her. Much better for him, too. A charming man. Did you see his *Miss in Her Teens?*"

"I've not been in England for a long time, Mrs. Foy."

"May I ask where you've been?"

"It would take too long to tell you. I'm a wanderer."

"And that's why you're off to America?"

"Yes."

She laughed. "You don't want to talk about yourself. That's odd, in a man!"

"Suppose," he said boldly, "you tell me something of *your*self."

"There's nothing to tell, Mr. Sudden."

He was tempted to ask her why she had married a man old enough to be her grandfather. Instead he said easily, "Perhaps you'll tell me why you wear white ribbons in your hats."

"How observant you are, sir!"

"In London," he suggested, "the white ribbon marks a lady of Jacobite tendencies. Is yours a symptom of the heart?"

"I don't wear my heart upon my sleeve, not even for such witty daws as you, Mr. Sudden."

"And what about the ribbon on your hat?" he insisted.

"Come, sir! There's nothing on my head at this moment but my hair, which is red—quite unpolitical and most unfashionable. Please talk to me. This is going to be a long voyage and I must have someone to converse with besides Mr. Foy and my maid and that black bear of a captain."

The night over the Downs was full of stars, and she had her face turned up to them, a pale oval in the dark. Experience tempted him. In the piquant piece which he had played so many times in so many places these were familiar cues: the woman's adroitly chosen time and place, the confession of loneliness, the stepping close, the mingled scents of perfume and soft flesh, the face upturned, the little waiting silence. There was even the spice of a husband somewhere in the offing. She was not beautiful, but she had a figure made for caresses, and there would be fire in her if the hair meant anything.

He slipped an easy arm about her waist and found it pliant, in spite of her stays, and warm under his palm. A promising waist, an exciting waist. In a moment now she would sway a little toward him and turn her head in unconvincing protest or perhaps only to laugh softly in assent, in any case to put her mouth in reach of his; and he would kiss her, lightly at first, while her lips waited, parted, for the next and deeper caress, her arms half lifted for the embrace that would bring them knee to knee and breast to breast. He felt her waist go taut.

But the blow came unexpectedly for all that, the back of a doubled left fist flung up with force. It caught him full in the mouth and he tasted the salt of a cut lip. He released her waist at once. He was furious.

She said quietly, "I've hurt you. I'm sorry."

"No." Liar! She had bruised his mouth and his self-esteem in a stroke.

"I don't like to be touched—by anyone."

"So I see."

She moved, a matter of inches, but the gulf was deep. "Please don't be angry. I'm not. Can't we talk about something? The weather? How long must we wait here for a fair wind?"

"That's hard to say," he replied coldly, and then, with an assumed lightness, "When you live in Kent the east wind seems to blow half the time; sailors waiting in the Downs for London say all the time, and those outward bound say none of the time. It's all in where you want to go or what you want to do."

"And what do you want to do? In America, I mean?"

"I told you once. To make my fortune."

"Many men have gone to America for a fortune and stayed for lack of it."

"Not I, ma'am. At the worst I can always put on a pair of tarry breeks and work a passage home."

"Where did you learn to say 'breeks'?"

"In my travels."

"You've traveled in Scotland, then. Tell me about Scotland."

His tongue went into his cheek. Then, wickedly, "A wild country, most of it too near the sky for comfort—a little too close to the weather. The men are wild like their country and rough as their weather, but there's a strain of music in them that deserves a better instrument than the bagpipe. A Highlander will kill you at the slightest insult and compose a poem over your corpse that would make the very mountains weep. The women——"

"Ah!"

"The women are strong and beautifully made, but there's more strength than beauty in their faces and more beauty than strength in their souls. They have the morals of the deer on the hillside. They don't wash as often as our London dames, but then town dirt is so much more dirty——"

"You're speaking of the Highlands"—her voice was thin-edged like the ice of a night's frost on a loch in the hills—"and thinking of some herdsman's women in a bothy among the glens. Have you never been in Edinburgh?"

"The women of Edinburgh are dirtier than the others and not so pleasant in their manner."

"You have a low opinion of Scottish women."

"On the contrary, I think them the finest in Europe."

"Do you speak from experience?" tartly.

"I do."

"And now you propose to sample the women of America?"

What scorn she put into those words! He answered deliberately, "I've put women behind me along with other things that have no more importance."

A silence. Then, lightly, "And what do you think of me, Mr. Sudden—from your experience?"

He had been waiting for that. She was very young in spite of her married poise and assurance. She had opened with a woman's gambit—asking a man to talk about himself—and it was inevitable that she would bring the conversation to herself.

"You are a Highlandwoman by birth, but you've spent much time on the Continent, no doubt following your husband's dragoons in the late campaign."

"What makes you think that?"

"My dear Mrs. Foy, I've lived the past three years on the Continent and met a number of people who spoke English fluently but with a trace of Scots or Irish, a sort of Gaelic lilt that is especially charming in a woman. Well, to go on . . . your husband seems a gentleman of means, yet he has no official standing in the expedition or you and he would have sailed with the captain general. So he must be interested in some commercial venture in the colony. I take it that you've no children or you'd have them with you—for you have the air of a woman who has burned her boats and sees nothing but the future."

Again silence. Then she said, "Mr. Sudden, there's a touch of wizardry about you. A dangerous gift."

She began to move away, and he said mockingly, "Are you afraid of it?"

She uttered a sound, a little cluck of annoyance, and said quickly, "I'm afraid of nothing about you, Mr. Sudden. Good night."

He watched the flit of her slender figure along the deck. The mast-head lanthorns of the fleet were swaying in the anchorage like a scatter of linkboys in a London street. A small shower of sparks flew into the sea from the *Fair Lady's* bow, where the anchor watchman was gently tapping out his clay on the bulwark. The fellow spoke as Roger stepped to the forecastle door.

"Wind's veering, I think."

Roger gave him a good night and passed inside. The crew snored in their hammocks by the light of a single lanthorn whose candle smoked vilely. He felt pleased with himself, as if he had scored some kind of victory over that cool, green-eyed young woman, but when he climbed into his hammock and lay there going over their conversation he knew what a fool he was. He had learned practically nothing about her. That did not matter very much. But in one way or another he had told her practically everything about himself. That was serious.

CHAPTER 12

Departure

THE WIND had not veered enough by morning to enable the transports to move, but Old Hux was anxious to show them what his nimble little snow could do. He came off Deal Beach in the first light with a red eye after the night's affairs, but in surprisingly good humor, and at once set about getting up anchor and making sail down the channel. It was a stiff business of long and short tacks, with incessant scrambling to halliards, braces, tacks, and sheets. A little sulkily, but putting a good face on it, Roger pulled and hauled with Tom Fuller in the larboard watch. Clever young Mrs. Foy sat with her husband on a bench against the cabin skylight, and Roger seemed to feel the play of the gold-flecked green eyes in all his movements. She was enjoying his awkwardness, no doubt, as she would have enjoyed a clown at Covent Garden. Whenever he thought of last evening's conversation he writhed.

Thus occupied in mind and body, he scarcely noticed the land slipping past until, hanging grimly to the maintopsail yard and striving with one hand to help reef the lively canvas, he saw Tom Fuller's jerking thumb and looked beyond the struggling men on the yard to a low shingle point off the starboard quarter.

"Dungeness! There's the last of old Kent!"

Aye, there it was, already no more than a shimmer in the haze. He thought piously, God send a good return!

On the following evening Old Hux dropped anchor among the idle warships at Spithead and went away with a bundle of papers in his gig toward the smudge of Portsmouth. Roger wakened in the night and heard a drumming of rain on the deck overhead and the harping of a rising wind in the rigging. Then the heavy clatter of restless Mr. Cheeny's sea boots and his voice in the forecastle, calling a few hands to "freshen the nip."

"What's the matter?" he asked of Tom in the next hammock.

"Hear the rain? Wind's come east, hard. She's swingin' to her anchors, and the mate wants to ease the cables a bit. The transports'll be up with us tomorrow night. A great wind for the outward bound."

In the forenoon Job Huxley came off in the gig, with a tarpaulin over his head against the downpour. His boat's crew looked like drowned rats. He ordered the gig stowed for sea, looked at the cables, announced that some important government stores would come off in lighters as soon as the weather cleared, that a sloop would come out of Portsmouth with fresh meat for the cabin table and a quan-

tity of sea stores, that the transports would be up by night, and that
he was to be called as soon as any of these things came to pass. With
that he dived into his cabin, bellowing for the steward, and did not
reappear until dusk, when the watch saw the first of the transports
looming through the rain. The others followed in slow file like a
herd of cows coming in from the pastures at nightfall, and there followed a good deal of backing and filling in search of anchorage, to
the accompaniment of profane advice by speaking trumpet from the
men-o'-war in the roads. Old Hux added some advice of his own to
the *Wilmington,* which blundered too close to the *Fair Lady.* He did
not quit the deck until all were settled.

Rain was still falling in the morning, although the wind had slackened a little. Mrs. Foy came on deck wrapped in a cloak and holding
an umbrella over her head. Her husband appeared in a double-caped
boat cloak and a common tarpaulin hat, gave a nod to Tom and
Roger, and commenced walking the poop with his wife.

Before long the rain ceased altogether, and Mrs. Foy ran a slender
hand up the umbrella stick and collapsed the thing like a tent. The
seamen stared.

Old Hux came from his cabin and peered toward Portsmouth,
where out of the light rain mist on the face of the waters there appeared presently the brown sails of a pair of lighters. They came
slowly and uncertainly in the wet, fluky wind off the Channel, and
Old Hux tramped impatiently up and down.

Alongside, their shallow bowels yielded mysterious machines in
wooden crates, followed by smaller boxes and cases, all marked with
the broad arrow of His Majesty. There was difficulty in stowing all
this, and Huxley stood at the open hatches roaring down to the
sweating seamen in the hold as if he could lever the goods into place
with his tongue. When all was stowed he walked aft, then forward,
peering over the side, announced fiercely, "I don't like her trim!",
and ordered some of the heavier goods, including the machines, transferred to the afterhold. This involved shifting other goods from the
afterhold to the forward. All in all the crew of the *Fair Lady* had well
earned their meager wage when the day began to wane.

Roger, in the hold, read the careful directions in black paint upon
the latest shipment: "Gifts for Indians" . . . "French Bibles" . . .

"Powder keep dry," and so on, but the crated machines remained a mystery until he clambered on deck with the others and found Old Hux loudly perusing his orders and a copy of the bill of lading by the hatch.

"Umph! *You are to make all speed to overtake or join the captain general upon the coast of Nova Scotia*—Zounds! Do they expect a bit of a snow to catch a sloop o' war?—*since your cargo must answer his immediate needs.* Needs, ecod! Beads, Bibles, brandy, hatchets, blankets, tinderboxes, gunpowder, fire engines—— Why, damme, barrin' the blankets that's all hell needs! What are ye grinnin' at, ye lubbers? Mr. Cheeny! Get the anchors up and make sail!"

The Channel and the sky over it were one leaden gray, the sky weeping once more, the sea tossing in uneasy lumps, the land a gloomy mass behind the rain. A melancholy scene for a departure. It seemed to affect the people in the transports, staring in silence over the rails as the *Fair Lady* went past. Below the transports lay decommissioned men-o'-war, one after another, with sails unbent and topmasts and upper yards struck, with no more than an anchor watch aboard, as if England had done with her wars forever.

Something disturbing about that. What? Roger wondered. The presence of France just over there to larboard? For years he had looked upon France as the faithful ally of his rightful king and all who fought for him. That notion had been shattered when France came to terms with England and thrust Prince Charlie from her bosom.

Now he sensed something intensely selfish and malignant looming along the south side of the Channel. The French had been playing a deep game, and the castoff Stuart cause was only part of it; the rest would go on and on. To what end? He told himself that he did not care and looked toward the west.

The *Fair Lady* sailed dead into a stormy sunset that promised a continuance of the useful easterly weather. Like a fire of cannel coal at the water's edge, the sun flared yellow behind black bars of cloud, touching the Isle of Wight with long pale rays that gilded the headlands and hilltops for a few moments and then were gone. The shadow of the heart of the land crept out, and now it was all a mystery, an illusion in the twilight, now near, now far, now part of the solid darkness in the east. A few lights pricked out of the dusk. Somewhere a sea bird cried, like a wail from the heart. Roger turned and saw the *Fair Lady's* whole company gathered along the starboard rail. He could not see past the foot of the mainsail to the poop, but he knew Old Hux was there and Foy and the green-eyed woman.

The wind, for the moment anyhow, was steady rather than strong, and the ship and all aboard seemed part of the enormous silence of the sea. Roger stood on the forehatch by the long boat. On his left hand the foremast raised its tower of canvas, the great course, the topsail, the smaller topgallant sail, the wisp of royal, all bellied out without a wrinkle by the steady wind and held there as if starched.

On his right hand rose the canvas of the mainmast, with the swell of the sails toward him like great breasts outlined against the night by the gleams of the masthead lanthorn. Not a block moved; for a space not so much as a reef point. The whole ship seemed to hold itself breathless in the spell that gripped the still figures at the bulwark, realizing suddenly the awful immensity of the sea and their loneliness on the face of it, and longing emptily for busy streets and rivers and roadsteads, the comfort of shipkind and mankind, and the knowledge that tomorrow's sun would rise upon things safe and assured and old-familiar.

Strangely, they did not think of America, where there were terrors enough, according to the tales. It was this final plunge away from the known that oppressed them, made awesome by night falling as they sailed, and terrible in its completeness. What awful curse had made the English the gypsies of the sea?

Whimsically, Roger saw Fate as a dark and inscrutable giant casting another two or three thousand English into the wilderness.

PART TWO

The New World

CHAPTER 13

Chebucto

THE LAND was a cloud at first, long and blue across the west, and then a low and ragged parapet traced in the flame of a fine sunset. Old Hux stood on for a time into the afterglow. Dusk had swallowed the east and was striding toward the ship on seven-league boots. He spread his chart against the cabin skylight, and Roger, at the wheel, had a long look at it. Nova Scotia leaned into the Atlantic, a narrow irregular country like Britain itself; but the chart had a vague look, there were long sections of coastline sketched uncertainly, "by some fool in a fog," Old Hux swore. His sailing directions—and the sailing directions for the whole fleet, for that matter—had been airy to say the least. They were to steer for the coast of Nova Scotia, and about halfway up its length they would find a great harbor which the savages called Chebucto. West of the entrance the shore line was white, and the shore to the east was red. And that was all.

Job Huxley stared at the long low wall against the twilight. "Struck it fair, damme . . . the whole stretch of it under my forefoot . . . but where? . . . And which way's this Chebucto?" He made an abrupt decision, bellowing, "Ready about!"

The men sprang, and later, as the snow hauled her wind, he grumbled in a great voice, "A fair wind and a good landfall . . . bad luck to turn your back on it . . . never did this afore in me life . . . passengers to consider . . . night comin' on . . . strange coast . . . no pilot . . . chart drawn by guess and by God . . . Um!"

He fortified his patience with gin and trod the poop most of the night, muttering piously for a continuance of the westerly weather. One breath from the east would smother him in that white bank fog again—and he had groped for a week in the stuff already, at the end of the long westerly voyage.

The *Fair Lady* stood off and on through the night. In the morning the wind had fallen light, and it began to baffle, with puffs of moist air from the southeast.

Huxley made all sail for the coast, as if pursued by demons. By noon they were close in. It was a low green mass with a gray thread of foreshore, with no large hills, with nothing remarkable that could be tied to that worthless chart. It trended northeast and southwest. In the end, savagely, Old Hux tossed a shilling, "Heads, east! Tails, west!" It fell in his big paw head up, and east he went. He spent most of the day in the fore-topmast crosstrees with a spyglass, bellowing his orders to the deck, and late in the afternoon he hailed Mr. Cheeny in sudden excitement. "A sail, there! A sloop or shallop o' some sort! Standin' in to the coast! After him! There's a pilot for us!"

The whole crew was on deck, and the passengers, straining their eyes to pick up the chase. The wind was strong at southeast now and dead aft as the *Fair Lady* swept toward the land, a cluster of irregular blue humps whose bases slowly joined as they approached. On its slim white wings the strange sloop fled before them like a gull. And now, to the east of the humps, appeared a low and featureless shore. But there was a narrow gap between, as if some sort of river flowed out of the forest there. The southeast sky was gray, a high canopy of cloud that hung in curious twists and folds like an enormous bedtester, wrinkled, soiled, and likely to collapse at any moment—and moving toward the ship at a great rate. Already there was a haze across the sun, and a wide dark ring appeared about it as the haze thickened and the weird, convoluted clouds moved up the sky. No one in *Fair Lady* had ever seen such a sky, but its meaning was plain to them all. A storm—and a lee shore. Old Hux held on doggedly.

Now and again there was a brief break in the overcast. In one of these moments the sun put a pale finger on the steep headland to the west and another on that low shore to the east.

"Look!" Mr. Cheeny cried.

The shore to the east had a reddish cast, a look of red claybanks.

But the foot of the headland to the west shone gray white in the sunshine.

"Chebucto!" shouted Old Hux. "Just"—with an almost audible swallowing of his own astonishment—"just where I figgered I was!"

The crew were not so sure. Old Hux stood on boldly in the wake of the little sloop, gambling everything on his luck, the brief break in the weather, the toss of a coin—so it seemed to them. The two headlands, whose doubtful colors might have fitted many a blind alley in the long ragged coast, seemed to creep out toward them, bent on their destruction. Now they could see the long swell breaking on the rocks inshore, and for that matter on reefs well off the west headland, where great spouts of white water leaped in the afternoon sun.

There was still no sign of the great harbor mentioned by the Lords of Trade, only a narrowing of the bay like the shoulders of a bottle. And there was a cork in the neck, a large island of some sort. The white sails of the sloop scudded into a passage to the west of it. Old Hux held on, but he shortened sail and put a man in the chains to heave the lead and another on the bowsprit to watch for the seaweed patch that might betray a sunken rock—as if, Tom Fuller growled, there would be time to do anything about it. They watched the lead line sliding away, noting the scrap of white calico at five fathoms, the red bunting at seven, the scrap of pierced leather at ten—and still no bottom. A pause, and then the leadsman's singsong, "Deep sixteen!"

"Sixteen faddom!" grunted Tom. He had guessed five or six at most, for they were well abreast of the island now and close in, with a long point of beach jutting out on the starboard hand and a steep wooded bluff on the other. The overcast had shut in and a bleak rain swept down on the wind.

"Heave again," said Old Hux calmly; and a roar to the masthead, "Don't lose that sloop!" Again the swing, and the line flicking out. "By the mark, fifteen!"

Some sort of creek opened to the northwest, dim in the rain. The flying sloop ignored it and held on to the north. Old Hux followed. A small island, cone shaped and covered with dark green trees, appeared ahead. But now the waterway was opening, and as the *Fair Lady* swung to starboard of the small green cone the main island closed the seaward view behind her like a shut door. On either hand

rose steep hillsides covered with wet pinewoods swaying and ruffling
in the wind, and the open water spread a good mile from shore to
shore, with the length of it running on for miles between the hills.
The lead gave eleven, fourteen, twelve fathoms. No sign of shoals,
even close inshore. Surely Chebucto, the great harbor of the French
maps and the tales of the New England fishermen! But all doubt
vanished as the *Fair Lady* passed inside the smaller island. There lay
a sloop of war with the flag of England fluttering, the *Sphinx* herself,
with the captain general aboard, and a harbor furl in her sails, and
the strange sloop running alongside her and putting a man aboard.
It was the twenty-first day of June. They had been eight-and-thirty
days on the voyage. There was no sign of the other transports.

On the second day the storm relaxed its fury, and Old Huxley,
dressed in his peculiar best, returned from a visit to the captain general in high fettle.

"Name's Cornwallis, all hot stuff and ginger, a man after me own
heart! Doubtful o' that red coat and gold lace, I was, knowin' sogers,
but he's all right, there ain't a pennyworth o' soger in him. Business—
all business! Cabin full o' quill drivers and ink flyin' like the rain.
Papers! Sealin' wax! Dispatches! He's got a pretty mess to straighten
out. The French are at Louisbourg to take over the fortress, and
Colonel Hopson up there's in a fine sweat—no ships to take his
troops away, nowhere to go, doesn't even know the captain general's
on the coast. Old Mascarene and his council's at Fort Anne, up in
the Bay o' Fundy, waitin' for orders. And God knows where the
transports and the settlers are—sunk, most likely, them and their
blessed ventilators!"

"Are you to carry dispatches?" John Foy asked.

"*Fair Lady?* Nunno! We've got that special gov'ment stuff aboard
—the Bibles and gunpowder and beads for the Indians and suchlike
that Colonel Cornwallis wants close to hand. No, there's two or three
fishin' sloops from New England he's usin' to run errands. All I've
got to do for the present, so I'm told, is to send a boat to explore the
head o' the harbor. Like to come?"

He said this with unusual deference. Some of his furious authority
had gone overboard with the anchors, apparently.

Old Hux had no immediate cause to regret the invitation, for Foy brought into the boat a basket of delicacies, with two wine bottles thrusting long green necks past the napkins. The cook passed down a mess kit of cold beef and broken biscuit for the men. Roger and Tom had been quick to leap when Mr. Cheeny called, "Hands to the gig!" and eight in all they rowed away in high cheer, watched by the two women and the glum remainder of the crew. They pulled over to the *Sphinx*, to pick up one of the New England pilots enlisted out of the fishing sloops by Cornwallis. He was a wiry man of middle height, not over thirty, with gaunt blue jaws and bright brown eyes. He gave his name as Barnabus Merrick and carried a fowling piece, bullet pouch, and powder horn.

Roger beheld for the first time an American. He was a little disappointed. Vague tales in England had given him a notion of pious Englishmen gone half wild in the American forest, and he had expected something between a dissenting preacher and an Indian. This fellow looked very ordinary in drab homespun and gray wool stockings, although he wore a cocked blue hat that must have cost him thirty shillings.

"What's that for?" demanded Old Hux, eying the gun. "Birds?"

"Of a kind," said Barnabus, settling himself on the thwart.

Huxley grunted, but John Foy leaned forward and said pointedly, "What kind of bird, precisely?"

The New Englander grinned a little. "A bird that walks like a man and howls like a wolf and ain't got no feathers barrin' one or two stuck in his topknot."

"Savages?" growled Old Hux. "These woods look peaceful as a church on Sunday morning."

"They always do," the pilot said, and spat. Boats from the *Sphinx* were moving slowly along both shores of the harbor as if they, too, suspected unusual birds.

"Why," declared the *Fair Lady's* master, "the forest comes right down to the water's edge, no paths, no smoke; I don't believe there's been a human foot in these parts since God made the world."

"Savages ain't human," the pilot said. "Besides, the Frinch was here three year ago, a whole fleet and army under the Duke d'Anville. Goin' to raise Cain with all New England, they was, but somethin' happened here to change their minds—smallpox, some say. I never did find out, rightly."

They followed the west shore northward for three or four miles. The wind fell, and the forest was a vast green silence gleaming with last night's rain. The east and west shores of the harbor drew together ahead, and Old Hux said, "Well, there's the head o' salt water by the look of it."

" 'Tain't," said the New England man.

"How d'ye know?"

"Been in here in fishin' vessels from home, fillin' water casks. That's the Narrers, up ahead. 'Bout half a mile wide. The harbor takes a turn to the west there, and then ye open the basin, five mile long and two or three broad, all shut in by woody hills. The whole o' the King's navy could ride in it, I guess."

"Gammon!" snapped Old Hux. "Have ye ever seen a fleet, Pumpkin?"

"Once."

"Where was that?"

"Louisbourg, the time us pumpkins took it from the Frinch."

"Umph!"

As the gig entered the basin the sun came out, and all cried out, seeing the broad reach of water and the perfect shelter of the hills.

"What water d'ye get here?" Huxley demanded.

"Fifteen to forty fathom."

"If ye know half as much as ye claim," said Old Hux in something close to awe, "this is the finest harbor in Ameriky. And that shore yonder is the place to build our town."

"No."

"Why not?"

"Too fur from the sea for fishermen. Town should be on the outer harbor, just inside the big island somewhere. Good beach on that island for dryin' cod."

"Cod! We've come here to build a fortress, not a stinkin' fish warehouse!"

Barnabus Merrick shrugged. "What'll ye live on? The King's rations?"

"For a year or so. After that our people will have their plantations."

"See the soil yet?"

"What about it?"

"I used to think," Barnabus drawled, "God dumped his leftover buildin' stores in Massachusetts, after He got through makin' the world. That was afore I see Nova Scotia."

"Rocks, d'ye mean?"

"And little else. On'y good soil in Nova Scotia's on the Bay o' Fundy side—and the Cajun farmers took up all that long ago. The on'y harvest ye'll ever see on this shore'll come from the sea, and it'll smell remarkable like fish."

Roger was enchanted with the fellow's lack of deference. Even Old Hux could not restrain a grin. The boat's crew were not so amused. Discipline had taught them to hold their tongues in the presence of superiors like Huxley, the master, and Foy, the gentleman. They resented this drawling fellow in the thirty-shilling hat. They were weary now from the long pull at the oars, and the sun was high and hot. The gig drifted on the wide glitter of the basin while Foy shared the contents of the basket with Old Hux, and the men munched the hard ship fare and washed it down with stale ship water from the *barrica*. The land was shuddering already in the June heat, and small islands toward the east side of the basin were going up and down like pumps in the haze.

"Now," declared Old Hux, wiping his mouth with the back of a hairy hand, "we'll push on to the end o' this basin and see if there's a river. Cornwallis says there ought to be a river somewhere."

"I can tell ye that without lookin'," Merrick said. "There's a river flows into the basin there"—pointing to the north—"but it's a small thing; ye could pitch a rock across it anywhere. There's no big river at Chebucto, nothin' but a couple o' fair-sized brooks."

"I see. Well, is there anythin' worth seein' up here? I've got to make a report to the captain general."

The New Englander considered for a moment. Then, in an odd voice, "Reckon there is—over yonder somewhere. On'y an Injun tale, mind. But there might be somethin' in it. I'm right curious about it myself."

They rowed in to the west shore, and as the gig drew into the shadow of the great pines by the waterside all the mystery of the new land seemed to rise before them like a wall. The forest was still as death. A smell of damp, of rotting vegetation, hung under the thick crown of the trees. The drip of yesterday's rain from the branches served only to emphasize the general silence. The seamen stared curiously at the great mossy boulders and the tall rugged trunks of the pines rising like pillars among them. They beached the boat cautiously and stepped ashore, Old Hux giving Merrick the lead— "seein' ye've got the only weapon in the company." Under the pines nothing grew but a mass of ferns, wet to the legs. The land rose steeply, and the steady climb brought the sweat to every face.

At last Old Hux gasped, with a clutch at his dripping beard, "Turn to the shore a bit, along the slope. 'Sblood! The country's hot as Jamaiky. Who'd ha' thought it, out there on the Banks in that freezin' fog?"

After a few rods of this there was a sound of water in the forest ahead. The little procession broke at once, the seamen scrambling wildly on, while Old Hux swore and Merrick halted, listening and staring from side to side like an alert cat. After a minute he went on, slowly, and came to a small stream running down the slope. There among the lush ferns squatted the seamen, scooping up the cool water in their tarry hands, or down full length, sucking and lapping like dogs.

Tom Fuller raised a dripping and beaming face and cried up to Roger and Foy, and Old Hux and the pilot, "At last, good, sweet, cold runnin' water! Arter forty days and forty nights afloat, like Noah in his blessed ark—on'y he could lower a bucket overside any time he was dry, whilst we had to drink that stinkin' Gravesend water all the way. Ah, take a drink, sirs! Take a good long swig of it! It's life, I tell ye! And to think on it runnin' to waste in these empty woods ever since the good God made the world!"

They abandoned their dignity and got down like the others, drinking long and thirstily, and lay in the ferns, dabbling their hot faces for the pleasure of it. They might have dawdled there an hour, but after the first fine ecstasy there were itchings and slappings, and they noticed suddenly that a host of small black flies hung over the brook in a gauzy cloud and crawled over their legs and hands and cheeks, whined in their ears, darted into their very eyes and the open cursing mouths of the seamen—and bit them everywhere.

They noticed Barnabus Merrick then. He was staring at an object just beyond the stream. It was a stump, cut with an ax, perhaps two, perhaps three seasons ago. They followed him in silence. There was a succession of stumps, the trace of a path which crossed some point of the land, apparently, for soon they caught a blue glimmer of the basin through the trees and in a few more steps emerged in a clearing of sorts beside the shore. A green tangle of undergrowth had sprung up since the trees were cut, and some of the larger pines still stood, as if the bygone axmen had been daunted by the size of them. A seaman yelled, pointing.

"Gad so!" ejaculated Old Hux, and stared, and they all stared.

Against the rough bark of one of the standing pines sprawled the skeleton of a man in the tatters of a white uniform. His shoes were off and lay at his hand, and the ten toe bones, upturned, shone white in the sunshine. A rusty musket leaned against the tree beside him, with the ruin of a hat hung on the muzzle. The eye sockets of the skull appeared to examine the Englishmen intently. The lower jaw hung open, as if in amazement, and they noted that most of the teeth were gone.

Roger moved a step or two toward the grisly thing and his shoe kicked something in the bushes. It rattled. He looked down and beheld another skeleton, festooned with the green of small creeping plants, and with a clump of ferns growing richly through the white basket of the ribs. The *Fair Lady's* party abandoned their awed silence with yells. "There's another!" "Look, there!" "Two more yonder!"

Dead men lay everywhere in that sunny space. The place was a charnel house. It seemed to have been cleared in great haste, trod by human feet for a space of weeks—two months at most, the New Englander said—and then abandoned by all but the dead. In the edge of the clearing were trees half cut and blown down in later winds, and trees with no more than the first bite of an ax. Often the ax was still there, wedged and rusting in the cut, or leaning against the trunk, or lying in the undergrowth and betrayed by the clink of metal against the seamen's shoes. And in the forest beyond, more dead men lay among the trees, half hidden in the ruins of brushwood shelters that had rotted and sunk upon their tenants in the suns and rains and snows of time gone by. The bones in the clearing, in the full blaze of the sunshine, were bleached and hard; but the skeletons in the gloom of the pines were stained with a green mold, so that each skull looked like a purser's cheese, and the bones had gone brittle and soft and had been gnawed by porcupines, so Barnabus Merrick said. Some wore the shreds of white regimentals, the brass buttons green with verdigris. Some lay in breeches only, the coat and waistcoat hung with care upon one of the rotten bivouac supports. Some were wrapped in blankets, moth-eaten and moldy, with swarms of gray wood lice crawling in the folds. Some lay naked to the world. The skulls grinned upward as if defying the Englishmen to guess their riddle.

Tom Fuller picked up a long black feather, and Old Hux snapped, "Savages!"

"Crows," said Barnabus Merrick coolly. "And ravens. What a feast they must ha' had! Lord! The stink 'ud fetch 'em from all the country 'round. Can't ye see 'em, eh?—peckin' and tearin' and clawin', and scufflin' and squabblin'?"

"Ah, but what killed these men, and who were they?" John Foy said. "I tell you, pilot, the savages must have surprised the poor devils, whoever they were, and massacred the lot."

The New Englander leaned on his gun, gazing solemnly about him. "I'll tell ye who they are—they're D'Anville's lot, that sailed for Nova Scotia from Brest, three years back. Goin' to drive the English from Louisbourg and Annapolis and ravage the New England ports. Started from France with half King Louis' navy and three or four thousand o' his best troops. Mounseer John-Care was with 'em, the governor o' Canady, and he'd arranged a force o' French rangers to come down from Quebec and join 'em here in Nova Scotia. I remember the fuss back home in Boston when we heard of it . . . troops called back from the march ag'in Crown Point . . . Boston full o' militia from all the country roundabout . . . hulks sunk in the channel . . . new cannon set up in Castle Willum . . . old uns scaled and fitted with new carriages . . . Lord! And prayer meetin's!

'Twas the prayers done it, I guess. The Lord riz up and smote 'em ag'in and ag'in. D'Anville made poor weather o' the westerlies and was all summer gittin' acrost. His fleet got off this coast dyin' o' scurvy—jeṣt in time to meet the Line Gale—it come a mite early that year, a week afore the sun crossed the 'quator—and there they was, caught on a lee shore with crews too sick to handle the canvas and claw off. Some was wrecked on the Isle o' Sable, some on the coast itself; some got dismasted and drifted off when the wind come 'round; some bore away for the Western Isles and the Caribbee waters. What was left gathered here to Chebucto."

"How d'ye know all this?" demanded Old Hux.

"From the tales o' the savages, partly. Partly from some New England fishermen that was caught here and held aboard one o' the French men-o'-war for a time. The Duke d'Anville poisoned hisself —died awful sudden, anyhow—and they buried him on that small round island in the outer harbor. The vice-admiral put the sick ashore and sent word cross-country to the Cajun settlements for help. The Cajuns cut a path through from Fundy Bay, and sent provisions and a mob o' Injuns for reinforcements. The scurvy was still ragin'—look at them skulls, hardly a one but spat out his teeth afore he died—and when that begun to clear up they all come down with the bloody flux and some other plague we never did figger out. The Injuns stole the dead men's cloes and caught the infection, and pritty soon *they* was dyin' like flies. They got scared and lit out. There was no sign o' the governor's troops from Canady. The vice-admiral give up in despair, locked hisself in his cabin and throwed hisself on his sword. I dunno where they buried *him*. Fact is, I never did know where they left their dead till I see this place today, though I heard tell of 'em chuckin' a lot overboard in the harbor itself. One way or another they left more'n eleven hundred dead here to Chebucto; and countin' what they buried at sea on the voyage out, they'd lost more'n twenty-three hundred sogers and sailors afore they quit this place and sailed for home. Preachers in Boston said there'd bin nothin' like it since the Spanish Ar-may-da."

"Let's get out o' this," Tom Fuller said. "Them bones give me a turn. Remind me of a shipmate that fell out o' luck——"

"We'll look a bit further," snorted Old Hux stoutly. "I've got a

report to make to Colonel Cornwallis, and I'll not have it said Job
Huxley turned back from a parcel o' dead bones."

Barnabus Merrick led off again, and for two hours they picked
their way through scattered clearings by the shore, separated by
patches of uncut forest. In some the bones lay thick, in others they
were few. In one spot there had been some proper burials; but the
stony soil and tough tree roots had been too much for the survivors,
and a dozen skeletons lay in a careful row, side by side, awaiting
graves that would never be dug this side of Judgment Day. The
single word *"Perdu"* was cut with a knife in a birch tree behind
them. There were inscriptions in other places, dates like *"15 Sep-
tembre 1746"* and *"Trepasse 2 Oct 46"* and the single word *"Dieu,"*
and someone with pride in his battalion had carved with skill in the
trunk of a maple, *"Regiment de Ponthieu."* The grim word *"Mort"*
was in several places.

Finally, as the Englishmen turned back along the shore toward
their boat, they came upon an inscription cut in a big birch at the
waterside.

"What's that mean?" Old Hux demanded.

"A l'Acadie?" Foy said. "Well, it's the French name for Nova
Scotia and——"

"Alackaday! A damned good name for it!" Old Hux looked over
his shoulder to that ossuary in the forest. "And this, ecod, is where
we've come to build a city!"

CHAPTER 14

Genesis

OLD HUX sent for Roger in the fine June twilight, and Roger found
him in the cabin with a case bottle and two glasses at his elbow.

"Sit down," the master said, "and help yourself. Tut, man! Shift
your hold. Always take a woman by 'the waist and a bottle by the
neck!"

Roger took a thoughtful sip of this unusual hospitality. What did
Old Hux want?

"Well, young feller," Huxley said, "ye've seen a bit o' the sea and a bit o' this Godforsaken country; what are ye goin' to do, eh? Take up a bit o' land wi' the rest o' that cockney mob and try to grub a livin' amongst the rocks and stumps?"

Roger sipped his gin again. "What else is there?"

"I'll give it to ye straight," said Job Huxley, fixing him with a bold blue eye. "Ye're a gentleman adventurer, I take it, and don't stick at trifles if I heard that bum bailiff in the Thames aright. Stay with me, then. I'm clearin' my passengers ashore—or to the transport that came in today, whichever they want—and sail for Annapolis in the mornin' to fetch Colonel Mascarene and his council here to start a gov'ment o' the province. In a couple o' months the *Fair Lady* goes off charter. Then for free-lance ladings and help-yourself trading up and down this coast—wherever there's a chance to pick up the pretty yellow boys." He rubbed his tarry thumb and forefinger suggestively. "Nova Scotia's all but an island—nailed to the continent like a cleat to the mast. Back country's got no roads and full o' savages anyhow. All settlement must be along the coast, and everything's got to move by sea. That's my chance—and yours."

"What about the other transports?"

"Too big, too clumsy for this coast—'specially the Bay o' Fundy, where I go tomorrow. In the bay harbors the tide rises and falls thirty or forty feet, and at the ebb ye're lyin' aground on your bilge and wonderin' where the ocean's gone. *Fair Lady's* got a good stiff back and ribs—Whitby-built, nothin' like 'em—stand hard lyin', winter weather, anythin' ye please. Only competition'll come from New England vessels, and there's room for all, 'specially after the fightin' starts. Wonderful how His Majesty looses his purse strings when the guns begin to pop. Now me—I know my ship and I know the sea, and in a month or two I'll know this coast like the palm o' me hand" —he spread his great paw on the boards, seamy and callused and none too clean (like his conscience, Roger thought)—"but I'll need someone like you that can talk the highfalutin lingo o' the captain general's staff."

"Why?"

"To bait the silver hook! The Lords o' Trade'll pour a flood o' money into this colony in the next few years, and that's a stream I want to fish."

Roger was silent. He did not love Old Hux, but he found the ruffian's bluntness engaging and even found something to respect in his energy and courage and his sea ability. Old Hux would not stick at law. Nor I, he thought—the law of the Hanoverians and the men who put them on England's throne! The money was the thing, the pretty yellow boys. Get 'em any way you could. Five years, ten years, and then home to Kent and the peace of Suddenholt. Still . . .

"Well?" the master grunted.

Roger's head wagged slowly. How to explain a whimsy that he did not understand himself? "I feel my fortune's ashore there, somehow. Because I'm a landsman, I suppose. I hate the sea."

"Who don't?" Huxley said.

"Well, it's more than that. It sounds silly, I admit. There's something about the country"—he nodded toward the open stern window of the cabin—"a sort of challenge, a riddle to be solved, a game of chance with strange cards . . . I don't quite know how to put it."

"Umph! Ye'll end as a pile o' green bones in the forest somewhere. D'ye know what's the matter with ye, Sudden? Ye're too damned romantic!"

Roger smiled. "What an epitaph!"

He left the cabin with an odd suspicion that someone had been listening at the bulkhead and that Old Hux knew it. The girl Jenny, no doubt; her servant curiosity.

In the forecastle he and Tom packed their duds under a gaze of silent men. The other "artisans" were staying with Old Hux, not liking the shore "till summat's been done to keep off the savages." Those dead men in the forest had impressed them. On deck Roger drew the American pilot aside.

"Merrick . . ."

"Call me Barney."

"Barney, then. What happened when you and Old Hux reported to Cornwallis? What's decided?"

"Nawthin's decided—yit. Thought we had big news, me and Old Bullroarer, but Colonel Cornwallis jest shrugged them fine shoulders o' his and went on to talk about somethin' else. Dead men don't bite.

It's live Frinch—and Injuns—he's got on his mind. But he agreed with me and the cap'n o' the *Spink* that the basin's no place for his town. I said 'twas too fur inland for the fishery, and the man-o'-war cap'n added that the town must command the outer harbor or all's worthless. Ye should ha' seen Huxley's face—enough to make a cat laugh. Well, then Cornwallis got sot on the notion o' buildin' the town on that pine point atween the harbor and the nor'west arm; argues he can defend the harbor entrance there and same time have a short bit o' land to watch ag'in the Injuns. That's the military mind for ye! Can't expect a soger to see the shoals off o' that point and the foul ground right ag'in the beach. Have to build long wharves to take the shippin', and the wharves wouldn't last any longer'n the first Line Gale—ye've on'y to look at that beach at Point Pleasant to know there's a tremenjus sea beats on it in southeasters. Rocks as big as tea chests hove up amongst the trees."

"What's your notion, Barney?"

"West side o' the harbor jest inside the small round island—the one they're callin' George's Island arter the King. Put cannon on that island and ye command the anchorage. Water's deep right in to the west shore, and ye've got a pritty level strip along the foot o' the ridge to build your warehouses and suchlike. The ridge rises to a peak that must command the country back of it for miles—a nat'ral citadel. Build the town on the lee side o' that hill for shelter from the nor'west wind—got to think o' the weather, see? The Frinch didn't think o' that when they built Louisbourg, and they freeze half to death in winter o' consequence. In clearin' the slope ye can get plenty o' good spruce and pine logs for spiles and cribs, and all the rock ballast God had left over from makin' the world—enough to build wharves from here to Jerusalem. Cornwallis is awful sot on a stream for fresh water, but I don't see what odds it makes. Plenty o' springs in the hillside, and ye can dig a hole anywhere in this country and git good water. 'Tain't like Injia or them other hot places that's nawthin' but sand and thirsty niggers."

"What does the sloop-of-war captain say?"

"The *Spink*? Agrees with me. All he cares about, o' course, is a good shore defense for the anchorage and a place to careen ships. A stiff-necked feller. I kep' callin' your skipper 'Cap'n Huxley,' and the

Spink man kep' remindin' me there wasn't any captains present but hisself—*Mister* Huxley bein' *master* of a snow under charter to the Lords o' Trade. Well, down home we call the master of anythin' bigger'n a shallop 'Cap'n'—and we talk the way we want."

There was something refreshing about that, and Roger grinned. The New World! It really was new, everything about it. A little too cocksure, perhaps, a little too scornful of what was old; but what other spirit could conquer this enormous green wilderness?

Seamen from the *Sphinx* had cut a clearing on the shore toward Point Pleasant and erected a few sailcloth tents, a little white cluster in the edge of the pinewoods, guarded by a handful of red-jacketed marines. A paltry beginning, but not much could be done until the fleet arrived. One or two transports had straggled in to the anchorage, and Old Hux now transferred the Foys and their maid to one of them, wanting their berth for Colonel Mascarene. Roger and Tom stood near the gangway, waiting for a duty boat from the *Sphinx* to take them to the tents ashore, when John Foy came with hand outstretched in farewell. The silver buttons gleamed in his scarlet coat, and the great full wig and dragoon hat made his long brown face seem longer still. The scar of the old sword cut twitched in his cheek.

"Good-by, Mr. Sudden. We'll meet ashore one of these days."

"Yes," Roger muttered lamely, gazing past the man to his wife. She came along the deck with her long light step, followed by the stolid Jenny.

"Good-by, Mr. Sudden." Her smile was impersonal—she turned to bestow it on several of the crew and passed down the gangway without a backward glance.

Her lips had that eager look which had nothing to do with men, and the male in Roger was piqued. In France he had seen novices look like that on the way to their wedding with Christ.

She did not fit his notion of beauty—too tall, too long in the leg, and red-haired women were bad-tempered and green-eyed women selfish and predatory. In Paris, Rome, or even London (where God knew most of the women were dull) he would not have noticed her at all. He put his interest down to abstinence, the long voyage, and the lone woman, a healthy male hunger asserting itself in spite of hardtack and saltpeter beef, the sort of thing that made men see a lush palm grove in the solitary thornbush of the desert. He seemed to see a sardonic look in Foy's eyes and flushed a little, muttering "Good-by" with lips unaccountably tight.

Their boat pulled away smartly, Mr. Cheeny at the tiller, the white hat ribbon of Mary Foy fluttering gaily in the harbor breeze.

Tom Fuller murmured, "As fine a leg as ever I see."

"Eh?"

"That maid o' m'lady's—Jenny."

"Oh!"

"Thank God there'll be some Englishwomen in this place."

The oars of the boat rose and fell like a machine.

Transports came in from the immensity of the sea in weather-beaten twos and threes. By July first not one was missing! Their re-assembly, safe and sound, in this vaguely known inlet of a savage shore three thousand stormy miles from Tilbury was nothing less than miraculous after D'Anville's fatal experience.

No wonder the French found the luck of the English incredible! The ships lay moored inside George's Island, their bulwarks lined with staring faces, so exactly like the squadron in the Thames that, standing beside his tent on the Point Pleasant shore, Roger had a whimsy that the voyage and these wooded hills were all a dream. Only the bumboats were missing. But there were other craft laden with fresh stores and the first consignments of sawn timber from Boston, slim New England sloops and schooners resting like gulls on the harbor water. From the ships there was a constant traffic of boats to the west shore. Mr. Inigo Bruce, the military engineer, and Charles Morris, the New England surveyor, were a-land every day with Corn-wallis and his staff, a little swarm of bright red flies that buzzed up and down the harborside and came to rest at last under the shoulder of the sugarloaf hill which Barnabus Merrick's shrewd brown eye had noticed from the first.

Roger and the handful of other emigrants in their small encamp-ment near Point Pleasant were thus left high and dry, and presently their little canvas oasis was invaded and overrun by a happy-go-lucky company in red coats with green facings and soiled white breeches and black gaiters—Warburton's Regiment, from Louisbourg. The soldiers fell to with axes and mattocks and a most amazing store of oaths, clearing a swath up the slope for the regimental camp.

Roger regarded them with mixed feelings, thinking back to Scotland, for this had been one of Johnnie Cope's regiments, scattered by Prince Charlie's men at Prestonpans. They maintained an indifferent guard and spoke of Indians with contempt; they had seen some at Louisbourg, "a lousy set of rascals without the spirit of a dog." That, my bold boys, Roger thought, is what you said of the Highlanders until you met them by the wall of Preston Park.

He picked up his worn portmanteau and trudged off along the shore, with Tom Fuller at his heels protesting emptily that a gentleman shouldn't carry his own baggage. At the foot of the sugarloaf they found a curious tumult: seamen from the transports clearing bushes from the water front and hewing down trees with more energy than skill; platoons of infantry strung like scarlet beads along the shore and through the hillside woods, bayonets gleaming, muskets cocked, watching for Indians but keeping a sharp eye also for the cockney girls; a swarm of emigrants about the harassed man Morris, following his every step, demanding that he lay off their fifty or their hundred acres—here—or over there—with gestures; army officers wandering in twos and threes as if for mutual support in the rabble, pointing canes and raising profane and ineffectual voices, or standing in scarlet groups, gold-laced hats together, hands twiddling canes behind, looking as if something urgent were toward —and probably discussing last night's play at cards; women squabbling or ogling the soldiers; small boys darting; babies shrieking.

Cornwallis and his staff were absorbed in affairs of state. Old Hux had brought Paul Mascarene and his council from Fort Anne, and about an oak table in the great stern cabin of the *Beaufort* transport they were holding a momentous meeting under the captain general's eye—the beginning of government.

The shore at the chosen site was now revealed as a narrow, stony beach with a strip of swamp behind it pocked with small stagnant pools. The seamen with axes had flung down logs to make a causeway to the hillside, and over this men were carrying the boards and timbers floated ashore from the American vessels. Two or three marquees were pitched over the stumps at the foot of the hill for the commissary, but there was storeroom only for immediate needs, salt beef, biscuit, a few hogsheads of rum. The great part of the stores must remain in the ships until there was permanent shelter ashore. That, Roger guessed, would not be for weeks, and probably months.

The hill shut off a light west breeze. In the narrow clearing by the shore the July sun fell like a bludgeon. Sweating cockneys cried that they had expected a cool country and, ecod, here it was as hot as Afriky! A moist reek of unwashed bodies rose and mingled in the clearing with a scent of new-cut pine and spruce and the tang of raw New England rum. Roger sniffed the queer blend pensively. Was this the smell of America? Afterward he knew it was, and would be for at least a century to come, until a clearing had been hewn far into the heart of the continent and men and women had leisure to be nice.

The cockneys had fared well on the long voyage. There was little sickness in the ships. For that they could thank the newfangled ventilators, but they were not a thankful lot. Their voices were raised now in complaint about the food, the lack of shelter, the flies, the climate, and the land itself. Axes had been put in their hands, but they would not cut a chip until their lots had been marked off by the surveyor. What! Cut a tree for someone else?

Barney Merrick growled, "Cornwallis is so busy bein' governor o' His Majesty's Province o' Nova Scotia that he ain't got time to set about buildin' his capital."

Roger smiled. "What's he done to displease you now?"

"Sent a sloop o' war off to the St. John River to watch the French there, another to see what's doin' up Canso way. Cap'n How's off overland to see about a treaty with the Injuns. Someone else is off to warn the Cajun French they've got to take the oath of allegiance to His Majesty. So it goes—the only officers with experience in this country sent over the hills and far away to chase wild geese—and nawthin' bein' done right here. These emigrants won't work 'less it's on their own lots. Cornwallis should tell 'em to pitch in first and clear the town site or by God there'll be no lots. If that don't fetch 'em, why, stop their rations—otherwise they'll stand about and jaw from July to Eternity—and Cornwallis ain't got that long. These fools think because the sun is hot today there ain't no winter in these parts. They'll larn!"

"What they really need," Roger suggested, not without malice, "is someone to show 'em how to do things. Someone like you."

"Um. Well, there's other men can show 'em. Cornwallis has done one smart thing—sent to Fort Anne for Gorham's company o' rangers. There's the lads! Backwoods Massachusetts men and half-breed Mohawks. Build a blockhouse while your reg'lar officer's drawin' up the plans. Know how to live off the country, and how to live *in* it, summer and winter. Go anywhere, any time, foot or canoe, it makes no odds. And they're skilled in fightin' Injun-fashion, which is what Cornwallis is goin' to need most. Reg'lar sogers in this country ain't worth His Majesty's sixpence a day—they ain't worth their rations. Pretty cocky now, o' course. But wait'll they've found a sentry or two with his head knocked in and his hair peeled off; wait'll they've seen a man cut up with knives and tomahawks till he looks like a lump o' offal from a slaughterhouse."

Barney smelled of rum, and the stuff had set his tongue wagging with a most unusual fluency. Roger listened with a faint smile on his lips. Old Hux was right, he thought; the man had Injuns on the brain.

"Did you ever," he suggested ironically, "see a regiment cut up with Highland broadswords?"

"Did y'ever," countered Barney, with eyes like slits, "see one o' your own friends knocked on the head and scalped while still livin', and then tortured for hours till the last gasp o' breath was wrung out o' him? Mind, I'll say this for the Micmacs, they didn't gather scalps till the white nations offered rewards for 'em. They tortured prisoners, but not with fire—which is hell's own delight—till the Frinch rangers and mission Injuns come down from Quebec and showed 'em how. Them mission Injuns can roast a man so delicate he don't die for two or three days—he's better eatin' that way."

"What! Cannibals?"

"Are ye surprised? All the tribes about the Great Lakes and south o' the St. Lawrence eat their enemies. Take a man, rip his scalp off, roast him to death, and pass him through your intestines as a final insult—that's the way to finish off your enemies! A woman's even better, to their way o' thinkin'. She yells louder when she feels the fire, and there's more fat on her, and her meat's more tender."

Roger felt a little sick. "Don't talk such filthy nonsense, man! You're drunk!"

"I'm sober as a judge! 'Tain't all one-sided, mind. Back home in New England and down York way we've made war partners o' the Six Nations—Mohawks and such—because they hate the Frinch and so do we. And a Mohawk is the devil's own. But at least he don't pretend to be a Christian! Them mission Injuns from Quebec . . . Listen, friend! There's jest two things a savage understands about the Christian faith—hell's fire and the Crucifixion. He's seen those things—he's *used* 'em all his life. The rest runs off him like water off a duck. He's got nawthin' to measure it by."

Barney's voice had risen with his memories. Roger sensed a peculiar hush about them and, turning, saw a gathering of emigrants regarding the New Englander with interest and awe.

"What's 'e talkin' about?" said one to Roger. It was Vace the journeyman barber. He recognized Roger as he spoke and set up a glad cry.

"Liz! Bob! Maggs! Oi! The lot o' ye—'ere's Mister Sudden!"

CHAPTER 15

Noblesse Oblige

To ROGER, in his self-seen role of foot-loose adventurer, the reappearance of Tooley Street was a confounded nuisance. What should have been an episode, to look back upon with amusement in some after-time of ease and well-being, had carried over into the present, where it had no place. It was not snobbery—he had rubbed elbows with common humanity too often, in too many places, to be finicky in this outpost in the wilds. But they clustered about him; they looked up to him; there was an air of relief about them as if—as if they had found an ass to carry their burdens. In his annoyance he was curt with them, but his curtness merely brought a wheedling note into their voices. There was no shaking them off; there was not room enough for that.

It was outrageous that in this enormous new world he should find himself confined to a five-acre clearing with this importunate rabble.

Well! The thing was to widen the clearing. He set them to work with axes and billhooks from the commissary. There was some murmuring about lots, but he crushed that in a voice whose cold violence astonished him quite as much as them. He took an ax himself by way of example and to satisfy a craving for action. The long idleness in Tooley Street and in the Thames and the monotony of weeks at sea had wound up his nerves like a spring.

The first bite of the sharp steel into a pine trunk was a joy, and as the white chips flew he wanted to sing. Sweat broke out on him, an ooze first and then a stream. He threw off waistcoat and shirt, regardless of the swarming black flies, and forgot the people, even the place. Nothing existed but the tall brown trunk and the white gash where the ax fell, seen through a glaze of sweat, and the lift and the swing and the satisfying *chock*.

This was the way you began, with one tree at the edge of the unknown; and from that you went on to the next and the next, leaving the chips behind, and the stumps, and the ashes of branches and leaves to enrich the soil. And as you stripped away the green pall which had covered it since Adam's time, the earth felt the warm kiss of the sunshine, as your own back felt it now, and stirred and was filled with new life. You swept away the shadow and the mystery and the menace, and opened it to the broad sky where the winds blew always and there was light. You were a god with a flaming sword, sweeping away the darkness that nourished things savage and evil, and while a tree stood high enough to cast a shadow you would go on and on and on! Down with it! Down! Down!

It was not so godlike after a time. The chips grew smaller, although he struck with the same furious energy. It occurred to him that the tree was very big. He shifted around the trunk a little and began again, and again for a time the chips fell large and fast. Then the narrow slot again, and the steel striking straight in, and the slow rain of little battered chips. He shifted again. He made a gradual circuit of the tree; then he was back to the original slot. He paused, panting. It was not so simple as he had thought. He would have to widen the cut. That was not so interesting or so satisfying. He wanted to get to the heart of the tree, and it seemed a waste of time and energy to hew a wider gash at the very outside.

He thought now of his little band of followers and inspected them, leaning on the ax. Tom Fuller, Bob, Killick, Maggs, Ned, and Jack, each had picked a tree and circled it in faithful imitation of himself. And there was the great creature Lumley, with her hairy and enormous forearms, swinging an ax as well as any.

The other women, and Vace the pale barber, were content to hack at the undergrowth with billhooks. Old Trope sat guardian on their poor baggage, a thin gray spirit of evil in the sunshine.

"Where's Little Bob?" Roger demanded.

Trope looked embarrassed. " 'E's orf."

"What d'you mean, off?"

"Orf for the cities of Ameriky in one o' the Boston vessels. Been talkin' about it ever since we got 'ere—didn't like the look o' the place—said 'twasn't what 'e expected and no chance for 'is profession, like. Asked one o' the schooner men if there was guineas to be 'ad in the Massachusetts colony, and the feller said, ecod, yes, the streets o' Boston was paved with 'em. So 'e's orf."

"There's others," added Mrs. Maggs darkly.

"Who?"

"Why, a lot o' them Wappin' men didn't never intend to chop no trees nor dig no plantations. All they wanted was a passage acrost— 'eard 'em jawin' about it in the ship comin' over. Said there was easy wages in the shippin' trade out o' New York and such places and the Lords o' Trade could plant their colony in 'ell for all they cared. They're slippin' away in the Boston vessels—seen some of 'em, 'aven't we, Missus Lumley?"

"Yes," uttered the Lumley hoarsely, "and I dunno but what they're wise. Plantations! These 'ere trees is too mortal 'ard to chop. Maybe we're doin' of it wrong."

"So you are!" said a new voice. They regarded a tall man coming toward them up the slope. He was gaunt and blue-jowled and loose in his movements, walking with a long stride and placing each step exactly before the other with easy precision, as if he had walked a tightrope all his life. He wore moccasins decorated with blue and red beads, and long leather leggings from ankle to crotch, with a fringe of jiggling leather points along the seams, and a loose hunting shirt of some soft thin hide. His hair was gathered into a short, stiff queue bound with a thong, and over it he wore a cocked blue hat much faded and stained. Three men stepped silent as cats at his heels, dressed like him except that their heads were shaven to a scalp lock stiffened with grease, and one had an eagle feather thrust in it; but they were not so tall, and their dark faces shone as if oiled and were hairless by nature, where his was shaven. Their cheekbones were large and square and their noses high like his but with wide-flaring nostrils; and their eyes were black and cunning like the eyes of a mongrel dog, where his were a startling blue in the brown face, like a glimpse of summer sky through a slit in a blanket.

"Gorham's my name," he said easily. "Cap'n Gorham, the shepherd o' the rangers. These"—jerking a thumb over his shoulder—"are some o' my lambs.'" He smiled.

Roger smiled and added coolly, "They look to me more like wolves."

The wolves stood, blank-faced, a pace behind him, regarding the cockneys with a faintly hostile contempt. Tooley Street stared back, astonished. This leather-clad group belonged in a booth at St. Bartholomew's Fair, with a barker charging tuppence at the door. The cockney mind clung to the things it knew: its notion of a plantation in the colonies, vague at first, made clear in the anchorage at Chebucto, seeing the settlement eventually as a sort of wooden London —on a small scale, of course—against a background of pines, full of familiar faces and things, and noisy with their own familiar speech. These visitors might have dropped from the sky. Tooley Street was not merely astonished, it was disturbed; as if, say, a tiger had come walking down the Borough Highway.

Captain Gorham picked up the ax. "If I talk like a schoolmaster," he announced whimsically, "blame Colonel Mascarene. I've spent the past five years showing his Fort Anne garrison how to get firewood and keep their hair on at the same time. Now I'm sent to another lot o' Johnnie-come-latelies. No offense, I hope? Now when ye go to fall a tree . . ." He explained the art of falling a tree, the wedge cut out low down on the side the tree was to fall, the main cut on the opposite side and slightly above, and hewn out wide from the start.

He demonstrated on Roger's pine. He did not seem to work very hard. He gave the ax a long swing and brought it whistling down, but his movements were leisurely, and after the first stroke he did not change his footing an inch. There was a magic about it. Man and ax were one thing, a whip with a lash of sharp steel. The movement began about his knees somewhere and traveled up his lean torso as he swung, and along the arms and wrists until at last the blade lashed home. A snow of large white chips flew and fell. The big pine swayed and began to fall, gently at first, gathering speed, hissing as it went, and at last smote the earth with a crash that shook it.

There was a large silence. Roger looked over his shoulder and saw Tooley Street in a wide half circle and a little in front of them a group of scarlet coats and gold-laced hats.

"Well, my man," said Colonel Cornwallis, "you seem to have made a start."

The captain general's cheeks were swollen with fly bites and beaded with sweat, and there were lines of worry in his forehead under the white edge of the wig. But his eyes were steady and there was a determined twist to his mouth. Beside him stood an aide, much like himself—Bulkeley, the Irish dragoon officer, his right-hand man. A pair of handsome military bachelors in the thirties, weary of London's drawing rooms, eager to do something solid in the colonies —written all over them.

"These people—you seem to have got 'em working. Working hard, by Jove! How did you do it? What's your influence with 'em?"

Roger shrugged. "They seemed to expect someone to tell them what to do. So I told 'em."

"And set 'em the example, eh, Gorham? You see, Bulkeley? The thing must be done in military fashion—divide the people into groups and put over them some fellow from their own ship's company, some energetic fellow like this, who's not afraid to tell 'em what to do and see that they do it. Hinshelwood! Make a note of this, please. A general order. Each ship's passengers shall be in charge of a man of their own company—they may select him if they wish—who shall be answerable to me. He shall be styled 'captain' of that company—I trust that won't offend your military sensibilities, Bulkeley—and shall be rewarded in the matter of rations and perhaps pay, later on. All complaints to be made through the 'captain'—I shall hear no others, mark that—and he shall draw his company's rations and tools and see that they are properly used—note that especially, Mr. Commissary, and notify the clerk of stores. Tomorrow after the noon meal I wish to meet all the 'captains' on the beach. See that this is faircopied at once, Hinshelwood. Nesbitt! Gray! You'll see that copies are distributed before night to each ship's company. That will be all for the present. The system can be elaborated as we go along. And—ah!—Hinshelwood, add that one of Captain Gorham's rangers shall be available to each company, to show 'em how to use an ax and build huts for 'emselves. You'll note that also, Gorham, please. Um! One other thing. Our present water supply seems confined to the small brook which runs down to the swamp behind the beach. Bulkeley, please see that a reliable man—one of Warburton's sergeants will do—is posted to patrol the stream. Any person, man or woman, committing a nuisance within twenty feet of the brook shall be publicly flogged on the beach by the stoutest drummers of the garrison. And that reminds me—Mr. Bruce, you'll kindly see that a whipping post and a pair of stocks are set up on the beach at the earliest opportunity."

The great man walked away and his perspiring staff fell in behind.

Roger turned to his ax again. There was no pleasure in it any more, none of that first ecstatic fury. It was labor now: sweat in the eyes and running down the loins, raw hands, sore muscles, the jar of ax blows running up the bones and smiting something sensitive behind the eyeballs, and thirst and weariness and flies, and knowing there were thousands—millions—of trees and that it took an hour, two hours, to hew one down and slash the branches off. For a tree was just a thicket on end; when you cut it down it cumbered the earth and your work was just begun. You could not count it finished, that one tree, until the trunk had been cut in proper lengths and rolled away to the hut sites, and the branches flung into a heap and burned to a flutter of ashes. It would take years! What a penance!

Thirst drove him at last to the brook, where already a solemn sergeant marched, full-buttoned in the heat, with halberd shouldered in witness of his authority. The stream was a poor thing; it would be dry, he judged, by mid-August, but a working party of seamen had made a rock-lined pool deep enough to dip a pail, and there he flung himself down and drank like a parched beast.

As he straightened his elbows, satisfied, he saw in the water a grim and sunburned visage, weary about the eyes, although the eyes themselves shone black and hard as jet. Drops of water glistened on the black-stubbled jaws. A large drop gathered on the tip of the fine curved nose, hung and glittered for a moment, then fell. The mirror was distorted with rings that spread across the pool, and the face became a gargoyle, dark and evil, with a mocking smile writhing on its lips. He rose, away from that grinning jinnee of the pool, thinking of the old witch in Spey glen and her whimsy that two creatures, saint and devil, lived within his skin. He could almost hear the cailleach now, the singsong Gaelic on her old cracked tongue, calling him "Saxon" and muttering of love affairs gone by, a safe enough guess with young men of the wandering sword. When he teased her for his future she had closed her eyes and cried, *"Luaidh mo chridhe, chan eil fhios agam fhin co dhiubh* [Dear of my heart, I do not know at all]." He had flung her a shilling for her honesty and gone off to Culloden. But he had wondered, since . . .

Another image fell across the pool, red-coated this, the guardian of the waters in urgent pursuit of a nuisance.

"What are ye doin' there?" it said.

"Inspecting the face of a sinner."

The sergeant looked in the pool suspiciously. "All I see is you."

Roger stood wiping his lips with a hand stained black with balsam. "Look again when I'm gone, my friend, and ask yourself if I lied."

CHAPTER 16

Halifax

THE SUMMER MARCHED—and its footsteps burned. Even the rangers complained of the heat. But it was the emigrants who truly suffered. They came ashore from the transports, the "husbandmen," the "artisans," their women and their noisy broods, pale from the London streets and the confinement of the ocean passage, twenty-five hundred of them swarming between the hilltop and the shore. The sun blistered them. The black flies tortured them by day and the mosquitoes by night. They rubbed the sunburns and scratched the bites, and broke out in sores and blamed it on the food. They chafed their hands on the ax handles and cut themselves with the blades. They felled trees on each other and suffered the crushing consequences. Children scorched themselves in the slash fires and were lost in the woods and fell off the makeshift wharves. The "reputed surgeons" of the Whitehall advertisement went from overwork to indifference and at last to disrepute. But the clearing grew.

They eked out the meager ration of salt meat and dried peas and hard ship bread with fish caught in the harbor, but symptoms of scurvy appeared. They drank from the guarded water supply—and from the stagnant pools above the beach and in every nook of the woods, which gave them dysentery. But the clearing grew.

They set the woods afire with their careless slash burning and had to fall on with branches of green spruce, with shovels, with sacks, with the very rags off their backs, to save the little they had won. They quarreled, man and man and woman and woman and gang and gang, with fists and claws and sticks and stones. They cursed the King, the Parliament, the soldiers, the sailors, the governor and all his staff; they cursed their "captains," they cursed the food, the tools, the rocks, the woods, the weather, the luck. Yet the clearing grew.

And the town began. It began with tents and brushwood bivouacs beside the first slender trail, which followed the south bank of the brook up the hill. Then methodical Inigo Bruce set his plan on a stump and measured off thirty feet each side of the trail, and Cornwallis called it George Street out of compliment to His Majesty. Then the huts began, with four walls of stakes driven into the earth cheek by jowl, with roofs of old sailcloth and boards from Boston and strips of birch bark, with chimneys of sticks and dried clay, and no light but the gleam of day in the open door. And the huts spread, so that Inigo Bruce must lay off a street parallel with the harbor and just above the beach and the swamp, this to be called Bedford Row out of compliment to the First Lord of the Admiralty. And the huts spread again, and Inigo Bruce laid off another cross street above

Bedford Row, and this was Holles Street, in compliment to the Prime Minister. There were so many compliments to pay for the patronage of the expedition—Granville, for the Lord Privy Seal; Sackville, for the President of the Council; Grafton, for the Lord Chamberlain; Argyll, for the Keeper of the Great Seal of Scotland; and of course the Prince of Wales must have a Prince Street not too far from George, and perhaps a Duke Street would do for the other noble lords—thank God there would be enough streets to go round when all were settled. And for the head of the Board of Trade and Plantations, whose finger was biggest in this affair? What less than the town itself? Halifax!

"Allyfax," the cockneys said, and laughed—and swore. They looked at "Bedford Row" and "Holles Street" and "George Street," the straggles of mean huts among the stumps and stones. Was it for this they had left the civilized comfort of St. Giles and Wapping and Whitechapel—and Pickle Herring Street and Dirty Lane and Bandy Leg Walk?

"Give me Tooley Street," said Mrs. Maggs, and voiced the sentiment of all.

American sloops and schooners were coming now in swarms—twenty in a single day, some with provisions, some with lumber, some with cattle and sheep. Others came to dry their Bank-caught fish in the new security of Chebucto. Some came with stocks of notions and rum—mostly rum—for sale to the townsmen. Some came out of sheer curiosity. They came and went—and when they went a few more names went missing from the roll call of the emigrants, a few more voices were silent at the ration drawing. It was not that fields looked greener to the south; they had seen enough of New World earth. It was the highways and alleyways of towns they wanted—real towns of brick and slate and cobblestones, and shops and carriages and chairs, and beaten streets and the reek of sea-coal fires. They wanted the jostle of town shoulders, the easy prattle of town tongues. They wanted to take up their old mysterious pursuits and leave this struggle with the forest to "them as had a taste for it." They wanted to be quit forever of flies and sweat and rocks and stumps and the eye smart of burning brushwood. They wanted to gape at fine folk a-Sundays, or a man with a dancing bear, or a Lord Mayor's coach, or anything at all so long as it was shut in by rows of proper houses. But most of all they wanted their alley-rat freedom again. This business of "captains" and orders and rations and inspections—why, you might as well go for a soger!

Yet Roger's own little company clung to him. They seemed to look upon him as some sort of talisman. He felt the drag of their minds like a physical burden, and cursed them and cursed himself—and went on with it. They had formed themselves upon him like a habit, and since one bad habit deserved another, he began to drink, as a relief from the daily drudgery.

A swarm of sutlers following the English troops from Louisbourg had set up stalls and small dark dens above the beach for the sale of rum, their chief commodity. It was cheap, to match the resources of the soldiers and the people, and strong enough to match their thirst. Roger began to imbibe a good deal of it in the long summer evenings after the day's work, returning with a solemn unsteadiness to his bivouac at dark. Often as he reeled up George Street in the darkness he was accosted by a woman; not always the same woman— a variety of saucy voices invited him to dally in some hovel of driven pickets, a tent, a brushwood lean-to, or under the sky itself, where the summer stars watched the world. Some hailed him by name, as if they had marked him and inquired. It was like Drury Lane— where a good many of them came from, he suspected.

Invariably he muttered, "Not tonight, ladies," doffed his hat gravely, and went on.

But one night a girl ran after him and caught his arm.

"I don't want your money, sweet. It's you. Don't ye know me?"

It was Sally Madigan.

She was in rags and her face was grimed with hovering about the fires, but she was pretty still. He considered her in the light of a rum-shop doorway and fished in his breeches for a coin which he put in her hand.

"It's my last sixpence, Sally. Take it and good luck to you. Now let me go."

They were standing near the top of George Street, and the girl turned and looked down the short length of it, past the rough knoll where the parade ground was to be—with a church at one end and a courthouse at the other—past the rows of hovels to the beach and the harbor. In the warm summer weather the people cooked outside their doors in the broad street itself. Their fires were falling into ashes now, but the embers glowed, a chain of winking red points in the darkness. From the grogshop came a rumble of boozy voices and a glimpse of unshaven faces black with the soot of slash fires, and far down the hill, among the sutlers' stalls along the beach, there was a sound of quarrel—soldiers and sailors, no doubt; they were always at fists and cudgels. The dark tidewater sparkled under the lantern glimmers of the shipping. Cornwallis and his staff still lived on board, and so did most of the better-class emigrants, the merchant adventurers, the substantial English farmers, the half-pay officers and their wives and families. They would not come ashore until the town had been laid out in full and materials for proper houses could be had. Evidently the Foys were among them, for Roger had not seen them since their departure from the *Fair Lady*. Old Hux he had seen once, in a grogshop on the beach, with a flash of white teeth in the black beard, demanding, "Well, young feller, solved your riddle yet?"

Sally Madigan gave the coin a little toss in her hand. She sang in the husky yet sweet voice he remembered from that day in Tooley Street:

> *"Sing a song o' sixpence, a pocketful o' rye,*
> *Four-and-twenty blackbirds baked in a pie.*
> *When the pie was opened the birds began to sing.*
> *Wasn't that a dainty dish to set before the king?"*

—and, turning swiftly, planted a kiss on his own grimy cheek and vanished.

On the hilltop, where his own little company lay in their brush-wood dens, he found the bivouac he shared with Tom and threw himself down. His bed was a heap of spruce twigs, once fragrant and green, but now brown and dead and full of little red spiders that ran over his face in the dark. Faithful Tom loosed his belt and took off his shoes, a nightly performance now for weeks.

"Tom," said Roger thickly, "I've spent our last sixpence. It's gone—our little fortune. Fortune! I used to think of fortune as a woman,

Tom. I used to see her very clearly. She sat naked in sunshine across the seas somewhere, with a sky behind her as blue as porcelain . . ."

"They're a-goin' to draw the lots in a few days now, sir. Fifty blessed acres each. That's the on'y fortin I know."

". . . and she had a golden skin and a queer sleepy smile on her face . . ."

"Some old sweetheart o' yourn, likely, sir."

". . . and she'd many breasts and . . ."

"Ecod, sir, you *are* drunk tonight! Go to sleep!"

The lots were drawn at seven o'clock on an August morning under the eye of Mr. Bruce and in accordance with a plan drawn up under the eye of Cornwallis. Heads of families, marshaled by their "captains," shuffled past a box and drew their slips. Single men, by order, formed "families" of four and selected a man to draw. As the slips were drawn a hubbub arose to the summer sky. Some of the most shiftless had drawn lots in the coveted area between the site of the governor's house and the beach, where there was easy commerce with the ships, protection from all dangers, and the convenience of the town well and the grogshops. Some of the more earnest laborers had drawn bits of swamp or a litter of boulders far up the hillside or in the still uncleared woods toward Point Pleasant or the north. What shocked them all was the discovery that the town of Mr. Bruce's plan occupied no more than two hundred acres, to be enclosed with palisades and guarded by four or five log-and-earth forts, and the "plantations" promised in the London advertisement must be laid out far into the wilderness—and even then reduced in size.

"What's it mean, sir?" demanded the little bald man, Vace. "There was to be fifty acres for me and ten for the old 'ooman and ten for each o' the kids—that makes ninety. I can add, sir, damme!"

"Can you divide?" Roger said. "Ninety acres would take nigh half the town—and what about the half-pay ensigns who were promised two hundred acres—captains four hundred, and so on?"

"Then it's a bloody swindle!"

"Call it what you like. The thing boils down to a town lot each—enough to build a hut on—and five acres a family somewhere outside the settlement, that way." He waved toward the woods.

They thronged about him, Trope and his hoarse woman, Bob, Maggs and his wife, and the Killicks and the others, shouting as if the whole thing were his fault.

He broke away from them, thoroughly out of humor with them and with all Halifax, and met Captain Gorham standing at the corner of George and Granville streets looking down at the mob.

"Where's your lot?" the ranger said.

Roger made a mouth. "A mile or more down the harbor shore, between here and the Narrows. A heap of rock and forest by the water!"

"That's better'n a lot inland."

"What do you mean?"

"The town might spread that way. It'll spread along the water front if it grows at all—and they say there's several thousand more people comin' next year. The future o' this place lies on the sea, not the land. Trade, fishery, His Majesty's naval station, all that."

"That's too vague, Captain. I wanted a plantation."

"Son, the on'y farmin' land in this province lies on the Fundy side —and there's a Cajun Frenchman squattin' on every acre of it, figgerin' how he can cod the English along and sell his produce to King Louis, same as always. He can't read nor write and he don't want to learn; he can recognize King Louis' mug on a coin, and that's all he cares to know. Cornwallis is tryin' to get 'em to sign the oath of allegiance, but he might's well talk to these trees. They're under the thumb of a wild priest called Le Loutre that hates the English like poison. The on'y way Cornwallis will ever get enough provisions in Nova Scotia for his garrison and fleet and town is to root the Cajuns out and settle English people on the Fundy farms. I don't mean people like these Halifax settlers, either. I mean folk from New England, that know how to live in this country."

"But you couldn't cut down the Acadians as you'd cut down these pines, man!"

Captain Gorham's eyes lit from within, and Roger thought of the hot blue brandy flames about a Christmas pudding.

"Couldn't I, though?"—softly. "Son, I've been fightin' up and down this country since '45. I've seen French and Injun war parties led down the valley to Fort Anne time and again by Cajun guides—seen my men killed and scalped in the wood choppin's, seen 'em carried

off to Quebec for ransom, seen 'em tortured to death on the spot.
I commanded the Massachusetts troops in that valley in '47, when
Noble's men were caught in their winter quarters in a Cajun village
—Grand Pré, remember that name!—and slaughtered like rats.
Cajuns? They're varmints same as Injuns; and they've got to be
rooted out, same as Injuns, afore there can ever be peace and plenty
for the English in Nova Scotia."

"Interesting," Roger murmured, but his indifference showed in his
face. Injuns, Cajuns, the Valley, Fort Anne, Louisbourg—all seemed
as remote as the moon. "I'm afraid all I can think about is Halifax—
and the fact that I'm out of cash."

Gorham looked at him keenly. "The fact is, you're workin' yourself
to death for nothin'. Cuttin' brush and tryin' to break up this rock
heap they've picked for a town! Take it easy. There's twenty-five
hundred pair o' hands to do that work, and more on the sea. Why
don't ye join my ranger company? I could use a man like you."

Churlishly Roger said, "Do I look as savage as all that?"

"Seen yourself in a glass lately? Besides, my lambs ain't all Injuns
nor half-breeds, son. There's plenty o' white adventurers in the
rangers—some of 'em's gentlemen, even. Come! What's here for a
man like you? A hut by the road and a cabbage patch? Or are ye
one o' those who think all hands can live by sellin' rum to each
other?"

"It might be an interesting experiment, Captain. What have your
rangers to offer?"

"A shillin' a day and the life of a lord. All the huntin' and fishin'
ye want, rum to drink, little to do, a bonus for scalps when the
fightin' starts."

"What else?"

"An education. Woods and Injuns and Cajuns and rivers and lakes.
The country itself. Not one in fifty o' those people"—he waved a disdainful hand down the hill—"will ever set foot outside the palisades.
Too scared—scared o' what they don't know. The man that's goin' to
count in this colony is the feller who can range up and down the
country, free o' blockhouses and forts. Oh, Cornwallis looks down
his nose at me and my lambs—no uniform, no discipline, no nothin'
—but when things get hot, and they're goin' to get mighty hot in

these parts someday, why, then I'll be heard respectful in the Council, and it'll be 'Cap'n Gorham this' and 'Cap'n Gorham that,' and 'His Majesty's corps of rangers,' where all ye hear now is 'Gorham and his crew of lazy scoundrels.' "

Roger shook his head resolutely. "I've done with fighting, Captain. Had my fill of it across the sea. There must be some other way to earn a shilling in this colony."

"Ha!" Captain Gorham's tone conveyed his opinion of a man who preferred working to fighting. "Well, as it happens, there's somethin'. Cornwallis wants a sawmill built, across the harbor where there's a stream flowin' out of a couple o' lakes. I've got my man Gilman posted over there with some o' the boys, for a guard, but he's had some trouble gittin' help. Now you and your little brood o' Londoners——"

"What sort is Gilman?"

"A good feller," Gorham drawled, and added, "Smart, too."

CHAPTER 17

Dartmouth

"A SHILLIN' A DAY, and rations, and all the rum ye can drink," Gilman said. His handful of wild men in buckskins had made a clearing in the pines above the shore and built a log house for their commander and a few brushwood lean-tos for themselves. The stream fell down the slope over a boulder bed and filled the surrounding woods with its hiss and pother. Tall spruce and fat white pine stood all about it, as if awaiting the saws. Gilman and his merry men had been there a month and so far had accomplished nothing beyond the hut and the small clearing, where two or three rangers were squaring a pine log for one of the mill sills, taking indolent turns with a broadax. A rum cask stood at Gilman's door with a cup hung on the spigot. A wisp of smoke curled upward from the ashes of a fire before the house, apparently the camp cooking place, a ring of fire-reddened stones crossed by a pole on a pair of forked stakes, and dangling from the pole a number of pothooks ingeniously fashioned from

forked twigs. Muskets leaned against the house wall in the sunshine.
Two bark canoes were drawn up on the shore and covered with old
moose hides to keep the sun from melting the gum on the seams.

There was no stockade, not even an abatis like the one now being
thrown about the site of Halifax. The only sign of defense here was
the half-dozen loopholes cut in the house logs. The whole place
breathed an air of leisured ease.

"Cut yourself some lean-tos and make yourselves to home," said
Gilman generously. "Don't kill yourselves. We've got all summer.
Time enough to work hard when cold weather comes."

The cockneys broke into delighted smiles. This was something
like! Ecod, this drawling colonial fellow was a bit of all right! Imagine Cornwallis saying anything like that! They slid into Gilman's
dolce far niente with all the righteousness of toilers come to ease at
last, though some of the women looked doubtful and Mrs. Lumley
declared outright that no good would come of it. The children fished
for rock cod at high tide and gathered lobsters among the weedy
rocks at low; and they wandered along the shore picking strange
and delightful fruit called blueberries and huckleberries, came back
wry-mouthed from an experiment with chokecherries, and discovered
that raspberries grew wild in this country and not in baskets at
Covent Garden as they had supposed.

The place was cool in the morning in the shadow of the ridge, but
from the time the ships' bells marked the forenoon watch with a
tinkling chorus over the roadstead the sun seemed to fall straight
down, and through the afternoon it poured a golden fire upon the
eastern slope of the harbor, tempered by the unfailing breeze along
the water. The black flies were gone and the salt breeze drove the
mosquitoes into the woods. A charming place, a charming country
after all.

Once a week Gilman sent across to the town for their rations and
another cask of rum. He posted a sentinel every day, and the man's
watch was fixed, not on the woods, but upon the shipping and the
town. When a boat drew across with one of Cornwallis' officers on
a tour of inspection there was a warning shout from the sentry post,
and there was a bustle, axes falling, chips flying, and three men
marching up and down with muskets along the edge of the clearing.

Roger was amused at first, then bored—and puzzled. He supposed the indolence of the rangers came partly from the Indian blood in so many of them, but mostly from their long sojourn at Fort Anne, where Mascarene had kept them close to the ramparts. Their business was to fight Injuns, they told Roger; these other things—with gestures toward the proposed site of the sawmill—were just a notion of those gold-laced gentlemen over there—a thumb at Halifax—who didn't want anybody loafing but 'emselves!

Captain Gorham was their beau ideal of a commander: lazy, genial, a wolf at the smell of an Injun or Cajun, a good forager in His Majesty's commissary or in the woods, as occasion demanded, a bland and ready shield against work of any kind.

Yet his lieutenant, Gilman, impressed Roger as a man of energy, with a keen eye to the main chance. He was not here for his health, he told Roger mysteriously. He looked and talked like one of the Boston traders who now swarmed in the lower town.

Across the water Halifax made a brown splotch on the green hillside. Its face was changing already with the influx of New Englanders. A growing number of the first crude huts were assuming the outward appearance of New England cottages, with clapboards nailed on over the logs, and small-paned windows added, and steep-pitched roofs to shed the winter snow. Here and there a frame house was rising, with sawn timbers, boards and clapboards from Boston, with an upper half story lit by dormers in the steep shingled roof, and a great square chimney of red brick. Cows snuffed among the stumps for bits of green. Pigs rooted among the thrown slops in the streets. Horses and oxen dragged a few heavy-wheeled carts painfully along the stony thoroughfares. There was a town pump now in George Street, where the drinking pool had been. The brook had gone dry with the clearing of the slope. An unending procession of women and children with pails in hand or slung from a wooden yoke moved to and from the pump. Roger wondered sometimes what they used it for; they all looked very dirty, and certainly no man drank it. Cornwallis, seeking to regulate the grog sellers, had imposed a license fee, and there were thirty licensed retailers, most of them in shanties grouped about the swampy strip above the beach. But drink could be bought in forty other places at least, with rum at three shillings the gallon, and red and white port at a shilling a bottle. There was talk of a government brewery and beer at tuppence a gallon.

There were still no defenses, except for the rude abatis of felled trees about the town and a swivel gun mounted upon a gravel-filled hogshead at each corner of the governor's modest dwelling by the town pump. Men who had seen Louisbourg laughed at the comparison.

There was some notion of a settlement about Gilman's sawmill when it was built—to be called Dartmouth, so the rangers said. Some patron's name, no doubt; but Roger thought of Dartmouth in the pleasant west country of England and was rather pleased. Not a bad place, this. He was astonished when in mid-September Killick returned from a trip across the harbor and told his wife to bundle up her things.

" 'Tain't that I don't like bein' with you, sir, but this layin' about and playin' at woodcuttin' don't strike me natural-like. Besides, I'm a waterman, and my old 'ooman dreams o' fish."

"What are you going to do?" Roger asked.

Killick ducked his head toward the harbor mouth. "Fish out there is thick as stones in George Street. All ye need is a canoe and a hook and line. There's some smart coves already in the business, and all the town for market. They sell their fish in that swampy square above the beach, a proper little Billingsgate; but that's for them as don't know better. I'm goin' to make my 'ooman a bit of a tray, and she can cry my fish through the streets and get the best price."

Away they went, rejoicing.

A few days later Trope and his bearded lady departed, declaring that the air was better on the Halifax side. Trope added, with his malicious old grin, that no man could respect hisself livin' off 'Is Majesty's bounty when the town needed an honest lodgin'house for strangers. They departed in the ration boat, Mrs. Lumley looking back with baleful eyes on Roger and Gilman.

"Is that a woman or a man?" muttered the ranger.

"A woman. She poses as Trope's daughter, but I think she's his doxy, really."

"What! That porcupine? Well, he's no beauty himself. He looks like the devil grown old."

Gilman thrust his hands into his belt and said abruptly, "Your little crew is thinnin' out. What's the matter? Don't I treat 'em good?"

"They don't like so much of their own company. They want the smell of the crowd. Besides," challenged Roger, "what's here for them? This sawmill—will it ever be built?"

Gilman's cool eyes twinkled and a grin spread over his thin lips. "D'ye want the truth? I'll tell ye, Sudden. It's every man for himself in a new country, and devil take the hindmost. This here's a mighty pretty layout for a sawmill, with the finest kind o' market right across the water. Now why should His Majesty get all the profit? Listen! Those quill drivers over there are countin' the cost, and by and by, along about October, say, it's goin' to add up to a nasty figger—and no boards in sight. Then Cornwallis'll get up on his high horse, declare the whole thing worthless, and decide to cut the loss. Then I'll buy it in—at ten or twenty guineas, say—half finished as it stands. Next spring I'll be sawin' as pretty as ye please and raftin' boards acrost the harbor like a good un. Cornwallis is payin' five pounds a thousand feet to those rogues in Boston—and drogin' it here at gov'-ment expense. Pity, ain't it, if I can't get four-pound-ten delivered on the beach? Why, if things go right, in five years I can make my fortune!"

"If it's as easy as all that," Roger objected, "why doesn't someone else build a mill?"

" 'Cause there's no other stream nigh the town that's big enough to turn a good-sized mill. A stream at the basin head, o' course, and a fair brook up the Nor'west Arm; but they're too far from the defenses. Sly, ain't I? You stick with me, Sudden. I like you. These rangers o' mine are good fellers, but they ain't the kind to stay, year in, year out, pullin' boards off o' the saws. I'll give ye a good lay, too, mind that."

"But is it honest?" Roger asked, and smiled.

Up shot Gilman's brows. "Who said anythin' of honesty? What's honest about this whole affair? Don't ye know the Lords o' Trade and Plantations made a pretty profit for 'emselves out o' the equippin' o' this expedition? Don't ye know His Majesty's purveyors in Boston —Apthorpe and Hancock and that lot—are makin' fortunes out o' the supplies they send up here? Don't ye know the men that's set up as merchants in Halifax are out to skin the gov'ment any way they can? Besides, what's honest about bringin' thousands o' poor devils acrost the sea on the promise o' plantation land—big chunks of it? What ha' they got, eh? A hut in that slum Cornwallis calls a town and five acres o' rock and forest outside somewhere, if, as, and when the Crown Surveyor can git around to layin' it out! They were promised defense. What's to defend a man tryin' to clear his five acres in the woods beyond the town? The troops? Those redcoats ain't worth a damn in the woods, and Cornwallis knows it; that's why he puts up with Gorham and his rangers—and people like me. But ye can't guard two or three thousand people with one company o' rangers."

"Who's to attack them?" Roger asked mildly. "We're at peace with France. And with the Indians—they came here and swore loyalty to the English king."

"Peace with the Injuns!" Gilman roared. "God's wounds, who ever heard o' such a thing? There's no such thing. Cornwallis has got their marks on a piece o' paper, that's all. And what's a mark on paper to an Injun? Not that!"—a snap of his bony fingers. "Sudden, those brown devils came here with their war paint on, bold as brass. There should ha' been a ceremony, spun out all the day and half the night, Injun-fashion, squattin' about a council fire, with each man jawin' a long spell and Cornwallis jawin' longest of all. Cornwallis should ha' insisted on 'em washin' off their war paint then and there, and they should ha' taken a hatchet and buried it deep, each one takin' a turn at scrapin' the dirt over it, and each one jawin' a bit in his own tongue—Cornwallis might ha' recited the Lord's Prayer if he couldn't think of anythin' else. Why, anyone that's been twelve months in this country could ha' told him what to do! But what did he do? He received 'em aboard the *Beaufort*. Can ye sit round a fire aboard ship? Can ye bury a hatchet in the ballast? He got a 'terpreter and jawed 'em about the way they'd been actin', demandin' to know this and that about the English they'd killed and carried off around the Fundy waters. Then he read 'em a long paper, got 'em to make their totems at the bottom with a quill, gave 'em presents, and sent 'em home—with the war paint still on their faces! Why, they even give a war dance and hollered their war whoop there on the deck afore they left—the English officers laughin' their heads off. Very quaint, these savages! Amusin', most amusin'! Off they went, with the bright new muskets and hatchets and knives he'd give 'em for to play like nice little boys, and he could hardly wait to see 'em over the side afore he was dictatin' a dispatch to the Lords o' Trade, tellin' 'em what a smart feller he was! The 'terpreter told me about it—said his hair stood on end the whole time; tried to tell Cornwallis the right of it but couldn't get a hearin'. Ye can't talk sense to an Englishman that's sot on bein' a soger and a gentleman in a country where a soger can't afford to be gentle any more'n a porcupine can afford a haircut. He'll have to learn the long way round; and in this country, Sudden, experience is a damned hard schoolmaster."

"At any rate," Roger suggested, "you're not greatly worried, it seems to me."

Gilman lifted a pebble with his moccasin toe and kicked it into the bushes.

"Us rangers can look after ourselves."

Roger sauntered upstream, where three rangers and his own little group were slowly gathering rocks to fill the cribwork of the dam. The green maple leaves had turned red in the past few nights, the bright red of fresh blood. Under this scarlet canopy, in shafts of sunshine through the branches, the men moved with the deliberate arms and legs of dreamers. A lethargy of rum and ease had come upon them like a blessing after the toil and trouble of the harbor's other side. To be sure, they groused about the rations—the salt pork from Boston had a taste of fish, for instance. Wasn't it true, sir, that the New Englanders fed their swine on cod heads and the like? And when in God's name would they get a bit of soft tack? This everlasting ship biscuit wore a man's teeth down.

But they were as near to satisfaction as cockneys could get beyond the sound of Bow bells, and their faces showed it. The women were not so sure; they missed the clack of tongues by day and did not like the forest sounds at night. The children rejoiced. It was odd to see how regular food, even the hard fare of the commissariat, had put flesh on their scrawny bodies, just as the sun had dyed their pallid

London skins a healthy brown. They ran all but naked, like young savages.

There was no thought of winter, and Roger was disturbed. His memories of cold weather in the Highlands came back to him painfully; the winters here must be ten times worse if the rangers' tales were true. If the cockneys thought of winter at all, it was in terms of London's rain and fog. Sometimes he envied their carelessness.

For some nights now there had been an intermittent rush of wings in the high dark—wild geese going south, the rangers said—and several times the pale fire of the northern lights, a wonder to behold. Along the harbor shores where the swamp maples hung over the water their leaves made a scarlet parade that put to shame the shabby coats of Warburton's and Hopson's regiments. There were calms when Chebucto gleamed and burned like a polished sword between the hills, and Halifax writhed and Citadel Hill quivered like a jelly in the haze, and all the distances were blue. "Weather breeders," Gilman said, and so they proved, for always they were followed by a gray scud whipping up swiftly from the southeast and a dank wind blowing in the harbor mouth, in small uneasy drafts at first, increasing to a gale whose fury seemed all the worse for the calm that went before. Rain came slanting down, hard-flung like spears, and all the hillside streamed. Trees swayed until it seemed they must go down before it, and recovered, thrashing, in time for the next gust. But old trees touched with decay sometimes snapped off like carrots and shook the sodden earth with their fall, and the cockneys, crouching in their half-demolished lean-tos, wondered if their time had come. The little clearing seemed very lonely then, for the Halifax side of the harbor vanished in a gray smother of rain and when night fell there was no friendly prick of lights across the darkness. The children whimpered and the men made frequent journeys to the keg outside the ranger's door. The women wished themselves in England.

CHAPTER 18

Into the Wilderness

THE LAST MORNING OF SEPTEMBER came after one of these storms, a flaring yellow sunrise, a sharp chill and a wet smell in the air, and the pungency of broken pine twigs. Roger's people turned out early, from no industrious desire. They had huddled eight-and-forty hours in their miserable bivouacs and were cramped and hungry. The fire was lit with chunks of split pine kept dry in the hut by the weather-wise rangers, and the whole crew clustered about it, shivering, while the salt .meat boiled in the great kettle and the ship biscuit was softened in water and then laid on the hot rocks to toast.

In an hour the men were off to the chopping, glad enough to set the chilled blood moving in their veins. The millstream was swollen to a torrent and foamed yellow down the hillside, filling the woods with its roar. Roger's chosen task lay at the millsite. He had acquired some skill with the broadax and liked his work of hewing white pine logs foursquare for the foundation of the mill. His only companion at this spot was one of Gilman's men, half Mohawk, a dark and silent person with the name of Silas. They fell to work at once.

The noise of the stream drowned all sounds but their own. Roger was a little astonished when, after ten minutes or so, there was a sharp ringing crack from the direction of the felling gang. In a moment there was another. Silas had thrown up his head at the first. At the second, without a word, he flung down his ax and dashed away through the trees toward the hut, bounding like a deer. Mystified, Roger clutched his ax and moved rapidly through the spruce thickets toward his gang. The roar of the stream filled his ears, but through it and above it there seemed to be a faint, high-pitched cry, going on and on in peculiar ululations like the sound of a horse in pain. He emerged into the open where his men had been cutting timber for the mill beams. No one in sight!

He stepped over a fallen pine trunk and beheld a phenomenon. A man lay in the trampled ferns with his knees drawn up and his thin, balsam-stained hands lying easily at his sides. The knees, the hands, the ragged shirt and breeches, the scrawny body belonged to Vace the barber. But they lacked the head of Vace the barber. That was gone, and where it should have been a torrent of thick blood was pouring from the red stump of his neck. Roger paused, revolted and amazed. Then, lifting his gaze a little, he saw one of the sedan chairmen—Jack, by the clothes—lying backward over a log. The legs were toward him, the belly formed the top of an uncomfortable arc, and the shoulders were only partly visible on the other side. He wondered if Jack, too, had lost his head. He observed a trickle of blood under the log.

He made a step or two away, uncertainly. His nostrils caught a whiff of something faint but tingling and old-familiar. Powder! He began to run toward the camp, and at once the figures of Ned, the other chairman, and Maggs, the chimney sweep, arose like apparitions from a brush pile in the middle of the chopping, running also, Maggs uttering a long wild cry. No lethargy about their movements now! They cleared logs and stumps and piles of slash in amazing leaps.

From the forest came a chorus of war whoops, harsh and high, and a ragged volley of muskets, sudden and wholly terrible in the peace of the autumn morning. Maggs stumbled forward several steps, head on breast and shoulders drooping, legs moving slower and slower, and knees sagging, as if in a moment he had grown tired of this violent exertion. He fell on his face at last.

A ball whined past Roger's head. And another. He dropped the ax and wished for longer legs. But he was running extremely well. The air seemed to rush past his ears. His hat blew off. He was overtaking Ned rapidly. Something whizzed past his shoulder, a hatchet hard-flung and bowling end over end. It struck Ned at the root of his pigtail. The chairman uttered an odd sound, more grunt than cry, and went down in a heap. Roger hesitated, but a yell of triumph close behind put new springs in his legs. He cleared the body in a leap and went on down the path. Now there was firing ahead, from the camp itself. Boxed, by Jove!

But there was no stopping, not with that hard patter of moccasins behind. He thanked God for the path, crooked and narrow, which forced his pursuers to run in file. Only the leading man could strike at him or shoot. His whole being dissolved into a pair of sprinting legs.

He burst into the sunshine, running hard, and there lay the camp clearing, the stumps, the scuffed brown mold, the bivouacs, the hut, the blue harbor water, all as if nothing had happened. There was no sign of the people. The fire still reeked; the big camp kettle had been scoured and set upside down against the scorched stones to dry and the wooden pothooks drawn to the end of the pole away from the heat. The hut door was closed. The tin cup dangled from the spigot of the rum keg, but it would not be needed any more; a brown stream was squirting indecently from the lower belly of the keg. All these things he noted clearly as he bounded across the clearing. The patter of moccasins stopped at the edge of the open, and his ears were smitten by a wild yell of rage, which was taken up by other savage voices all around the clearing. A flung tomahawk struck the ground ahead, flung up a little spurt of the dry mold, and slithered to a stop in front of the door.

At the same time he noticed a musket muzzle staring like a round and intensely evil eye from one of the hut loopholes, saw a fierce bearded face in the flash of a pan inside, and then a gush of flame and white smoke. The ball sang past him and struck something behind him with a vicious slap. From the direction of the path came another yell, of anger, derision, pain—he could not tell what.

But now white puffs of powder smoke spat from the bushes all about the clearing. He reached the door in a swarm of terrific bees which thwacked into the logs.

He flung himself against the door, gasping, "Open! For the love of Christ!" and heard the slither of the bar, felt the door yield, and fell among silent women and children on the puncheon floor. He had not run far, perhaps two hundred yards, but he was spent as if it were a mile. He lay there panting in a cold drench of sweat for several minutes, hearing a furious *splat* against the logs from time to time, and the more frightening boom and jump of the door, as if under the hammer blows of a giant, and the drone of a ball across the room. Like the steady flicker of summer lightning the gloom of the hut was lit at regular intervals by the flaring gun pans of the rangers.

Nobody said a word. The women and children watched the men at the loopholes warily because their musket butts came rattling along the floor when they reloaded, with no respect for fingers or faces.

Suddenly all was silent. No shots. No yells.

Gilman's voice, cool enough: "Take a squint at the harbor, Nahum. Gorham's boys must be on the way."

Roger was skeptical. The sound of the fight must have alarmed all Halifax by this time, but he could not imagine those lazy fellows of Gorham's moving so fast.

But the ranger at the west loophole cried, "Here they come like blazes—dozen canoes or more—whaleboat full o' sogers behind!"

"Um! That's why the devils lit out. Well, they ain't got much start. Anybody hurt?"

A chorus: "No!"—"Not here"—"None o' mine, thank 'eavens!"

But Mrs. Maggs rose up on her knees and cried to Roger, "Where's my man?" And lean Mrs. Vace called out, "Will, Mr. Sudden—have you seen my Will?"

He shook his head, sick, and glad of the half-dark that obscured his face and his lie.

Gilman said, "Open the door—easy-like. Keep down, everybody!"

He and two others stood well back in the room, aiming their muskets into the widening shaft of sunshine as the door swung open. Nothing happened. The ranger Nahum stepped outside cautiously. Still nothing. And now a chorus of fierce yells from the waterside and a rush of men in buckskins, Gorham among them.

Roger stepped out of the hut and picked up the tomahawk which had missed him so narrowly, a well-made thing with a slim ash handle, brown and polished with use and decorated with a little knot of yellowhammer feathers at the butt. Its slender, triangular blade was of brass, incised with tiny manikins, canoes, wigwams, moons, and suns, and with a piece of fine steel set cunningly into the broad end and ground to a razor edge. No trade hatchet, this. Made in an armorer's workshop probably, at Louisbourg or Quebec, for someone of importance to the French. It balanced in his hand beautifully, and while he dandled it Gorham, in a few terse questions, gained all that Gilman knew. It was not much. The men at the camp had heard a couple of shots up in the chopping and quickly gathered the women and youngsters into the hut. Then hell broke loose.

"Micmacs?" grunted Gorham. "Malecites? Abenakis?"

"Micmacs, by the whoops. We didn't git a square look at any of 'em."

"After 'em, boys!" Gorham cried. His fifty rangers swung into a long file trotting up the path, like a human snake in the woods. Roger fell in behind, urged by some bloodthirsty instinct which seemed to come from the deadly thing in his hand.

Behind them boomed the cannon of alarmed ships in the roadstead, firing into the woods at half a mile, a sad waste of His Majesty's powder and shot. Behind them also sounded the cool voice of Gilman reassuring the hysterical women. He had stayed behind—to look after His Majesty's sawmill.

They came upon Ned first, stripped of his jacket and breeches, the top of his head a raw horror, roughly circular, with the white of the skull showing partly through the bloodstains. The body was warm and flaccid. The blow of the flung hatchet had stunned him and thrown him down, and then a triumphant savage had leaped upon him with a knife slash at the throat that nearly severed the neck. Farther on lay Maggs, scalped also—a poor prize, for his hair was thin. His staring eyes directed a look of mute inquiry at the sky. The rangers went on swiftly, questing like dogs along the edge of the chopping, while Gorham and Roger paused at the bodies of Vace and Jack.

"Micmacs," Gorham said with finality. "They like to take the whole head if there's time. Must ha' been scalp-and-run with the other two. Well, a head's a heavy thing and awkward carryin'—we may come up with the devils."

The rangers were off again. One of their scouts had found a game path scuffled by moccasins. It wound up the slope, roughly following the course of the stream.

"Mark this," Gorham said to Roger as they joined the pursuit. "Never linger by fallin' water if ye can help it. It drowns all sounds but a shot or a war whoop. And when ye hear *them* ye've heard your last."

"But if you want to build a sawmill . . ."

"Get some other fool to take the risk and stay where ye can hear a twig snap—like Gilman."

For a time the long file trotted up the slope. Then something happened at the head of it. Shouts. A shot. Then three shots and a wild yelling. A quiver came back along the human snake. Without an order, without a word spoken, it disintegrated, some men plunging into the woods on the right of the trail, others to the left.

Gorham kept on the path, and Roger followed. It was admirable, the instant arrowhead formation in case of ambush, the swiftly wheeling flanks to bring the whole company into line toward the front, and the commander in the center where he belonged. All done as if by instinct. Shooting continued ahead. It lacked the flurry of a fight. A steady pop-pop-pop as of men firing at a mark. The woods began to open, and Roger saw on the pine trunks above his head the speckled reflection of sunshine on water. In another minute or two they were standing on the shore of a lake in a bowl of low, forested hills. Upon its surface, at two or three hundred yards and rapidly drawing away, were ten canoes. Seen thus from astern, with their low hulls and the furiously plying arms and paddles, they looked like brown grasshoppers walking on the surface of the water. A number of rangers were kneeling in the bushes, trying hopeful long shots. At every futile splash the fleeing war party uttered a derisive howl.

A ranger held up two human heads for Gorham's inspection. They did not belong to Vace or Jack. The faces were broad and dark as old leather, and daubed with red ocher in angular streaks, with rings of charcoal about the eyes. The long, coarse hair, stiff with grease, was gathered with a thong on top of the head. The raw edges of the severed necks dripped a red patter on the ground at the ranger's feet.

"Micmacs, all right," Gorham observed. "Why didn't ye jest scalp 'em?"

"A head fer a head," the ranger grinned. "We got three. Cass is scalpin' t'other."

Roger walked over to a little knot of buckskins regarding with interest some object on the ground between them. An Indian lay there shot through the back. A small stone ornament hung about his neck, crudely carved in the shape of a fish. He was quite naked except for a leather clout slung about his privates from a thong around his waist. The red pool beneath him was spreading and trickling slowly toward the lake. The ranger Cass knelt on the brown hairless chest, busy with a scalping knife. He ran the sharp point expertly around the head. A line of bright blood appeared, swelled, stood out like a red cord for a moment, and then broke in little dribbles down about the ears. Cass slipped the knife point under the skin at the back of the head and turned up a flap of the scalp. He rose and put a foot on the neck, grasped the thick black topknot, and made a sudden wrench. The scalp came away in his hand with a nauseous peeling sound; and there was the bare skull like an acorn uncapped. Cass held high the limp black wig and uttered a long harsh cry that rang over the lake. But Roger was staring at the human wreck on the ground. It was alive! The glazed black eyes seemed to bulge from some emotion within; the lips snarled apart and showed two rows of strong white teeth. They uttered no sound, yet those eyes and lips conveyed to Roger a vast and terrible hatred that would go on, long after the flesh was dead. Weird! We can kill, but can we conquer *that?* he wondered.

Two men picked up that dead-alive thing by the feet and shoulders and swung it into the lake with a cheerful "Heave-ho!" The head lolled; the brown breast rose, gleaming, for a full minute, rolled a little, and went down.

"Well," Gorham said, "we've got some hair to show Cornwallis, anyhow."

"Reckon he'll pay fer it?" Cass asked.

Gorham shot a swift side glance at Roger and winked at Cass. "Reckon not. 'Tain't accordin' to the laws o' war as the cap'n-general knows 'em—not yet, it ain't. But those devils'll come again, and this is the way they'll come, 'slikely, not down that river at the basin head, where Cornwallis wants me to build a fort."

The retreating canoes were vanishing into the woods at the far end of the lake.

"Aren't you going after them?" Roger demanded, with a wave of the tomahawk.

"What'll we use for canoes?" retorted Gorham humorously.

"We can run around the shore. The lake is small."

"Son, where there's one lake there's usually another—a string of 'em perhaps. And beyond that there'll be a portage and another stream goin' the other way. Them brown devils prob'ly came fifty, maybe a hundred miles, maybe a whole lot more. The Micmac country runs clear up to Gaspé."

"Then carry your canoes up from the harbor. It isn't far."

Some of the rangers grinned. The friendly note went out of Captain Gorham's voice.

"Don't try to teach the old bull while your horns are green, Sudden. All right, boys, lead off in file. Let's hope Gilman's got some rum in that cask o' his."

Back they went. But Roger remained by the lake shore. It stung him to think of some filthy savage displaying the unfortunate barber's head as Cass had displayed that hideous black wig. Perhaps the Micmacs had cast aside those grisly souvenirs when Gorham's scouts came up with them. He began to search the bushes along the shore. The leaves of the red maples were falling now. Dry and crisp, with edges curled and stem upturned, they sailed on the water like little scarlet boats. From a rock at the waterside he could see the dead Indian lying on the bottom a few feet away. The dark body was the color of the bottom, a mat of last year's sunken leaves gone rotten. If he had not known it was there he would not have seen it at all. He pushed on around a point in the shore. Gorham and his rangers! He wondered what to make of them. Their spirit seemed composed in equal parts of courage and cowardice, indolence and energy, with a strong dash of cruelty thrown in. When idle, they passed the time in almost maniacal drunkenness and would lie down with anything in petticoats, however ugly or depraved. Yet on a trail that suited them they would go for weeks with little rest and less food than a dog, and at the end of it they would turn back like poltroons or fight like heroes, according to which mood they happened to be in. All this he knew from their own tales. He wondered if he would ever understand them. English officers who had seen only their sorry side declared them worthless. Others with experience of their tougher qualities declared them the only troops worth His Majesty's pay in all America. Many of Gorham's crew were half-breeds, and these he could understand—half man, half beast. But the rest were white men from the Massachusetts frontier, with a sprinkling of English and other adventurers, and they were beyond his mind's grasp. Someday I'll know, he thought. One thing was sure: they were a part of the country. Some instinct of his horse-breeding ancestors gave him a notion that someday, somehow, the country would produce a kind of men with less of those faults and more of those virtues, and they would sweep away the terror and the mystery of this silent green hell and march like gods across the continent. How long would it take? He thought of that feckless mob across the harbor. A century, certainly. Longer, probably.

The bushes were mostly huckleberry, still laden with small black fruit and the leaves beginning to show signs of the autumn red. He came upon a small reedy finger of the lake reaching a few yards into the shore and overhung at its tip by a mass of huckleberry leaves. The outlet of the lake was just beyond; the beginning of the mill-stream—he could hear the rush of water. In thrusting his way through the bushes he put his foot on something that yielded and, looking down, saw the gunwale of a bark canoe, cunningly concealed.

"Ah!" he ejaculated. His whole sensation was of triumph. The greenhorn had found something that the forest-wise ranger had not even bothered to seek!

There was a mighty convulsion in the bushes. In a moment he was clutched about the throat from behind and thrown off his feet. Three savage figures flung themselves upon him. Wildly he clawed at the hard fingers at his windpipe. Useless! It was all over in half a minute. Swiftly his ankles were bound together with a thong. Another fastened his wrists behind him. A stick was laid across his mouth and pushed violently between his teeth, and fixed there like a horse bit with a thong around the back of his head. The three stood up, grunting, and he lay at their feet and looked up at them. They were armed with cheap trade hatchets and muskets of an old French pattern, and wore nothing but breechclouts and moccasins. One had a pewter crucifix on a thong about his neck. Their long black hair was gathered on top of their heads in the queer womanish fashion of the Micmacs, but there was nothing womanish about their stocky, well-muscled bodies nor their broad faces daubed with ocher and charcoal. Their brown skins stank and shone with rancid bear grease.

They were looking at the tomahawk, turning it over and over and grunting one to another. Two of them went away in the direction of the trail. Whatever they sought they did not find, for he read dissatisfaction in their faces when they returned. When they looked at him their black eyes were hot and merciless. What animals! He had forgotten his scorn of Gorham now, hoping desperately that the ranger captain had missed him by this time. But he thought of the long, winding file and Gorham's thirst. The emigrant would not be missed until the whole company stood lamenting about Gilman's bullet-pierced keg.

His captors came to a decision. He was swung into the canoe and lay face upward on the bottom. Two of the savages took their places at the bow and stern paddles. The third, he of the crucifix, sat on Roger's chest, a crushing weight. Roger gasped for breath and continued gasping all the way up the lake. His bound hands, tortured by the tight thong and pressed under his own weight and the Indian's, sent waves of agony along his arms and into his shoulders. He could see nothing but the man's gleaming back and parts of the gunwales and the blue sky. As the journey progressed he saw less of these things. A dark mist gathered before his eyes and a great drum beat slowly in his head.

CHAPTER 19

Shubenacadie

THERE WAS A PORTAGE not far from the first lake. Or was it the second, or third? He was only half conscious. But the portage was clear enough, for he was slung out of the canoe there like a sack of meal, the thong was removed from his ankles, and one of the savages beat him unmercifully with a stick because he could not walk. His feet were numb and swollen, and he fell on his face. They wrenched off his shoes and threw them away and dragged him to his feet again. Again he fell. Again the stick. His body was one big pain now, and his nerves accepted the new burden dully. There was some debate among them. From his gestures, one was for killing the captive then and there. The others did not agree.

Finally he was slung over a brown shoulder and carried along a faint path in the shadow of big trees. Then sunlight and lapping water. Another lake. Another voyage on the canoe bottom with the hard brown buttocks on his chest. Again the hard-fought breathing, hissing past the wooden bit in his jaws. Again the darkness for a time. Then the canoe grated softly and the weight sprang off his breast. He was hoisted out and placed on his feet. With the thong gone the life had come back to them. He swayed a little. They were at the tip of a narrow lake that seemed to stretch on for several miles. The sun sat on a pine ridge to Roger's left. In a few moments it was gone and there was twilight. A path disappeared into the bushes a little way up the bank. There was a chill in the air and he shivered.

Soon he shivered much more, for after concealing the canoe and paddles in the woods the savages stripped him to the skin. One put on the tattered breeches, another the shirt. They grinned at each other—the first sign of pleasure he had seen in them. The third, having no share in this poor loot, contented himself with cutting a stiff maple switch. They arranged themselves in a little procession in the path: first he of the breeches, then the captive, then he of the switch, and finally he of the shirt. The switch came down with a terrific cut across Roger's back, and he leaped into movement like a stung horse. This was desired, apparently, for they all broke into a trot up the path, the savages lifting their voices in long, cracked howls. There were answering howls in the woods ahead, and after fifty yards or so their small procession came into an open space where several fires were burning and a rabble of painted Indians came running and squalling toward them, catching up sticks of firewood as they ran. There were twenty or thirty of them, all young and active males. In a moment the prisoner was surrounded by a whooping swarm all trying to strike at once. He fell to his knees under the sheer weight of this wooden torrent and thought dimly, *It is all over; this is the end*.

A voice cut through the wild chorus. The rain of sticks died away in a patter which he scarcely felt, and one last vicious cut of the maple switch that he did. The crowd opened a little. Roger was

still on his knees, bowed against the storm. He tried to stop the
trembling which shook his beaten flesh, and failed. But he managed
to lift his head. He was aware of an awful necessity for courage,
or a show of it at any rate, an insistent something, sheer Kentish
stubbornness perhaps, arising from some unbeaten part of him inside.

His captors seemed to be telling their tale, a gabble of three voices
going on and on. The tomahawk was displayed and passed from
hand to hand.

A strange voice said sharply, "Stand up!" in English.

Roger rose unsteadily and perceived a small man, brown and
gleaming like the others, in clout and moccasins and with a hawk
feather thrust in his topknot. A necklace of bear claws hung about
his neck with a tobacco pipe of polished gray stone slung by a
slender thong. His black beard marked him for a European, or a
half-blood more likely. The beard had been trimmed carelessly, probably with a sharp knife. A pelt of curly black hair grew on his lean
breast and down his belly, and his thin, corded arms were as hairy as
a bear's. He displayed the brass tomahawk.

"Where you get dees?"

"I picked it up."

" 'Ow you get dees?"

"It was thrown at me and I picked it up."

"Th'own? What mean th'own?"

Roger repeated his words in French. The man's small brown eyes
gleamed. In the Acadien dialect he spat out rapidly, *"Tiens!* What
is this that you speak French? You are English, you!"

"I have lived in France."

"Are you one of Gorham's men?"

"No."

"You are one of Gorham's men. What did you do to Peyal?"

"I do not know Peyal."

A flourish of the brass tomahawk. "This was Peyal's. You are one
of Gorham's men and you killed Peyal and took his head."

"I killed no one. I am a woodcutter. I found the hatchet by the
shore of Chebucto where your people killed my friends."

The fellow uttered a few gutturals over his shoulder, and two of
the savages fetched a pole with two heads dangling from it. Darkness

was falling fast, but in the flicker of the fires Roger recognized the waxy faces of Vace and Jack, eyes closed, mouths agape, expressionless as masks.

"Are these your friends?"

"Yes."

"*Eh bien*"—maliciously—"you have found them. What did they at Chebucto?"

"They wished to live there, I suppose."

"How many redcoats at Chebucto?"

"Two regiments."

"How many?"

"I do not know."

"Fool! You must tell me or *these* will roast you in the fire."

"The fire cannot tell me what I do not know."

"You are one of Gorham's men!"

"I am a woodcutter."

"Where is Peyal?"

"I do not know."

So it went on, for a long time, and the savages grew restive. Several shook their hatchets in the prisoner's face. At last the Acadien wearied of this circular catechism. Roger's hands were fastened behind his back again and his feet hobbled with a thong. The savages returned to their meal at the fires. After a time they slept. There was dew on the grass, and it chilled Roger's naked flesh to the bone. Even the stars were cold. His feet were at ease in the hobble, but the tight thong about his wrists called up once more the throbbing agony of the journey from Chebucto.

In the morning a mist hung like a cold fleece on the still surface of the lake. He was put in a canoe. The Acadien sat in the stern, a savage in the bow. When the sun broke through the vapor in the forenoon he saw that they were moving toward the north or northeast. On all sides he could hear paddles and occasional talk from the other canoes of the war party. After about four miles the forest came together and there was a river, shallow after the summer drought but growing in volume as the miles went past. A chill wind worried the treetops, but inside the canoe, where the sun fell, there was shelter and warmth and he was grateful. The river widened steadily, and after a time there were red claybanks. Toward sunset they came to a place where there was a grassy slope above the river with paths trodden bare in the red earth. Roger was lifted out of the canoe. The hobble was cut away from his ankles. He saw a village of bark huts, some of them square and not unlike the shanties at Halifax, most of them cone shaped—evidently the "wigwams" of the rangers' tales—and at least two buildings of logs stood on end with red clay plastered in the chinks and covered with a roof of bark. The village was overhung with a blue mist of wood smoke, and it sprawled over the slope in a clearing so old that the last trace of stumps and roots had gone.

The war party set up that painfully familiar squalling, and the village gave tongue in reply: a swarm of men in leather clouts and women in greasy buckskin smocks and children naked as the wind came howling down to the bank, catching up sticks as they ran and accompanied by a rabble of dogs.

Roger's personal captors formed their little procession for the triumph; a stick lashed his bruised skin cruelly, and he broke into an obedient run toward the huts. In a moment he was surrounded by a mad mob, shrieking, clawing for a chance to strike at him, a whole forest of sticks rising and falling, even the gaunt wolf dogs burrowing under the tumult to snap at his ankles. He went down under it and lay among the snarling dogs. There was a momentary respite while the dogs were beaten off. He was jerked to his feet again, and again the howl went up, and again the sticks rose and fell. He was barely conscious of them now. The uproar came and went in waves like a mirage of sound. He was aware of a fatuous smile upon his lips.

Darkness. Not the whole darkness of night nor the cool gloom of the forest. A brown darkness, warm somehow. A mingled smell of wood smoke and stale tobacco and food and of unwashed human flesh. He opened his eyes and saw that he was lying in a wigwam made of broad sheets of birch bark wrapped about a cone of standing poles. Daylight entered at the apex, indirectly, for he could not see the sky. His faculties came back slowly. Hearing, now. A chorus of wild sounds outside somewhere. His nerves shrank and something inside him whimpered. But it was not the witches' Sabbath he re-

membered last. These were mournful sounds, the wailing and shrieking of women. His flesh was awakening now, and he was sorry, for it
crept with pain from head to foot. It began inside with an ache in all
his bones and oozed toward the surface where his skin, or what was
left of it, burned as if with fire. He had to lock his teeth to keep from
crying out. He lay on a low couch of fir twigs with a ragged and
filthy blanket over him. The wigwam's entrance was a triangular gap
in the bark sheets reaching up to the height of a man's shoulders and
screened by a soiled blue stroud blanket like the one which covered
him. Beside it, on a mat of woven rushes, crouched a very old woman
in a filthy buckskin smock, sucking slowly at a short and very black
clay pipe. She was watching him with one black malevolent eye; the
other was a blue-white horror, blind with cataract.

The door blanket jerked aside and the Acadian man stepped in,
dressed now in gray homespun trousers and a linsey-woolsey shirt. A
wooden canteen hung from his shoulder by a strap. He unslung it
and knelt beside the couch to pour a trickle of harsh trade brandy
into Roger's mouth.

"You are sore, my friend. Can you speak?"

"Yes."

"What happened to Peyal?"

"I do not know Peyal."

"He was the sagamore, the leader of these people. You hear those
women? They mourn for him."

"I did not kill him."

"Who, then?"

"Gorham's men killed three Indians near the lake above Chebucto."

"Did you see them?"

"I saw one. He had a small stone fish slung about his neck."

"Ha! Did they scalp him—Gorham's men?"

"Yes."

"That was Peyal. Did they take the totem from his neck?"

"The fish? I do not think so."

"Did you take it?"

"No."

"How did you get the hatchet of Peyal?"

"I picked it up."

"You lie. You killed Peyal. Where is the totem?"

"I do not know."

The man squatted on his moccasin heels and whittled shreds from a piece of stick tobacco with his belt knife. He rubbed them in his strong, hairy hands and took the gray stone pipe from the thong about his neck. A grunt sent the old squaw forth, evidently for a coal.

"Listen, Englishman. I am your friend, me. A Frenchman and a Catholic. My name is Gautier. I live with these savages here at Shubenacadie. I buy their furs for brandy and such other matters as they desire. I have an Indian woman. I am one of them. I hunt with them sometimes, as you have seen. And if sometimes there are a few *chevelures* to be had . . ." A shrug, a roll of the small dark eyes, a wry smile. "What would you? A fur trader cannot afford to be nice about the pelts his clients take, you comprehend. There is a good price for such things at Louisbourg, a better at Quebec if one wishes to send his goods so far. But that is not what I wish to talk about. I wish to talk of you, my boy. The savages want your life—for the life of Peyal, you comprehend. That is only justice. But it is not your English justice—they will not dance you on a rope. No! No! They do not understand such methods. It must be done slowly . . . slowly, so that death may come to the captive as winter comes to the earth, a little cold, a little warmth, a little storm, a little calm, a time to think, and a time to cry out . . . so!" He put his black-nailed finger tips together and drew them slowly apart. "Mercy they do not know. Pain they know . . . theirs is a painful world . . . and there is pleasure in the pain of others."

Roger wondered dully how he could be in greater pain than now. There was a limit. The notion gave him a feeling of resignation, almost of indifference.

He muttered, "What will they do?"

Again the shrug and the wry mouth. "Fire, perhaps. Fire is not a custom of the Meeg-a-maage, but they have joined in war parties with the Abenakis, and then always there is fire with captives. But there are other ways of drawing pain from a man's flesh, you comprehend. The tender parts first, the fingernails, the toenails, the privates, the mouth, the nostrils—but never the eyes or ears, for always the poor devil must see and hear. *Tiens!* The things I have seen! And the women . . . the women are the worst of all. When they turn you over to the women you have passed the portals of hell, my friend. I have seen a man skinned alive. You think I am trying to frighten you? I tell you the truth. I tell you the devil himself must have turned his face from certain affairs I have regarded, me!"

"Why are you telling me all this?"

Gautier brought his beady stare close to Roger's face. "Because you can do something for me and I can do something for you. An affair, that! I am a trader, *hein*? The amulet—the little stone fish. I want it! Why? Because it is a totem of these people, a thing that brings good hunting, good fishing, good wooing and begetting, good everything. It is very old; they do not know how old. They say it came from *Sakawachkik,* the Ancient Ones, who journeyed to this country from the south when the earth was young and there were giants in the forest. They believe strange things, you comprehend. The missionary Le Loutre comes to this place, this Shubenacadie, several times a year and sings Mass in the little chapel by the river and teaches them to cross themselves. He talks about the flames of hell, and they go in great fear of him. He brings them gifts of meal and blankets and hatchets and guns, and they look upon him as their father. He informs them that their Munitoo, their Maker-of-the-world, is none but the devil himself and must not be worshiped any more; and he gives them little pewter crucifixes and says they must not wear the old charms any more. But what is the good father's paradise compared to their own Good Hunting Place? They do not want his heaven, although they greatly fear his hell. So they say *'Ayah! Ayah!'* and cross themselves and go on worshiping the devil and wearing the ancient charms together with the crucifix. So! You see? The little stone fish is important. With a talisman like that one can go anywhere, do anything, in the country of the Meeg-a-maage. No savage would dare to harm a hair of his head who wears it. On the contrary, they would ask him to come amongst them so that they might enjoy the influence of its magic."

"It did not save Peyal from an English bullet," Roger said.

"That was to be expected, my friend. It is well known amongst the Meeg-a-maage that the English have an evil medicine that the ancient totems cannot overcome. Nor can the totem of the abbé's god, for the savages remember the Frenchmen of D'Anville perishing by hundreds on the shores of Chebucto despite the crucifix about their necks. That, too, was wrought by the evil magic of the English. Against the English there is no talisman but that of bullet and tomahawk. The stone fish is for other matters. The stone fish is for peaceful things."

"I tell you where to find the amulet and you save my life, is that it?" A great clarity had come upon Roger's muddled mind. The little stone fish was slung about the neck of that *thing* in the lake above Chebucto, of course! But if he told what he knew, Gautier would journey there and get it, and whatever influence went with it; and how far was Gautier to be trusted then? Not a bit!

"But yes!" Gautier cried. "Where? Tell me!"

"First, how do you propose to save me?"

"That is easy—for me, my friend. I send a canoe to Beaubassin and fetch here the Abbé Le Loutre himself! He does not permit the slaying of English captives who may be worth gold alive. He uses the ransom money to buy guns and hatchets for his savages—for the glory of God."

"You are cynical, Gautier."

"I am a Catholic"—simply. "The Holy Church is not to be condemned for the actions of a half-wild priest. Père Le Loutre is a little cracked on the subject of the English. That makes him equally useful to *Le bon Dieu* and the devil."

"I cannot tell you where the totem is."

"*Sacré nom!* You wish to die?"

"It seems to me that while the totem remains unfound I have a chance to live."

Through his thin brown nose, with the sound that only a disappointed Frenchman achieves, Gautier cried, "You really think so, my poor friend? The thing is not so important as all that!"

The old squaw returned with a coal, caught between two chips. Gautier clutched the unlit pipe in his fist, dashed the coal out of her hands, flung a parting *"Sot!"* at Roger, and vanished beyond the door blanket.

CHAPTER 20

Education

In the next fifteen or twenty days—he soon lost count—Roger was convinced of his own shrewdness. The crone rubbed his cuts and bruises every morning with an evil-smelling salve of grease and crushed herbs, and twice a day brought him food, usually a bark dish full of boiled venison, partridge, hare, or porcupine—once or twice he suspected dog—and various kinds of fish, the chief of which was very bony but rather sweet, apparently caught in springtime and partly sun-dried, partly smoked. The ache went out of his bones and the smart from his flesh.

His chief discomfort was the multitude of lice. His bed blanket fairly hopped with fleas as well, but his nakedness saved him from their worst ravages.

There seemed to be no guard except the old squaw, but there was no chance of escape. From dawn to dark a succession of brown faces—men, women, and children—examined him with the bright eyes of animals. And at night the animals themselves, the dogs, those half wolves, prowled about the silent huts.

As the object of so much discussion, Roger heard a vast amount of the Micmac tongue. It was guttural and monotonous, with a peculiar singsong intonation at the end of a phrase. When his ear became accustomed to the simple vowels he could distinguish many French words in the medley, adapted to their tongues by substituting *l* for *r* and making one sound of *b* and *p*, of *d* and *t*, and of *g* and *k*.

Gautier, who visited him from time to time and brought a clay pipe and tobacco to help him while away the hours, enlarged upon these matters with the rather droll air of a schoolmaster.

"You are surprised at their mixed tongue, monsieur? But why? These people have known the French for at least one hundred and fifty years. And before that the Basques, who came to fish on the Banks and dried their codfish on these shores, two centuries ago." Roger could not help thinking of Nova Scotia as a new country. It was a little bewildering to suggest that Europeans had frequented this coast when Queen Bess took the throne of England.

"*Ces sauvages-là*"—an airy wave toward the glitter of black eyes in the doorway—"are all baptized with French names, as their fathers were before them, by the missionaries. So they are Jean, Pierre, Bernard, Martin, Claude, Gabriel—and call themselves San, Peyal, Penaul, Malti, Glode, Cobleal, because that is the best their tongues can do. Sometimes they bear a byname, after the ancient fashion of the savages, and so that one you killed, you comprehend, was known as Bright Sun to mark him from the other Pierres among them. It is written in the abbé's little book thus, Pierre-*dit*-Beau-Soleil." And significantly, "You will remember that name!"

Roger shrugged. That blend of self-confidence and indifference, born of a belief in his luck, the true mark of the adventurer, was again strong in him.

There were other matters to be explained, and Gautier explained them, with gestures, with the self-important air of one whose wisdom is enormous in the presence of a child. The Micmacs—properly Meeg-a-maage—were hunters and wanderers who scattered up and down the coast in small family groups in summer, when clams and fish were plentiful and the sea breeze kept away the flies. In winter they gathered inland, where the moose and caribou hunting could sustain them, away from the coastal storms. There were numerous petty chiefs like the dead warrior Peyal, but they recognized no supreme authority as a tribe, except in the region of the Bay of Fundy. There Le Loutre exercised his remarkable sway over them, partly religious, partly mundane—for his bounty often kept them from starvation in the snow months—but chiefly by the force of a personality that stalked the forest like a flame. And by the fortune of coincidence, which made his family name that of an animal well known to the Indians, Le Loutre translated perfectly into Micmac. The short black-robed figure, the brisk and restless movements, the sharp and cunning eyes, the courage amounting to ferocity, the scorn of weather and distance, the faculty of bobbing up in unexpected places, all made him perfectly The Otter.

These Micmacs who wintered at Shubenacadie probably were the largest single group in the peninsula. Another vague gathering wintered in the interior somewhere toward Cape Sable, and a third in the island of Cape Breton. There were others along the Gulf of St. Lawrence shore as far north as Gaspé, but of these Gautier knew little. Roger had pictured the great forest infested with these two-legged wolves, and it was a shock to hear Gautier suggest that all the Micmacs in the peninsula did not number more than two thousand and at most could not put more than four hundred warriors on the warpath. "And," the trader added emphatically, "only a prophet—or Le Loutre—could get them all together at one time!"

Roger thought of Cornwallis and his thousand redcoats at Halifax, and Paul Mascarene and his regiment at Fort Anne, all held within their palisades by the notion of a forest full of savages.

"It is incredible," he said.

"Incroyable! You think of your soldiers, no? Those! Besieged by phantoms! It is the forest they fear. That is a big enemy. Long ago we discovered, we French, that the forest is a friend to the swift and the bold and is merciless to all others. Voilà! We range the great forest from Quebec to Mexico and the continent is ours, while you English sit with your tails in salt water like the butcher's cat."

"And if the English learn to move in the forest?"

Gautier was amused. His small brown eyes twinkled. "The English," he said profoundly, "never learn. Regard yourself! I have told you how to save yourself and——"

"Let us not return to that," said Roger coldly.

To liven the monotony of these long and empty days he set himself to learn the language from Gautier, from the ancient squaw (whose toothless gums and withered lips, however, made her difficult to understand) and from the solemn children at the door. The men he never addressed. Something in their eyes forbade it, and there were times when that silent malevolence brought a chill to his self-confidence and again a reckless longing to have it over with, whatever *it* was.

The language was copious, with a word for everything under the sun, and a word for every variation in form and substance of that thing. Verbs could be enlarged, or whittled down, and fitted to parts of other verbs similarly whittled or enlarged, to express exactly the thing in mind. He was appalled to realize that the conjugation of a

single verb might run to several thousand forms. But this word carpentry made it possible to express a whole sentence in a single word,
shorn of all excess syllables, admirable in its directness. In Micmac
you said exactly what you thought and nothing more, not by so much
as a grunt. He came to realize that the most ignorant savage could
put his thoughts in words that had the pith and simple dignity of,
say, the English of the King James Bible.

Roger applied himself with a perseverance that would have astounded his Oxford masters. He had a gift for languages. In the
Highlands he had mastered Gaelic—surely the most difficult of
tongues. On the continent he had acquired a perfect fluency in
French and a good deal of Italian. His progress in Micmac delighted
Gautier, carried away by his role of schoolmaster, but after a time
the trader showed less pleasure.

"Do you hope, my deluded friend, that you can *talk* yourself out
of the hands of these savages?"

"It passes the time."

"Ah, I am not sure that I should do so in your place. Time . . .
life . . . these things are short sometimes. One should wish them to
go slowly."

"You are morbid, Gautier."

"And you are mad."

From time to time the humdrum of this life was broken by the
arrival of another party from the summer wanderings along the
coast, a single family in a couple of canoes, or five or six families together. Roger listened for that painfully familiar yell which meant a
prisoner, but there were none. There were scalps and heads, however,
and then always there was an uproar lasting through the day and the
night, with much dancing about a fire in the midst of the camp and
the slaying of dogs for a feast. These were uneasy occasions, with a
succession of grotesque painted faces thrust abruptly into the wigwam door, emitting blood-freezing howls and regarding his white
nakedness with the eyes of wolves.

Gautier vanished from these scenes as if even he did not feel safe
and later explained—a little shamefaced, it seemed to Roger—that
no white man was permitted to look upon a head dance. The trader's
eyes were uneasy. They were hounding him for *booktawichkc*—"fire-

water"—and he dared not let them have it. He kept his kegs hidden in the woods down-river because in the frenzy of the head dance they often came and rummaged his store. It would not be safe to give them brandy till the cold weather had set in and chilled their lusts a bit. Then he would buy the scalps they had taken during the summer and send the collection to Louisbourg for the French king's bounty. Furs? They would have no furs worth buying until the snows came.

"Where do they get all these scalps and heads?" Roger asked one day.

Gautier pushed out his lips and looked exactly like an ape. "You will remember those four from Chebucto? *Bien!* That is a beginning. We shall have good hunting there next year. There are always some to be gathered in the region of Fort Anne, as you call our old Port Royal—deserters and wanderers outside the *banlieue*. But the best hunting, truly, has always been along the coast, where the *Bostoon* fishermen come in to lonely harbors for fuel and water. They are watchful when they go ashore, but when they return on board they have that droll belief of seamen in the security of their ship. So . . . a rush of canoes in the dark, a shout and a squeak, and all is over . . . five . . . ten . . . fifteen *chevelures* to hang in the sun to dry. It happens every year, up and down the coast. You never learn, you English."

"Someday we shall teach, my friend. And we shall teach a lesson that your savages, yes, and you Acadiens, will remember forever."

"God let me live so long!" cried Gautier merrily.

The pursuit of such strange knowledge and the steady shrinking of the daylight hours made the days pass quickly enough. But the growing nights became a burden on his nerves. He could not sleep soundly, for lack of exercise, and in the long wakeful hours of darkness his thoughts galloped furiously and fruitlessly like a caged squirrel on its treadmill. Sometimes, desperate, he resolved to break forth, regardless of the old woman, the dogs, and the rest, make a dash for the riverbank, seize a canoe, and attempt to escape down that mysterious red river in the dark. But when he stepped, however stealthily, toward the door the squaw stirred and muttered, the gaunt dogs growled outside, and discretion swallowed valor.

The wigwam was a good two hundred yards from the river. There appeared to be fifty or more of these dwellings arranged in a rude U with its open end toward the stream. The space down the middle was beaten bare and pocked with the shallow pits of cooking fires. On the riverbank itself stood two large log huts, one of which he knew was Gautier's store. The other bore a rude wooden cross and was evidently the chapel of M. Le Loutre.

He had questioned the trader adroitly about the locality and, despite Gautier's evasiveness, had learned that the Shubenacadie River flowed into a great arm of the Bay of Fundy somewhere to the north. But if he escaped down the river to the bay, he would be farther from Halifax than ever, and in the country of the Acadien farmers, who would turn him over to the Indians without hesitation. Thus Gautier. The way was upstream, then. He must follow the river to that long and narrow lake between the pine hills, find the portage to the lakes above Chebucto, and follow them to Gilman's mill-stream. He guessed the distance as fifty miles. That was not far as distances went in this country, but a bark canoe was a tricky thing and a lone man pushing upstream would be overtaken in a few hours at most. To attempt the journey naked and afoot was madness. There was no way out. The treadmill had come full circle now, and he gave it up—until the next wakeful night.

For some nights there had been hard frosts with a frigid mist in the mornings. But the days were bright, and a cool west wind hissed in the pine tops and chased masses of white cloud across an indigo sky. The hardwood leaves across the river were in full color now, a miracle to his English eyes. How splendid and barbaric! He had always loved the woods at Suddenholt and sometimes tried to picture them as they stood across the whole of Kent before the Romans came. Here was the reality, yet like no forest that England ever knew, as if the old Weald had come to life far in the west and dressed itself in war paint and feathers after the fashion of the country. The display was best at sundown, when the red blaze in the western sky lit a new flame in the yellow and scarlet maples and gilded the edges of the yellow birch leaves and added richness to the brown hues of the old oaks and the wine purple of the sapling oaks and turned the huckleberry bushes to a sea of blood. And in the afterglow one lone poplar on the riverbank became a torch of ruddy gold, flickering against the forest shadows on the other side.

During the summer at Halifax he had come to think of the forest as a somber and terrible wilderness. Now he saw it as he had seen it first, from the deck of the *Fair Lady*—as an invitation and a challenge. He longed to tread beneath that splendor, to have the feel and smell of it, to seek out the secret heart of it. To be in it! To be part of it!

CHAPTER 21

Toujours la Femme

THERE WAS A YELL from the riverbank one afternoon, with the usual outcry and scurry in the village, followed by a prolonged babble in the midst of the camp. Gautier squatted at his favorite place inside the door, stricken silent in the midst of a lively tale of moose hunting in the Cobequids. Roger sprawled on his bed, smoking the frugal mixture of trade tobacco and willow bark which the Micmacs called *tabagy*. The door blanket was flung aside, and into the wigwam stepped an astonishing figure, taller and leaner than the common run of Micmac men, and wearing, in addition to clout and moccasins, the red coat of a British soldier and a thrice-cocked hat of black felt bound with silver lace. Bracelets of hawk bells jingled at his wrists and ankles. Roger noted swiftly the faded buff facings of the coat— the uniform of Philips' Regiment at Fort Anne—and thought joyously, "By Jove! A friendly Indian!"

His pleasure faded swiftly. There was nothing friendly in the painted face. The hard, thin mouth, the set of the gaunt jaws, the bloodshot eyes with their black pupils dilating cat-like in the gloom of the wigwam, all exhibited a ferocity beyond anything he had seen since his capture.

The familiar smell of the hut was overborne by a new sharp reek of sweat and bear grease. The strange Indian examined Roger from head to foot with a glare that could be felt. After a full minute of it he turned to Gautier.

"Ho!"

"*Kway!*" returned the trader politely.

A sort of confessional followed, the Indian grunting questions and Gautier stammering replies. There was something cringing and servile in Gautier's voice and manner. They were discussing him, Roger knew. He could follow some of it. Finally the visitor jerked his chin toward the door and stepped outside, followed quickly by Gautier. The voices drew away and became part of the chatter still rising from the midst of the camp. The old woman spoke. "You will die."

Roger made no answer. His skin was prickling from that long and furious stare.

Toward evening Gautier came back. The man's bronze cheeks had turned a sickly yellow. He was sweating. "You are lost," he said simply. He remained standing. There was a nervous air about him, as if he were ready to bolt at any moment.

"What has happened? Who was that man?"

"That was Koap, who bears the baptized name of Jean Baptiste— San Badees, as the Micmacs say. The foremost warrior of these people now that Peyal is dead. And"—with an expressive roll of eyes— "the right hand, the forerunner of Abbé Le Loutre in all his machinations against the English."

"But this is good news!" Roger cried. "You tell me this missionary does not permit them to kill captives!"

Gautier burst out harshly, "Exactly! And they never do—in his presence. But he is not present, my poor friend. He is on his way by canoe from Beaubassin. And Koap says you must die because you killed Peyal—you must die now, before the priest arrives."

"There will be gossip,'" said Roger desperately. "You tell me the warriors confess to Monsieur Le Loutre . . ."

"You are to be taken into the forest by the squaws. What happens there will be their secret."

"But if he learns?" persisted Roger.

"The warriors will blame it on the women. Squaws have no souls, that is well understood by M. Le Loutre." The trader lifted his shoulders and spread his hands, with a roll of eyes toward the smoky peak of the wigwam.

Voices approached, the clack and titter of pleased and excited women. Gautier dived past the door blanket like a frightened hare. Roger rose slowly and passed his little black clay, still fuming pleasantly, to the old woman. She took it, wordless, regarding him intently with her one good eye. There was no emotion in her wrinkled face. He had the impression that she had seen many like him come to be healed of wounds and beatings, to be fed, to be made whole for the supreme rite of torture and death.

Two stout matrons entered, with an eager and important air. They were dressed for a festival in the bright rags of petticoats and bedgowns got, no doubt, from Louisbourg, with strings of colored trade beads around their fat necks and wound about their wrists, and fillets of red cloth about their hair. They jerked his wrists behind him and bound them together tightly. He was pushed outside.

The flood of sunlight dazzled him for a moment. A screaming chorus rose about him, and he saw a mob of females of all ages arrayed in buckskins and queer tatters of European finery, each armed with a thin rod of peeled maple or birch. So! Another beating! They scurried, giggling, to arrange themselves in a double line leading toward the trees. Pleasure shone in all their faces—commonly as dull as wood. His skin crept, awaiting the pain. It was not long in coming. He started violently at the first vicious slash and ran his best. The women set up a cry, a long-drawn "Aaaaeeee!" and his back, his bound hands, his buttocks and thighs were assailed by a swarm of red-hot wasps as he passed. The air seemed full of the swish and whistle of descending withes. They seemed to create a wind that blew him along. The faces on either side were a laughing brown blur.

The way led into the woods, a path made by fuel-gathering squaws. He had a wild resolve. After he had passed the gauntlet he would keep on, running like the wind, straight into the forest, and on and on.

But after he passed the end of that squealing avenue the slashing at his back continued, with a patter of moccasins added to the shrill laughter. The younger squaws were running at his heels as easily as deer. Fortunately the path was narrow and not more than two could strike at a time. But after a hundred yards or so the woods opened and he found himself running into a considerable clearing surrounded by large hemlock trees. A stick was thrust expertly between his legs and he went down on his face. He was dragged to his feet, gasping, and pushed backward against a slender post or perhaps a sapling tree. His wrists were untied, passed about the thing, and fastened again behind it. Instinctively he looked at the ground about his feet. No sign of past fires there. Gautier had given him a gruesome list of agonies, but it was death by fire that he feared most. A silence fell. The women faced him at a little distance, the whole panting mob. Their eyes still glittered with excitement and expectancy but only the older ones were laughing now; the young squaws seemed a little awed, nudging each other and wriggling uneasily. The switches had been thrown aside and he noticed the women in front fingering clam shells and leaf-shaped flints. It dawned upon him in a cold fit of horror that these were the tools they used in skinning and scraping hides. His gaze fastened itself upon these simple but now incredibly evil objects with a dreadful fascination.

The fleet-footed younger women made the forefront of the crowd. There were a few self-conscious giggles among them now, and they began to edge toward him under pressure from behind. A bold one touched his naked stomach lightly and pulled her hand away, laughing. Soon there were several exploring his white skin. There were remarks which he could not catch because, apparently, they referred to things not mentioned in his lessons, and at each there was an outburst of merriment that spread over the whole gathering. He felt sick. He lifted his gaze resolutely, staring past that brown sea of greasy grins, and saw Koap standing in the path. The warrior called out something angrily, and an old gaunt squaw came muttering to the front, thrusting the young women aside. The laughter ceased.

She stepped forward with one of the sharp flint flaying tools clutched in her bony fingers and made a sudden but expert slash with it, slitting the skin across his stomach from hip to hip. He was aware of a thin burning, as if a red-hot pencil had been drawn across the skin, and he could feel a dribble of blood down his belly and flanks. The women uttered a long, low "Ah!" and began to press forward, thrusting out their flints and shells. He would not look down. But he shrank against the post. He could not help it. His starting eyes were fixed on the foremost squaw, a creature fit for this bad dream. She had appeared from the back of the crowd, her face rubbed with a compound of grease and charcoal, her long black hair all wild about her shoulders. There was nothing festive about her clothing. She wore the shapeless buckskin smock, reaching to the knees, with a knotted thong about the waist, which was the common dress of women in the camp. She might have been any age from sixteen to sixty. In the black mask her dark eyes burned like coals.

Without warning she turned her face to the sky and uttered a long and high-pitched cry. It was familiar, the mourning cry of the women on the day after he came to Shubenacadie. It startled the other women quite as much as the captive. They drew back a little, staring at her. She dropped on her knees and rocked back and forth, uttering that weird sound of a bereft she-wolf. The clearing rang with it. Koap came thrusting through the women. The man was furious. He flung a question at the she-wolf, yelling the words. Without rising from her knees she shrieked up at him a long harangue broken only by an intermittent sharp, hissing intake of breath.

Once or twice Koap tried to break in, but it was useless. Roger strained to catch her words. In that harsh, cracked voice he could recognize nothing except "Peyal," repeated frequently with the second syllable drawn out in a peculiarly dismal way. The other squaws were murmuring now. Koap snarled at them, and several old hags cried back at him in a manner quite different from their usual meek tones in the presence of men. Clearly a point had arisen on which the women could speak with impunity. There was even a strident satisfaction in some of the voices, as if they rejoiced at the chance. Koap scowled. He made as if to strike one of them, and all the voices rose at once to a howl. He turned and strode away, and as he disappeared there was an outbreak of laughter and one or two unmistakable catcalls. Roger might have relished that if he had not felt an urgent need to retch; for Koap was very like a cat indeed, a gaunt and furious tomcat worsted by a party of indignant tabbies.

Someone unfastened his hands. He was borne along the path to the village in a stream of excited women all talking at once. The woman with the blackened face had vanished. In the common ground between the rows of wigwams the men of Shubenacadie were

gathered, hearing with impassive faces a tirade from the angry tongue
of San Badees Koap. The women pushed him into the familiar bark
prison, and the door flap closed. Roger eased himself down upon the
couch. From his nape to the backs of his knees the skin was afire.
Compared to that misery, the score across his upper belly, little more
than skin deep, was a mere irritant. He was completely mystified at
the turn of events. He had a pessimistic notion that worse was to
come.

Gautier came, grinning and excited. *"Hola!* What a man! The luck
of the devil! How many come back whole from a caressing by the
squaws?"

"Well?" gloomily.

The trader squatted. His small brown eyes gleamed slyly. "You are
favored, my friend. The widow of Peyal has decided to take you to
her bed."

Roger started up, and the movement sent a wave of fiery agony
up his back. He sank back again. "You have a droll humor, Gautier."

"I am serious."

"What! You mean that black-faced one? That animal?"

Gautier looked at him curiously. "They are not so bad when you
get used to them."

"Impossible!"

"But possible! My God, are you the fool you seem? I have lived
twenty years amongst these savages, and in that time I have seen
many captives die in such ways as I have related to you. Few—very
few, you comprehend—were spared by the whim of a woman as you
were today. Regard you, it is an ancient law amongst them that the
widow of a warrior slain in battle may take a captive to her bed if
she desires—to breed a son to take her husband's place in the tribe.
Parbleu! That is a custom in all these fighting races whose warriors
die faster than their women breed."

"A custom of mongrels."

"Call it what you like." Gautier was laughing. "You are sore, and
when one's flesh is in pain one cannot . . . Well, no matter. These
women understand the flesh of mankind perfectly. You will be healed
by your protectress . . . with the most tender care. And you shall
have time to adjust yourself to your new life. The woman has a long

period of mourning to observe. When the moment comes—and she will choose the moment, not you—shut your eyes and play your part gallantly. Use your imagination, my boy! You must pretend she is a beautiful virgin under the spell of a sorceress, like the old hag in the tale!"

"Impossible!"

Gautier's expression changed swiftly. He snarled, "Impossible! Always this impossible! You wish to live? Even a fool wishes to live. *Bien,* here is your life. A gift from God or the devil or whatever it is you English worship. Take it, then! You belong to her now, whether you wish it or not. You are her captive, understand? You will hunt and fish with the men of her family. Your food, your clothing will be prepared for you as becomes a man. But you will have no privilege beyond these. If you attempt to escape you will be slain like a dog—or handed back to those she-devils to be flayed alive. Listen, my friend, it is a good life out there in the forest. It is the way a man was meant to live. When you have spent a year with these people you will never wish to leave them. There are hundreds like you, mated to savage women in the woods between here and the great lakes of the St. Lawrence."

"When does Abbé Le Loutre arrive?"

"*Peste!* You still hope for ransom? You will never see the priest! Tomorrow you depart with the woman Wapke, with Luksi, her father, with her brother, Le Bras d'Or, and his squaw and little ones."

"Where?"

The shrug, and the expressive hands.

And on the morrow they departed, in two canoes, with an east wind keening in the bare trees by the river and a cold rain slipping down. No one came down to the bank to see them off, there was no word of farewell at all; a few curious heads at the doors of wigwams, that was all. There was no sign of Gautier. Nor of San Badees Koap, except that the door of the small log chapel was open and a squaw was sweeping it out with a bundle of birch twigs in preparation for Abbé Le Loutre.

CHAPTER 22

Morning Light

LIKE Theseus entering the labyrinth, Roger embarked upon this new journey into the unknown with a careful eye for marks along the way. But it was such a long way, and with so many marks, that he forgot them. He could look for no help from his charcoal-smeared Ariadne. She took the squaw's place at the bow paddle, where he could see only her swaying buckskin back, and she stared straight ahead and said not a word. Luksi, her father, sat on the stern thwart, steering. The captive lay on skins along the bottom, lifting himself—warily, because all movement was painful—to stare at the passing banks from time to time. Stowed on the bottom also were a brass kettle, a musket, a pair of French hatchets, a fish spear, and a pole with one end sharpened and hardened in fire, which Luksi used to punt the canoe upstream in shallow places. The rest of their household goods were stowed in a pair of large baskets of maple splints, shaped like a peddler's sack with a broad base and narrow neck, the top sealed against the weather by a circular wooden lid, and the whole fitted with leather straps for carrying.

Roger's back was a torment. He could put his hand behind and feel the scourged skin of his buttocks and loins, a mesh of fiery ridges. Farther up, between his shoulders, many of the old cuts had opened under that enthusiastic welting by the squaws. The cold rain chilled him in his nakedness. He was tempted to pull one of the furs over him but refrained for fear of seeming womanish in the eyes of old Luksi, who wore nothing but a clout, or the eyes of the children in the canoe behind, who wore nothing at all. Not far from the village Luksi left the broad stream of the Shubenacadie and turned his bow into a shallow tributary flowing from the east. A struggle began. There were long stretches where the stream rattled thinly over gravel bars, and all had to jump out and wade upstream pushing the canoes with their hands—all except the youngest child of Le Bras d'Or, an infant of three months or so, strapped to a carrying board in the canoe bottom and gazing up at the rainy sky with eyes like small black buttons. The banks were low and featureless, pine and hemlock forest fringed with red maples whose last lone leaves shivered forlornly in the wet October gale. Flocks of wild duck went up with a great splatter and quacking from the occasional stillwaters that wound, deep and dark as ink, through strips of wild meadow. Once in such a meadow they came upon a dome-shaped beaver house and Luksi got out and stood upon the mound of turf and gnawed sticks speculatively. But his daughter cried an impatient *"Boosenech!* Let us paddle on!" He got in with a rather comical reluctance, licking his old lips as if the smatch of stewed fat beaver tail were in his mouth already.

They did not break their fast until midafternoon, when the canoes were drawn up on the bank and Luksi conjured a fire of pine splinters with the aid of a battered French tinderbox. The meal consisted of *moosok,* lean moose meat cut in strips, dried in the sun, pounded to a fibrous mass, mixed with blueberries to give it a tang of sweetness, and molded in round cakes—a journey ration with which Roger was to become wearily familiar. They squatted about the fire in the shelter of a massive hemlock tree while the meat stewed in the pot, and the squaw of Le Bras d'Or untied her smock and fed her infant, still strapped to the board, from a brown breast that hung long and flaccid like a half-filled shot pouch of polished leather.

Later Roger was mildly astonished to see her chew a mouthful of the stringy journey meat and place some of it in the child's mouth with her work-callused forefinger. She was a plump and shining creature, well named Swaakwe—"She-seal," although she bore the Christian name of Mahlee—from the Ste. Marie of the missionaries.

Her husband was a stocky man, rather ugly, with broad, flaring nostrils and a face deeply pitted with the scars of smallpox. His name puzzled Roger until old Luksi informed him casually that Le Bras d'Or was born beside the shore of an inland sea which the French knew by that name.

"Where is that?" Roger asked. Gold was an intriguing word.

"Oonamaagik—the Foggy Country," with a gesture toward the east.

Golden Arm and the Seal had two youngsters besides the infant, a boy about five years and a girl of eight or nine. The boy had a parted upper lip and was known appropriately as Little Hare. The girl was Mahlee, like her mother. The baptismal zeal of the missionaries had filled the Micmac villages with Mahlees.

Luksi was an active old fellow with fine teeth and keen black eyes. There was much gray in his topknot, and his face was deeply lined. Roger guessed his age at sixty. It was quite fruitless to hazard the age of the women. He had observed at Shubenacadie that the female savages matured early, became thick and stolid after bearing the first child, and were hags soon after thirty.

He studied Wapke whenever he got a chance. She renewed her greasy black mask from time to time from a small earthenware pot in one of the basket packs. She smeared it on thickly, and the stuff sagged with the warmth of her face and gave her the look of a haggard Negress. The long hair flittered about her face in untended tangles. He wondered how long this mourning ritual would last.

The others talked to him freely. Wapke held herself aloof and was silent except when making a direct request or a command. The buckskin smock gave no hint of her figure. She was active as a cat, but so were all Micmac women except the very old. Her hands were long and strong. Her legs below the smock were smooth and round, and she had the thick ankles of her people.

She had a charming name. Wapke—Morning Light. It was even more charming than that, for this Micmac word for dawn pronounced with the proper nuances meant literally "The opening eye of the day." But he had seen a fat and hideous squaw named Shining Star.

When evening came the little river had dwindled to a shallow brook overhung with naked maples and bordered by a crimson mass of huckleberry bushes. The voyagers waded now, working the canoes along with care, for the least touch on a sharp stone meant a slit in the bar and a long halt to melt balsam and mend the leak. Roger's teeth chattered. He wondered what Charles would think if he could see him now—naked in the rain, in October, in the wilds of America. Charles with his mulled wine and a good fire leaping on the hearth at Suddenholt!

The hanging bushes rasped his raw back and the stones of the stream bed bruised his bare feet; he was weary and cold, and his belly groaned for food, but for all that something in him exulted when he thought of Charles. Charles and the Fiat Club—Boyce and the parson and John Harroll and old Sir Jeremy and the rest, toasting King James over the water perhaps at this very moment. By Jove, they'd have died, the lot of them, in half an hour of this!

A gap in the bushes and the ghost of a path, a trace, no more, running off into the dusk under the trees. A portage, evidently. Luksi swung the canoe on his shoulders, upside down, with a quick powerful heave, and walked off with it. Golden Arm followed with the other. The Seal burdened herself with her family goods and her husband's gun and set off in the wake of the bobbing canoes, which seemed to swim, capsized, a foot or two above the bush tops. Her infant was strapped to her broad back and she herself was a waddling bundle of skins and baskets.

Wapke stooped to her own goods, checked herself sharply, and turned her black inhuman mask to Roger. She pointed imperiously. "*Pemadega!* Carry it!"

He hesitated, filled with a male resentment. "That is women's work."

"Thou art less than a woman. Thou art a *thing*. My *thing*. *Pemadega!*"

She picked up a stick, and he saw that she meant to be obeyed. He stooped and awkwardly began to sling the baskets about himself and picked up the bundled skins. He could not remember how the Seal had done it—she must have had four hands. How could anyone carry the bulky skin bundles, the fish spear, the setting pole, the kettle, the musket, and two hatchets with a single pair? Wapke picked up the gun and the tomahawks. Unwilling to trust him with the weapons, probably. The rest he managed somehow, but he staggered under the load, and the baskets galled his sore back. Wapke walked behind.

"Someday," he said aloud in English, "I shall pay off all these scores, my fine she-wolf—on you and your whole howling pack."

If she understood she made no answer. He was tempted to say it in her own tongue, but he could not think of the word for revenge.

The bushes opened and surrounded an old camp site, apparently not used in a long time. There was space for three or four wigwams. The ashes of the fires had long since melted away and grass had grown about the charred knots that remained. The Seal had dropped her load, except for the solemn child strapped to her back, and was busy cutting poles for her wigwam. Roger wondered if he should do the same. Luksi and Golden Arm squatted under a big pine, watching with a glint of amusement in their black eyes. But Wapke had decided not to trust him with the hatchet, that was clear. She cut the poles herself and set up the wigwam with a swift skill that he had to admire. The Seal hacked firewood from an old pine snag behind the camp site, and Luksi's tinderbox provided the magic flame. They ate stewed *moosok* again—Luksi and Golden Arm first, then the squaws and children. The leavings went to Wapke's *thing,* last of all. He was impressed with his insignificance. But he thought whimsically, It is something to be less than a woman, after all; you can't be expected to cook or make garments—or have babies. He wondered how she proposed to divide the labor. Would she do the hunting?

In his naked state it was a boon to have shelter at last from the wind and rain. Luksi's couch of fire twigs was in the place of honor opposite the door. Wapke lay down on the right side of the wigwam and motioned Roger toward the left, tossing him a bearskin for bedding. Luksi snored loudly. The warmth of the fur was grateful, but Roger could not sleep. He twisted and turned for a long time, always with due care for his tender back. At last Wapke came and bent over him.

"Why do thee not sleep? Tomorrow will go hard with thee."

"I wish to sleep, but my back does not."

Her dim form glided to the baskets. In a moment she was back again.

"Lie on thy belly," she commanded, and rubbed his inflamed back with bear grease and herbs of the kind used by the old squaw at Shubenacadie. Her fingers were gentle. He went to sleep almost at once, lying on his face.

In the morning the sky was clear and cold, with a nipping wind from the west. Even Luksi and Golden Arm were glad to squat by the fire, and the old man motioned Roger to come and warm his nakedness there also. Wapke busied herself with some scraps of caribou hide and her bone needles. When evening came she flung at Roger's feet a pair of moccasins and a breechclout with its thongs attached.

He put them on and said, *"Kaan*—I thank thee." She sniffed and busied herself with the evening meal.

The clout was barely enough for decency and of no use whatever against the cold, but with his loins thus girded he felt better. He stepped up and down the little clearing to get the feel of the moccasins, and in his satisfaction whistled a bar or two of "I'd Fee'd a Lad at Michaelmas" and performed a few steps of the Highland fling.

The Seal and her children gaped in sheer astonishment. Golden Arm scowled, but old Luksi grinned. What Wapke thought was not apparent.

Three days they lay at this place while Luksi and Golden Arm hunted for fresh meat without success. Roger was eager to go with them but Wapke forbade it. He put it down to malice and was sulky at his squaw tasks—fetching water from the brook, gathering deadwood for the fire, and ferns for the added comfort of their beds. Each evening she rubbed his back with the evil-smelling salve and examined the stone cuts in his feet with the brisk and impersonal air of a groom with a horse. On the fourth morning they struck camp and moved off along the trace toward the south, Luksi and Golden Arm carrying the canoes, then the children, then the Seal and Roger with their multiple burdens, and Wapke bringing up the rear, and late that day emerged from the forest on the shore of a small lake, where they camped.

Here they stayed a week. The two Indians hunted every day. They were eager for moose or caribou, but nothing came to the pot except the flesh of porcupines, which tasted to Roger like elderly mutton steeped in spruce gum. They were stoical about their ill luck until a day when Golden Arm came into the camp grunting that his gun was "sick" and flung the thing to the ground. He had come upon a moose, a fine fat cow, and when he put the gun up there was nothing but a flash in the pan. He had reprimed hastily while the cow stood, as if she knew that Golden Arm had a sick gun. He pulled the trigger again, and this time the gun would not move at all. The hammer, "the little thigh," would not fall. And the cow ran away.

The gun lay by the fire where he had thrown it, a rusty old French fusil with a split stock bound in brass wire. It would be left there when they moved on, Roger knew. He had seen such weapons on the refuse heaps behind the wigwams at Shubenacadie. A gun out of repair was sick and in fact dead. The traders encouraged this belief, and so the tribes offered an insatiable market for firearms. He sauntered over to it carelessly, conscious of their eyes, picked it up and laid it across his knees, asking them the names of the parts. They were used to his linguistic curiosity by this time, and there followed an odd little recital.

"What do you call it?"—with a finger on the barrel.

"*Webaagwik.*"

Finger on the stock, "*Paskowaogum.*" The muzzle, "*Wedoonik.*" The ramrod, "*Sensakudaagun.*" The trigger, "*Wegwadakun.*" The pan, "*Emkwonejit.*" Each was a picture word drawn with unerring skill. Finally with an immense casualness he picked up a broken knife used by the Seal for scraping her pot, and unscrewed the lock; the cock first, then the pan spring, the pan guard, and finally the long brass screws that passed through from the left side and held the lock plate in place. Their eyes bulged.

The hammer spring and the cam of the trigger were crusted with rust, and the whole movement was choked with the fine dirt of—he guessed—forty or fifty years in the forest. He scraped the parts carefully, dug out the dirt, and rubbed all carefully with bear grease dipped with an impudent finger from Wapke's little pot.

Now he put the gun together, reamed the touchhole with a piece of wire, and handed the weapon to Golden Arm.

"Behold, this gun is well."

Golden Arm took it dubiously and tested the charge, still in the gun, with his ramrod. He caught up his powder horn and primed the pan, and aimed the weapon at a boulder in the lake. As his brown finger pulled the trigger home, the pan flamed, the muzzle jumped, belching fire, and a small feather of water leaped and died beside the rock.

"Wah! Indeed this gun is well!" An incredulous smile broke over the pocked face.

The Seal pointed to Roger with wide eyes. "He has magic."

"Fool!" snapped Wapke. "He has only the wisdom of those who make these things."

Luksi addressed her sharply and with an air of finality. "This now is a man."

He did not use the general term for men but the precise word *cheenum,* meaning man as distinguished from woman or child.

Or *thing!* thought Roger triumphantly.

"Still he is mine," she insisted.

Luksi made no answer, but his eyes met Roger's in that whimsical look which means the same thing in all languages, man to man.

Next morning, when the men rose in the frosty dark for the day's hunt, Luksi grunted "Come!" and Roger went. If Wapke heard, she said nothing.

Every morning in the still air of daybreak, when no scent would carry far, the Indians hid in a clump of hackmatacks in the midst of a wild meadow a mile from the camp, while Luksi mimicked the mating call of a cow moose with the aid of a birch-bark horn. The old man was hopeful, although, he admitted, the mating season was nearly past. To Roger it was simply a study in endurance. Each took a fur which he draped about his shoulders against the morning cold, squatting in the frosty wild grass for an hour, two hours, three hours, while Luksi made the ridges echo with that wild and weird sound. It afforded Roger a certain satisfaction to observe Golden Arm's brown buttocks turning faintly purple and prickling with goose flesh, and to hear old Luksi's teeth rattling between the calls. He decided they were no tougher than many white men—the Highland Scots, for instance. What the savage had was an ability to retire within himself, to the comfort of some inner warmth, abandoning his skin to the cold. An effort of will.

There were several of these aching vigils in the frosty dawns, all fruitless, and Roger was glad when the day wind sprang up in the west and put an end to them. The rest of the time was spent in still-hunting along the marshy swales which lay between the pine ridges. These bottoms were studded with clumps of hackmatack and black spruce which offered cover to game, and in places there were acres of tall brown grass and well-spaced trunks of swamp maple, like an English deer park gone wild. In the afternoons the late October sun fell hot between the uplands and the goose flesh of the morning gave way to streams of sweat.

On one such afternoon Golden Arm, suddenly despondent, passed his gun to Roger. "This thou hast made well. Can thee make it see meat?"

Within twenty steps a pair of caribou rose from the waist-high grass. They seemed to come out of the earth, an apparition of dark brown hairy bodies, astonished eyes, and horns like bare thorn trees. Luksi fired hurriedly and missed. Roger fired. The bull went down and kicked in the grass. The cow ran off a little way and stood, snorting and staring toward her fallen partner after the stupid manner of caribou.

Luksi addressed her aloud, thus, "O Ka-le-bo, stand whilst I put new fire in my *paskowa*, for my belly rumbles empty and I need thy skin for winter"—all the while reloading his musket with deliberate movements, not to startle her.

When he put up the gun again he said reverently, "I thank thee, Shining One," and pulled trigger. Down she went.

They ran forward, whooping and pulling forth their knives, and when the throat veins had been cut to bleed the meat, Luksi said solemnly to Roger, "There is luck in thee." And Golden Arm grunted, "From this time the gun is thine as much as mine."

They walked back to camp and in the lordly Micmac fashion told the women where the meat lay, drawing a little map with a stick. The Seal caught up her hatchet and skinning tools and started off at once. Wapke hesitated, her fine eyes gleaming in the horrid black mess of her mourning.

Arrogantly Roger said, "I have killed meat and am a man. *Jegulaase* —away with thee!"

Her nostrils flared. She sucked in a great breath and looked at Luksi in appeal, but her father's eyes were hard. She turned and rummaged viciously for her skinning tools, hurling the contents of her basket right and left. But she went, and the hunters lazed beside the fire. Golden Arm chuckled from time to time, and old Luksi said in mimicry, *"Jegulaasel Hél Hél"* They all grinned at each other across the fire.

It was dusk when the squaws returned, weary and bedraggled, each dragging a quarter of caribou by the shank. Perspiration and the scrape of twigs and bushes had done queer things to the stuff on Wapke's face. The mourning mask was no longer horrible, it was ludicrous. He smiled, and she saw the smile and thereafter kept her back toward him while she and the Seal prepared the meal.

Roger ate with the other hunters, as of right, and the meat was doubly sweet for the knowledge that the woman must follow him at the pot.

CHAPTER 23

Bosoley

THUS THEY JOURNEYED, pausing to hunt at intervals, a feckless existence with fits of furious energy and periods of lethargy when the men sprawled or squatted by the fire, smoking the harsh *tabagy* in Luksi's little pipe, passed from hand to hand, and talking of old hunts and journeys in the droning voices of dreamers, while the women sat silent in the wigwams working on fur garments for the winter, and the children, with bright-eyed interest, tortured frogs and snakes and other small creatures that came easily to their hands.

Their slow wanderings followed the course of a stream called by a long name, Musquodoboit, in whose upper valley they had determined to winter. Their hunting luck was like the weather, good and bad. Roger's first blind stroke of hunting fortune was not repeated often enough to justify that superstitious faith of Golden Arm, but he acquitted himself well. It was a business very different from stalking deer in the corries of Argyll, but the principle was the same —the stealth, the patience, the ever-vigilant ears and eyes, the over-mastering resolve to find and kill. He learned the language of the forest, whose words were a broken twig, a print in the mud, a leaf displaced, a few hairs caught in the bark of a tree, a hundred other matters written plainly for the seeking eye, which together made a tale. He threw himself into it and enjoyed it, striving to outhunt the others, to outendure them in the chase, to outsuffer them in hard weather.

Always he had been muscular in a slim, well-molded way, in the fashion, say, of a well-born Englishman of athletic tastes. Now his thews were hard, his skin a smooth and polished brown, like good saddle leather. He kept his hair in a queue, tied with a thong. When they found a dead eagle by one of the streams he thrust a long tail feather in the root of his pigtail for a whimsy—and kept it there. Because his beard itched and became greasy with hand-to-mouth eating, he shaved it frequently, using Luksi's hunting knife, carefully whetted on a piece of slate stone, and a bit of looking glass from Wapke's basket—a process of never-failing interest to his companions. The Indians were hairless about the body except at the crotch and armpits, and they plucked out the few black wisps that grew on their faces. His habit of bathing in the cold autumn streams was likewise a source of interest, especially to Wapke. Her menfolk never bathed except when necessity forced them to plunge across a stream. Then they swam like otters. They kept their bodies oiled with bear grease, a useful habit when flies were thick; but there were no flies now, and they showed a queer reluctance to admit their superstition that men might absorb the great courage and strength of Moween by rubbing their skins with his fat. It kept them warm, they said. It also made them smell very rank whenever the sun was warm.

The women went down to a secluded part of the water at certain times, but whether they bathed whole or merely dabbled themselves Roger did not know. Wapke always looked bathed, anyhow. Her skin gleamed. Not that he saw much of it. Most of Wapke's person remained a mystery in the shapeless *atlei* which covered her from neck to knees; but her arms, bare to the shoulder, were shapely and strong, and the short smock exposed a pair of round knees and gave her the rather charming look of a pubescent girl outgrowing her clothes. There the illusion ended. The quick black eyes which gleamed in the loathsome mask were those of an Eve who had eaten the fruit of the Tree and had found the taste to her liking. And when she was vexed—which was often—they burned with an anger which amounted to hatred. It was quaint to see the awe in which her father and brother regarded her then, for all their lordly maleness and her inferior status as a woman; and it was this, no doubt, that gave Roger their secret sympathy. For he was undoubtedly hers. They made that very clear to him. Their insistence on his rights as a man sprang simply from a male instinct to keep women in their place. Nevertheless a sense of humor lurked behind those grave brown faces; they seemed to see a piquancy in his situation and watched him, making the most of it.

The Seal watched Wapke. And Wapke reserved her gaze for the captive who belonged to her. Only the children seemed indifferent to this contest of wills and curiosities.

The men addressed him as "Thou" and sometimes, "O Man," for Wapke's ears. But one night at the fireside Luksi said, "What is thy name amongst the English?"

He answered carefully, "Roger."

"Lojul!" Luksi could not get his tongue around it. Nor could Golden Arm.

Wapke was listening in the wigwam door. Her eyes glowed like a cat's.

"O Man," she called, "thy name is Bosoley."

He turned his head and said deliberately, watching Luksi and Golden Arm, "Beau Soleil is the name of one dead. I am a living man."

He saw the hostility rise in their dark eyes as he said it.

Luksi spoke. "This that *was* Bosoley is no more. The woman has taken a captive in his place, after the custom, to lie with her and breed sons in the name of him that *was*. Now thou art Bosoley, O Man. Speak no more empty words, for the woman is my daughter and I will not see her shamed before women."

"*Ayah!*" agreed Golden Arm, opening his sleepy pig's eyes very wide.

The Seal looked alarmed.

"For how long?" asked Roger. "For how long am I Bosoley?"

"Thou heard!" snapped Golden Arm. His cheek worked under the pocked skin. "Thy life is hers. How long is a life?"

Deuced long! thought Roger. But he said no more. There was too much violence in that air about the fire.

Winter crept upon them like a ponderous white beast out of the north, with cold, seeking claws in the wind, with pauses now and then as if crouching for a spring. Snow flew in small hard specks that rattled on the wigwam skins. One night it whitened the ground along the river and vanished in the afternoon sun.

The hardwood ridges now were a dun bristle of naked trunks and branches, but here and there a big old oak clung stoutly to its leaves, and the beech saplings still rattled their brown wisps harshly in the wind. In the swamps the hackmatack had turned a delicate yellow at last, a pale flame in the river meadows at dusk, and already began to shed its needles and expose its knotty twigs, as if after seeing that orgy of the maples in October, and after due consideration, it had decided to drop the modest existence of an evergreen for one blaze of pleasure and an end.

The game paths on the uplands were deep in dead leaves, which rattled underfoot in dry weather and made hunting difficult. Ferns were crisp and brown and the swamp grass whispered dryly in the wind, and often the pools in the wild meadows had a skin of ice in the mornings. The last of the wild duck were passing southward now. Woodcock had appeared in great flocks from the north in October, haunted the alder covers for two or three weeks, and now vanished in a single night as mysteriously as they came. The squaws laid snares for hares, whose coats were turning gray white from the summer brown; and once the Seal found a covey of spruce partridge roosting in a fir beside the river and took them all, one after another, with a little noose of rawhide on a stick, a quaint affair to Roger, who had never seen a bird so stupid. The wary grouse were not to be taken except by shot, which was too precious to waste on such small game.

The woods seemed hushed now, lacking so many departed voices. Only chickadees twittered in the thickets. At night and in late afternoon owls could be heard in the big timber, but even they had a subdued note and did not seem so many or so talkative as in warmer weather. It seemed to Roger's whimsy that the forest waited, resigned and with a stoic calm, for the onslaught of the Frost Giants of the Indian tales.

And then miraculously, out of the frosts and the first tentative snows, out of the dreary November rains, came a St. Martin's summer of hot and drowsy days that hung the shallow river valley in a blue haze and turned the night air soft as a woman's breath. It was all very unreal—as if you had braced yourself for a blow and felt only a caress. And it came at the time of the new moon.

Wapke pointed out to Luksi and Golden Arm that yellow slanting sickle in the west and talked to them briefly in a low voice.

In the morning she struck the wigwam and carried the skins and baskets down to the river. She returned for a haunch of moose meat hanging in a birch tree by the camp and motioned Roger to pick up the paddles.

Luksi sat with Golden Arm beside the fire, smoking the little pipe. From her wigwam the Seal and her children watched. Roger turned to Luksi with an inquiry on his lips, and the old man said curtly, "Go!"

At the river, where Wapke waited beside the laden canoe, she motioned Roger to the man's seat at the stern. He took it, mystified, but pleased at the prospect of steering the craft. The river had risen under the rains, and the passage upstream called for every bit of wit and strength he had. But he enjoyed it thoroughly. There was a happy sense of mastery in it, like riding a good horse at the hurdles. Again he thought of Charles and the Fiat Club. How very far away all that seemed now! At sundown they came to a glen where the pinewoods rose in shadowed walls and a strip of wild meadow ran beside the river. A small brook fell down the hill among the pines, and near the point where it boiled into the river was another ancient camping place. There were the usual fire-reddened stones all intergrown with grass, the space for three or four wigwams, the surrounding trees bearing the healed scars of old hatchet marks, the indefinable air of a place where humans had tarried awhile and gone. Roger came to know these for signs of the old savage life, since diverted by Le Loutre and other agents of the French king and made to flow and even to clot about the Acadian settlements, where it could be most influenced and controlled.

The Micmacs, all but a few bands of outcasts and primitives, had abandoned the ancient ways for something made in France.

"In this place we shall winter," Wapke said simply, and busied herself setting up the wigwam and preparing the evening meal.

"And the others?" he asked, waving a hand downstream.

She answered indifferently, "They will come."

"Tomorrow?"

"When the moon is round."

Sunset burned along the western rim of the glen with the final flare-up of a dying fire. The pine tops made a black saw edge against the glow. The river writhed and gleamed along the glen floor, reflecting the swiftly changing colors of the sky and lifting its voice now in the evening hush. And now came that soft and unreal darkness again, the still and humid air of a summer night falling magically over a landscape already given up to winter.

Relaxed after the day's exertions and comfortably aware of a full belly, Roger sat by the wigwam door watching the tip of the young moon rise above the trees. He longed for tobacco. Wapke had gone down to the river. A fire of dry pine roots from a stump at the waterside made a fine red glow in the dusk. From a still water up the river came the long call of a loon, weird and mournful, like the voice of all this emptiness.

When Wapke returned to the fire he looked up diffidently—and looked again, startled. His first wild thought was that he was under visitation by one of those lascivious night fairies of whom the young braves jested sometimes by the morning fires, a sort of Micmac succuba. Certainly it was not Wapke. No daughter of the Meeg-a-maage would let herself be seen thus by a man, even a husband. For this creature was entirely nude—and unabashed. She came to the fireside all wet and gleaming from the river and stretched her arms across the blaze toward him, regarding him with large and glittering black eyes.

He had come to accept Wapke as a shapeless caribou-hide smock with a black repulsive mask at one end and a pair of muscular legs at the other. The bronze pixie before him was young and slender as to waist, with rounded hips and plump thighs and a pair of breasts neither large nor small, pink-nippled and erect. Her cheeks had that light olive hue of Micmac girls and young women before too much weather and the smoke of cooking fires had darkened them, and before the endless drudgery had coarsened and lined the skin. Her hair showed the ministrations of a wooden comb, sleek and black, falling loosely behind her shoulders.

Thus she stood, with knees together and arms outstretched, letting the fire glow play upon her skin and watching him. Roger trembled with some emotion he did not recognize. Lust he had known. And fear. It was neither of these things. He crouched in the doorway, waiting. After an intolerable time she spoke—and the voice was the voice of Wapke.

"O Bosoley," she said softly, "this is the moment I have longed for ever since I saw thee at the killing place."

He made no answer. He felt himself blushing. He had foreseen something like this, of course, although not in this shape; but now that it had come he was profoundly disturbed—he was shocked. He felt absurdly like a prim girl confronted by her first kiss. That cynical advice of Gautier! He had prepared himself for the amorous demand of a middle-aged squaw, protecting himself with an armor of disgust. With Wapke in this form his guard was gone, and all that was English and aloof in him resented his defenselessness. He shivered, for she was tempting.

In a nimbus of firelight the golden flesh stood lit and glowing against the darkness, as if she were the living heart of the night, of the whole black wilderness. On the pivot of bare toe and heel she revolved herself slowly, bathing herself in the warmth—or was it in the somber gaze of the white man in the wigwam door?—and as she turned, erect, with head flung back, her hands moved sensuously over the skin, stroking her sides and hips, patting lightly the curved golden belly, and cupping and releasing the round breasts, which now had lost some of their stark rigidity, like green fruit turning soft and ripe and drooping a little on the vine, as if the fire were some sort of sun.

He was struck with a preposterous thought. Was it She? Was this the Golden Woman after all? Had it all come to this, a union with Wapke in this desert of shadows?

She observed his hesitation and said, like any woman anywhere, "Is there some other? Had thee a woman at Chebucto?"

He answered honestly, "No."

"The white squaws look sick always," she announced contemptuously. "Look at me, Bosoley! I am strong and alive. I am like a young maple by the water. In my arms thou shall find such pleasure as no *sakumaaskwe* could give thee. Also," she added practically, "who is there to cook thy meat and make thee garments against the cold?"

He shook his head woodenly. Who, indeed?

"Am I not well made, Bosoley?"

"As the moon," he answered. She was turning herself again, displaying all her perfections with the pride of a naked child, but at his words she broke her pose and dropped upon her knees before him, saying softly:

"Then let us make love together, Bosoley."

How many women had said that to him in other lands and other tongues! And how easy it had been to take what they offered and pass on, without the shadow of a thought! Yet it was just that, the shadow of a thought, that hung between him and the splendid animal at his feet—the notion of a plunge into darkness from which there was no return. Gautier's voice came back to him: "When you have spent a year . . . you will not wish to leave . . . hundreds like you mated to savage women in the woods . . ." All his impressions of this enormous loneliness confirmed the Acadian's words, and all his instincts rebelled. To mate with this wild thing, to produce hybrid things, half beast and half himself, and to live year in year out among these mockeries, like a man shut up in a room hung with distorted mirrors . . . ugh! Darkness! Darkness!

"No!" he said violently.

She sat back on her heels and said in a trembling voice, "Thou cannot refuse me, Bosoley. Thy life is mine."

"My life is my own," he answered stubbornly, "and I must follow my own destiny which I have seen in dreams. Let me go back to my people!"

Her face was shadowed by the fire glow at her back, but he caught the white flash of her teeth as she answered, "No! Never!" Then, in a wheedling voice, "I am *nedaje* for thee, Bosoley. I too have my dreams. I dream of thee at night. I cannot eat for thinking of thee. Yet"—her voice went hard as flint—"if thou refuse me and make me a thing of laughter to the squaws at the camping places—I shall have thee slain!"

He stared past her into the darkness from which there was no escape. Alone, he would perish in this winter-touched waste—and he was quite sure that his destiny lay other ways. He tried to conjure up that sunlit vision of the Golden Woman, for strength or guidance, but she would not come. Instead, strangely, he seemed to see that scornful young woman in the Downs, with her red-gold hair and enigmatic eyes.

"Wapke," he said desperately, "many moons ago, across the Big Water, I made a vow on the totem of my fathers that I would have no more to do with women. I have kept my vow and want no woman. If I should break my vow . . ." He groped hopelessly. The Micmacs had no word for sin. "If I should break my vow, some great evil surely will befall me—and thee!"

Her eyes went wide. He had struck the one chord in her that vibrated more loudly than pride or hunger or lovesickness—the superstitious one.

But shrewdly she said, "This promise to thy fathers cannot last forever. There must be a woman, else their seed will die."

"I must wait for a sign," he declared with a preposterous smugness.

She nodded slowly, as if this were the most reasonable thing in the world.

Then, with the utmost innocence, she uttered a piece of wisdom straight from Mother Eve. "Bosoley, lest my people laugh at me, lest my menkind kill thee, we must share a wigwam, thou and I. In the fullness of time there will come a sign."

CHAPTER 24

The Forest

WINTER WAS A BITTER THING. Life was a thread, no more, quivering in the north wind, never far from breaking. When they ventured into the great cold they wore leggings to the crotch, hooded cloaks of beaver skin, separate sleeves of fur which tied behind the shoulders, huge fur mittens, and wrappings of thin caribou hide about the ankles and feet, which were thrust into great moccasins stuffed with dried grass. Within each wigwam the squaws kept burning a perpetual fire that filled the cone with smoke and forced them to lie close against the floor. The Frost Giants screamed and smote them furious blows, besieged them with white armies and tree-cracking frost artillery, and paused with a silence that made the ears ache, and baited them with two- or three-day thaws, and leaped to smite again. The stream was too rapid to freeze completely over the run past their camp, but the white banks put forth lips of ice that grew as the winter deepened, and the dwindling gray water yielded up a mist that hung like a cold white smoke along the valley.

In the vast silences the least sound carried far. From the forest, now near, now far, came those mysterious knockings which the savages knew only as *keaskunoogwejit*—"the ghostly woodcutter." And on nights of intense frost came the steady woomp-woomp-woomp of pressure cracks ripping the thick ice of lakes upstream and echoing down the wooded glen like thunder. No wonder they believed in giants!

They recited their weird mythology when snowstorms pinned them to the shelter of the wigwams, saying the world was made by Munitoo, the great spirit, who sent a giant named Gluskap to create the Meeg-a-maage and guard their fortunes. Gluskap made the first man from a tree. And sometimes, because he was a whimsical giant, he changed men back to trees—or any other object he fancied. Thus the forest was filled with things which might or might not be changelings, and must therefore be regarded with the respect due to those touched by the gods. Again, when a warrior died his spirit ascended to the sky and traveled the Spirit Road, which white men called the Milky Way, and reached at last the Good Hunting Place of his earthly dreams, where there was no winter and no night. But if in this paradise of fish and game he hankered to visit earth again, he could do so in the guise of his old totem. Thus any beast overtaken in the hunt might contain a spirit from Beyond, and must be addressed with reverence and favored with an apology for the killing, as Luksi had spoken to the caribou on that day of the first lucky hunt.

It was a little startling to think that Peyal, say, might return to visit Wapke in the shape of a sunbeam. Sometimes, peering past the door flap at the whirling snow, Roger wished he would. The name he had inherited from the dead man was a mockery in this environment. Beau Soleil—pah!

Spring was a joy that came slowly, with fits and starts, with sunshine at hide-and-seek with snows and rains and fogs. Roger had lost count of the weeks, but sometime in April or May they broke camp after daubing the canoe seams with fresh gum and paddled down the river to the sea. There they lived easily on clams and fish and ducks, wandering slowly eastward along the coast.

Sometimes they encountered groups like their own and tarried together a day or a week, exchanging tales of the winter past. Roger was accepted as one of them, addressed always as Bosoley. His black eyes and dark skin and the nose bequeathed him by his Norman ancestors made this acceptance easy, and if they noticed the European cast of his features they said nothing. The long intercourse of French and Micmacs had produced so many who looked exactly like him.

This provided an unpleasant surprise for a St. Malo trader whose small lugger lay in one of the wild rocky harbors conducting a brisk barter for furs. For the winter's catch of Luksi's group the shrewd Malouin offered two gallons of rum, an iron hatchet, half a dozen hawk bells, and four handfuls of beads. He gave them a sup of rum first, to put the hankering in their mouths, passing to them in turn a pewter mug that held about a gill.

It was not even good rum, an acrid *tafia* from Guadeloupe or the Haiti plantations, and when Luksi nodded in agreement Roger cried out in protest, launching into the trader with epithets of particular force and piquancy.

Assailed thus in idiomatic French by an apparent savage, the Malouin was taken aback, and before he recovered he had paid for the furs an additional iron pot, a knife, a fusil in good repair, five pounds of gunpowder, a hundred balls, and two dozen flints.

"Wah!" cried Luksi afterward as they sat drinking about their fire. "Thy tongue speaks fire in the Wenjoo language, Bosoley. Now this is a great thing. Fortune it was that set my daughter's eyes upon

thee at the killing place. Thou shall bargain for us in all the springs
to come."

"All the springs" rang unpleasantly in Roger's ears. The sight of
the lugger had awakened his hopes. He was resolved to wait until
they were drunk and then slip away, to persuade the trader to take
him away to Louisbourg. But second thought showed him the hope-
lessness of that. Wapke would not let him out of her sight. In any
case the sly Malouin would hand him back to the savages for the sake
of their good will. He drank himself into a stupor and made himself
sick and Wapke angry. She had expected a more amorous result. She
settled herself to wait with an enormous patience for the sign.

Luksi and Golden Arm drank more cannily, working themselves
up to a fine frenzy for a dance about the fire, screaming war whoops
and slashing imaginary enemies with their hatchets while the Seal
and her brood admired them from the safety of their wigwam door.
The orgy lasted two days and nights, and when they sobered at last
the trader's lugger was gone. Golden Arm grumbled that Bosoley
should have bargained for more firewater and less of the other things.
But he took the trade gun and passed Roger his old one. Luksi took
the knife and later shared the powder, shot, and flints among them.
The women divided the beads, and Wapke made a pair of anklets
with the hawk bells. They tinkled pleasantly when she walked and
when she stirred at night.

Summer was the time of ease, of warmth, of indolence. If hunting
or fishing failed, the squaws could dig up a meal with a stick on the
nearest clam flat. Hence all their camps were pitched by some sandy
inlet where the mingling of fresh water with salt produced at low
tide a stretch of malodorous mud.

When autumn painted the hardwoods they moved inland, thrusting their canoes up another lonely river to a wintering place somewhere toward Oonamaagik, the Foggy Country, which Roger now
knew to be Cape Breton. He cursed himself for not paying more
attention to that crude chart of Nova Scotia which Old Hux used to
spread upon the hatch. He had a vague picture of a peninsula jutting
into the Atlantic with a large island at one end, but he had no notion
of the distances.

Winter again, and another struggle to keep alive. Another long, heartbreaking spring, another journey to the coast, another lazy summer. So it went.

Roger had long ceased trying to count moons and reckoned in winters as the Indians did. From time to time in the fleeting summer moons Wapke asked solemnly if his fathers had given him a sign. Always the answer was no.

He marveled at her patience, but it irritated him. In the other seasons there was no question. The mating urge went out of her then as it went from all the savages, as the sap withdrew from the trees. Life was too hard, too starved, too cold. They lived and endured together in an amicable sexlessness like brother and sister. He saw no more of the Golden Woman. When he dreamed it was of food.

Sometimes in summer, lying beside the Big Water, he tortured himself with memories of England, of Kent, and all the pleasant things that lay beyond. He thought of Halifax a good deal, wondering what had become of the emigrants he knew, especially Mary Foy. And it was strange how, whenever she was in his mind, Wapke came with an instinctive jealousy to break in upon his thoughts. Wapke was uncanny. Whenever they were camped with other wandering savages and the young squaws were laughing about the cooking fires, she watched him with the eyes of a hunting cat.

In these encounters there was news to which he always listened carefully. The English town was growing at Chebucto. Konwallich had gone back across the sea—this was a surprise—and the sagamore of the English now was "Opsum." Evidently Hopson, the cool soldier who saw the usefulness of ranger troops when Cornwallis could see only their undiscipline. Opsum had raised new ranger companies with volunteers from the regiments, from the emigrants and the footloose New Englanders, and was sending them deep into the forest to punish the Micmacs for their raids. Even the stiff regulars had been thrust out boldly from the palisades of Halifax. The mutinous regiment at Fort Anne had been brought to discipline by ruthless shootings and hangings, of which the Indians spoke with awe. And as a result of all this the English were getting a firm hold on the Acadien country where Le Loutre had reigned supreme so many years.

And Le Loutre? The Otter was gone *eloowawe*—crazy. He talked no more of Sessooglee (Jesus Christ) and Kejnoomahlee (Virgin Mary), but raved instead of fire and slaughter, threatening the dull Acadiens with the wrath of the savages if they took the oath of allegiance to King George, commanding them to burn their farms along the south side of Fundy and withdraw toward the St. Lawrence.

Ayah! the Indians said, The Otter himself had burned the Acadien village of Beaubassin, church and all, for an example.

But the most astonishing tale concerned the fierce San Badees Koap of the Shubenacadie mission—Koap had proclaimed himself chief of the Micmacs, had gone to Chebucto and made a "peace" with the English in their name!

What did that mean? Roger asked. They answered with glee that Koap had fooled the English. Even now he was sending war parties to take scalps at Chebucto. But they added casually that Le Loutre was urging the tribes to remove beyond the reach of the English rangers—toward Louisbourg, where their families would be safe and whence they could launch war parties against the English at their pleasure.

What did it all mean? Something lay behind all this—it was in the wind. Open war between England and France? An end to that ill-conceived peace of '48? That would mean, ultimately, a struggle to the death between Halifax and Louisbourg. These speculations aroused a ferment in Roger at a time when apathy had almost taken possession of him. His hopes of escape had faded and gone long ago. He was watched too closely when they were on the coast, and the interior in winter was a prison in itself. At the approach of this year's warm weather he had become aware of a growing fascination in the savage life, and in Wapke, as if in his veins too the sap had begun to flow according to the seasons. This is the way it goes, warned the voice within. You hope for a time, then bit by bit you let yourself go, and the woman and the forest do the rest. But the voice was feeble now, and he heard it with indifference.

All this the watchful Wapke knew. After her long waiting she began to see a glimmer of the sign. And one lazy summer afternoon she resolved to put it to the test.

The camp was by a brackish lagoon, common along the coast, which the Acadians called *barachois*. A small river flowed through a beach of fine sand when the tide was low. As the tide rose the stream was thrust back upon itself and the combined waters filled a wide and shallow trough between the beach and the pinewoods. At ebb tide the mingled waters rushed out again and there was a flat of reeking mud where clams were plentiful and fat.

Roger had gone around a pine point to bathe in the *barachois,* and he was lying naked in the sunshine to dry himself when Wapke came.

She sat beside him, playing with her ankle bells.

"Hear me, Bosoley. For a long time we have been man and wife in the eyes of our people, and long ago I put my father from the wigwam lest he know the truth, saying it was a custom of the Aglaseaou to have their wives alone. All this time I have been faithful to thee and thy promise to thy fathers. But, Bosoley, I am a woman, and too soon I shall be old and ugly in thine eyes. Now is my summer, and I wish to love and bear fruit before my winter comes. Bosoley, the Seal looks on me with a smile in her eyes because I am not fruitful. When we camp with others of our people the women ask where are my children, and I lie and say they died in the winters, as I did when Peyal was my man. But I cannot lie to my own heart. I wish for sons, so that when I am old I can look upon them with content and say, This is the fruit of Bosoley and me. I am young and of good parts, and thou art strong and well made for the satisfaction of women. Must I live and die a barren thing?"

He was silent for a time, lying with eyes closed against the sun. At last he raised himself on an elbow and said slowly, "Wapke, I have thought upon these things, and this is what I see. Look there at the Big Water. It is clean and beautiful, like thee. And there is the river, clean and strong. Yet where they mingle"—stabbing an accusing finger at the steaming flat—"is mud and a stink. That is the wisdom of Munitoo who made these things—and thee and me."

"It is false!" Her voice went hoarse with rage. "What of Gautier and his squaw at Shubenacadie? What of all the other women who have taken white men to their beds? They breed like mink! It is well known amongst our people that the white man's seed is more copious than ours and has the power of making women fertile."

"Thou know what I mean, Wapke."

"Ayah! I know—there is some other woman in thy heart."

"Yes."

"And this promise to thy fathers—that was a lie?"

He groped for the words he wanted. "When I was young I took the warpath, far across the Big Water. It led into strange places, and there were women along the way. But at last I wearied of the warpath and of them. For war and women come easily to a young man, but they leave him no reward. I said in my heart, No more. But when I came across the Big Water there was a woman. She had no eyes for me, and I told myself I did not want her—but I did. Something in my heart was troubled when I thought of her. She was the first woman I had wanted that I could not have."

"And thou wish to go back to her—to this woman who does not want thee!" she cried scornfully.

"She would not have me now—and there are other things I want far more. I wish"—he groped again. The Micmacs had no word for riches. "I wish to be a trader like Gautier, but at Chebucto. I wish to have a great store of goods and live as white men do. And when I have gathered enough I shall return across the Big Water to live in the home of my fathers."

"Without a woman?" she asked, astonished.

"No woman will matter then."

"What is she like, this *saakskwe?*"

He smiled. "You would find her very ugly, Wapke. She has red hair and green eyes and there are small brown speckles on her nose."

"Heugh!" She spat. "All this is true?" she added suspiciously.

"May the flesh rot from my bones if I lie to thee."

She shrank at that. In a world haunted by whimsical gods it was not safe to make such dangerous suggestions.

But she said proudly, "I too am wanted by a man I have denied."

It was Roger's turn to be surprised. "Who?"

"San Badees Koap. His heart is sick for me."

He was disturbed. Koap was not good enough for Wapke.

"You like him—San Badees?"

"He is strong and well made, Bosoley. He would give me sons."

He did not miss the challenge in her voice. She added, "If my father knew the truth of thee and me he would slay thee."

Roger was silent. Then she said carefully, "But if I say that I am weary of thee, that thy seed is barren and I wish for sons, that I would mate with San Badees who is the great sagamore of our people now, as Peyal was . . . and if I say I must have blankets and bright cloth and many ornaments as becomes the bride of San Badees . . . then my father will sell thee to the whitecoats at Louisbourg."

He opened his eyes and sat up then, startled. "Louisbourg!"

"War is coming between the Wenjoo and the Aglaseaou, and this time one will drive the other out. Then thou can return to the home of thy fathers, Bosoley."

For a moment he was stunned, but when he turned to her in a rush of gratitude she leaped up and stood aside, looking down at him with proud dark eyes.

With dignity she said, "Do not touch me, Bosoley. Not now. For I go to meet the father of my sons."

"I shall never forget thee, Wapke."

"Thou never knew me," she answered, and was gone.

PART THREE

The Totem

CHAPTER 25

The True Cuckoo

THE OFFICE of the *commissaire-ordonnateur* was in a large and busy building of Caen stone at the corner of the Rue St. Louis and the Rue du Quai. Like a drift of brown leaves twenty or thirty savages squatted in the autumn sunshine of the Quai, talking in slow gutturals and gazing past the Cale de l'Intendance, where their canoes were drawn up, to the bright blue harbor water. From the stony beach east of the quay arose a strong reek of split codfish drying in the sun. The anchorage was dotted with fishing vessels gathered for the return to France with the summer's catch, and farther out in the roads three or four French West Indiamen awaited convoy across the Atlantic.

The water front swarmed with fishermen chattering in Norman, Breton, and Biscayan dialects. A few soldiers in grubby white uniforms wandered aimlessly along the quay. Outside the commissary door lounged a corporal's guard of the Compagnies de la Marine in white tunics and blue breeches and gaiters, admitting the savages in small groups. Most of these brown wolves had come to cadge powder and shot for the winter's hunting, but several had English scalps for barter, and there were three or four gaunt and naked prisoners for sale, New England fishermen by the look and speech.

Slowly the Indians filed through the doorway. It was three hours before Luksi and Golden Arm were admitted with Roger between them.

The commissary was an irritable man in the fifties with rheumatic movements and a sickly face. Beside him sat the town major of Louisbourg, a pair of fierce mustaches, addressed as "Loppinot."

The sale of Roger to His Most Christian Majesty was soon completed. Luksi tried to haggle, but Aide-Major Loppinot cut him short in brusque and badly accented Micmac. The old man turned away with a little billet addressed to the keeper of the King's stores. Golden Arm went out before him, licking his animal lips as if he tasted firewater already, but Luksi turned in the doorway and looked back at Roger, saying uneasily, "Bosoley, this is my daughter's wish, not mine, for I had come to look upon thee as a son. Yet," he added indignantly, "you are strange men, you English, who cannot abide an old man in the wigwam with your women! Now I go to join her with San Badees, who will let me place my blanket opposite the door as an honored guest."

With that he was gone, and Roger had a twinge of regret, almost of self-reproach.

Major Loppinot fingered his superb mustaches and said in unskillful English:

"Your name, prisoner?"

"Sudden. Roger Sudden." A pen scratched somewhere in the chamber.

"You from Fort Anne?"

"No, from Halifax."

"Ha! You soger, eh?"

"A settler, from London."

" 'Ow long you weeth those savage?"

"Four years. I was taken soon after I came to this country."

Major Loppinot was plainly disappointed. "You know not'ing, then. *Eh bien*, you are now a prisoner of France. You 'ave friend at Alfax weeth money, eh?"

"No."

A mouth and a shrug. "That ees un'appy for you. But *mordieu!* it is a better place to leev, our Louisbourg, than that meeserable Alfax." And briskly, "You shall work on the walls weeth other prisoner. If you are gentle you shall 'ave a leetle leeberty about the town. Eef you try to run away you shall 'ang. That ees all!" He bawled an order to the corporal outside, and Roger was marched away by two blue-legged marines. The narrow, cobbled streets rang with the sabots of fishermen and townsmen, and there was a clack of women's tongues from every open casement, but no one gave Roger more than a glance. The passage of a naked English prisoner was too commonplace.

They crossed the town and emerged into an open space under the ramparts at the east end. There in the shadow of a tall bastion sat a long low building of black stone with narrow, heavily barred windows. Inside Roger found a dim cavern where forty or fifty ragged and half-naked men sprawled on pallets of straw after a day's work on the fortifications. They leaped up at once, crying questions, but, finding that he knew nothing recent of Halifax and nothing at all of Fort Anne or Boston, they drifted away to their pallets again.

The majority appeared to be New Englanders, fishermen captured by the Indians while getting wood and water on the Nova Scotia coast. There were half a dozen soldiers of Philips' Regiment and one or two of Warburton's. Some had been there for years, and all assured him he was lucky to be alive. Most English captives taken by the Micmacs fell into the hands of Le Loutre, who ransomed those whose friends had money and collected a handsome profit. The rest he turned back to the savages as worthless—and the savages promptly took them into the woods, knocked them on the head, and sliced off their scalps. Le Loutre then bought the scalps, which had a firm price at Quebec and Louisbourg. Only those savages who distrusted the mad priest in matters of payment made the long journey to Louisbourg with their trophies, living and dead.

The prisoners complained of His Most Christian Majesty's fare: "Codfish and rotten olive oil, the whole town lives on it!"; the work, "Patching the ramparts and walls all spring and summer, digging coals at L'Indienne" (they called it Lingan) "all fall, and shoveling snow from the streets all winter"; the prison itself, "The Rat Nest," "The Icehouse," "The Château Louis-damné." But it was wonderful to hear and speak the English tongue again. He talked incessantly until the first delight wore away and no one listened any more. As the last-comer, he was allotted a pallet near the door where the drafts would be worst in winter and far from the single stove which stood like a rusty puncheon against the far wall.

The men were clad in the most miserable rags, castoff clothing of a townsfolk who, with French thrift, cast off nothing until the very patches were threadbare. Some had sabots; some wrapped their feet in bits of cloth or sail canvas; most were barefoot. They were shaggy and unclean from long lack of soap.

Roger mentioned the word "escape," and they told him in a sort of humorous despair that there was only one escape from Louisbourg. They pointed it out to him from the ramparts where the prisoners labored with pick shovel and wheelbarrow one sunny October day— a cleared knoll in the scrub forest to the west, with a gibbet stark against the sky. Gallows Hill!

Roger shrugged and, leaning on his shovel, turned and looked northward over the town. It was compact, not more than fifty or sixty acres within the half circle of the walls, yet in its narrow streets swarmed a population of close on three thousand. Some buildings were of stone, some had a stone lower story and a wooden upper; most were of wood, shingled in the American fashion; all dominated by the fine brick-and-stone mass of the hospital of the Frères de la Charité and the similar mass of the Royal Barracks in the Bastion du Roi, with their tall belfries over all.

Louisbourg had been a-building thirty or forty years, not long as Europe measured time, yet the weathering of the unpainted wooden houses had given it the gray and ancient look of a garrison town in, say, Brittany. He had an impression of great strength. The fortress stood on a point of bleak moorland between harbor and sea, the land side guarded by massive walls of earth faced with stone and standing thirty feet above the general level. There were six bastions, the Bastion du Roi a citadel in itself, separated from the town by a dry moat and containing the main barracks and the residence of the governor. All of these were well supplied with cannon.

Beyond the walls lay the moat, wide and deep, bristling with sharp stakes for lack of water; then the stone-faced counterscarp, the smooth green fall of the glacis, and finally an open moor half a mile wide, bare as a billiard cloth between the fortress and the woods. No man could cross that space alive while a single musket pointed from the ramparts.

And from the sea? The harbor entrance was guarded on the east by a battery on Lighthouse Point, where the tall stone *tour du fanal* burned cod oil in a huge and ingenious lantern every night; Battery Island sat in the very mouth of it with thirty-odd cannon in its embrasures. From the town the battery of La Grève watched the anchorage. And at the head of the harbor squatted the Grand Battery with its twin sixty-foot stone towers and its heavy artillery, ready to rake the entrance or the anchorage at will.

He thought of Halifax, its miserable wooden palisade, the pitiful log-and-earth "forts," all dominated by undefended Citadel Hill; the forest which came to its very skirts, a perfect cover for hostile war parties; and the town of squalid huts and the people, unfitted to make a living on land or sea.

What a comparison!

The French were not hard taskmasters, and if the prisoners' fare and lodging were miserable they were not much worse off than hundreds of poor fishermen who lived like barreled herrings in the Rue du Pont and Rue Toulouse and along the Quai. The worst hardship, and the one which reduced the inhabitants of the prison to despair, was their mere situation—prisoners of France in what the diplomats of Europe pretended was a time of peace. Only the soldiers had the faintest hope of ransom, mumbling of a time when Cornwallis had ransomed a Lieutenant Hamilton and sixty others taken in a raid by Le Loutre's savages. But that had cost Cornwallis well over eight hundred pounds, and the governor now was tough old Lawrence, who was not likely to pay a penny's tribute.

The work on the defenses was not bad. What they hated was the quarrying and breaking of stone at Cap Noir for the facing of the walls and counterscarp. In the late autumn they were taken up the coast in sloops to L'Indienne, where in shallow pits they dug coals for the Louisbourg garrison. And through the winter itself they were generally busy clearing the streets of snow, cutting firewood in the garrison fuel yard, on stormy days picking oakum on the drafty prison floor. Sometimes there were odd jobs to be done about the houses of army officers or their merchant friends, and then there was usually a small gratuity, a few sous, an old coat, a *manoque* of tobacco leaves, or even a small jug of thin wine. In this way Roger covered his nakedness with a pair of worn sabots (stuffed with straw against the winter cold), a pair of homespun breeches patched like Joseph's coat, a linsey shirt, a red flannel nightcap of the sort worn by fishermen, and the red-and-blue rags of a French artillery tunic.

He thought he had known every vicissitude of the climate in his wanderings with the savages, but winter in this corner of the Cape Breton coast was a thing beyond his experience. The site of the town had been chosen with a view to defense and nothing else. It was exposed to every wind that blew, and the gales were more frequent and blew longer and harder, and the snow was deeper and the frost sharper than anything he had known. Snow driving in from the sea choked the streets and formed steep, sloping drifts that sometimes reached the top of the ramparts. Sentries froze fingers and toes, even in the shelter of the *guérites*. On bitter nights the sound of frost-drawn nails rang over the town like musketry.

The northeast and southwest arms of the harbor froze over, but the anchorage remained free until spring, when the great sea pack came drifting down the coast, poured past Battery Island like an invading fleet, and filled the harbor with grinding floes. But long before the sea ice came, before the first breath of the wet spring wind, indeed while ramparts, streets, roofs, the Quai, the decks of wintering ships and all the country roundabout were still crusted white in the harsh cold, Roger found hope in a most unexpected place.

He was sent to shift some wine barrels in the cellar of a cabaret in the Rue du Quai. He found the Veritable Coucou without difficulty by the sign that swung in the February wind and, turning inside, was blinded for some moments by the dim interior after the dazzle of the snow outside.

He announced in French, "I have been sent from the prison on the orders of Captain——"

"*Zut!*" snapped a woman's voice. "There is no need to cry my affairs to the world!"

His eyes had grown accustomed to the indoor light by now, and he saw that the place was empty—it was about nine o'clock, the quiet hour between the morning drams and the forenoon calls for dinner wine—except for himself and a brisk black-eyed woman in a brown gown and white handkerchief. She came from behind the bar, inspecting his rags, his beard, his shaggy hair with an impersonal contempt which doubtless came of much dealing with the canaille of the water front. Her face was rather thin, which made her eyes seem large and bold and drew the eye to her full lower lip. Her waist owed something to tight laces, and her bosom filled out the bodice in a manner that suggested a sylph gone a little to flesh.

"What are you staring at, *cochon?*" she said coldly.

"At a ghost, madame. It is—let me consider—seven years, eight years—since I saw it in the flesh—not quite so much flesh, if you will pardon me. What are you doing here, so far from Paris, Madame Ducudrai?"

Her eyes were enormous now. She stared at him with a furious curiosity. Then, in a startled whisper, "It is you, Monsieur Soudain— Roger! My God, what have they done to you?"

He stepped toward her with a thin smile, and she backed away.

"One changes one's appearance with one's fortune, madame."

She had her taut back against the bar now. She protested hoarsely, "You were so young, so gallant, Roger! Now—now you are——"

"Ragged and very dirty, madame, that is all."

"No! There is something else—don't come nearer. Don't touch me! You—you have changed. You look cruel. You are like a savage!"

He stopped and said ironically, "My dear, I am a savage. I have lived for years with savages. But you, madame—you have not changed so very much. How charming and how fortunate that we should meet again! Your husband—does he still conduct the dancing lessons?"

"He is in New York," she said in that whispering voice and with that incredulous stare.

He raised his eyebrows. "So far?"

"He is a dancing master there."

"I see! And in his absence it is only right that a captain of the Compagnies de la Marine should keep an eye on the Veritable Coucou—a witty name, that!—and send a bit of prison labor now and then to see that Madame keeps her pretty hands from toil!"

"He has been kind to me," she returned defiantly. "But you—how comes it that you, an officer of the Prince Charles, are in this prison here?"

"How, madame? When France kicked out the Chevalier Charles I came to Nova Scotia—Acadie, I beg your pardon—with the intention

of making a plantation. The savages removed me, with some violence I may say. The *commissaire-ordonnateur* buys English prisoners for the work on the fortificatiôns. *Voilà!*"

"But you are not an enemy of France!"

"I seem to be an enemy of all the world. Don't look like that,
madame. I do not quarrel with my fortune; why should you?"

"There never was any man like you," she murmured, as if to herself. "You were all that a woman dreams about and never finds. It
was marvelous. But"—she checked herself sharply—"that is all past
and gone, you comprehend? Captain Johnstone——"

"Ah!"

"He has become my very dear friend. I could not let him know
that you—that I—we——"

"One understands perfectly, madame. And one congratulates you
both. You may rely on my discretion . . . don't look so incredulous,
ma chère! Four years among the savages have taught me many things
I lacked across the sea. And now . . . there are some casks to be
moved . . ."

"Roger," said Madame Ducudrai, "you will not so much as whisper . . . ?"

He gave his mouth a twist. "One gossips a good deal in the Château
Louis-damné . . . to pass the time, you understand. And the guards
of the Compagnies-Marine . . ." He shrugged expressively. "Those
dogs have long ears! Now if one had employment in the town all
day . . . posting a ledger for some merchant along the Quai, for
example . . ."

"You must know that prisoners are not permitted on the Quai."

"But why?"

"There are English ships, smugglers from Alfax, from Boston, in
the summer."

"Ah! Precisely why I could be very useful to some merchant on the
Quai, madame. I speak and write English and French well. After all
I, too, have bled in the service of the Chevalier, like your very dear
friend—and surely France owes me something for my pains?"

"If I persuade my friend to arrange this," she said with a hard
mouth, "he must never know who you are. You must never reveal . . ."

"*Ma chère,* your friend never did know me as well as I knew him. But have no fear, I am silence itself. Four years in the forest! *Mordieu!*"

"You swear?"

"Upon my heart!" A hand on his heart, a bow, a wide sardonic smile.

CHAPTER 26

The Door

THE ESTABLISHMENT of Rodrigues *et fils* was on the Quai near the corner of the Rue Dauphine, with a fine view and smell of the fish market and within convenient reach of the fuel yard. It had other conveniences for trade and profit. To the east ran a narrow lane bordered by fishermen's huts and sheds and ending at the shore of a small lagoon. The lagoon lay half in, half outside the walls, presenting the military engineers with a very pretty problem. They had solved it by running a pile bridge across from the Maurepas Bastion to the shore battery of La Grève and facing its outer side with sharp palisades. Sentinels patrolled the bridge constantly or inconstantly, according to the wishes of M. Rodrigues and others who dealt in contraband, and with a suitable bribe to the officer of the guard it was possible to pass the slender bateaux of the fishermen under the bridge and between certain of the palings. A long stony beach ran between the lagoon and the harbor to the flank of lonely Rochefort Point. And so the business of M. Rodrigues flowed in two distinct channels, not very far apart; legitimate trade with France and the French West Indies and Canada passed over the cobbled Quai under the eye of the *ordonnateur;* the no less profitable trade with Halifax and New England went by way of the beach and lagoon. All of which interested the prisoner bookkeeper Sudden very much.

M. Rodrigues found him intelligent and attentive to his duties. After a time he was glad to make a permanent arrangement with the director of the prison. The Rodrigues *comptoir* was a small chamber at the front of the big warehouse, facing on the Quai. The chief clerk was a Basque like Rodrigues himself, a thin man with a hacking cough and a face as yellow as snuff, and he and Roger worked side by side at a simple desk of planed pine under a large leaded window looking out on the harbor. From the interior of the warehouse came mingled smells of wine and spirits, vinegar, sugar, tobacco, coffee, tea, bacon, tar, and gunpowder, a not unpleasant blend, to Roger the very smell of prosperity.

He thought, This is what I want. Someday I shall have it.

His belief in his destiny, his faith in the Golden Woman leaped in him fiercer than ever. Nevertheless adversity had taught him more than the mere discretion he had mentioned so flippantly to Madame Ducudrai. He had learned that whether you hunted caribou or cash, you must have perfect knowledge.

And so as his careful quill recorded casks of molasses, of tafia, of right Jamaica, of sugar, of olive oil; and tobacco pipes and Negro slaves and butter and flour and stockfish; and casks of wine, Bordeaux, Aubagne, and Saintonge; and herring nets and *doré* anchors and candles and nails and silks and sails—he committed these matters carefully to memory, with their cost and selling price, their origin and destination.

So too he watched and listened when men came with goods to buy or sell, especially after the ice went out of the harbor and traffic began with the open sea. Above all he listened for English accents. Sometimes he heard them, New England accents usually, but always beyond the *comptoir* out of sight.

After such occasions Rodrigues conversed with his chief clerk in Basque, with a careful eye on the *prisonnier-commis* Sudden.

But there was much to be learned for all that, from the ledger entries and particularly from a small journal which came under his eye from time to time, recording the bribes, large and small, in Halifax and Boston, as well as Louisbourg, which paved the way for contraband and broke the laws of King George and King Louis in a stroke. There was an enormous profit in all this.

The rate of profit on legitimate trade was comparatively small: Rodrigues' books for the previous year, 1753, showed a mere thirty per cent. But the volume was immense.

Louisbourg was headquarters for the French codfishery, to which fifteen or twenty thousand men came every year from the old country, quite apart from the busy shore fishery of Cape Breton itself. And there was the rich matter of supplies for the garrison, and for outposts as far away as Beauséjour in Acadie, and for the warships and Indiamen which rendezvoused at Louisbourg for convoy across the Atlantic. But more than any of these matters was the fact that Louisbourg stood at the sea crossroads of Canada, France, and the West Indies, and flourished as an entrepôt.

The quantities of goods which passed through the Louisbourg warehouses in the three-way trade were immense, and at thirty per cent the merchants long established in this bleak gray town had become as rich as rajahs.

Roger's labors in the countinghouse brought him a small wage which he was obliged to take in goods. In the course of four months he got himself coat and breeches of stout blue cloth, a pair of square-toed French shoes, a hat, a change of shirts and stockings. In addition Rodrigues awarded him wine and tobacco, which he shared as far as possible with the inmates of the onetime magazine in the angle of the Bastion Brouillant.

They were inclined to resent his prosperity at first. They knew it began with his errand to the Veritable Coucou. He knocked down a sallow corporal of Philips' Regiment who sneered that, damn his blood, there was no accounting for the itch of women. But on the whole they admired his good fortune, welcomed him when he returned under guard each night, and grinned and winked when he talked of his labors with pen and ink.

Spring dragged its dreary length across the calendar. It was June before the last of the ice vanished from the deep woods, and Louisbourg sat shrouded in gray sea fogs with occasional bursts of burning sunshine. Fishermen and traders found their way in and out of the harbor by some instinct of their own, and the Quai roared with life. The Rodrigues warehouse, like a vast cow stomach, swallowed and disgorged masses of merchandise while his clerks drove their quills furiously to keep pace. There were rumors of war—the annual canard, said the sick Basque indifferently. What did it matter if those people in Europe called it peace or war? Between French and English in

America there was war always. One day in August M. Rodrigues confirmed this, bouncing cheerfully into the *comptoir* to announce that "we French" had drawn blood in the far reaches of the Ohio. Coulon de Villiers had done it—ah, Coulon, what a boy!—and this time his *coureurs de bois* and Indians had taken a force of English provincials under some young idiot named *Vashinton.* A place called Great Meadows—a coincidence, *parbleu!* Wasn't it at Grand Pré here in Acadie that Coulon slaughtered the English seven years ago? A traveler, that one!

Well! A beginning! Next year, who knows? One certain thing—next year the Louisbourg garrison was to be increased by two battalions—regulars!—Regiment Bourgogne, Regiment Artois—straight from France! How that would brighten the bored eyes of our little ladies!

Certainly it brightened the eyes of M. Rodrigues. His thick fingers twitched as if he felt the fat contracts for supplies already.

Three or four days later he twitched a single finger at the prisoner from the door of his private *cabinet.* Roger laid down his pen carefully and walked inside. He had often itched for a peep at this little chamber, which had a separate entrance on an alley which led into the Rue L'Estaing.

Mysterious callers came that way, officers of the army, of the navy, a priest or two, women, Indians, seamen—some of them New English —and others whose calling was as mysterious as their presence itself.

A worn drugget covered the floor and a painted King Louis looked down from a painted horse upon the wall. There were three chairs, a stove, a window of opaque glass lozenges, and a shelf which held nothing but a rusty fragment of bombshell left by the New Englanders in '45.

M. Rodrigues (nobody had ever seen the *fils,* who was said to manage a branch of the family business in Rochelle) was a squat and swarthy man with an enormous head, which he made even larger by a wig of a queer rusty color and of a texture like picked oakum. His eyes were large and black and a little bloodshot, and his face was round and tight and rough with little pimples—like a Seville orange gone brown. His mouth was a knife slash across the lower section of the orange, with a glimpse of bad teeth when he smiled. He had small silver earrings and wore on each of his little fingers a gold ring set with a large emerald. He closed the door and stood for a full minute with his thick cotton-stockinged legs well apart and staring hard in Roger's face.

"M. Soudain," he said at last. "You are a gentleman of fortune, I believe."

"Of ill fortune so far," Roger said.

"Ah well! It seems, M. Soudain, that your fortune has changed." Another hard glance at the prisoner. Then, with his gaze fixed on the old bomb fragment, "One is given to understand that you served as captain in the army of the Chevalier Charles Stuart, in that unfortunate affair eight or nine years ago. You fled to France and spent some time in exile there."

"That is correct," murmured Roger politely. "I suppose Madame Ducudrai——"

"No names!" cried Rodrigues severely. "One learns also that you were one of the settlers at Halifax, where you have land granted by the English government."

"Correct."

"You asked for employment at the Quai because you entertained some hope of escape that way, did you not?"

Roger's cheek went warm. "Yes."

"Ah! But escape is not easy, as you have seen. What were your desires in Halifax?"

"To gather a little money and commence a business of some sort."

"What sort of business?"

"I do not know, monsieur—but yes, I do! I am familiar with the savages, and it seems to me that I could do well in the fur trade."

Rodrigues pinched his round, blue-stubbled chin with a thick forefinger and thumb, and it made a little rasping sound.

"An Englishman in the fur trade in Acadie risks his own pelt, my friend!"

"I am prepared to risk mine."

"Ah! There you speak well! And a trader who moves about the country and uses his eyes and ears can no doubt find other ways to turn a sou, eh?"

"That is my hope, monsieur."

"M. Soudain," announced Rodrigues, inspecting the scrap of iron with undying interest, "I have watched your work and I am impressed. You seem to realize the importance of figures in the conduct of affairs. Yet—it seems a pity that a man young and ambitious should be tied to a stool in a *comptoir*. Now I am a man of broad affairs. I am always seeking ambitious men who know how to move about the country and have no fear and—shall we say, not too fine a scruple?"

Roger thought of the Rochester coach and smiled. "You interest me, monsieur!"

"Good! Good! Well, there is unfortunately a state of strain between the English and French in America. I say unfortunately because I am aware of business opportunities in the English portion of Acadie which as a Frenchman I cannot pursue. I have surmounted this obstacle in other places with the aid of such intelligent gentlemen as yourself. Business," said M. Rodrigues grandly, "knows no boundaries."

"Exactly," murmured Roger politely.

"Very well, I have an affair to propose to you, M. Soudain. I propose to enable you to reach Alfax——"

"Eh!"

"—in order that you may pursue the fur trade and such other matters as you desire. Do not interrupt, please! I have an agent there, a private banker who will advance you certain sums for my account. You will pursue your affairs in your own name, you comprehend, but I shall require a semiannual statement of profit or loss, and you must provide exact vouchers and inventories. You will render these accounts to my agent, who has my complete confidence."

He paused and then snapped, "You find this acceptable?"

"Yes!" Roger stammered. "Yes, of course! I—am a little overwhelmed, monsieur."

"You are a gentleman, one learns, a man of honor," pursued the merchant harshly, "and I give you my confidence. I give you also three fourths of the profits. Is that enough?"

Roger gaped at the man. He had a whimsy that he would wake up any moment and find himself on his pallet in the Château Louisdamné.

"You will never mention my name nor that of my agent in your transactions in Acadie," continued the rasping voice. "You will on no account speak of your little stay at Louisbourg. You will inform your friends that you have been in the hands of the savages—and no more. You understand"—in a smoother tone—"that a merchant like myself, who does business with all the world, must preserve a secrecy in certain matters."

"I appreciate that, monsieur."

"Tonight you will be conducted from this place to a smuggling vessel bound for Halifax. You will have with you a sealed paper, which you will on no account open until you reach that port. Upon it you will find the name of my agent. As soon as possible you will present the paper to him—you will go discreetly, you understand?— and he will have his instructions. You will govern yourself by his advice. That is all, I think. No! One thing more—you will need some English money until you reach my agent. *Voici!*"—a small trickle of guineas into Roger's unsteady palm.

A dozen questions fluttered on Roger's lips, but Rodrigues fore-stalled them with a brusque, "Not another word! I shall expect you to be diligent and faithful—and discreet. I give you far more than freedom, M. Soudain. I grant you an opportunity such as few young men receive in the New World or the Old. Be sure you make the most of it." He paused. Then rapidly, "You shall not return to the prison in the usual manner this evening. I shall make an excuse to the officer of the guard. You will remain in the *comptoir* until dark. After that you will be guided by Manuel . . . and now, *au 'voir!*"

"*Au revoir,*" Roger said huskily, "and one thousand thanks——"

"Bah! *Bon chance, monsieur,* and remember . . ." A thin smile, a brown glimpse of teeth, a thick finger against the lips.

The supper hour came with a clatter of sabots homeward from the Quai. The warehouse fell silent. The clerks departed. The summer run of mackerel had appeared off the harbor two days ago, and from the frying pans of the Rue Dauphine now came the smell of them in oily gusts.

The silent Manuel brought a hunch of bread, an onion, and a piece of cheese, which Roger washed down with a mug of sour wine from a cask in the warehouse. He settled himself to wait for dark. It was an eternity.

Dusk at last, and the sea fog creeping in gray wisps between the warehouses, and the scrape of a fiddle somewhere down the Quai, and Breton voices raised in song. A woman's laugh in the alley behind, a slap and a man's voice urgent in the dialect of St. Jean de Luz. A roll of drums from the ramparts beating the retreat. The gray of the dusty windows black at last. A scurry of rats in the silent Magasin de Rodrigues.

A cautious knock on the door, Manuel opening it, and a bustle of purposeful figures trundling ankers of brandy, bolts of sailcloth, coils of rope, and a number of small boat anchors into the dark lane toward the lagoon.

Manuel's whisper, "After them!"

He stepped into the foggy dark and stumbled at the tail of the furtive procession until the water of the lagoon gleamed dully before him.

A French voice: "Are you monsieur the passenger?"

"Yes."

"Into this boat quickly, then!"

Stealthy oars across the water, a glimpse of the sentinel's bayonet in the fuzzy glow of a lantern, a cautious wait while his footsteps boomed across the wooden walk toward La Grève. A quick passage of the palisades beneath, just room for a boat to squeeze through. Oars again. The yellow candle pricks of the town shut off by fog and the dark bulk of the ramparts. A grating of keels on beach stones. A swift portage of kegs and bundles to the seaward side, and the dim shapes of waiting men and boats, into one of which he was pushed. Oars again and a low calling of farewells in broken French to the vanishing figures on the shore. A long and silent row in the clammy dark, from which at long last the shape of a vessel loomed. A passing of stuff aboard, a securing of boats, a scramble over the bulwark. An immediate sense of familiarity.

Then, "Where's that hell-confounded passenger?" in a voice like no other in the world, the voice of *Fair Lady,* the voice of Old Hux himself.

CHAPTER 27

Out of the Night

It was like a return from the dead—but after twenty years, not five. The mere existence of Halifax was a miracle after all this time. For five years his mind had been filled with memories of that cockney swarm and their bivouacs on the hillside, a cluster of lonely fires in the darkness of a continent. He remembered the "town" as a brown sword cut in the green flank of Citadel Hill, festering under the heat and flies, erupting sores of canvas and brushwood, and swarming with human maggots. It had an incredible air in those days; he expected to wake any morning and find the maggots gone, the sores vanished, and the wound healed green again. Only the transports, lying week after week in the harbor, had any appearance of reality—and their very presence had given the whole affair a transient air, the look of a great migration at a wayside halt.

All he had heard in Louisbourg of the English settlement at "Alfax" confirmed the impression of a hopeless enterprise, a clot of English exiles living a hand-to-mouth existence on the side of a hill at Chebucto, a "fortress" which had in fact no citadel, no walls, no bastions, no ditch, no magazines, nothing but a few rickety blockhouses and a rotten palisade. Many of the emigrants were still dependent entirely on the meager rations of the commissariat—six pounds of ship biscuit, four of pork, and one of peas per head per week. After five years! Those plantations of the early plans had never come to fact. On the peninsula between Northwest Arm and Bedford Basin a scatter of small farms had been grubbed out of the rocky soil, guarded from the Indians by a blockhouse line across the neck, but their produce was a mouthful, no more.

Cornwallis and the other governors had sought to tap the rich farms of the Fundy side, and for a time succeeded in tempting the avaricious Acadians with gold and silver payment. But Le Loutre had put a stop to that.

Louisbourg and the French forts at the head of Fundy Bay were getting all the Acadian supplies; as if Halifax did not exist, as if Nova Scotia had never passed from the rule of France! All Canada was laughing over this pitiful English venture at Chebucto, this would-be rival to Louisbourg which after five years of enormous expense remained nothing but a palisaded almshouse.

But now, as Roger wandered through the steep and stony streets, a lean and shabby figure in the throng of soldiers, rangers, seamen, townsmen, and fishermen, he had a strange impression of permanence. He could not understand it. There was nothing to warrant it. Sprawled over the hillside facing the harbor were seven or eight hundred houses of all sorts from the simple log hut to the one-and-a-half-story dwelling of New England, with unpainted shingles or clapboards, with dormers peering from steep-pitched roofs, and squat square chimneys of imported brick. Most of the houses stood on walls of dry fieldstones to keep their sills above the muck of the streets.

There were still many stumps in the public thoroughfares, but they were rotten now. In another year or two the traffic of heavy two-wheeled carts would grind them into the general mud. Their battered presence called attention to the barren streets, shadeless in the summer weather. Within the town limits almost every tree had been cut down ruthlessly in that first passion to get rid of the forest. This stripping of its cover had dried up the small stream which flowed down the north side of George Street to the beach. Its bed was filled with rubbish, and a town pump stood where the drinking pool had been, within an easy stone cast of the governor's modest door. The swamp above the landing place was well-nigh filled with rubbish and silt from the hillside, and now formed a rough esplanade along the head of the wharves, lined on its upper side by grogshops and ship chandlers' stores. The part which lay at the foot of George Street was known as Market Square; the rest was still simply the Beach. At the foot of the "square," untouched for superstitious reasons probably, the old gnarled hardwood tree remained, the town's first gallows. The stocks and pillory had been removed to the Parade.

He went up there and saw a company of grenadiers changing the guard. They were sweating under the hot sun in their tight stocks and wigs and heavy red coats and waistcoats. He recognized them for some of Warburton's by the green facings on their breasts and cuffs. His Majesty's 45th Foot—all regiments went by numbers now, it seemed—looked rather the worse for their years of service in these wilds; the long black gaiters were patched with leather and the red coats much torn and much mended and all stained with sweat and dirt and streaks of dried balsam. He thought dourly, You've come a long way since Prestonpans, my lads! The Parade was simply a narrow space along the rough hillside, and as the company faced up the slope for inspection the noses of the rear platoon were on a level with the knees of the foremost. Something symbolic about that! An uphill climb for Halifax forever and ever, Amen.

He turned away to look at the high wooden rear of St. Paul's, the finest building in the town, erected of timber from Boston at the king's expense. It had a Londonish look. St. Peter's in Vere Street? Modeled from one of 'em, certainly. But it lay north-and-south. Odd, that. Wasn't there a rule about building churches east-and-west? Of course you couldn't build anything east-and-west in Halifax without digging a hole in the hill. Um!

He walked to the summit. Women and youngsters were dotted over the slopes picking blueberries among the stumps and boulders. Looking back on the town, he noticed at once the state of the defenses. Troops still manned the five log forts which careful Mr. Bruce had built about the perimeter, and lived in barracks under the north shoulder of the hill by Grenadier Fort. But the palisade between the forts was falling down. Whole sections were gone—for firewood, probably; he pictured the cockneys after dark. The town had outgrown the thing anyway. Houses were scattered all along the harbor slope now, north and south, and settlement was creeping over the shoulders of the hill toward the west, where an expanse of wild meadows and sedgy ponds had been set aside as a common. Beyond the common began the little farms and pastures of the German folk. Oats were ripe in their fields, and he could see the flash of sickles. Goldenrod was in bloom, a deep yellow fringe along the dusty roads. It would be autumn soon.

He came upon one of Gorham's rangers sprawled with a slattern in the shade of an alder clump and spoke the question foremost in his mind.

"What's become of all the English settlers?"

The pair were none too pleased with this interruption. The ranger turned on an elbow and regarded him with a cold eye, but after inspection the fellow checked the retort twitching on his mouth and said carefully, "Go down the south slope o' the hill, mister, and foller the palisade till ye come to the south gate o' the town. It's right below Horsman's Fort. Ye'll find a lane runnin' off toward P'int Pleasant that some folk call Pleasant Street. Naow, jist aoutside the gate, on the west side o' the lane, ye'll find the English settlers—most of 'em, anyhow. O' course a lot run off Boston and York way, or cadged a passage home."

"My thanks." As Roger turned away toward the south he heard the woman giggle.

The south gate lay on its back at the side of the road with grass growing through its weathered timbers. It had not been closed in many moons. A bored redcoat, half asleep in the sunshine, regarded Roger indifferently from the sentinel's walk outside the tumble-down log fort.

The lane with the pleasant name ran toward the south through pinewoods and scattered clearings. On its west side, just outside the palisade, a large field climbed the slope, pimpled with low green mounds and here and there a heap of fresh-turned earth. Most of the mounds were marked with a chunk of rough fieldstone at head and foot.

He cursed the ranger's humor and was about to leave when he noticed a woman sitting in the rank grass. She had a bunch of wild flowers in her hand. He ran to her, crying "Mrs. Killick!"

She jumped up, wide-eyed, and put out a large red hand as if to stave off a horror. "No!" she gasped. " 'Tain't you! You're dead— dead five year come Michaelmas!"

"I'm Roger Sudden," he said impatiently.

She went on in a somber voice, "It all comes of 'angin' about the graveyard, just like Killick warned me. God save me, a Christian woman that never done nobody 'arm. In the broad afternoon, too!"

"Nonsense! Look here, I was carried off by the savages. And now I've come back. Look at me!"

"You always was a decent gentleman," she said timidly after a pause. "Not one to play nasty pranks you wasn't—livin' or dead. Is it reely you, Mr. Sudden?"

"Of course it is! Tell me—where's Killick . . . and my friend Tom . . . and Trope and Mrs. Lumley . . . all those people?"

She sat down rather violently on a small mound and began to cry. "Oh, Mister Sudden, sir!"

"Tell me—everything!"

"I 'ad a baby that autumn you was took, Mr. Sudden. A proper darlin'—and me childless all them years. But my little boy died, sir, in the winter, in the cruel weather." She put her head in her hands and wept without restraint. Roger waited.

At last she lifted a tear-smeared face and began in a hushed voice. "We 'ad a terrible time, sir, all of us. The Injuns didn't bother us much that first autumn 'cept now and agin, like that time you got took—and Maggs and Bob and poor Will Vace that wouldn't 'urt a fly, skelped, 'ead and all, so they say. . . . God save us all, what murderin' 'eathens to be cast amongst! But it wasn't the Injuns, sir, it was the winter—that was what done for us, sir. I dunno which was the worst off—them as stayed aboard the transports all winter or them like us that lived ashore in an 'ut made o' brushwood and old sail canvas—bare earth for the floor, fire in the middle, smoke fit to choke ye, and that orful wind a-stabbin' through the walls like baggonets. There wasn't 'ardly any stoves, afloat or ashore. The food was all salt provisions, o' course, and that brought scurvy. And the water—the sogers tried to keep it clean, but ye know what it was like —all that filth about the 'uts, drippin' down into the town well in the thaws. It killed us, sir. By the 'undred. Dretful, sir. Nobody knows 'ow many died, but it was close on a thousand; some say more. The gov'nor 'ad to make regulations orderin' people to put out their dead o' mornin's, and make proper coffins, and go with the corp to the buryin' place—this place 'ere, sir.

"It was like the great plague o' London in King Charles' time, sir. When the warm weather come we prayed for a great fire, same as then, to sweep the town away so Mr. Cornwallis 'ud take us 'ome. But there wasn't any such luck, sir. Just them Injun scoundrels 'angin' about outside the palisade, killin' or takin' off the woodcutters and women pickin' berries and childer that straggled into the woods. So we 'ad to stay—what was left of us."

"But the town's grown!" protested Roger.

"Oh, so it 'as, sir. After that first summer Mr. Cornwallis sent for Dutch and Swiss settlers—people that knew a bit o' farmin'. And they come by thousands—too many for a place like this. The gov'nor sent a lot of 'em down the coast to make a town o' their own. But nearly all the farms ye see now 'tween the town and the blockhouse line was made by the furriners. Desperate poor—us London folk was rich beside 'em—but good people, a patient lot, and 'ard-workin'. But the biggest change is the New Englanders. They've come in droves o' their own accord—a thousand the fust year. They know this sort o' country—say it's like Massy-chew-*sets*—and don't mind the winters nor the savages. Traders and fishermen mostly—say the soil this side o' the province is sour as vinegar and ain't wuth time nor sweat—work very 'ard, talk through their noses, and pray to Gawd in a meetin'ouse just like the chapel folk at 'ome. They showed Killick 'ow to catch salmon and codfish proper-like. 'E used to sell it 'isself in the market place, but I got 'im to make me a fish tray to carry on me 'ead so I could cry it through the streets and get a better price."

"And you're getting along all right?"

"Right as rain, sir"—proudly. "Got a nice little 'ouse down by the water where the fishin' folk live. A bit o' garden in the back and a wild-cherry tree that's white as snow come blossomtime. Killick with a boat of 'is own, too. And me"—she cast her eyes down bashfully—"expectin' again along about Christmas time."

"That's nice. But—the others—the people I knew?"

Her mouth went mournful again. "Mrs. Maggs and three of 'er young'uns perished o' the plague that first winter—t'other's in the gov'ment orphan house. 'Member the little Vace gel wi' the crippled leg? She got done in by Injuns the second summer, pickin' flowers in the common land. The ones with 'er got away, but she couldn't run fast enough, along of 'er leg, and the devils knocked 'er down and skelped 'er in sight o' the palisades. 'Eld the skelp up, they did, and 'owled frightful at the sentries. Lovely yeller 'air it was, too. Mrs. Vace went barmy after that. Leastways she run orf with a soger, which is much the same. 'Er other young'uns is bound out for orphans and got fair enough 'omes, considerin'. Bob's widder, she marrit one o' the Dutch settlers—they're Germans, reely—and seems to be 'appy. They've got a farm on the block'ouse road."

"But Tom—Tom Fuller?"

"Oh, 'im! Tom, 'e up and joined one o' the ranger companies— Bartelo's, I think—arter you was took, sir. They're posted upcountry somewhere."

"And Trope and the Lumley woman?"

She made a mouth and a nose. "Them! Got a lodgin'ouse in Prince Street, down by the dissenters' meetin'ouse. I sell 'em a bit o' fish sometimes. They seem to do well. Very respectable lodgers, so *she* says. Clerks and such. Not like Tooley Street. But the likes o' Lumley turnin' up 'er nose!"

She stood up and brushed the grass from her broad skirts. And timidly, "I've got to get along 'ome now, sir, to get supper for my man. Would you—could you come and 'ave a bite with us, Mr. Sudden? 'Tain't much to offer a gentleman . . ."

Roger refused, promising to come some other time. There were so many things burning to be done. Nevertheless, after she had gone he remained for a time musing over the graves, seeing the pits in the snow that first winter, and the fires to thaw the ground, the watchful redcoats standing guard at the edge of the woods, and the poor human rubbish thrown into the holes, three and four deep because the soil was precious in this stony land.

So it *was* an omen after all—that grisly scene on the Basin shore when they found D'Anville's men. Death had sat grinning at them all that summer afternoon—the poor fools who saw no danger but from Indians!

He turned back along "Pleasant Street" into the unclean town and stopped at the first tavern for a stiff dram of Jamaica. He drank it at a gulp and shivered as if he had been touched by ghosts.

Had *they* too dreamed of a Golden Woman?

He found the lodginghouse of Trope in Prince Street between Hollis and Granville, just above the little dissenting meetinghouse, precisely as the old den in Tooley Street had stood in the morning shadow of St. Olave's. There was something nostalgic about that. They greeted him unemotionally, but the eyes of Trope and Lumley glittered with a sly curiosity. They, at least, had not changed.

Mrs. Lumley appraised his sober clothing with a fishy eye and declared, "Five shillin' a week," folding her great paws over the bulge of her apron and sniffing as if to say, "Stay or leave, it suits me."

He took it without question and climbed at her slovenly heels to just such an attic as he and Tom had shared in Tooley Street.

He observed whimsically, "All it wants is Sally Madigan."

Surprisingly the hairy creature grunted, "Well, Sal's in Allyfax, if ye want to know. But ye wouldn't catch Sal in your attic now! She's an officer's doxy and lives in a big clapboard 'ouse in Granville Street with servants at 'er beck and call. A fine lady now, I tell ye! A major o' Lascelles' Regiment took a fancy to 'er—always a pretty slut, Sally was—and treats 'er like a queen. That's what she acts like, too."

She flumped away down the stairs indignantly.

Roger stepped to the narrow gable window and peered across the ruts and stumps of Prince Street to the green rectangle of the governor's plot, where the little wooden residency stood in the heart of the town. This is the beginning, he told himself. Someday you'll hobnob over there, and they'll turn out the guard for you. He thought then of the sealed billet in his pocket and broke the wax casually.

The name, in Rodrigues' spidery scrawl, seemed to leap at him from the paper: "John Foy."

CHAPTER 28

The House of Foy

THE HOUSE was an unobtrusive one in Hollis Street a few doors north of George, two stories of brown-painted shingles and a gambrel roof, with a kitchen garden at the rear enclosed in a high fence of pickets.

His fingers closed on the knocker, a lion's paw of polished brass, and the echoing rat-a-tat made him smile. Door knockers in Halifax! Somehow all the changes of five years seemed manifest in that.

The maidservant Jenny admitted him with no more emotion than

the Tropes had shown, but with the same glint of curiosity. This
casualness nettled him. It was as if he had not been missed for a
moment of that long five years.

He stalked, hat in hand, into an elegant little parlor. A shaft of
sunshine from the west window pierced it like a sword. There was
a warm Turkey carpet on the floor, and the walls were wainscoted
in curly maple to the ceiling, with blue flock panels. The furniture
was of mahogany, shaped in the rather lascivious curves which his
mind's eye associated with French interiors. Indeed the whole chamber had a continental look which made him wistful, for exactly what
he did not know. Mary Foy? He had not lied to Wapke when he
told her of the green-eyed woman. But now that freedom blew about
him like breeze in summer, he was filled once more with visions of
that golden idol under the fabulous porcelain sky. He knew no more
than ever where to find her, but he felt quite sure his feet were on
the road. He awaited impatiently the banker's step in the little hall.

Instead, with no more warning than a quick froufrou of petticoats,
Mary Foy swept in, wearing a sacque dress of some light muslin
stuff. The loose fall of the sacque behind gave an artful dressmaker's
emphasis to the taut figure in front, indeed gave her the look of a
slim figurehead springing from the full bows of a ship instead of a
sacque and hoops. It belonged to her, that look. That was how he saw
her always—a tall, eager figure leaning into a wind. She wore no
cap. The red hair was gathered away from her forehead and from the
back of her head a thick bunch of curls fell to her shoulders.

He had expected her to look older, and there was a riper swell to
the breasts in the telltale bodice, her chin was softer, she had lost
that tomboy look, and yet—and yet she still had that air of innocence
avid for experience, the yearning for something momentous outside,
which could be described in one word only—virginal. A silly thing
to say of a woman married since sixteen, but there it was, and there
she was, an enigma.

"Mr. Sudden—Roger!" she cried, coming to him with both hands
outstretched.

He bent over the slim, strong fingers politely, aware of Foy coming
into the chamber behind her. Then he was shaking Foy's hand and
both of them were crying congratulations on his escape. Clearly

Rodrigues had sent an explanatory letter by Old Hux. He was a little disappointed. He had nursed a dramatic scene in which they would be dumfounded (like poor Mrs. Killick) and he the cool adventurer. But at least they were pleased at his appearance in the flesh, and Foy called Jenny for wine and insisted on his story.

He yielded the tale reluctantly, a little resentfully. He felt suddenly the instinctive hostility of a soldier toward those who live at ease far from the battle. His phrases were curt. He shrugged off half their questions.

The sunbeam crept across the room. Roger sipped his wine from time to time. Mary's stood untouched. She was watching him with wide eyes and parted lips. But Foy drank thirstily and replenished his glass and drank and refilled with an eager clutch on the decanter, protesting jovially that, egad, this August weather parched a man. Mary glanced at him—a little mournfully, Roger thought—and presently she rose with a diffident, "Well, I daresay you men have business to discuss." And from the doorway, lightly, "We'll be seeing you frequently, I hope, Mr. Sudden?"

"I shall be very busy, I'm afraid, ma'am."

"Ah!" Her eyes were chilled. He rose and bowed, and she was gone.

"Now, sir," Roger said bluntly, "you've heard from Rodrigues, I think?"

Foy moved his wet lips several times before replying. "Rodrigues? Yes. Yes, of course! You seem to have made an impression on my—ah—client, Sudden."

Roger's mouth tightened. Words! Words! Words—when the Golden Woman waited for him somewhere in this wilderness!

"I think I can be of profit to your client, Captain Foy—and to myself. To be quite frank, at this moment I'm thinking entirely of myself—and I want five hundred pounds at once."

Foy's brows shot up comically. "That all?" in a sour voice.

"That will do to begin with. I want wealth, position, the amenities which make life bearable—the sort of things you enjoy, for instance, Captain."

"The things that I enjoy have a rather high price, Sudden," Foy answered harshly. His snuff-dyed fingers lifted and fell in a little

dance on the table edge. "I like you, Sudden, you understand. I liked
you from the first, from that night you boarded the *Fair Lady* in the
Thames. A gentleman and a man of action. Well! As one gentleman
to another, I'm happy to lend you the money you require. As a
banker I must bring up the matter of collateral security."

"I have none."

Foy leaned forward. "Ah, but I have my security, I have the fact
that you are Captain Roger Sudden, late of the Manchester Regiment, so called in the rebellion for Charles Stuart, a refugee from
England for your Jacobite sympathies—sit down, please!—and now
resident in a colony very much under the military government of
King George."

Roger frowned. Rodrigues! And Madame Ducudrai, of course.

"I see what you mean," he said.

"Good! Since we're about to become in a sense partners, it's just
as well to have fundamental matters clear between us, Captain
Sudden."

"So far you have the advantage, sir"—stiffly.

"And I intend to keep it, my dear Sudden!" Foy's smile was bland.
The scar twitched in his cheek. "I shall furnish you with London
drafts for five hundred pounds. Your first venture is to be in the
Indian trade, I understand. That will take you away from Halifax
for the autumn and winter, but I shall expect you in April, say, with
a full accounting. If you have done reasonably well you shall have
further credits. In fact if you show diligence and enterprise I am
prepared to finance anything you undertake—always providing your
proposal is convincing to my own good sense."

He paused. "One or two cautions—a young man seeking his fortune cannot afford much notice in a gossipy outpost like this. Live
quietly, dress thriftily, drink cautiously. Trust no one with a word of
our affairs. Especially a woman. . . . Are you partial to women,
Sudden?"

"I don't think so, no."

"I suspect that women are partial to you. Um! Well, your affair, of
course. I ask that you be discreet—in all things. Henceforth you must
never come to my house except at night. In the street I shall not
acknowledge you, so don't speak to me. Bear in mind that I am not

only the silent partner, I am the invisible partner as far as Halifax is concerned. I shall expect full and frequent accounts of your doings in the province. Keep your eyes and ears open. Information is the life of trade. Um! One more thing—I'm absent from town at certain intervals. At such times you will render your account to my wife. She is thoroughly familiar with my affairs."

"Including this?"

"I shall acquaint her with it. I may say, Sudden, that she was delighted when we heard of your escape. She'd always hoped you were alive. Insisted, in fact! Ah, the ladies, Captain Sudden! Whatever should we do without 'em?"

"What indeed?" murmured Roger politely. He had found them a confounded nuisance. And now, by Foy's airy breach of his own rule, that baffling green-eyed creature was to have a hand in his affairs.

He wasted no time. By first postbag upcountry went a packet containing seven guineas and a note addressed to Tom Fuller in Bartelo's company of rangers at Fort Lawrence: "Choose six good men, buy your discharge and theirs, and come to Halifax at once."

He laid out his funds carefully, chiefly on rum at two shillings a gallon. He wanted a number of muskets, but Mr. Thomas Saul, the great merchant of Halifax, looked down a long nose and said frigidly that the Indians were a lot of murdering devils not to be trusted with such things.

"If we don't trust 'em, the French will, Mr. Saul."

But Mr. Saul's mouth was tight. He was quite sure he had no muskets. So, it seemed, were Joshua Mauger and the other merchants.

Roger laid out the rest of his credits in coarse blue stroud blankets and the usual knives, hatchets, hawk bells, beads, red cloth, looking glasses, and tinderboxes of the Indian trade.

From the dissolute Micmacs who sold lobsters on the Beach he haggled and bought four large bark canoes which he overhauled himself, paying the patches and seams with tar.

On the seventh day Tom Fuller came, thin and brown in buckskins, with six men who looked exactly like him. The light in his gray eyes was the light of a happy dog's.

" 'Struth, sir, I allus *knowed* ye'd turn up sometime, and when ye did, why, orf we'd go agin. What is it now?"

Roger told him and watched the lift of the bold black brows.

"Ho! Peddlin' trade rum to the redskins!" He grinned. "Well, I bin liftin' their scalps all this time—'twon't hurt to poison 'em for a change."

"What about these others?"

"Stake your life on 'em, sir! I picked 'em careful—Findlay and Pell was seamen once like myself, and Corcoran and Ricker and Kelligrove are woodsmen from Noo England, and the little feller Bloy that's shy his starboard ear . . . nobody knows where he come from, and he won't say, but I reckon there's a drop o' Mohawk in him somewheres. It took all your guineas to pay the smart money, sir. Bartelo gits paid accordin' to the ration stren'th o' his company, so he don't like lettin' men go for keeps."

"That's all right. How soon can we start?"

"Now, if ye say."

"Tomorrow will do. Here's another guinea—find the men lodging somewhere, and come and sleep with me at Trope's in Prince Street."

After dark Roger called at the house in Hollis Street. The stolid Jenny admitted him, and after a moment Mary appeared.

"John's away," she said at once.

"Then I'll report to you, ma'am." He drew papers from his pocket and spread them on the little mahogany table. "Here's a list of my disbursements. You'll observe I had to buy some men out of the ranger corps to look after my trading posts. We start in the morning."

She looked astonished. "You're as sudden as your name, aren't you?" And, with a gleam of mischief, "One would have thought that after your long denial in the wilderness the society of our Halifax ladies . . ."

"You forget I have learned the refinements of the forest, ma'am."

"I see," she murmured, displeased. She asked a number of questions, all shrewd and to the point. When she discussed his purchases a distinct Scots accent crept out of that too-perfect English of hers, and he was amused. She seemed satisfied, however, and to end the interview put out her hand briskly, as a man might. He made a leg and touched her fingers with his lips, murmuring, *"Au revoir, madame."*

She flushed a little and the green eyes were annoyed. "Until spring," she answered in English, severely.

The little expedition crossed the harbor with laden canoes in the first light and journeyed toward Fundy by the Micmac war trail of Roger's painful memory. At the first lake—called by the Indians "Banook," which meant just that—Roger called a halt, without explanation, and began a careful search along the shore. There was no sign of Peyal's bones in the shallows where he had seen the corpse flung. Perhaps some Indian party had found the thing, or a party of loggers from the Dartmouth sawmill. He was disappointed and baffled. But it occurred to him that in the natural process of decay that bloated carcass must have risen to the surface and drifted toward the outlet of the lake.

He had an odd qualm at the spot where he had been kidnaped, and gripped his hatchet instinctively, as if those brown brutes might rise again from the huckleberries. But the bushes were empty and he passed on, wading slowly close to the bank, disturbing a host of frogs. He reached the rattling outpour of the lake—and there *it* was, sunk against the upstream side of a great boulder where it had drifted and caught. That mangled and hate-distorted flesh had rotted and sunk and dissolved, and nothing remained but the bones, furry with green pondweed—and the crude little amulet still slung against the breastbone by the thong.

He expected to find Shubenacadie well-nigh deserted, and it was. The migration from the coast was still a moon away. A scatter of human dregs, too sick, too old, or too lazy to make the spring journey to the sea, spilled out of the wigwams and regarded the white men in an apprehensive silence.

Gautier's cabin was empty. The door swung wide in the wind along the river and there was a drift of last fall's leaves in the corners. The trader had not been here since last summer, then. Why? He walked the length of the camp and found the wigwams in a state of disuse for the most part. The rush matting was rotten, and the brush-wood on the bed places was so old that the brown needles had fallen from the twigs entirely. The ashes of the cooking fires were sunken and caked. An air of neglect hung over everything. Even the cross on the little log chapel hung awry.

He peered into the lodge where he had been a prisoner and was astounded to see the old woman squatting there silent and alone, as if she had waited all this time for his return.

"Kway!" he said.

"O Man," she answered in a rustling voice, "I cannot see thee, for my eyes are dead, but thy voice is the voice of Bosoley."

"I am Bosoley, mother. Where are the people?"

"Thou know where the people go in summer," she answered evasively.

"They did not winter here. Think thou I am blind, like thee?"

She rose and put out a withered claw, fumbling slowly at his breast. When her fingers passed over the amulet she uttered in a small squeak, "Ehhhhh!"

"How did thee know?" he asked.

"Thou came, and only the power of the totem could have brought thee back. It belongs to the Meeg-a-maage, Bosoley. The little fish cries out to be restored to them."

"Perhaps the little fish will tell me where the people are," he taunted.

Her eyes, those dead disks, stared at him horribly. "The women and children have gone toward Oonamaagik, to the great town of the Wenjoo there. The warriors gather with The Otter at the end of the Great Bay."

"At Beauséjour?"

"That is the Wenjoo name."

"The Otter has gathered them for Jesus-talk, perhaps?"

"For war. War is in the wind."

"What wind, mother?"

"The springtime wind, which blows from the southwest, from *Bostoon*."

He put a stick of trade tobacco in her hand and left her mumbling of a forest turned red before its time.

CHAPTER 29

The Path to Fortune

IN APRIL, the *Punadumwegoos* of the Micmacs, Roger returned to Halifax with his store of furs by sloop around the coast from Fundy Bay. He found the provincial capital ankle-deep in the spring thaw. A black ooze dripped down the streets toward the harbor, as if Citadel Hill were some sort of mud volcano in slow eruption—ooze fetid with slops and refuse flung from the houses during the winter and exposed now with the melting of the snow. The drab wooden houses had the haggard look of prisoners emerging from long and dark confinement, huddling together against the cold spring rain, blinking in the fitful bursts of sunshine.

But the people were brisk enough. The lower town was thronged. And its voice now was unmistakably the nasal drawl of New England, with undertones of cockney, of throaty Swiss and German, of sonorous Huguenot. And here and there he met the chatter and gesticulation of traders from the Spanish Main, the glib and comical English of slaves from the West Indies, the reedy monotones of Micmacs peddling fish and furs. He discovered a group of Portuguese from the Azores. And there were the varied accents of the garrison: the 47th Foot—Lascelles' Irish—in their red coats and white facings, the Englishmen of Warburton's 45th in red and green, the mixed English and colonials in the red and buff of the 40th—the regiment which was formed at Fort Anne after the conquest and, like the Israelites of old, had spent forty years in the wilderness. And the polyglot rangers, those scoundrels and adventurers in buckskin, who counted in their ranks all sorts of men from a petty Sicilian nobleman to a half-breed Mohawk, a Cape Cod deacon, and a cashiered captain of His Majesty's Foot Guards. A few carriages splashed along—he noticed Sally Madigan in one, laughing beside a middle-aged major of the 47th—and a small rank of sedan chairs stood for hire at the Parade; but horseback was still the accepted mode of keeping genteel feet out of the mire.

Roger sent Tom Fuller with a note advising Foy that he would call that night. In the small chill attic at Trope's he changed reluctantly from the comfortable buckskins, worn to his lean shape by nine months' travel, to the coarse and ill-fitting garments which proclaimed him a townsman of the poorer class. Rain was falling steadily when he set forth. He picked his way along Hollis Street with care to avoid the deeper holes. There were lampposts at every corner, and Cornwallis and his successors had made attempts to keep them lit; but the posts were only ten feet high and the lanterns too easily stolen or smashed by roistering seamen.

An east wind wafted through the dark a salty reek of harbor water. At his knock the door opened on a stout chain and the woman Jenny inspected him for a moment by the light of a candle.

"Oh! It's you!"

"The bad penny," he said coldly.

Mary Foy was in the parlor, wearing one of those green things that went so well with her eyes and hair. He paused in the doorway and bowed, saying handsomely, "Green's your color, ma'am—and I like the smaller hoops. A new mode you're setting?"

"An old thing from London," she said quickly. "Do sit down."

He faced her across the glow of a bright fire, and a spaniel got up from the hearthstone, sniffed his knee suspiciously, and then nuzzled his hand. He stroked the dog's ears and looked upon Foy's wife appreciatively. Spermaceti tapers in a three-branched candelabra competed wanly with the firelight, which struck gleams of copper from her hair and gave her eyes the dark look he remembered.

"I've come to report to your husband."

"John's away again. You can make your report to me."

"May I ask where he goes so frequently?"

"You may not, Mr. Sudden."

His lips twitched. "Well, ma'am, I wish to report a very successful season. I've established posts at Piziquid, Minas, and Fort Lawrence, as your husband wished. That gives us a steady sutling trade with the troops stationed at those places—mostly in drink, of course. There's some business with the friendly Indians who hang about the forts, but they're a drunken lot, too lazy to catch much fur and too careless in the skinning and curing of it. So I left a man in charge of each post and sent the others through the wild country where there's more and better fur."

"And much more risk!"

"We managed very well. One of my men, Ricker, was murdered by savages at a place called Merigomish." He frowned. "I recovered most of his goods—and took hard pay for what was gone."

"I don't understand."

"It was nothing, really. I borrowed the services of a few rangers from Gorham's company at Fort Lawrence and journeyed through the woods on snowshoes. Came upon the savages camped in a snowstorm by a frozen harbor called Piktook, where the French come in summer to cut mast timber for Louisbourg. Six men, one or two squaws, a few youngsters—we killed and scalped the lot. Most of the stolen goods were in the wigwams, and we found Ricker's head, hard frozen, in one of their pack baskets. I had to pay the rangers for their time and trouble, of course, but fortunately the governor's paying a good bounty for Micmac scalps just now. They'll fetch twenty-five pounds each, which will pretty well repay the loss all round."

He lifted his gaze from the dog, wriggling with pleasure at his knee, and saw her eyes wide with horror. She shivered and burst out, "Ah, how could you? And how can you talk of it in that cold-blooded way? If you knew how terrible you seem!"

An indifferent hitch of his shoulders. "Fur is fur, whether you skin it from an Indian or a mink. Have you ever considered the sufferings of a trapped mink? Besides, the Indians suffered a more merciful death than they gave Ricker. The point is, ma'am, I couldn't go on trading in that wild country with Ricker unavenged. 'Twould have made me an object of contempt throughout the tribes. As it is, the wind carries a whiff of a different sort. The Micmacs will respect the name of Bosoley because he took a stiff price for his man."

"Bosoley?"

"Beau Soleil—my name among the Indians."

"Oh!" Her tone had an edge. "How very odd! I should have said you were neither handsome nor sunny, Mr. Sudden. What did the savages do to you, to make you so very cruel?"

"I'm afraid that's too long a story, ma'am—and much too dull. Here's the inventory of stock on hand in my truck houses as of March thirty-first."

She gave the sheet a glance, but her clouded eyes lifted at once.

"You'll see," Roger pursued a little impatiently, "that our goods need replenishment, especially the rum. I can take care of that with the proceeds of my furs, of course. Here's a list of the furs . . ."

"Tell me the main things. I can go over your reports with John later."

"Well, to begin with"—he tried to keep the satisfaction out of his voice—"I've about three thousand pounds' weight of beaver. I could sell 'em in Halifax to Joshua Mauger, say, but I propose to ship 'em to Boston for the best price. Apart from beaver, I've a hundred otter, a hundred and forty-six marten, and four hundred and twenty-three assorted fisher, mink, fox, ermine, wildcat, and bear skins . . . not worth as much as the beaver, you understand. Perhaps I'd better explain the trade a bit . . . the standard of currency's the spring beaver skin. Two spring beaver are reckoned worth three fall skins. To go on from there, a pound of prime spring beaver's worth three of marten, or six mink, or two fox, or ten muskrat, or——"

She broke in, "You'd better put that on paper. It's rather confusing."

"It's written; it's here in my report," he said curtly. "Well, if you want the bones of the matter, ma'am, we've a profit, based on the current price of prime beaver in Boston and allowing for freight and insurance—I'll get Mr. Saul to underwrite the shipment, I think, the stuff's too valuable to risk even on so short a voyage—a profit of something like fifteen thousand dollars."

"Why," she asked, "don't you reckon in English money? I'll have to reckon it in pounds shillings and pence before I understand what it means."

"There's little or no English currency in the province. The governor has to fetch Spanish silver from the West Indies to pay the troops, and that's about the only hard money in circulation. So I reckon in dollars."

She stepped swiftly to an escritoire and figured intently with pencil and paper, catching the pencil end from time to time reflectively in her short white teeth.

"In other words," she announced, looking at him over a slim green shoulder, "there's a clear gain of something like 3,750 pounds—and of that 2,800 pounds or so is yours under the agreement. I should say you'd spent a very profitable winter, Mr. Sudden!"

The Scots accent had crept into her voice again, but the note of contempt was there too. She was charming in the mingled light of fire and candles, and it was queer to hear a pretty woman calculating with that precise rolling of the *r*s which his memory associated with canny men in the countinghouses of Glasgow and Auld Reekie. He had a swift suspicion that she was more than her husband's assistant, that she was the banker herself. But what was strange about that? The world was full of clever wives and tipsy husbands.

She added, seeing his hesitation, "I hope you're satisfied?"

"Not at all," he said bluntly. "The woods are full of opportunities, and there's precious little time. That's why I want to see your husband. I want to reach out in several directions. That means more capital. I must have a ship of my own, for instance."

"Why?"

"To supply my posts—they're all on or near tidewater—and to obtain those supplies in the first place. Prices in Halifax are an outrage. No wonder Saul and Mauger and their little clique are getting rich! Well, I propose to buy my goods in Louisbourg."

She looked at him oddly. "But isn't that against the law, Mr. Sudden?"

"Why don't you call me Roger? We're partners, after all."

"Are we?" She lifted an eyebrow. "I'm not sure I want to be partner in a smuggling venture—Roger."

He snorted, "Why not? Every Halifax merchant smuggles when he gets a chance; and from what I saw in Louisbourg I should say every merchant in Boston as well. Look here, I have to compete in the woods with French traders who offer the Indians better stuff at lower prices. And the savages are accustomed to French goods; they like 'em and ask for 'em. Mary, with a ship of my own to assure a supply from Louisbourg, I can push my posts far to the eastward, where the Indians haven't been spoiled and the best fur's to be had."

"And where you're very likely to be murdered, Roger Sudden!"

He shrugged cheerfully. "Fortune's for those who don't mind risks. Besides, the savages are afraid of me; I have a talisman. But we're getting away from business. I want to charter a couple of brigs in addition to the one I buy outright."

"Whatever for?"

"There's going to be a pretty penny in Bay of Fundy freights this summer. Several thousand New England troops are coming to take Fort Beauséjour without the formality of declaring war."

"How do you know?" she said shrewdly.

"A friend, an officer at Fort Anne. The governor sent Colonel Monckton to Boston last year and it's all arranged. But that's not all, Mary. I'm ready to gamble on some fat shipping business after the siege. One can't be sure, of course. It's like an idle exercise in arithmetic: you pick up figures here and there and add them up, and they make a sum. It may mean something or nothing. I'm thinking of the Acadians in all those settlements along the Fundy shore. They've always refused to take the English oath of allegiance, always kept on the sunny side of the Micmacs and Malecites, always sent tithes to Quebec, always given a hand when their French compatriots came down to strike at Fort Anne. Some of the younger and more reckless men have taken part in Indian raids on Halifax."

"Well?" Mary was frowning.

"Cornwallis and Hopson thought they could win over those people by tolerance and a show of force—hence the little English forts along the Fundy side. No good, of course. Le Loutre was too much for 'em. But now there's a very different sort of governor, this tough old soldier Lawrence who got a nasty whiff of Le Loutre's powder at Chignecto four years back. And he's got the governors of New England at his elbow urging him to stamp out French influence in Nova Scotia once and for all."

"Well, Roger?"

"It's whispered in the officers' mess at Fort Anne—and at Fort Edward, Fort Vieux Logis, Fort Lawrence—that after Beauséjour falls the Acadians will be removed from Fundy, lock, stock, and barrel. That'll take ships, Mary. Ships!"

"Where will they take them?" she asked in a hushed voice.

"Who knows? Not to Canada, certainly. Lawrence wouldn't hand over such a fine lot of *coureurs de bois* to swell the forces of France."

"What do they think . . . in the messes?"

"Some say France, but that's absurd on the face of it. Some say England; but I've a notion Whitehall won't want anything to do with it. No . . . somewhere this side the ocean . . . some of the southern colonies . . . or Louisiana. A good long voyage at any rate . . . and I hope to get a good rate."

"And a long speculation, it seems to me," she objected. "I don't think my husband will lend you a shilling on it."

"That means you know he won't!" The Sudden chin came up. "Very well, Mary, I'll borrow the money elsewhere. There must be someone in Halifax——"

"Please! Not so hasty!" she returned quickly, with a pink spot in each cheek. "I merely said it wasn't the sort of business we—my husband's principal—had in mind when he offered you a partnership. It's like—it's like chartering in the slave trade. I mean the money's tainted. And——"

"Pish! All money's tainted. But it's mighty useful stuff, and I intend to gather all I can. Now in this matter of ships, I propose to buy outright the *Fair Lady*. She's handy for smuggling, and Old Hux is just the man for it. And I'll charter two stout brigs—although something bigger might be better for the Fundy business. Some of the old transports are still on the coast. I happen to know the *Duke of Bedford* can be had for seventy-five pounds a month."

"As you wish," she said in a dull tone. "But it seems to me you'll arouse some unwelcome curiosity in Halifax. If I—if we finance these schemes of yours, how shall you account for your sudden wealth?"

He grinned. "Sudden's my name! And this is a country where no one can afford to be surprised at anything. In ten or fifteen years there'll be wealthy men in Halifax who yesterday hadn't a decent bit of leather underfoot."

He glanced whimsically at his own cheap clumps and so did she.

"My dear lady, I've told you only a few of my 'schemes' for making money. I'm as full of notions as a German clock."

She said tartly, "Don't you think of anything but money, Roger?"

He regarded her curiously for a moment. She tossed her head back as she said it, and the red-gold hair glowed in the firelight. The slender nose was up and the lips pressed very straight. In the lace-fringed yoke of her bodice the rounded white skin lifted and fell indignantly.

"What else is there?" he retorted, and bowed and left in eager search for Old Hux.

CHAPTER 30

Contracts

So MUCH TO DO, so little time! In an effort to be everywhere at once, Roger commenced the swift canoe journeys back and forth across the province, following routes known only to the Indians and him-self, which were to make him a legend in Halifax in the next two years.

The matter of ships was soon settled. He bought the *Fair Lady* outright and engaged the services of Job Huxley with her.

"Ecod, I never thought I'd come down to taking orders from a man out o' my own fo'c'sle," declared that ruffian cheerfully.

"There must be a first time to everything," Roger laughed. "I may yet make an honest woman of *Fair Lady,* who knows?"

"I'll chance that," Old Hux said, and winked.

Next came a year's charter of the *Duke of Bedford,* which cost him ninety pounds a month instead of the seventy-five pounds he had so confidently expected. But he did not hesitate. And he snapped up a roomy Salem brig, *Sea Horse,* at forty pounds. Not a day too soon. Things were astir in Boston. By the first week in May preparations were well advanced for the expedition.

Through shrewd and all-powerful Mr. Apthorpe at Boston (whose commission was a thumping twenty per cent) he succeeded in char-tering *Fair Lady*—after two quick and furtive trips to Louisbourg— at £200 a month, the *Duke of Bedford* at £300 and *Sea Horse* at £150.

"Not unreasonable Rates," wrote Apthorpe smugly, "considering the Dangers of Navigation in Fundy Bay at the foggy Time of Year, and the Risques attendant upon the carriage of Troops engaged in War."

Roger was at Fort Lawrence when the fleet arrived, and watched the army disembark. Most were Massachusetts men in coarse blue regimentals which they laid aside as soon as they got ashore, working in soiled leather breeches and a great variety of ragged shirts. The only regulars were a few companies of the 40th from Fort Anne in shabby red and buff, and Lawrence had sent up a battery of brass field guns from Halifax.

They made a busy and purposeful swarm on the low ridge in the marshes, and the French watched them carefully from the ramparts of Fort Beauséjour across the red stream of the Missaguash.

It was a temptation to stay and see the fighting. But pshaw! what was a skirmish in these woods and marshes to an affair like Culloden? What mattered was the presence of several thousand soldiers and camp followers, all working up a famous thirst in the hot weather. Some hopeful sutlers had come from Boston with the expedition, but Roger had the advantage of a truck house well established at Fort Lawrence in charge of the old ranger Corcoran.

He made sure that Corcoran was well supplied—and saw to it that additional supplies were carried free of charge up the bay in those handsomely chartered vessels. Then, with Tom Fuller at the bow paddle, he set off for Halifax by way of Minas Basin and the Shubenacadie, using a light canoe made for him by friendly Micmacs.

The old war trail was now familiar to the point of monotony, but their journey was enlivened by an odd little encounter at the almost deserted Micmac town. On the riverbank they met Gautier, armed with hatchet and gun and wearing nothing but a skin clout and a draggled eagle feather. His hairy body glistened with bear grease and his dark face was bizarre with red ocher stripes. Behind him stood a short dark man with piercing black eyes, dressed in homespun breeches and a grimy waistcoat that hung open and exposed a silver crucifix hung about his neck. He had buckskin leggings and beaded moccasins.

Their canoe lay on the red claybank with a pack basket and a pair of blue blankets.

"You leave?" Roger said.

"For Beauséjour," Gautier answered. Roger wondered if they smelled what was afoot there. If not, why Gautier's war paint?

"Beau Soleil," Gautier announced in his strong Acadien accent, "this is Père Le Loutre." He said it a little too loudly, as if it were the priest he wished to warn.

Roger started. The Otter! So! He had pictured the missionary as a tall, gaunt creature roaming the forest in a cassock. The man before him might have been any Acadian farmer from the bay settlements. Except in the eyes—the priest's monomania glittered there.

"Beau Soleil!" Le Loutre repeated, looking him up and down. "So you have stolen the name of Peyal as well as his woman!"

It was clear that Koap had managed to conceal from the priest his acquisition of Wapke, fearful of sin, that mysterious thing for which the Micmacs had no word.

Roger checked the retort on his lips and muttered in a surly voice, "The woman took me, a captive, and gave me the dead man's name in the custom of her people."

"Did she give you the pagan thing you wear at your throat?"

Roger's fingers went instinctively to the little stone fish. "That I found."

"*Scélérat!*" the priest cried. "You come to live in sin among these people and corrupt them with your English goods! It is a part of the English plot!"

"My goods are mostly French, monsieur. And if I live in sin, what of my good friend Gautier there, whom you approve? Come, monsieur! Let us be consistent! I am no English plotter—but if I were, is that worse than to come among these poor savages as a missionary of Christ and preach nothing but hatred and bloodshed?"

"Thieves! You have no right in Acadie, you English!"

"We are here by right of a treaty signed by France nearly half a century ago, and by which we have abided. You and your Acadians are here by tolerance under that same treaty—which you have broken again and again, as well as the laws of God whom you profess to serve."

"You dare say that?" the madman cried in a strangled voice.

"I dare say that and more, monsieur. It is time someone told you these truths. Your hands are stained with blood, and your soul—

you have no soul!—you have involved the Acadian people in your
crimes against God and man. Now there is a debt to be paid and the
Acadians will have to pay it—for you will save your miserable skin,
I do not doubt."

"What do you mean, infidel?"

Roger put his tongue between his teeth. It was a rich temptation
to tell the man of the storm about to burst. But Le Loutre confounded him. A fanatical smile convulsed the narrow features.

"You mean this English venture against Fort Beauséjour? Pfui!
One is aware of that! One has eyes, Monsieur Beau Soleil—and ears
in unexpected places! I have been gathering my savages and Acadiens, and we shall entrap the English as they try to cross the Missaguash. They shall never get in cannon range of the fort. The good
God fights for France, always for France!"

"*Le bon Dieu* may change his mind, monsieur."

"Infidel! The good God does not change his mind! But if he did—
bien, I have used every means in my power to remove the Acadiens
beyond the tyranny of the English. Those imbeciles who stay must
suffer the consequences of their own folly. I wash my hands of them."

The little black eyes blazed.

"Come, Father," murmured Gautier uneasily, seeing the twitch of
Tom Fuller's fingers on the tomahawk at his belt. "The tide goes out
of the river."

Abruptly the priest turned. They pushed off down-river without
another word and in a few moments had vanished around the bend.

"Phew! There's a rum cove!" Tom observed. "Who might he be?"

Roger looked at the deserted chapel, the broken door, the fallen
wooden cross.

"Lucifer," he said.

The agent-victualer of His Majesty's Navy at Halifax was a bony,
blue-jawed man with ferret eyes and a Semitic nose.

"My name is Sudden," Roger said.

"I've heard of it," Joshua Mauger returned sourly. One of the irons
he had in the provincial fire was a trucking trade with the Indians.

"You'll hear more from time to time," Roger assured him coolly.
"But here's a matter we can work on together. Britain's at war with

France, declared or not. So the North Atlantic fleet will rendezvous here this summer."

"What makes you think so?"

"Because that's what Halifax was built for. Now a fleet must have supplies—and that's what you're here for. I have in mind the matter of beef."

Mauger smiled thinly. "I suppose you've picked up some cattle somewhere, Mr. Sudden. But have you any notion how much Admiral Boscawen will require? I'm afraid this is a matter beyond your resources, my enterprising young friend. I have arrangements to obtain beef in New England."

"At Boston prices, which shave your profits rather thin! The admiral holds you to the Halifax market price, isn't that the truth?"

"Suppose it is," Mauger challenged.

"Admiral Boscawen will come from England provisioned for three months. That's usual, I believe. By September, when he leaves this coast, he must victual again. Now you may call me a gambler if you wish, Mr. Mauger, but I'm ready to risk a substantial specie deposit that in three months' time I can supply you beef enough to victual the whole fleet."

"At how much the pound?" demanded Mauger, Shylock in a tie-wig.

"Fourpence! That will give you a profit of tuppence—twice what you'd get on New England beef."

"Halifax currency?"

"Sterling!"

"You mean barreled beef, of course?"

"Of course not. I mean fresh beef dressed and ready for the barrel.'

Mauger stared. "It will take two or three hundred tons of dressed meat—at least a thousand cattle."

"I know."

"How do you propose to make delivery?"

"At the town slaughterhouse. You can bring your salt and barrels there."

"And where do you propose to get the cattle?"

"That's my affair, sir."

"Humph! You can't buy from the Acadians—they sell all their beef cattle to traders from Quebec and Louisbourg."

"Yes."

"You can't buy beef in Boston and deliver it in Halifax at four-pence the pound."

"True."

Mauger sucked in a long breath of annoyance. "You seem to be an energetic young man, and I've heard something of your success in the fur trade. But"—sharply—"you should stick to things you know, my friend. I can't afford to risk His Majesty's appointment on your mysterious supply."

"How large a deposit do you wish?"

"One thousand pounds sterling." Mauger smiled cynically as he said it.

"You shall have it in the morning. I shall require from you a sub-contract, signed and witnessed, acknowledging receipt of my deposit and warranting fourpence the pound, sterling, sixty days from de-livery."

The ferret's eyes examined Roger fully half a minute.

"You've made a bargain, Mr. Sudden."

John Foy had been drinking. Beads of boozy perspiration gleamed on his sallow brow. The pink coat, flung open, revealed a dribble of wine stains down his long white silk waistcoat. His stock was un-fastened, his wig awry. His pale blue eyes were deeply bloodshot, and the fleshy pouches beneath them had gathered in deep puckers that made him look ill as well as drunk.

"Look here," he said loudly, "you're overstepping our agreement. 'Twas no part of it that you should supply His Majesty's forces. I forbid it"—waggling a finger—"ab-so-lute-ly."

They were alone in the now-familiar parlor. Halifax sweltered in the mid-June heat. The night was still and airless, and through the open casements came the hot fetor of Hollis Street.

"Why?"

"That's no affair of yours, Sudden."

Roger fingered a silver bottle screw lying on the table.

"I'll tell you why, Captain Foy. You're a paid agent of France. You were sent here for the sole purpose of espionage in the very beginning. Banker! But it's ingenious, damme, all of it! There's Rodrigues, whose business touches half the world. His little *cabinet* at Louisbourg's a handy clearinghouse for information, isn't it? The spider in the web! Why, I even know some of the threads! Quite apart from you and Mary there's charming Madame Ducudrai of the Veritable Coucou, who so adroitly questions the foreign sailors; and there's her husband the dancing master—the chief French spy in New York; and there's that young fool Roger Sudden who thinks he's gathering information for commercial purposes. . . . God's blood, Foy, did you think I was that blind?"

"I think you're mad, sir!" Sweat was streaming down the drunkard's face now. The pale eyes bulged.

"Mad or not, I can add two twos. I've wondered about you ever since we left the Thames. And when you became my 'banker' your thirst for information intrigued me mightily. I suspected . . . but I didn't care, really. I don't care now. I owe nothing to King George."

"I know that," Foy said eagerly.

"What you don't seem to realize is that I owe King Louis nothing either. My loyalty belongs entirely to one Roger Sudden. And tomorrow morning Roger Sudden wants a thousand pounds in specie."

"You shall have it, Roger"—in a whisper. "All of it, I swear!"

"Mary——"

"For God's sake, say nothing of this to Mary!"

"Very well. We understand each other." Roger laughed without pleasure. "And now I've a bit of news you can pass on to your 'principal.' Beauséjour fell two days ago."

"Impossible!" Foy gasped. "The place has been invested a bare fortnight."

"A poor affair, truly," Roger said indifferently. "Monckton had to fight his way across the Missaguash, but after that the French simply shut 'emselves up in the fort. You can imagine the rest. Monckton set up mortars at his ease, a little way up the ridge. 'Twas like pitching coins into a hat at six paces . . . only Monckton used twelve- and sixteen-inch bombs. The fort was in poor condition, and when one of the bombs burst in a casemate and killed a few men the garrison lost their courage. They were sadly outnumbered, of course, and Louisbourg was too far for hope of relief."

"What of Le Loutre?"

"Stole out and away—disguised as a woman. Droll, wasn't it? For rumor says the bishop of Quebec unfrocked the man some time ago. Was he one of your 'principals'?"

"Roger, I swear we—I never sent that cunning devil a word. I've never condoned his mode of warfare. I'm an old soldier, damme!"

"But you've been very useful to the French at Louisbourg?"

Foy drew himself up with drunken dignity. "I've striven to serve His Christian Majesty King Louis, in whose service I have the honor to hold a commission—like many another honest Jacobite, sir. Not all of us are able to forget the past, like you."

"That's why none of you have any future," Roger said.

CHAPTER 31

Agent de Confiance

ON THE LAST DAY of July 1755, Halifax prickled with news of battle in the far Ohio woods, and the petty triumph of Beauséjour was washed away in a flood of gloom. "Braddock's defeat" was on every lip, always in a hushed voice, as if it bespoke the end of the world. A picked force of British regulars defeated, aye, slaughtered like sheep by a handful of naked savages and *coureurs de bois*. Good Gad, what next?

As if in answer, came tales of a great French armament on the sea, destined for Louisbourg, aye, for the final reckoning with Halifax. The town was in a ferment of alarm and speculation. What of the defenses? The palisade and its log forts were falling down. Governor Lawrence had built three or four small batteries of logs and earth along the water front, and of course there was the Eastern Battery, a simple picketed thing on the Dartmouth side; and the old battery on George's Island. All good enough against Indians or a venturesome privateer; but men who had seen the fortress of Louisbourg rolled their eyes and spat in despair.

These tales of disaster and doom soon reached the Acadians of Fundy Bay, and Roger's traders reported a new defiance in them. When Governor Lawrence summoned thirty deputies from them and demanded for the last time a general oath of allegiance to the British king, they refused him flatly and went home. Roger had been called to the meeting as an interpreter, and he returned to his lodging thoughtfully. All this chimed with a new arrogance among the Indians. The Otter was gone—had vanished utterly—but the policy he had preached so long now bore its fruit. The Micmacs were in slow but full migration toward the east end of the peninsula and Cape Breton, were concentrated for the first time in their history, a striking force at last.

The French at Louisbourg would not overlook so powerful a weapon in their hand. Nor could Governor Lawrence. And there were the English forts upcountry surrounded by hostile Acadien villages like stack poles in a hay meadow in September—doomed at the first spark in the grass. That tough old bachelor in the Halifax residency would have to do something decisive—and quickly.

With this cold logic Roger soothed his own anxiety. He had gambled simply on the instincts of Lawrence after the fall of Beauséjour cleared the way to a final reckoning with the Acadians. He had been certain of the Acadians' attitude. He had not foreseen such strokes of fortune as the Braddock affair, with its far-reaching effect on British military minds, or the French armaments, real or fancied, now said to be gathering at Louisbourg. Now all these men and things combined to make his gamble an absolute certainty.

And it was confirmed in August, when a smug letter from Apthorpe informed him that *Fair Lady, Duke of Bedford,* and *Sea Horse* were to take part in a mass deportation of the Acadians, beginning in September. "Poor devils, but I suppose one should not pity 'em. Some are for Louisiana, 'tis said, but the general plan is to scatter 'em in small groups up and down the seaboard from Massachusetts to Mexico, where they can't do harm."

Roger set out at once for Fort Edward at Piziquid and gathered there a band of select spirits, most of them former rangers. There followed a time of waiting. To pass part of the time—and pay a debt —he paddled a canoe down the broad red estuary to the home of one Muise, who had been of service to him in the fur trade. It was a typical Acadian farm: a small clearing at the edge of the upland, a few staked fields in the wild meadows, a miserable cabin of logs (overflowing with children, dogs, fowls, and lean pigs), a crazy barn, and one or two outhouses. The people were small and lean and sharp of feature, living in a sort of dour content with themselves and at odds with the rest of the world. The women were shapeless in homespun, none too clean, and the men wore a mixture of homespun and buckskin. They were satisfied to till a small part of the tide meadows, keeping great numbers of cattle and horses on the wild hay which abounded there, and in general too indolent to clear the rich soil of the upland except to get the winter's fuel. The young men hunted a good deal with the Indians; over a century and a half their casual amours with the squaws had produced a visible strain of French blood in the Micmac tribes.

Once settled down with an Acadian wife, they were virtuous enough and made fond husbands and indulgent fathers. Each year the process of nature brought a new mouth to feed in the household and a corresponding increase in the cattle in the meadows, a manifest arrangement of *le bon Dieu* which saved the menkind all unnecessary labor in the clearing of new farmland. Their wealth was on the hoof in the meadows, and since there was a constant demand for cattle in the garrisons of Louisbourg and Quebec, they demanded and got payment in coin, for which they had an insatiable greed. The governors of Quebec and Louisbourg grumbled continually over this disappearance of their specie, but their grumblings made no impression. The Acadians leaned toward Quebec out of sheer hatred and suspicion of the English, but their interest was solely in themselves. Pious and extremely ignorant—not one in a hundred could read or write—they depended utterly upon their priests for knowledge of the world. Hence the sway of Le Loutre, whom they feared but did not dare to hate.

They were hospitable in their own poor fashion, and apart from avarice their only vice was squabbling with each other over boundaries in the meadowland. Their long and close relations with the Indians had given them a half-savage outlook which astonished Roger at times; indeed they were primitives, hating the English as the Micmacs did, yet suspicious of the *Quebecois,* who haggled over the price of beef and talked uncomfortably of tithes and taxes, and friendly only to the savages who were, in fact, a part of them by blood as well as association.

With these things in his eye and mind, Roger talked to Martin Muise in the dusk of an August evening. The vast brood of children had gone to their pallets in the low upper story of the dwelling, and Madame (seven months gone and round as a rum puncheon) prepared the fire for the night, sweeping ashes over the coals with a dusty duck wing. He sat on a birchwood stool facing Martin over a greasy pine table. The kitchen was lit by a single candle of dull yellow tallow, and the Acadian had a ragged elbow on the board, stuffing trade tobacco into a short black clay. Roger's "pocket pistol" stood between them, a metal traveling flask of rum, and they drank and pushed it back and forth.

"My old one," said Roger in the patois as Madame wheezed off to bed, "you've been a good friend to me, and I give you a favor in return."

"And what is that?" demanded Martin, belching comfortably.

"A bit of advice—either go to Fort Edward within the next week, and take the oath of allegiance to King George, or remove your family and cattle across the Bay of Fundy to the French side. I have three vessels in the bay. The little snow will take you over if you decide quickly."

"But why?" Martin's eyes were quizzical. He glanced at the bottle.

"Suppose I told you that sometime soon, certainly within a month, all the Acadian people in the peninsula are to be taken from their farms and transported to the English colonies as far south as Georgia?"

"I should say that you were very drunk, my friend."

"I am sober—and I tell you now."

"But why?" said the Acadian again. His narrow face, all sharp lights and shadows in the candle glow, was suspicious but only vaguely alarmed.

Roger heaved his shoulders. "There is war between England and France."

"They are always at war, those!"—contemptuously.

"Ah, but this time it is for the possession of Canada, once and for all. You saw what happened at Beauséjour. The English intend to take Louisbourg in the same way, and then Quebec. But first they must clear their flank in Acadie. That is only good sense, you will admit."

"But what have we done, we Acadians? We are neutral in these eternal quarrels of the English and French."

Roger twisted his lips. "Oh, come, Martin! Let us be honest with each other. You people have harbored every French expedition against Annapolis for years. You sent provisions, guides, pilots to D'Anville at Chebucto in '47. And what have you to say of Beauséjour? There your Acadians fought openly against the English, in the woods and in the fort."

"Père Le Loutre forced us to do so"—sullenly.

"A poor excuse in English eyes. Besides, your young men have taken part in the Micmac raids on Halifax ever since the English came there. All those raids began on this side of the province. You must share responsibility with the Indians, for you are one with them."

"What proof is there?" demanded Muise cunningly.

"None in written law, perhaps. But the English in Acadie face great dangers, and the law of self-preservation comes first with them as with everyone. They have seen too many of their people murdered and scalped to have room for mercy now, and here you are, the source of the trouble. With you and your priests removed the savages would make peace. While you remain the bloodshed will go on."

Muise took a long pull at the bottle. "My friend, you are a clever man, but when you speak of removing the Acadian people you talk nonsense. There has been bloodshed, yes. Suppose I admit that I myself have gone on the warpath with the Indians, that I myself have taken scalps at Halifax and sold them to Le Loutre. Suppose I admit that others of our men have done the same. The Indians are our brothers, after all, and we must prove our brotherhood from time to time lest they turn their face against us. Suppose we admit also that we have fed and sheltered and guided the French troops from Quebec whenever they came against Annapolis. Suppose we admit everything." He swept his brown hand across the board violently and nearly upset the candle. "What can you do, you English? You dare not try to murder us. And where," he demanded triumphantly, "shall the English find ships enough to take our people away to these places of which we have never heard? Why, there are hundreds, thousands—yes, two, maybe three thousand of us!"

Roger clucked his tongue. There were nearly ten thousand of them. What folly to be wise! He persevered.

"There are ships enough in Boston alone to carry your people to the end of the world. And there is the will to do it."

"And our cattle and goods?"

"You will have to leave your cattle and goods, except such as you can carry on your backs."

"But that is infamous!"

"It is war."

"Bah! You talk like a soldier. That is what they all say, English and French alike, when they do something of which they are ashamed. *C'est la guerre! C'est la guerre!* How often I have heard that mumbled over the scalps of women and children! That is what Coulon's fellows said that night at Grand Pré when we showed them how to pull the Bastonnais out of the houses and butcher them in the snow. That is what the Bastonnais themselves said in the old days whenever they plundered Port Royal and the farms along the river."

"Why not take the oath? A matter of words."

"Our faith is in France."

"This country is English. You know that. Acadie has been English forty-five years."

"We do not recognize the English. We do not understand their language, and besides, they are heretics. *Le bon Dieu* himself does not recognize heretics."

"That is a matter of opinion. One thing I can assure you—*le bon Dieu* will not interfere when you and yours are transported to the south. There you will find yourselves in strange lands, dependent on the charity of heretics whether you recognize them or not. Go across the bay, you fool, while there is time!"

"My people have been here four generations. Not the devil himself could make us leave our lands. Why should we go for the English, who are only in league with him?"

Roger gave it up. He slept the night on the kitchen floor and returned in the morning to Fort Edward.

The long-awaited spectacle unfolded suddenly. Winslow's blue-coated New Englanders had been quartered about the basin of Minas, chiefly at Grand Pré, since mid-August, with a sprinkling of redcoats of the 40th—for the look of the thing, no doubt, like a splatter of official wax upon a document.

There were four chosen centers for the business, all on tidewater, where on various pretexts the Acadian men and boys were gathered at harvesttime. They vastly outnumbered the troops and were all active males accustomed to the use of weapons, consequently the officers in charge—Handfield at Annapolis, Winslow at Grand Pré, Murray at Fort Edward, Monckton at Chignecto—took the most elaborate precautions before breaking the news of the expulsion. Monckton retained the larger part of the troops, of course—he made sure of that; a domineering man full of his own importance. Handfield, the stolid regular, had his shrunken garrison at Fort Anne, and Murray a handful of regulars at Piziquid. Winslow, with his scant three hundred New Englanders, had the task of seizing all the inhabitants between Minas Basin and Annapolis.

Roger's dealings in supply and transport had brought him into intimate contact with these officers. He detested Monckton for his bullying way with colonials and despised Handfield for his weak soul, but he had found a congenial spirit in the lighthearted and courageous Murray and had a hearty respect for Winslow, the fat, warmhearted man from Massachusetts on whom the greatest burden fell. Winslow hated the whole business, considering it unsoldierly, but he carried it out with vigor and skill and maintained in his force a Puritan discipline that put Monckton's regulars to shame. He carried his discipline so far as to forbid card playing in his camp, and quoits because the game tore up the Acadians' grass; and Roger saw a man strung up and flogged for stealing fowls.

"Why so tender?" he asked whimsically.

Winslow's round red face was sweating under the hot wig. He

rested his double chin on the breast of his fine coat and uttered gloomily, "I know, I know! If the shoe were on the other foot they'd shoot us down like dogs—or rather get the Indians to do it. Still, I can't find it in my heart to hate 'em as my men do. I raised my regiment for war, not for this. These peasants are a stupid and stubborn lot—don't believe we mean business—think it's all a scare to frighten 'em into taking the oath. Suppose they refuse to go when the time comes? My God, Sudden, have I got to kill 'em? My men would, quick enough. I tell you, this business haunts me. I wish to God they were aboard the transports and the whole thing over."

Roger was watching when Winslow read the order to the men of Grand Pré in their church overlooking the meadows. The Acadians heard it stolidly, though some looked worried. Though the words were in French, they obviously believed the whole thing just another trick of the unbelievable English, and when the ships failed to arrive they were sure of it. They showed their hatred and distrust in all things, even refusing to eat the English rations, demanding that their women bring them food from the farms.

But at last the ships came, and the moment. It was tense. Winslow was obliged to show his bayonets to get them moving down the road toward the landing place. Then at last the stolid faces broke into prayers and tears, and the women, who until that moment had seemed utterly indifferent, rent the autumn air with lamentations.

With the men safely aboard the transports, the women and children were taken off, a pitiful procession, and behind them the troops put torch to house and church and barn. The long valley lay under a haze of smoke in the warm September weather, and other smokes arose from Piziquid, Cobequid, Chignecto, from the farms along the Acadian isthmus and beside the Petitcodiac.

It was astounding now that it was done—this thing which Roger had so long foreseen and on which he had gambled so heavily. The affair had an uncanny quality. He felt as a prophet might, seeing the destruction of a world he had foretold. There was a temptation to linger and gaze upon the tragedy in all its aspects. What would posterity say of all this? Poets and romancers would have a theme for the next five hundred years. He wondered how many would make an honest search into its causes and stab their pens where the guilt lay most. But there was work to be done! Posterity was a long way off, and the poets be damned!

He set his men to gather the abandoned cattle, first at Grand Pré and gradually westward along the valley. The hungry beasts had found their way into the garden patches through the broken fences and into the fat green aftergrass of the hayfields. Roger sent them down the winding road to Halifax in herds of fifty, each in charge of a pair of his rangers jolting merrily along on the backs of scrawny Acadian ponies.

Now and then a provincial officer, brave in blue and scarlet, questioned his right to these spoils. He waved his contract with the agent-victualer under their noses, saying the cattle were for His Majesty's fleet and who the deuce were they to question it? The officers shrugged and said no more. They were not in love with their task. But the rank and file had their hearts in it. The long hatred of the English colonists for the French was flaming here, fanned by old memories of the frontier wars. The rangers and the Massachusetts troops had charge of the whole expulsion, except in the vicinity of Annapolis, where Handfield's 40th Foot, many of them married to Acadian women during the regiment's long station at Fort Anne, performed that awkward task themselves.

The situation there was touchy, and Roger did not venture to assert his peculiar rights. The halfhearted expulsion of the Acadians from Annapolis was to him the most curious part of a strange affair; for Fort Anne was really governed by the old matriarch Marie Magdalen Maisonat, a Frenchwoman and a devout Catholic whose daughters had married officers of the garrison, some of them in high rank now. The close-knit relationship of all the Acadians within the *banlieue* must have made it very difficult for Handfield to select his sheep from his goats.

For other reasons Roger kept his men away from Beauséjour (now officially "Fort Cumberland") and its marshlands. One reason was Colonel Monckton, that stiffly pipe-clayed regular, with his contempt for all colonials. Monckton had made a point of insulting the Massachusetts officers and men; what would he not say to a cattle-hunting civilian? Another potent reason was the swarm of Acadians and Indians led by skillful young Boishebert, who were making things very hot indeed for Monckton's destroying columns about the head of Fundy Bay.

"We're not here to fight," said Roger to his men.

But there was fighting for all that along the Annapolis valley and about the shores of Minas Basin, where parties of young Acadians had taken to the woods with musket and tomahawk. His herdsmen had several brushes with them in remote pastures and once or twice managed to take scalps, which they showed to Roger in high glee. He was surprised to find himself a little sick.

Perhaps it was the melancholy atmosphere of the Fundy settlements, especially in the Cornwallis valley. Under the blaze of September sunshine the countryside was at its loveliest: the long green hills and the flat floor of the valley, checkered with squares of ripe wheat and rye, with orchards marching in orderly ranks along the slopes, the apples red and gold among the leaves, with the broad and carefully diked marshes where hundreds of ownerless cattle now munched hock-deep in uncut hay. The smoking ashes of homes and barns were like the hoofprints of Satan in some earthly paradise.

And he could not dismiss from his mind the hopeless faces of the Acadians, trudging the dusty road down to the boats between the bright bayonets of their guards. The sound of those shuffling sabots and moccasins seemed to hang in the air long after the red dust had subsided and the ships were gone. A man could let himself get dangerously sentimental in such a scene.

He hardened his soul at Grand Pré, the saddest and most lovely scene of all, by walking past the black shell of the village to the slopes where Noble's men slept their last sleep in shallow graves under the apple trees.

It was easy there to call up the winter's night of '47 when Coulon's war party, guided from billet to billet by the Acadians themselves, had dragged the New Englanders from their beds and tomahawked them, bayoneted them, shot them down in their shirts. Dead men *did* tell tales.

And now the harsh sequel was being written. He shrugged and went his way.

John Foy stared at the neat figures on the sheet before him. They made an impressive little sum:

	£	s	d
1024 horned cattle, dressed wt. 223 tons @ 4d per lb.	8325	6	8
1018 hides (6 spoiled) @ 5/-	254	10	0
Gross	8579	16	8

Less:

	£	s	d		£	s	d
30 herdsmen 30 days @ 2/- per diem	90	0	0				
Rum & provisions for herdsmen	22	10	0				
Tavern bills do.	16	4	3				
Butchers, etc. Halifax ...	51	4	0				
Fees, surveyor of hides, @ 3d per hide	12	14	6				
Sundry other matters	10	2	8		202	15	5
				Net profit	8377	1	3

"It's—it's incredible!" he muttered.

"It's a fact, nevertheless," Roger snapped. "And a very good beginning, you'll agree."

"And an end, man, an end," returned Foy irritably. "You've supplied the fleet with three months' beef, enough to give Boscawen a final cruise in these waters and to take him home to England. What then?"

"He'll be back in the spring, Captain Foy—and the next spring—and the next. This is going to be a long war, a fight to the finish this time, make no mistake. Halifax and Louisbourg, each with a powerful nation behind it, and an empire for the prize! Who takes Louisbourg can take Quebec and all Canada with it. You told me that yourself, long ago. On the other hand, if the French can take Halifax, they'll have Boston under their gun muzzles—and York a step away

And here we are in the midst of it! Exactly placed to profit by it!
Quite apart from the fleet, sir, you seem to forget His Majesty's
forces in Nova Scotia. They eat beef too—seven pounds per week per
man. Now why must it come from Boston? Eh? Why should Messrs.
Apthorpe and Hancock reap all the profit? They've had a monopoly
of provisions ever since Halifax was founded because there was no
other supply this side the water. But now, by Jove, there are fifty or
sixty thousand cattle running loose about the ruined Acadian farms,
and Lord knows how many sheep and hogs. I'm gathering 'em in
large pounds near the better shipping places—Grand Pré, Piziquid,
Cobequid, and so on. There's plenty of fodder, and I'll put up sheds
to shelter 'em through the winter. Next summer——"

"Next summer you'll have competitors," suggested Foy dryly.

"No doubt. I've had a little trouble with the Germans from Lunenburg, coming across country to forage on their own. I've complained
to Mauger about that, and he's putting a stop to it. And doubtless
there will be a few New Englanders coming up the bay next year to
pick up what they can. They're welcome to what I leave."

"Who's to protect your cattle?"

"My man Tom Fuller and his lads—a brisk little company, Captain
Foy. I've picked up good men wherever I could find 'em. A rough lot,
but they suit me. D'you know what they call us in the messrooms at
Fort Anne and the other posts along the bay? 'Sudden's Wolves'!"

He laughed, leaning back in his chair, and Foy looked at him
sourly.

"Are you really so proud of these activities, Sudden?"

Roger let his chair come down with a thump. With all the black
Sudden temper he jerked out, "Why not? Have you any notion how
contemptible you seem to me?"

"Roger!" Mary's voice, indignant in the doorway. She swept into
the chamber with a swish of quilted silk. "What do you mean?"

Foy's eyes rolled toward the ceiling. Roger hesitated, but only for a
moment. Thought and tongue moved together adroitly and acidly.

"It's all of you," he dissembled. "You comfortable townspeople!
The clothes you wear, the food you eat, the fuel you burn—all
brought to you by men like me, who must risk their lives in some
fashion to get it here. Why, your hoity-toity ladies and gentlemen

daren't venture outside the palisade even now—except for the afternoon promenade towards Point Pleasant. Under guard of a company of redcoats and paced by fife and drum! What a spectacle! It's the jest of every barrack in the province!"

"What touched off this explosion?" she asked suspiciously, and her glance fell on the sheet of figures. Foy's mouth sagged as she picked it up. There was a painful silence. Slowly she said, "So this is what it meant—all those cattle pattering through the streets and everyone saying they belonged to that remarkable young Mr. Sudden. I thought it a joke. Now I see!" Her indignation flared. "You've been supplying Boscawen's fleet, Roger—using our funds—funds that belong to France!"

"Mary!" Foy cried piteously.

She ignored him. She was superbly angry. Her eyes blazed green fire at the adventurer. "I don't care—why shouldn't he know? You see, Roger—you who think of nothing but money, money, money!— we hoity-toity Foys live in the shadow of the gallows, year in, year out, for nothing but our faith in France and the cause of our rightful king!"

The obvious retort curled on his lips, but he checked it there. Instead he said soberly, "Has it occurred to you, Mary, that your faith in France may mean the death of many men whose faith is in King George?"

"Och!" she cried. "King George and his men were sib enough with death in the Highlands. Have you forgotten the road from Culloden so soon?"

"My feet are on a new road now," he answered gravely. "Why should I wring my neck with looking back?"

She put up that shapely chin of hers with a jerk that set the chestnut curls dancing. "Oh, you—you Englishman!"

He could not help smiling a little, she sounded so very feminine and Scotch.

She whirled about and marched, chin up, to the door—and turned for the last word. She addressed herself to Foy.

"You must dissolve—I think that's the word—dissolve this business with Mr. Sudden at once. He will refund the money we've advanced —it isn't much, in the light of his new prosperity."

"But, Mary!" Foy put out an imploring hand.

"Yes!" She stamped a silk-slippered foot imperiously. Her eyes glittered with angry tears. Roger gazed at her with admiration in his own, and she saw it and flounced and was gone. The door slammed like a cannon.

Foy looked unhappy—more, the man was in a fright. He kept his bloodshot gaze on Roger's face and ran his tongue tip back and forth across the doleful mouth. Roger stepped to the sideboard and poured half a tumbler of brandy from the decanter. The spy drank it in a long gulp, and the ripe Nantz made him splutter. He daubed at his lips and streaming eyes with a yellow handkerchief and took off his wig and mopped a head as bald and shining as an egg.

"My God!" he wheezed. "I'll have to do as she says."

"Don't take it so much to heart, man! Better to lose a client than a wife. Besides, I never liked the feel of your money, Foy. Tomorrow you shall have it to a penny. But if you think to sever all relations between me and Rodrigues *et fils,* there I say no. Rodrigues is much too useful to me."

"But M. Rodrigues——"

"Has a sound commercial instinct, like my own. What are these squabbles of states and kings to the march of commerce through the world? For men like Rodrigues and me, wars are merely opportunities. You have regular means of communication with Louisbourg. I have not. So I'm afraid you must continue to act as go-between, whether it benefits His Most Christian Majesty or not."

"I see." Foy licked his lips again. "Brandy . . . the decanter, if you please. My thanks. Your health, sir!" He tossed off another stout dram and drew a tortoise-shell snuffbox from his waistcoat, applying a pinch to each nostril with shaking fingers. "Ha! Tcha! Hum! There are certain—tcha!—things I must tell you, Sudden . . . for Mary's own sake, you understand? For myself I care nothing. I am old and disillusioned. She is young, romantic, infatuated with a shadow. She dragged me across the sea in pursuit of it. Give ear now . . . Mary's the daughter of a Highland family impoverished by the '15—long before she was born. She grew up in an air of blind loyalty to the Stuarts. When she was fifteen the Chevalier came to the Highlands, and you know what it was like. Prince Charlie in his person embodied the Stuart cause for all of us. He was young and gallant, at home on the ballroom floor or in the field, a prince out of a fairy tale. Women went daft about him, old and young. Mary was no exception, though she never saw him but twice—once at her father's house in the winter of '45, and after Culloden, for a moment only—he was flying for his life. She saw the wreck of the Highland army, her only brother in flight, her father's gardener dragged from his bothie and shot because he had a claymore on the wall."

Foy paused for breath. The brandy had loosened his tongue, and the words fell from it in a spate.

"All that, you understand, made a desperate impression on a spirited girl in her teens. Her brother James—ten years older than Mary and a very canny man—fled into England where he'd not be looked for. There he lay holed like a fox. To provide his escape Mary journeyed to London and thence to Holland in the train of Lady Jean Douglas, with James in the guise of a manservant. They came to Paris, where I'd spent my life in exile since the '15. They . . . we were all part of that hopeful Scottish colony which lingered in Paris on the charity of King Louis. Then came that miserable treaty of Aix-la-Chappelle, where France agreed to expel the Chevalier in return for the fortress of Louisbourg—a pretty bargain. That was the end for Prince Charlie and all of us. The charity stopped like that!" He attempted a snap of his snuffy fingers and failed. "The Scottish officers were offered commissions in the army of France, that was all. Most of them accepted, were sent to remote garrisons, vanished. James dallied in Paris . . . the wine, the pretty little ladies, all that. . . . When he was down to his and Mary's last sou he entered the Compagnies de la Marine and was ordered on foreign service, to Louisbourg—the end of the world. Mary was afire to go too. She was devoted to him, the douce elder brother, the bonnie companion and protector of her childhood, the gallant young soldier of the Chevalier . . . Well, you see what I mean. She fair worships that scamp Jamie to this day. But he was bitter then; he was moody and aloof; he flung off to Rochelle and a ship for Cape Breton without so much as a 'God be wi' ye!' The puir lassie was heartbroken and alone. So she turned to me."

"I see!"

Foy mopped his brow again. His eyes avoided Roger's hard gaze. "I had no money, no influence. In any case, I didn't want to leave Paris, where I'd lived in a shabby comfort all those years. I was too old for military service in the colonies. But Mary kept at me to cross the sea, to be near that scapegrace Jamie if not with him. And she wrote him letters—letters, without a scratch of pen in return. Then one day in the spring of '49 there came a note from Jamie suggesting a post in the confidential service of France for Mary and me. I wanted no part in it. But Mary gave me no rest. Finally she went herself to Rouille, the Minister of Marine, and he offered me—us—because of our 'special qualifications'—this post we have. I was to go to London with Mary and join the expedition for Nova Scotia which the English government was advertising so boldly in the *Gazette*. We would become citizens of the new English fortress and I was to report to Louisbourg everything that passed. In two or three years at most, Rouille suggested, France would be triumphant in America and we could remove to Louisbourg or anywhere we pleased, with a rich reward. He was delicate. He didn't use that word 'spy' which comes off your lips so readily, my friend. *Agent de confiance*—that is what I am."

"One moment," Roger said. "Why tell me all this?"

"Because I want you to understand."

"You mean you're afraid!"

"For Mary, yes."

Roger made a mouth. Well, he had deserved it.

"Rest easy, then," he said stiffly. "I've always felt that Judas was a fool—selling his happiness for the price of a hang rope."

"I'm afraid I don't understand . . ."

"I don't understand myself, Captain Foy. I've never cared more than a snap of my fingers for women. I care less, now. And yet—I covet your wife."

A rush of blood darkened Foy's sallow cheek, and the old sword cut stood out livid as lightning against a stormy sky. In his wide, pale eyes Roger watched a flicker of emotions: doubt, suspicion, a puzzled alarm, a flare of anger, finally a glitter of malicious amusement. His lips writhed and then parted in a long cackle of laughter, and there he sat, head thrown back, wig on the floor, clothing disordered and splattered with brandy, a picture of Bacchus grown old and thin and daft.

Roger left him abruptly. As he stepped out of the chamber there was a froufrou in the dark hall. He called "Jenny!" but there was no answer. He groped for his hat and let himself out into the street.

CHAPTER 32

Contredanse

"DIRTY CARGO," Old Hux growled, and took the stubby black clay from his bearded lips to spit in the cold fireplace. "Besides, 'tain't like French rum and suchlike that ye can land on old Mauger's beach at the harbor mouth and run up to town in small boats."

"I propose to bring the ship to my wharf."

Huxley stared. "With coals from Cape Breton? You *are* a bold un."

"Not at all. I shall enter the coal as produce of this province."

"Pooh! His Majesty's customs officers ain't so blind as all that. The on'y coal in this part o' the world is up at Lingan in French territory."

"Wrong, Job, my friend. There's coal up the Bay of Fundy, sixteen miles this side of Fort Cumberland. I've seen it."

"On tidewater?"

"Yes. A place called Joggin. The garrisons of Fort Anne and Cumberland get all their winter coals there. They send up working parties, dig the stuff out of shallow pits, and load it into sloops and brigs —just as the French do at L'Indienne."

"Then why not get your coals from Joggin, honest-like?"

"You know why. L'Indienne's only half the distance, and no lying on your beam ends at low tide as you must in the bay. Besides, the French coal's better."

"Umph! Who's to dig your coals at Lingan—me?" Old Hux cocked a black and ironic eyebrow.

"Rodrigues will arrange that. For a few sous a day those poverty-stricken French *pecheurs* would dig coals in hell itself. The place is just around the headland from Glace Bay—you'll see the old blockhouse the English troops built to guard their working parties there in '46. A watch is kept in the blockhouse, and when wind and sea are right for loading they hoist a pennant on the staff. You go in, take your hatches off, and the shore gang does the rest."

"S'pose I run afoul of a French man-o'-war?"

"That's a risk you must take anywhere in these times."

Huxley pulled at his beard. "Why not send the *Sea Horse* or that new brig ye bought this year, the *Venture?* Why me?"

"I'm sending all of you. I want at least two thousand chaldrons here before cold weather."

" 'Od's heart! That's a lot o' coals!"

"With all Halifax for market? The townsfolk have cut all the firewood that's easy to get at. They're bringing it now in vessels from as far as Lunenburg. Last winter the price was twelve to twenty shillings the cord; this year it'll be twenty or thirty. Now a chaldron of good L'Indienne coal should give twice the heat in a cord of wood—and takes far less storage room. I'll sell my coals at forty shillings the chaldron, and they'll scramble to buy it."

"Zounds!" cried Old Hux. "Ye make the damned stuff sound like money itself."

"It's as good as gold in this climate, Job. I expect a profit of three thousand sterling at the very least, each winter."

Job Huxley sat back in the chair and admired his employer.

"Ecod," he chuckled, "it's true what they say about ye, Roger—everything ye touch turns to money. Is it true ye've made fifty thousand quid just off beef to His Majesty?"

"In that and other ways—but go on!"

"Well, there's your big warehouse chock-full o' goods, and your new wharf, and your truck houses all over the province, your fur trade, your ships, your distillery, all out o' nothing in three years or so . . . What's your secret?"

Roger fingered his wineglass and smiled into the burgundy.

"Would you really like to know?"

" 'Od's blood, all Halifax 'ud like to know!"

Roger unfastened his stock and parted the ruffles of his cambric shirt.

Old Hux stared at the little stone fish. "That? In God's name, what is it?"

"A trinket I picked up in the woods. Its name is Good Fortune."

"And ye believe that?" Old Hux favored him with an incredulous leer.

"I only know that Fortune has smiled on me from the moment I hung it about my neck."

"Smiled!" said the ruffian coarsely. "She got into bed with ye, man! When do I sail for Lingan?"

"I'll have your stores aboard tomorrow morning. As soon after that as the wind serves."

"Umph! That means a fair wind as soon as the hatches are battened if that heathen thing's half as good as ye say."

"A good voyage, then."

"And a safe return," intoned Old Hux piously.

Swaying through the town in a sedan chair in the early October dusk, Roger felt an agreeable complacency. Huxley's ribald compliment still tickled his ear. In three years his persistent wooing of the Golden Woman had yielded him in cash and property something like seventy thousand pounds. Indeed the flood of money had presented him with a pretty problem in investment.

Halifax had no real trade yet, no opportunity for the employment of large funds. A city founded by decree and kept alive and vigorous by subsidies, by the rich bounty of King George. Contractors like Roger were able to batten on His Majesty with absurdly little capital, and their profits had to be sent abroad for interest. Thus Joshua Mauger had long been laying up treasure in England.

For Roger, England seemed too far away and much too perilous. He wanted his money under his keen nose. A year ago he had begun sending large sums to Rodrigues for investment in the shrewd Basque's vast and profitable enterprises. He was pleased to find a quick and sure return on all he cared to invest. The bulk of his fortune now was in Louisbourg safe and sound. It pleased him to reflect that he had by proxy a considerable finger in the trade of the world.

All these matters with Rodrigues had been arranged through the reluctant Foy. Sometimes Mary was present at the furtive conferences; usually she withdrew after a polite exchange of compliments. For a long time after that memorable dissolving of their partnership

her attitude to Roger was cold and disapproving—when she noticed
him at all. Yet there came times when Roger felt her gaze on him as
he talked to Foy, and it was oddly like March sunshine striking
through a frosty pane when all outside was ice and snow. She was interested in what he had to say, in spite of herself. And once or twice
he saw in her eyes a desolation and a longing that astonished him.

Of course, he reflected, Foy was a poor sort of fish to be mated to
such an ardent creature. Was it possible that now and again the Jacobite frenzy which possessed her had to give way to something merely
womanly? Ten years ago he would have been sure of it; but he was
sure of everything then, especially women. Now he inclined to judge
Mary by himself, who had shed all fleshly inclinations in his one great
purpose. His indifference to women was so complete that at times he
was disturbed by a fear of atrophy, even by a sense of loss, as no
doubt eunuchs felt, indifferent in the presence of the harem. Mary
Foy was so completely self-contained that he saw in her a feminine
replica of himself, and, Narcissus-like, admired the image—and
wondered.

Abroad, of course, he did not recognize the Foys by so much as a
nod, keeping the rule laid down by Rodrigues in the beginning. Not
that he saw much of Foy in the town; but Mary was everywhere, in
winter dancing at the frequent assemblies or flitting about the streets
in a smart sleigh turnout piled with furs; in summer riding, driving,
sailing on the harbor, always in company with officers of the garrison
and fleet. Sometimes he felt a pang, not of jealousy so much as resentment, that Foy should let her expose herself to gossip and worse
for his own ends. But he knew that here, too, she kept the fortress of
herself.

At bachelor affairs, when tongues wagged over the wine, her name
was invariably mentioned with lickerish sentiments by the gay young
dogs, but no one, even the drunkest, ventured to boast success in his
pursuit. She was a teaser, some said, and that was the only uncompli-
mentary thing said of her.

Poets were busy, and bits of verse went the rounds of the messrooms indited to "Chloe" or "Phoebe" or "Amaryllis," describing the
eyes, the hair, the other charms that were unmistakably Mary Foy's,
and breathing sticky sentiments that went very ill with the lusty de-

sires of His Majesty's young gentlemen. Some had put their inclinations to the test, with rueful results. She was made of ice, they said. But a merry captain of the 45th declared that chilled wine gave the best glow in the drinking, and there was no noticeable slackening in the chase. There was some stout betting on the leading contenders.

What the Halifax ladies thought of all this Roger could only guess. No doubt they admired Mrs. Foy's skill in walking the tightrope over such continuous perils (for wasn't this the feat that every woman longs to perform and so few achieve?) while watching cat-eyed for her fall. It would have been interesting to hear the comments that passed behind fans and bed curtains. It seemed to Roger that all Halifax waited like a crowd in an arena to acclaim the victor and turn a thumb upon the victim.

He could not resist saying to her one night in the summer of '57, when Foy had gone for the wine and was long about it, "Isn't it rather dangerous—all this?"

She was dressed for a rout somewhere in the town and sat drumming her finger tips on a chair arm, awaiting Major Boutlow's chaise, which was to take her there. She gave him a green look, sitting straight in the chair, and then, animatedly, "After all, a spy, Roger . . . have you forgotten? You told me once that fortune's for those who don't mind risks. Well, this is the fortune of war. I've had to learn my trade. I was stupid at first. I thought a spy must be unnoticed, but after the first few years I came to know that to see one must be seen, and to hear one must learn to prattle the right thing in the right ear at the right time. After that my course was easy and"—with a note of challenge, a quick toss of the chestnut head—"I enjoy it! Danger's charming, isn't it, Roger? What a bore this life would be without it! Is anything worse in this world than waiting for a battle that never comes?"

"Suppose you're caught?" he said.

Her eyes lit. "Do you think I'm afraid? When I think of my kinsmen who were hanged ∴ . ."

"It's not your neck I'm thinking about."

She paused, flushing. Her eyes were annoyed and then amused. "Are you concerned about my virtue, Roger? That's nice of you. I thought poor John was the only one who fretted on that score." She opened her fan, examined the painted silk for a moment, and shut it with a click. "Well, there's spice in that sort of danger too, Roger. Not to say exercise to the wits. The young blades I don't mind; they're pathetic in a way—like children pawing after sweets, and just as easy to deal with. The older ones are more dangerous, more sure of themselves and you, and so you hate 'em, and it's more fun making fools of 'em. This is the pleasure Atalanta knew—and mark this, Roger—I've no taste for golden apples."

"Atalanta! You mean you dangle yourself like a carrot before every ass in the garrison!"

She laughed. "You sound like an elderly uncle—or a husband. A carrot indeed! Are you referring to my figure or my hair?" And defiantly, "Well, a carrot, then. It's something to be a carrot, a slim and juicy and well-scrubbed carrot, and to know that you mustn't dangle too far out of reach lest the donkey lose his interest—and that one slip means being crunched and swallowed."

"And how do you feel inside? Do you scrub your conscience?"

Her brows went up. "What a thing to ask! Do you scrub yours, Roger?" Then, with an impatient flutter of her shoulders, "Ah, why do we talk like this? Playing tennis with words!"

Roger's tongue curled sourly on some quip about honesty between rogues. He was surprised to hear himself saying slowly, "Tennis—that's it. A net between us always. And somehow I hate the thing."

For a long moment his black gaze met the green—and the net was gone. Then the chaise came and she was off in a swirl of cloak and silk petticoats.

The woman Jenny, returning from the door, paused in the parlor entry with a look of anger in her dark and heavy face.

"You!" she accused. "Why don't you do something?"

"About what?"

She jerked her head toward the street and the retreating sound of carriage wheels.

"My good girl, what on earth could I do?"

Jenny was breathing hard. "Everything! I've got eyes—and ears. You're the only one of the lot she cares a fig for. And you . . . I never liked you . . . black eyes, black heart, I always say . . . but,

well, you'd be a lot better for her than those rakehell officers and
such."

The notion of himself as the lesser of evils made him grin wryly,
and Jenny snorted and tramped off down the hall as Foy appeared
with the decanters.

Now it was autumn again, and the hardwoods seemed to reflect
the gold that poured into the coffers of every Halifax merchant. The
war went ill with England, and the worried gentlemen at Whitehall
were spending treasure in a panic to repair the army and navy they
had neglected ever since '48.

In that strange fancy of Roger's the Golden Woman had developed
new and unexpected breasts, and more and more and more of them
swayed within his reach. There was the encounter with Sally Madigan last spring, for instance. She had stopped her carriage in Argyle
Street and beckoned him to her side.

"Things go well with you, Roger?"

"Yes, Sally," he said pleasantly, and bit off an instinct to return the
compliment.

Sally's lover, the major, was now on Governor Lawrence's staff and
a power in the land.

"Why don't ye go in for army and navy contracts?"

He pursed his lips. "They're pretty much in the hands of Mauger
and Saul and Butler. I've had a good share, of course."

"It's time ye had a better! I'll speak to O'Rourke."

"That's very good of you, Sally. But why trouble your pretty head
about me?"

Her blue eyes twinkled. "Well, you're the best-lookin' bachelor in
Halifax and one o' the richest—got every miss, japers! and half the
married women, pantin' for a soft word or a touch o' your hand. And
ye're not afraid to step up to my carriage in the broad o' day, in the
most fashionable street in the town, and stand with your hat doffed
as if I was the finest in the land . . ."

"Who says you're not?" laughing and putting a quick hand to his
hanger hilt.

"Ah, that's what I like about ye, Roger—ye don't care a tinker's
damn for anyone. It's a good thing I love my old Tim. But that's not

why I want to help ye with the contracts. D'ye remember that evenin'
on the hillside when ye gave me your last sixpence? That's it, Roger."

He had smiled and said, "That little rhyme you sang, 'Four-and-
twenty blackbirds!' "

She tipped her nose disdainfully and cast a blue glance along the
"most fashionable street."

"I still think it's a dainty dish to set before the king—seein' what
it's cost him so far. Mother of God! They've poured enough gold
down these filthy gutters to build a new Jerusalem. And this year—
keep a close tongue on it, Roger—there's an army comin' under Lord
Loudoun, regiments *and* regiments, and the good yellow guineas
flowin' like wather. Well, see that ye get your full share of it, darlin'—
and God bless ye!"

Within a week the commissaries had come to him, in a quaint mixture of bewilderment and respect, and offered him what must have
seemed to them the moon and stars. Roger accepted, with a noncha-
lance that left them gasping, and busied himself laying in great stocks
of war supplies from ship bread to gunpowder.

In the early summer Lord Loudoun had come to conquer Louisbourg with his army and Lord Holborn's fleet; a windy man, concealing his doubts and fears and ineptitude in a thundering pompos-
ity that deceived no one. Roger and the little coterie of contractors
waxed rich. For Loudoun's army had not budged from Halifax but
sprawled all summer in tents on the Citadel slopes and common and
upon the low ridge to the southwest which now went by the name
of Camp Hill, drinking too much rum and eating too little fresh provisions and sickening of scurvy, smallpox, and the bloody flux. Loudoun had set them planting cabbages against the scurvy, and toward
the season's end, alarmed by secret information of a great French
armada at Louisbourg, he had taken them off to New York again
without stopping even to gather their crop!

As Roger's chairmen turned the corner of Duke Street and dived
downhill toward the Great Pontack Inn, he could see the lantern
glimmers of Holborn's ships in the harbor. The sailor, bolder than
Loudoun, had cruised off Cape Breton well into September, only to be
caught in a hurricane on a lee shore. He had clawed off somehow and
brought his shattered ships to Halifax, and now was refitting feverishly

("and hang the expense, sir!") for a return to England. Next year they and Loudoun's army would come back again and there would be another fiasco for the amusement of the French and the enrichment of the Halifax contractors.

Roger's mind turned on the prospect. There was money in masting. This winter he must send a gang to cut masts up the Bay of Fundy somewhere—the pines grew very straight and tall in those parts. Bring 'em around the coast to Halifax in the spring. A stiff price and a certain market with a big fleet on this windy shore. And why not export as well? Good masts and spars were precious things in England nowadays. Write London and find out the prospects. Um!

And the matter of ship bread. Why not build a bakery and undertake the supply of biscuit when the fleet came on the coast? Something there! Indeed, why not supply the troops as well? Loudoun's thousands, not to say the garrisons of Halifax and the chain of forts up Fundy-way. Ecod!

Mauger wouldn't like it, of course, and Mr. Saul would look down his long nose and grumble about a gentlemen's agreement—they were importing ship bread stale from Boston and charging famous prices. But hang Mauger and hang Saul!

As for beef, Tom Fuller and his lads were finding plenty of Acadian cattle still. Having to fight for it sometimes—that French fellow, what was his name? . . . Boishebert? A damned nuisance. Clever, though. If Boishebert ever got his Quebecois bushfighters and the Indians and refugee Acadians rallied en masse, there'd be the deuce to pay in Nova Scotia!

In the meantime cattle were still coming down the Valley road. He was salting the beef himself now and selling it in cask for the full profit—he had got as high as three shillings the pound for salt provisions to Loudoun's troops. The look on Mauger's face! And Mauger's sour prediction: "Someday, young feller, you'll overreach yourself." Music!

And now here was the Great Pontack, the pride of Halifax, named for Pontack's famous club in London. The windows blazed with candles for the farewell rout for Holborn's officers—common tallow in the less important chambers and the Long Room glowing like a lantern with the best of spermaceti.

A powdered Negro in blue coat and white silk breeches took Roger's hat and cloak and sword cane, and he passed inside, into the glitter and hubbub of fashionable Halifax at play. Musicians on a dais at the far end. A candlelit transparency over their heads set forth an illumined ship and declared "A Happy Voyage and a Safe Return." At the other end another transparency: "Health to His Majesty." Festoons of bunting along the walls, and branches of maple leaves in autumn color. The tinkle of a pianoforte, the zoom of a bass viol, the plunk of fiddles tuning for the next quadrille. Holborn's officers in blue with touches of white, the naval uniform now, a whim of His Majesty's. Fat George had been greatly fetched by the Duchess of Bedford's riding habit and adopted its colors for his fleet—so ran the gossip. He had the German passion for uniformity—and pretty women. Well, who hadn't that? There was pretty stuff here, wives and daughters of the garrison officers and the leading merchants. Not their Sallies, though—he saw O'Rourke alone.

There was Governor Lawrence, the unbending bachelor, now bending very gallantly over pretty hands. A tall and powerful figure, a heavy face florid with the effort of the last dance, pleasant enough at the moment, but not the face of a man to be crossed lightly. The poor stupid Acadians had found that out. And there was Bulkeley, at forty still looking more the handsome dragoon than the plodding provincial secretary. He had just married young Amy Rous, and Roger moved across the floor to congratulate him, aware of many eyes and an acidulous female voice cutting the din with, "There goes that young Midas, Roger Sudden. Why don't he marry some nice gel and play the gentleman?"

Bulkeley acknowledged Roger's felicitations pleasantly and drew him aside.

"How is it, Sudden, that you always know where money's to be had?"

"What it is now?" parried Roger cautiously.

"His Majesty's dockyard. We've got a careening wharf and one or two buildings, but there's need of a sail loft, a masting pond, a hospital, and heaven knows what besides—all to be built next year. And what do we find when we search out the title of the land we want? That some was granted to Captain Gorham, that ranger man, and the rest to one Roger Sudden, as far back as '49! Are you in league with the devil? And how much d'ye want?"

"I'm afraid you'll have to extend the dockyard in the other direction, Captain. I don't want to sell. My distillery——"

"Oh come, Sudden! Your distillery's only a mask for the rum you smuggle in from Louisbourg. How dense d'ye think I am?"

Roger looked in the secretary's eyes. Something cool behind the smile. Bulkeley was incorruptible, the only incorruptible in Halifax barring Governor Lawrence himself.

"How much d'ye want for it?" Bulkeley repeated. "You and the devil!"

The musicians struck up "Country Garden," and the floor filled and swayed with uniforms and hooped gowns. Laughter. A running fire of quips and compliments. Warm essence of women. Powder. Patches. Slither of small silk shoes. Tap and scrape of leather. The candles fluttering. Lawrence towering in the midst of the swirl, lively as a subaltern in a red coat richly laced. Hands lifting and falling. Bows and curtseys. A popping of corks somewhere in the offing, and a smell of food—the buffet tables in the side room.

Zounds, what a change since '49! Forty-nine, and Gorham drawling, "The town'll spread that way . . . bide my time . . . trade, the fishery, His Majesty's naval station . . . " Eight years ago. Or was it eighty?

"Five thousand pounds," Roger said.

"You're joking, Sudden, of course. Be serious, man! These patched-up ships of Holborn's show the need of a proper dockyard if we're to wage a war against the French in these waters. And things have gone deuced badly everywhere . . ."

"Three thousand," Roger said.

"Surely you'll make it two?"

"Three," he insisted coldly.

"Very well!" A twist of anger on Bulkeley's tongue. "Your patriotism, sir . . ."

"Is exceeded only by my sense of money's worth, Captain Bulkeley."

They parted, too politely. I've made another enemy, Roger thought, and did not care. Those who sought the Golden Woman could waste no time with incorruptibles.

Mauger's beady ferret face peered at him from across the room, and yonder was long-fingered Thomas Saul, musing, no doubt, on the cost of the night's entertainment, and beside him John Butler, who had done so well in army contracts. And there were the lesser moneybags, not so long acquainted with the Golden Woman or with the right officials. Grant, Salter, Steele, Prescott, and the rest, thrusters all, some with wives and some without, held in contempt by the military gentlemen but sure of themselves and their fortunes. And the powerful men of the Council—Collier, Rous, Cottrell, Green, and dignified Jonathan Belcher, the chief justice. Wealth, power, and chivalry, with odds on the chivalry if red coats and blue meant anything.

Roger ran a dark glance over the women. They did not seem so charming now—was it the taste of money in his mouth? Lean old and fat old; horse-faced but sometimes handsome middle-aged; and vapid young faces and some clever ones. Bulkeley's bride easily the belle, nineteen, fair and fragile as a flower—consumption, probably. Small hoops the rage now and stuffs lighter, a good thing, too. But older women clung to heavy brocades and broad hoops, sailing ponderously behind the fashion, like three-deckers in the wake of brigs.

His roving glance found a patch of green in this desert and halted there. She, of course. No other woman could wear that color as if it belonged to her, and few would have dared those sharply narrowing hoops which shaped the silk like a pagoda roof, rising in a series of flounces from a wide and sweeping hem to beautiful hips which were her own. From the apex of that cone, like Aphrodite from the sea, she emerged in a close and downward-pointing stomacher that drew the indignant glances of the dowagers—or was it the laced bodice that fitted her long waist like a skin and made a green stem of it to support the white fruit, half seen, half hidden in a foam of Valenciennes? A gold clasp fastened a narrow band of black velvet about her throat; otherwise she wore no ornament. Her face was powdered lightly but not rouged, and she lacked the coquettish black patches of the fashion. There were prettier women in the room but none more shapely or more self-possessed, and she was surrounded by ardent young naval and military gentlemen wriggling like puppies about a dish.

Something she said in her light voice set them all in a gale of laughter that shook them apart a little, and Roger's gaze met hers. The Long Room of the Pontack was not very long and certainly not wide. And at this moment, in one of those silences that come upon a crowded company like a bolt from the gods, smiting all tongues at once, her voice was heard saying clearly:

"There's that mysterious man Sudden. Do bring him over, some-one. I want to see if he bites."

In the stillness, in that sea of stares, she made a *moue* and brought the closed fan up to her lips. One or two of her admirers moved to carry out her wish, but Roger was crossing the floor already. There was nothing else for it. He was furious. But as young Barry of the 45th stuttered an introduction he bowed over her hand with a chill politeness, and then the governor's voice cried in the silence, calling for another dance, and all the tongues began to clack again, the pianoforte tinkled, the fiddles wailed, the chamber frothed with petticoats and nimble legs. She dismissed the young men to their duties and after a moment, in the privacy of the very commotion about them, murmured in Roger's ear:

"I must talk to you. Away from here."

"Your house?" he asked doubtfully.

"No"—quickly. "John's well set on an evening's drinking; he may take home some of his friends. I'll come to your house."

"Is that discreet?" he asked.

She shrugged, smiling brilliantly for the benefit of passing eyes. "I confess I'm devoured with curiosity, Roger. One hears that you have a little mansion in the outskirts—on the track they call 'Pleasant Street,' isn't it?—attended by blackamoors and surrounded by high stone walls. In fact, one hears all sorts of tales. Some say you're a Bluebeard and some that you're a monk. Some call you Young Hunks the Miser and others swear you're lavish to the poor—especially the London emigrants."

"We can't leave the assembly together."

"Of course not! You'll disappear in the next few minutes—it's well known you only attend these affairs out of policy. And after the next dance I shall plead a megrim and have my chair called. If I go home by way of Pleasant Street, who's to know?"

"You're being very rash," he warned.

"With you?" she retorted impishly, and dismissed him with a flick of her fan.

CHAPTER 33

The Vestal and the Flame

ROGER HAD BULT THE HOUSE for a number of reasons, not least a desire to get away from the Trope lodging with its eternal reek of boiled codfish and the faint yet unmistakable air of squalor which the ape-faced Lumley woman had brought with her somehow from Tooley Street and imposed upon the "genteel furnishings" of her Halifax establishment. He required a place apart from his too-public count-inghouse where he could consult men of devious affairs, of smuggling affairs especially, and so the site had been dictated by the need—Pleasant Street on the ridge south of the town proper, and hard by the tumble-down palisade, where Old Hux and the others could slip in quietly from boat landings on the Point Pleasant shore. And it satisfied an instinct for a roof of his own, a retreat where he could keep some choice wines and brandies and gather a few books, with comfortable furniture and perhaps later on a horse or two and dogs.

Not that his old vision of a return, rich, to Suddenholt had lost a whit of its savor. After eight years that was stronger than ever. Like any Englishman abroad—like hundreds of them in this unlovely wooden town—the word "home" meant for him one thing alone, and four walls and a roof on the wrong side of the ocean could not take its place. But something in him demanded a payment on account.

Hence the "mansion," a modest thing in all truth, two stories and a garret of pine clapboards with a steep shingled roof. It was set well back from the highroad in a garden made of earth carted from the woods, the whole surrounded by a high wall of fieldstones topped with broken glass, and approached by a forbidding iron gate. His servants he bought of Mauger, who had dealt in black ivory in his West Indian days and still manned all his ships with Negroes. Tall and very ugly men and very black indeed, they spoke a jargon of

English, Martinique French, and pure African—and understood Roger very well. Their names, Quashie and Brass Pot. The loneliness of the house, the uncompromising wall, the huge blacks, the wild men in buckskins who called by day and the mysterious visitors who came by night, the enigmatic owner himself, all these had set the tongues of Halifax a-wagging.

He awaited Mary with a rather brittle patience in the chamber where he received all his visitors, a plain apartment paneled in hard maple and furnished with a Turkey carpet, a desk, a round table of black walnut, a small Dutch-footed sofa from Philadelphia, and three or four New England chairs.

A musket and a fowling piece lay over the mantel upon the horns of a caribou he had shot himself. The panels were decorated with hung pieces of Indian dyed quillwork, a pair of crossed snowshoes, a curiously carved powder horn taken in a brush with Boishebert's men, a shot pouch made of a human scalp with a design in red and blue beads. A rack of pipes hung by the fireplace with a bark box of tobacco beneath. A wooden corner bracket supported a painted plaster figure of St. Joseph from the ravished Acadian chapel at Grand Pré.

A fire of split birch flamed upon the hearth. The man Brass Pot had drawn the heavy velvet curtains and placed a two-branched candelabra on the table. Roger bade him fetch sweet biscuits, glasses, and a decanter of the best claret.

The big Negro wrinkled his brows for a moment; he was used to bringing rum and snuff for visitors. He departed and was about to enter the chamber with the unusual refreshments when the gate groaned on its hinges and a light, quick step came up the walk. Roger motioned him to put the tray down and depart. He went to the door himself.

Her tall figure was wrapped in a blue cloak with a hood thrown over her hair. She put the hood back as she entered his chamber and looked about her in frank curiosity. He found himself nodding in approval. Most women would have gone into the vapors at the mere notion of coming to this house of dark rumors.

"So this is where you live, Roger!" She went on with her inspection, seeking, he knew, some sign of other women.

"Do sit down," he murmured, putting forward his most comfortable chair.

She sank into it with that lithe grace of hers and laid the cloak aside, probing her chignon and its fall of curls with' her slim fingers in the charming gesture which women make so artlessly and so disturbingly. Her self-possession piqued him a little, but he glanced at her bosom and observed the fluttered rise and fall of her breasts, drawn taut in the thin silk bodice by her lifted arms.

"Well?" he said.

She turned her face to him, saying nothing for a minute, looking full into his eyes.

"Roger, would you think me very bold or very mad if I asked you to take me in your arms and kiss me?"

A flush crept up her throat and stained her face as she said it. Something within him, the old Roger of the continental days, dead and buried all this time, leaped alive at the familiar invitation. Yet his harsh tongue found the word it never could say then.

"Why?"

"Because!" She heard his cluck of tongue at that silly womanism and added in a little rush, "Because it would be so much easier then to say what I have to say."

He brooded on that, all the cynic in him suspicious and alert.

"Once . . . do you remember that night in the Downs, Mary? . . . I misunderstood a mood of yours and paid the penalty. What mood is this?"

"Ah!" she cried, sitting straight in the chair and regarding St. Joseph (all scratched where the rough New Englanders had thrown him down on the day of the expulsion). "That was so long ago—and I didn't know you. I didn't know you! I didn't want to be touched, by you or anyone. To be touched was horrible, except in the way of ordinary politeness. From a child it was like that to me . . . I can't explain . . . like snakes . . . or toads. I had to leap back and strike. Does that seem very strange?"

"It seemed strange," he said brutally, "in a woman who presumably had known the kiss-and-tumble of the marriage bed."

Her lips went white. "You don't understand. My husband——"

"Are you going to suggest that your husband never touched his wife, like St. Joseph over there?"

"Please—please don't speak like that, Roger! I'm trying to tell you that a woman like me must have time to see and learn and know a man . . . to love him."

"You don't mean that you've learned to love me?" he said, incredulous.

She looked at the tip of her shoe and said in a low voice, "I'm saying that I wish to be loved. I've never been truly loved in my life . . . and I'm twenty-seven, Roger."

She turned to him then, her proud face in its frame of ruddy hair, the moving lips, the fine-carved nostrils with their eager upward tilt, and slowly rose and came to him. She was as tall as he, and when she flung her arms about his neck her eyes came close and were enormous, inviting, promising, yet with some quality reserved, a challenge of hidden strength, like the green depths of a sea pool on a summer afternoon. He felt a wayfarer's hot and dusty urge to plunge. His arms slipped about her and found her warm and pliant in their embrace. She closed her eyes and offered a mouth alive with passion, fear, prayer—he did not know and did not care. He was aware of a triumph, feeling once more that leaping belief in himself and the little totem which had brought so many treasures to his feet.

She drew her lips away at last with a small gasp as if for breath. Her eyes opened with mingled emotions in them, shy and bold—and inquisitive.

"It's been a long time," Roger said, and felt himself trembling.

"Only a little time more," she whispered. "I promise you that."

"Is that all?" he protested. "A kiss and a promise?"—all savage impatience at such a timeworn subterfuge. Every coquette played this card at just this moment, for the pleasure of being coaxed. Well, he was in no mood for coquetry. He seized her and kissed her long and long. She submitted ardently, and yet he sensed that reserve in her, some sharp anxiety that spoiled her for love-making as love should be made. The notion troubled him, for all his swift and greedy want.

He paused, baffled, and she said impulsively, "Oh, Roger . . . Roger, say you'll be good to me!"

"I will."

"You won't think I'm a trollop?"

"I know better."

"You know what people will say?"

"I never cared what people said or thought." But a shadow crossed his mind like a reproach. What about Mary? Even in this raw outpost the little circle of gentility kept its forms and covenants. Poor Sally Madigan, happy enough with her·O'Rourke but unable to mingle in polite society with him, for all his rank and money!

He said carefully, "John . . . ?"

She flushed and lowered her eyes. "He will return to France. He was never happy away from Paris."

"You've discussed this with him?"

"Yes"—simply.

He was astounded and a little chilled. He was not afflicted with morality; it was the banality of the thing; the elderly spouse, the young wife, and the lover—the oldest jest in all the taverns of the world. He did not feel sorry for Foy, that sot. He felt that Foy had taken advantage of the girl's loneliness in Paris and her *idée fixe*. That! Was that obsession of hers a part of . . . this?

He demanded abruptly, "Which means most to you, Mary, your hatred of England or your love for me?"

It stung, for she returned with spirit, "Which do you love most, Roger Sudden, your money or me?"

A neat retort, and because he could not answer it he snapped churlishly, "What makes you think I love you at all?"

"Ah, now you're angry, Roger! You sound as you did that night in the Downs. How difficult you are! But I know you love me. Long before we reached Nova Scotia in the *Fair Lady* I knew that—it was in your eyes whenever you looked at me, all that long voyage. I don't think you knew it yourself, then. But I did—and yet I knew it could mean nothing to me. I put it from my mind, though it tore my heart when you were taken by the savages; and all that long time afterward, the waiting and the scheming for France that seemed to have no end, the false life that we lived—as if life in this place were not misery enough. When you came back I was glad, but all my thoughts had fastened themselves upon the cause of King James and the wrongs of the Highlands—and my brother fretting his heart away alone in Louisbourg. And you . . . your eyes were different, Roger. You were hard and cruel. All you wished to talk about was money. We were oceans apart then, you and I. Then one night in Hollis Street I overheard you telling John you wanted me. I went to bed and wept, for happiness, yes, and for sadness, because I was quite sure I couldn't bring myself to do what I'm doing now. Then came that quarrel over your supply contract, and all seemed over.

"Tonight when you entered the Long Room all those young and old fools and their compliments seemed like a chatter of apes. I hadn't even seen you come in, yet I knew. There's a force in you, Roger, that can be felt across a room by any woman. I wonder how many women? Poor things! What a forlorn sensation—the knees shivering and yet a fever in one's cheeks and palms, and a sudden alarmed awareness of all one's cherished mysteries—like those nightmares where you find yourself abroad in nothing but your stockings. Why are you smiling, Roger? You should feel appalled. But there was something else. When I looked across the room I seemed to see the message I wanted in your eyes, and I knew you belonged to me and no other, and I to you—after all this time consumed in other things. And so . . . you see? . . . I've come to offer myself like a strumpet . . . and you ask me which is stronger, love or hate!"

"What are we to do?" he muttered, amazed and strangely helpless. How long was "only a little time more"?

Her eyes danced. *"Och, mo chridhe,* don't you see how simple it all is now? We've had our triumphs, you and I. You've grown rich— surely you must be satisfied? And I've seen, after all this time, the failure of a great English expedition through my efforts—mine! For it was I who warned Louisbourg in time, I who suggested that a French ship fall into Holborn's hands with dispatches that 'revealed' the size of De la Motte's fleet! It frightened Loudoun half to death and kept him here at Halifax, planting cabbages and watching his army go to pieces with sheer idleness. Loudoun, that man—that Campbell! Of all people! What a revenge for Scotland! I feel awed, my Roger, when I think how that fox of Skye was given his English rank—was given this very command in America—for his services against Prince Charlie in the '45. And heaven put him in my hands! All the world's laughing—the great John Campbell, Baron Mauchlane, Earl of Loudoun, defeated by a scrawled lie in a barrel of French fish!"

She had swayed her chestnut head back, resting her eager hands upon his shoulders. Her face was alight, she was laughing with the world. He was uneasy and a little shocked. With such a passion in her, was there really room for love?

He said, "I feel as if I were seducing a vestal."

She stiffened and said in an odd voice, with color staining her cheeks, "Whatever made you say that?"

"This sacred flame you keep."

A silence. Then, reproachfully, "You were eager enough to seduce me once—have you forgotten? Do you remember what you said of women then?"

"I was young and a fool then."

She looked astonished and indignant. "Roger Sudden, are you telling me you've grown too old and wise to seduce me now? After I've flung myself at your head?"

"I'm telling you I love you, and I wish to heaven——"

"Roger! Oh, Roger!" Her voice quaked and her eyes went very wide. "Why didn't you say that before? Why didn't you *say* it? Don't you understand? I thought you wanted——"

A sound toward the road, the rattle of a stick on iron. Flustered, she cried, "There's my chair at the gate—I must go." She whirled the cloak about herself and stepped into his arms.

"Kiss me, a long kiss, Roger, for I shan't see you again till you come to Louisbourg."

"Louisbourg!"

"Yes—you've always intended to remove to Louisbourg, haven't you? Isn't that why you've sent the great part of your fortune to Rodrigues? We go tonight, *a ghaoil mo chridhe*—in a smuggler's sloop; John says we are suspected at last and must run. Now do you see? Do you see why I had to come and bare my heart to you tonight? Kiss me and swear you'll come to me soon!"

He put his hard mouth to her eager one and clutched her against him desperately, as if her supple person were the one thing certain in a suddenly risen sea of perplexities, while her chairmen beat a tune upon the frosty gate outside.

CHAPTER 34

Enter a Ghost

JOSHUA MAUGER's predatory fingers picked at the sheet and poised a quill.

"A gentlemen's bargain, good round figures, Mr. Sudden. Two thousand for the wharf and warehouse—too much, you know, those spruce piles don't stand water rot like good red pine. One thousand for the merchandise, including coals, now in the warehouse and the fuel yard adjoining. Three thousand for the truck houses upcountry, with all goods and chattels and all furs in transit—you're to notify your factors of the change in ownership at once. Two thousand five hundred for the ships and all spare cordage, sails, and stores . . . excepting and reserving the *Fair Lady* snow. Um! I make it eight thousand five hundred pounds."

"Guineas."

"Oh? Oh! You drive a hard bargain, my young friend."

"You're getting a flourishing business at the price of dirt and you know it, Mauger. I want specie, please."

"Oh, come, Mr. Sudden! Where should I lay hands on so much currency so quickly? A bill of credit on London, now—or Amsterdam, say . . ."

"Specie! Boscawen's fleet is in the harbor and the army's here again, pouring guineas across every counter in the town. Besides, you're the wealthiest man in Halifax—that's why I came to you. I set my prices low for good hard money and that's what I want."

The ferret's eyes regarded him curiously. "If you insist, Mr. Sudden." What an oily voice the fellow had! And softly, "Would you mind telling me, Mr. Sudden, why you're selling out now, of all times? It isn't like you—with all these opportunities."

"I'm sick of shaking the guinea tree."

Mauger smiled slyly. "Do you expect me to believe that, Mr. Sudden?"

Roger's tongue coiled in his cheek. The long contest of wits with

Mauger had been meat and drink to him, and there was a sour taste of surrender in selling out to the dark and greedy man just when the Golden Woman seemed to present her very choicest charms. And yet . . . and yet it might prove the greatest coup of all if Louisbourg won the coming summer's battle. All the news from Europe told of British incompetence and defeat, a state of affairs well demonstrated in the New World by Lord Loudoun. Old Hux said the streets of Louisbourg were full of veterans from France, and the French fleet had arrived on the coast again, commanded by Des Gouttes this time instead of old Bois de la Motte.

Another fiasco like last summer's campaign and the French would be in Halifax. True, this new expedition in the harbor seemed larger and better equipped than any British force yet seen in America, but most of the regiments were fresh out from garrison towns in England, the very worst material for a war in the Nova Scotia wilds, and many of Boscawen's ships had been shattered on this coast last year and patched anew—eighteen of his captains had served under Holborn in that infamous affair. Loudoun had been replaced by Jeffrey Amherst in the supreme command—a man who had never seen America.

All the signs pointed to a disaster worse than any yet suffered by British arms in a war of disasters. It would be something, Roger mused, to see the look on Joshua Mauger's face when all this came about.

He said with an elaborate indifference, "I told you—I'm tired. But if you want a better answer, why, I've gathered the fortune I set out to seek and now I propose to enjoy it while my health and thirst are sound."

"In England, I dare say?"

"Eventually, yes."

He was surprised to see the wily eyes turn dreamy for a minute. "Ah! That's what I intend to do myself someday. After this campaign, perhaps. England! A house in London, a place in the country, buy a seat in Parliament and play the gentleman. All my life I've dreamed of that."

He blinked and opened his eyes on Roger and the present.

"When do you leave, Mr. Sudden?"

"I'm not sure. A week or a month, perhaps."

"Ah, then we'll see more of you before you go. You are a remarkable young man and we shall miss you very much." The oily smile again. "And now . . . here is the agreement of sale, and the pen."

With the quill in his hand Roger paused. "This clause—'full payment of which is hereby acknowledged'—I don't quite like that."

"Ah, my dear Mr. Sudden, what a question to raise! A common business formality, as you surely know. The specie will take some days to collect. It shall be delivered within a week, you have my word. A matter between gentlemen." But, seeing the doubt still in Roger's eyes, "After all, Mr. Sudden, you're a man of influence in Halifax, you have friends in high places . . . if I were a rogue, at least I am not a fool!"

Roger signed without further ado. But he refused Mauger's notion of wine and "a toast to our mutual advantage," pleading other urgent matters, and walked out breathing a sigh of relief. There was a taint in air that Mauger breathed.

It was Maytime and Halifax basked in sunshine under a blue spring sky. The grass was fresh and green at the sides of the less-traveled streets and on the broad flank of Citadel Hill, but the hardwood ridges on the Dartmouth side still wore the dun tint of winter. A breathless air hung over Halifax and the leafless countryside, the deep pause of the earth itself before flinging into summer like a woman into the arms of a lover. The throng of ships in the roadstead and the swarm of redcoats ashore gave that breathlessness another and sharper significance. All America, aye, and Europe, waited like this, watchful and motionless, for the flowering of this struggle in the northern wilderness.

The hubbub of English soldiers' voices in the streets was like old days in '49 before the advent of the Germans and New Englanders. Some of them were Kentish—Kentish as the chime of Canterbury bells. He resisted an urge to stop and ask if any were from Suddenholt way. But now rose a sound of music wild and high, fantastic on this side the sea. It brought people running from the houses and halted Roger like a shout. Along Barrington Street, forerun by a rabble of delighted urchins, came the skirl of bagpipes and a gallant rattle of drums. Astounded he beheld a regiment marching past in short red coats and waistcoats, in kilt and plaid, in blue bonnets with

scarlet pompons, in diced red-and-white stockings. The spring sunshine glinted on musket and broadsword and the long Lochaber axes
of the sergeants. Leather sporrans danced and kilts swung to the
ordered thrust of hairy knees, the quick, springy step of men of the
hills.

Frasers, by the plaid. What were they doing here in the forbidden
Highland dress, in those red jackets, with the hateful *G.R.* stamped
upon their cartridge boxes? Frasers, fighting for King George?

He turned away abruptly as a prophet might turn from a chosen
people gone to Baal. Good God, what next! The lilt of the pipe tune
mocked him all the way to Pleasant Street, with his feet falling instinctively into the march step and memories whirling through his
head. In this state he entered the chamber hung with tokens of his
new life and found Tom Fuller awaiting him.

The sight of Tom was like a breath of the forest. Years on the
narrow trails had given him the look, even the pigeon-toed walk,
of an Indian. He was dark and gaunt, and the fringed buckskins
seemed a part of him. Only his speech and the scarred hand recalled
the seaman of the Rochester road. The savages, fascinated by that
twisted but powerful hand, had given him a long name meaning
Bosoley's Claw. They had felt that claw in many ways in the past few
years.

"I got your letter—and the money," Tom said in a dull voice.

Roger avoided his eyes. It had seemed so easy to put his farewell
in a letter. He might have known that Tom would come and face
him with it.

"I've made my fortune, Tom. There seems no reason to stay on."

"But," protested Tom, "a-partin' company like this, sir, arter all
we've seed and done together!"

"It had to come to this, old friend. You wouldn't like it where
I'm going, and besides, you've wandered long enough. Take the
money home to England and buy an inn down Kent-way somewhere.
That old affair's forgotten now. Someday I'm going home to Kent
myself. You'll find me then at Suddenholt and we'll have many a
good glass together and talk of these wild times."

"Is it—is it a woman, sir?"

"Yes."

Tom made a mouth and nodded slowly, a philosopher in buckskins. "I see. 'Tain't nothin' to be said, then. But I'm glad. 'Tain't nateral for a man to sheer off women all the best part o' his life—not a man like you, sir, that a woman 'ud give 'er 'eart to quick as wink." He added dourly, "I on'y hope she's worth it, damme!"

Brass Pot brought rum and lemons, and they drank to eternal fellowship and the meeting in old Kent.

"Till then!" said Tom at parting. "If the war spares me as well as you."

"What d'you mean?"

"Me and the lads is a-goin' into a reg'ment o' rangers that the gov'nor's raisin' for the new campaign."

"What! Why?"

" 'Cause we're sick an' tired o' seein' things go from bad to worse, sir!" Tom burst out savagely. "Ever since the old ranger companies was disbanded, barrin' Gorham's, there's been no safety for settlers outside the forts. Boishebert's war parties range the whole province. Even our troops can't pass along the Annapolis valley 'cept in large parties and well armed. The gov'nor's had to give up his pet settlement down Cole Harbor way. Last year a war party come down the old canoe trail from Shubenacadie and killed some inhabitants at Dartmouth—a thing they ain't tried in a long time. Why, last summer a party o' seamen got scalped in the woods at Point Pleasant—right under the nose o' Loudoun's whole army! An' them poor Dutch at Lunenburg live in hell the whole time, day an' night. Well, all that—that's why."

He stuck out the scarred right hand, and Roger shook it hard. There was a lump in his throat. The seaman's hard gray eyes were saying something that his loyal tongue withheld. Does he know? wondered Roger. The door closed and the iron gate clanged dismally.

He dined alone, eating little but drinking Madeira in a way that made the eyes of Brass Pot bulge. Afterward he wandered up and down the chamber, hands in breeches, while the long May twilight faded slowly into darkness. A black mood settled on him like the night itself. His two selves were at war again. Good and evil? That was what the Spey wife said. But which was which? One could not wait for a sight of Louisbourg and Mary Foy. And surely that was the end of the road he had followed all this time, the way to love and fortune? Two insisted, Stay. But why? he asked. What was here now?

The big Negro came in with a taper to light the candles and the evening fire. Roger drew up a chair to the blaze, staring into the flames for a glimpse of Mary's face, conjuring a memory of her strange flecked eyes which always had golden glints in such a light as this. She would say Come, at any rate. But all he could hear was the pipe tune in the streets and all he could see was Tom Fuller and the look in Tom Fuller's eyes. Doubt! Doubt! Just when he had been certain of his destiny! I must be very drunk, he thought.

There were sounds outside, a rat-tat on the stout front door, an altercation of some sort in the hall, and finally the flinging open of the chamber door itself.

He sprang up, crying, "What the deuce . . ." and saw Captain Bulkeley standing there in a cloak and laced hat and looking as dour as death.

"Sudden," the tall secretary said, "you must come with me at once."

"Why?"

"The governor wishes to see you."

"I'm afraid I have other plans for this evening, Captain Bulkeley."

"I'm afraid you must give 'em up. My carriage is outside."

"I don't like your manner, sir. One would think he was under arrest."

The Irishman's eyes flashed in the firelight. "You are, sir! You are!"

Roger stared beyond the man and saw a sergeant's halberd gleaming in the hall. There was a shift of other feet outside. Without further word he passed the gibbering Brass Pot into the night, seeing faintly, in the hazy starlight, the forms and dully gleaming musket barrels of the sergeant's guard. Bulkeley addressed the sergeant curtly:

"Stay and arrest anyone who attempts to enter or leave."

The carriage lurched along Pleasant Street, down the stony drop of Sackville Street and along Granville to the governor's house. The new residency stood ghostly and unfinished in the flicker of the chaise lamps; the fashion of Halifax were fitting costumes and counting the days toward a grand housewarming ball. The old, that relic of '49, sat small and shabby in the corner above Market Square. It was headquarters now for the expedition, and every window blazed.

The guard turned out and presented arms as Bulkeley stepped from the chaise. He and Roger passed inside. Bulkeley left his prisoner in an anteroom jammed with orderlies from a dozen regiments. He reappeared in a moment.

"This way, Mr. Sudden, please."

Roger found himself in the large presence of Governor Lawrence. The door closed quietly. They were alone. A coal fire glowed in an iron basket on the small hearth—coals supplied by Roger himself under that lucrative fuel contract which now belonged to Mauger. Quaint, that—the commander of this British garrison warming his labors at a fire of smuggled French coal.

The big ruddy man behind the paper-littered table wore the red coat and blue facings of his own regiment, the Royal Americans. He looked up, grunted, waved a hand toward a chair.

"Mr. Sudden, I find myself in a painful position. You've been denounced as an accomplice of the French spy Foy, who decamped from the town with his wife not long ago."

"Ah!"

"As a soldier, I've put you under arrest. As governor—and one who has admired your energy and courage if not your principles—I'm strongly inclined to doubt the—ah—person who makes the accusation." He thrust forward his big face, framed in the tight white wig. "Damme, Sudden, you're an Englishman, you've fought and suffered, you've labored in this wild country, you've seen and know the malice of the French. You've made a fortune here—and a good part of it, I suspect, from supplies to His Majesty's forces. You've no reason to be anything but loyal. What the devil does this mean? What d'you know about this fellow Foy?"

"Very little, sir," coolly. "He was a passenger in the ship which carried me here as an emigrant. I met him subsequently about the town. He seemed to have no source of income. I often wondered how he lived."

"Umph! Our—ah—informant says you've been seen to visit him in Hollis Street and—ah—that his lady has been observed to enter your house under rather romantic circumstances. Alone, I mean to say, and at night. What about that, eh?"

Roger looked hurt. "You surely understand, sir—you are a bachelor and a gentleman—that in honor I can't answer that question."

A smile broke over the heavy face. The governor's great fist came down with a whack amongst the papers. "Exactly! Precisely what I thought—precisely what I told Bulkeley! 'A young bachelor and a pretty woman,' I said. 'If dalliance were treason, damme, I'd have to gibbet half Halifax.' Pshaw! I was young once myself, Sudden. These little affairs . . . ha! Well! Mind you, I doubted Mauger's story from the first——"

"Mauger!"

"Yes—a man I detest as I do a skunk. Gives me more trouble than the French. Is he, by chance, an enemy of yours?"

Roger burned. It was a struggle to keep his voice steady. "In matters of business, yes, sir. I've scored some triumphs at his expense. And just now . . . well, Mauger stands to gain close on nine thousand pounds if he can so much as smudge my reputation."

Lawrence opened his eyes very wide. "God's death! You play for pretty stakes, you commissaries, don't you?" His thick fingers drummed. "I command the forces—nominally you understand—until Amherst arrives. He's still at sea somewhere. But the actual commander, Amherst or no Amherst, and quite unofficially mark you, is one of the brigadiers, a favorite of Mr. Pitt's, a feverish young madman who's never seen America till now and says Pish to all advice. Talks of landing the army boldly on the Louisbourg beaches in the teeth of the French entrenchments, in broad daylight, and from open boats, begad! Says Boscawen's ships could take Louisbourg alone . . . says the army should do it in ten days and push on to Quebec! Pooh-poohs the corps of rangers I've raised and says colonial troops are all cowardly dogs that 'fall down in their own dirt at the first musket shot.' Hates Scotsmen like poison—yet proposes to lead 'em into battle. 'Od's life, he talks like that fellow Braddock—and you know what happened to Braddock!"

"What," demanded Roger, teeth on edge, "has this to do with me?"

"Everything, Sudden! That cunning fellow Mauger's gone to him with his information, knowing I wouldn't give it the grace of a second thought. So . . . you see? I wanted you to know the sort of man you have to deal with—they're awaiting you in the right-hand chamber at the end of the hall. Go on then, tell him what you've told me. He's a bachelor himself and about your age. Think of it, thirty-one and a brigadier! What's the British Army coming to?"

Roger was tempted to answer that. The French would either slaughter them on the Louisbourg beaches or ambush them in the woods between the shore and the fortress. But he was consumed with hate for Mauger and the desire to meet him face to face. He passed swiftly down the hall, rapped on the right-hand door, and stepped inside.

There was Mauger warming his raptorial claws—and doubtless his courage—at the fire across the room. But Roger saw him as a secondary figure in a startling little tableau. His whole attention was drawn and frozen by the figure at the desk. Years shrank to hours, the Atlantic to a step, and here in this chamber he could smell again the reek of the Thames marshes, hear the rattle and splash of the fat yellow coach, the echo of his own voice crying, "Stand!" and the creak of rusty gibbet chains as Jemmie Calter cocked his hollow eye along the Rochester road.

As the first great suck of breath subsided through his taut nostrils, so his mind subsided to a rueful resignation. A long run for the money, after all. Six guineas? Seven guineas? He could not remember now.

Ah well! The clockwork of the world was queerly meshed, and the little wheel that seemed to run so fast could turn the big one only a cog or two at a revolution. Tick! Tock! and there you were, and there was the thin ridiculous young major of the 20th Foot, with his sandy brows and hot blue eyes and his face of a starved rabbit as plain as yesterday.

CHAPTER 35

The Toils of Circumstance

"So," UTTERED THE APPARITION. "We meet again, Sir Highwayman!"

"I'm afraid you're mistaken," Roger said.

"Oh, come! Your name's Sudden, I'm told. Mr. Roger Sudden? Mine's Wolfe—you must remember me! I was . . . let me see . . . 'on old Hangman Hawley's staff at Culloden' . . . ha! . . . 'safely removed from the broadswords' . . . eh? . . . and 'robbing the Highland gentlefolk in the name of King George' . . . I think that was the way it went. What it is to have a memory!"

Damn your memory, thought Roger violently. He said, coldly enough:

"I don't know what you're talking about, my dear sir, and I wish you a very good evening . . ."

"Stay!" snapped the voice like a pistol. No escape, of course. Face it out, then! After all, what proof was there?

"I want you to meet an old friend of yours, Mr. Sudden."

"Mr. Mauger is no friend of mine."

"So I gather! So I gather! But Mr. Mauger, a painstaking man, seems to have found someone who was . . . Mr. Mauger, will you be so good as to call in your witness?"

Mauger sprang to an inner door, and in shuffled Isaac Trope, hat in hand, soiled white hair bound with a ribbon of Lumley's, his old limbs clad in a suit of wrinkled drab. He turned his disreputable head from side to side, bestowing a thin malicious grin on Mauger and Roger and General Wolfe impartially.

"This is the man?" snapped Wolfe to Old Evil.

"Yes, that's him. Roger Sudden. Come to my house in Tooley Street one night in Jannivary '49, along of a seaman, and both a-stink o' horse sweat. Rented my garret and kep' 'emselves pretty close, though they used to go down the river to Wappin' quite a bit."

"Um! And they'd plenty of money the night they came?"

"Hear the guineas clinkin' and rollin' now, I can, sir, t'other side o' the door. 'Fust we'll divide the spoils,' says Mr. Sudden, offhand like. And the sailor says, 'No, ye done it all. As bold a piece o' work as ever I see.' But Mr. Sudden had his way—he usually did, did Mr. Sudden—so they talked o' what they'd do. The seaman wanted to go for a pirate, but Mr. Sudden says No, there's better ways to fortune. They talked o' the colonies . . . all that."

"And have you any proof of all this?"

Trope fished in his unclean coattails and with some diffidence laid a pair of shabby leather objects on the table. "Them purses, sir. Found 'em in the alley under their garret window next mornin'. Nice things, they was then, one quite plain and t'other with 'E.B.' sewed on the leather in white silk . . ."

"Colonel Belcher's," said Wolfe to Roger cheerfully. "Remember?"

"So I kep' 'em, sir, thinkin' as I might find the owner, like. Used 'em a bit, after a time, and hopin' ye don't mind, sir, bein' a poor old man in the lodgin'-keepin' way—me and my daughter . . ."

"Any others in Halifax who'd recognize this man as your lodger in Tooley Street?"

"Ho yes, sir! They wouldn't like to come here and speak up, bein' friends o' his, but ye could make 'em talk, sir. There's Sal . . . she's an orf'cer's lady now and needs takin' down a peg or two, and there's Killick, he's a fisherman . . ."

Wolfe turned the hot blue gaze to Roger. "Are you satisfied or shall I send for them?"

"Don't trouble them."

"You admit the robbery?"

"Yes."

"Ha!" cried Mauger from the fireside. Wolfe regarded him with distaste.

"That will be all. Take your witness and get out." And as the sinister pair departed through the side door, "Well, my Jacobite friend, you seem to have made an ill choice in your company from first to last. From Chevalier to Shylock in three moves—a proper rogue's progress! What have you to say for yourself?"

"Nothing."

"It's a poor dog that won't bark in his own defense."

"It's a worse that whines at the whip."

"Umph! What about this matter of espionage? This man Foy, eh?"

"Nothing to say."

"You admit Mauger's charge?"

"Not at all—but nothing I could say would make any difference in view of what's just passed."

"You admit it then!" Wolfe sprawled his ungainly person in the chair. How *long* he was! A good six-foot-three if an inch. "D'ye know you intrigue me, Sudden. I've never forgotten that day on the Rochester road—I've never seen anything so devilish cool in my life. I'm told you've done remarkable things in this country, that the savages look upon you with the fear of God, and I don't doubt it for a moment. Now I can understand a Jacobite up to a point—to the point where he betrays his own blood to the French. An Englishman —from Kent, like me, if I know Kentish speech—and his country in peril of conquest . . . all Europe in arms against her, one might say . . . ninety millions against five, as Mr. Pitt puts it . . . and nothing to look back on but a record of failure and defeat! And a gentleman! Why, I've an army of rogues and drunkards, the sweepings of England, but they'll fight for her—they'll fight for her!"

Wolfe sprang up and began to pace the room on his thin, ridiculous legs, fluttering the candles as he passed and repassed the table. "All bungled so far, damme! Minorca . . . there we lost the whole Mediterranean . . . and the fleet that should have turned the tables ran away . . . Parliament! . . . Parliament should have hanged itself for folly and neglect . . . they shot the admiral instead. . . . Poor Byng! . . . and Rochefort, a melancholy mess . . . after all our high hopes. . . . Fumbling! Bungling! . . . Councils of war! . . . What we need is less councils and more war . . . Good God, what a spectacle! . . . Well, I'll have no Rochefort here! . . . Get ashore, somehow or anyhow. And fight! Fight!"

He fired off these ejaculations as he strode up and down, covering the chamber floor in five extraordinary strides each way, shaking an irritable fist at every point. His high voice broke sometimes into a squeak.

Roger was forgotten. With a cynical amusement he watched the performance of this odd red-coated Hamlet. At last he broke in savagely.

"If all this is true, what are you doing here with all these ships and men? Why aren't you and Boscawen ranged along the Channel?"

Wolfe halted in mid-stride. "What! Sit and wait for destruction? A man with the odds against him must leap out and strike—strike where his force will count the most!"

"You don't mean Pitt's chancing everything on this wild stroke in America?"

"I mean England must take chances right and left, and she's taking this one for a start."

Roger stared at the man, a fit choice for this folly. His mind reeled back to the Highlands after Culloden, when the glens were filled with hope of a great French armament fitting out at Brest. That was D'Anville's force, which was rumored for Scotland, for a direct blow at the English from the north. But D'Anville sailed across the sea for a blow at the English in America—and laid the bones of his army on the wild shores of Chebucto. And now—and now England was repeating history with the roles reversed! It was incredible.

Wolfe seemed to recollect himself. He threw his ungainly length into the chair. His mouth was petulant, his large blue eyes as hard as chinaware. He stabbed a long, accusing finger. "You were in love with this Frenchwoman Foy?"

"Yes."

"And Mauger says you've sold out to him, that you've transferred your fortune to Louisbourg over a period of many months—d'ye deny it?"

"No."

"Well, you're honest about it. I don't believe you're a spy. You're just a Jacobite rogue who's picked up an itch for the bawbees amongst the Scotch. Orderly!"

A grenadier-capped head at the door.

"My compliments to Captain Bulkeley and ask him to come here, please."

The secretary entered, with an impersonal glance at Roger.

"Captain Bulkeley, I wish this man confined to jail awaiting His Majesty's pleasure."

"Very good, sir. The charge is treason, I take it?"

"Not enough evidence. But I've evidence enough to hang him on quite another matter. That must wait until I come back from Quebec, however. In the meantime let him cool his heels in your lockup. That will keep him out of any possible mischief with the French."

Wolfe nodded in dismissal and turned to the papers on the desk, shouting in a high voice for his orderly.

Roger marched before Bulkeley out of the room. A file of grenadiers conducted him in silence through the dark streets. The military prison, a stone house built by Colonel Horsman in the early days, stood in the shadow of the fort he had commanded overlooking the south gate of the town. The way lay past Roger's house, and he saw a little knot of soldiers with a lantern, engaged in argument with a burly man in seaman's dress. Old Hux! As the file tramped past, the master of *Fair Lady* turned his head and met Roger's gaze for a moment. His jaw dropped. As the prison door closed behind him Roger found that he could smile at the memory of that amazed O in the midst of Job Huxley's whiskers.

The little prison lacked the bonhomie of the Château Louis-damné, for its inhabitants were soldiers of the garrison confined for petty military crimes and kept apart in narrow stone kennels like unruly dogs. They conversed by shouting through their small grilles into the corridor, and Roger was quickly assailed with cries of "You! New man! What are ye in for?"

He told them highway robbery, and there was a chorus of astonished oaths and an indignant Welsh voice spluttering, *"Mawdredd an'll* A townss-man—and a ploody thief att thatt! Itt iss an outrage!"

But in the succeeding days, when his few guineas bought the good nature of the guard and procured some rum and corned meat to liven their fare of water and hard biscuit, they mended their opinion, vowing that, Od's bob! he was a jolly good fellow, the old stone jug had come up in the world. And the one called Taffy went so far as to pronounce him "A chentleman, py Gott!"

One or two departed, having served their sentences, and others came to take their places. One man, straight from a stiff two hundred at the regimental triangles, set the place echoing with howls and curses for twelve hours on end. No one paid any attention except the corporal of the guard, who looked in upon the fellow's raw back once or twice and said, "Ah, Jack, ye'll change your tune afore the army sails for Louisbourg."

And so Jack did, for within three days he was fretting aloud like the rest of them lest his regiment go off to fight the French without him.

Roger marveled. Their life was a red-coated slavery at best, and in these colonial posts the harsh discipline was matched by the severity of the climate and the violence of the diseases which afflicted them. Their pay was sixpence a day, out of which they had to pay for their own leggings, shirts, stockings, shoes, their washing, the services of the company barber, and the daily ration of spruce beer. Active service changed none of these things but added the hazards of wounds and death. Yet they sought for it eagerly and were in a fever lest they miss the chance.

Roger asked his right-hand neighbor what he wanted to fight for, and the fellow replied, after a little consideration, "Why, damme, I never thought on't much, but I s'pose it's to strike a blow for old England. What else?"

By standing on his stool Roger could gaze through a small barred window high in the wall. It faced toward Pleasant Street, and he could see the south corner of his own garden wall and catch recurring glimpses of a bored redcoat facing about at the end of his beat. He wondered about Quashie and Brass Pot. The removal of their master and the presence of the soldiers at the gate must be harrowing their thick skulls. It was amusing to fancy the blacks, with their quaint knowledge of English, trying to make any sense whatever of the Yorkshire oaths of the guards. But chiefly he whiled the daylight hours looking down the slope to the harbor. What went on there was interesting enough.

The expedition was busy rehearsing its descent upon the shores of Cape Breton. Every day, at a signal, a swarm of boats put off from the anchored transports, each crammed with soldiers and seamen pulling furiously for the Dartmouth shore. It made a curious spectacle at this distance. The laden boats were like bright red insects, many-legged, running over the water toward the forest as if in haste to devour it. From the bushes along the shore came small white puffs of powder smoke and a delayed pop-pop-pop, very faint and far; but the insects came on gallantly, abandoned their dark beetle cases at the waterside, and with much wriggle and scurry formed along the beach a narrow and continuous red mass, tipped with steel. Then at a further signal the mass plunged into the woods. The trees seemed to swallow them as a vast green frog might lick into its maw a wandering column of red ants. For a time the popping continued, and a murmur that might have been cheers; then silence, and at last a reappearance of the ants, straggling now, a leisurely resumption of their beetle form and a journey back to the ships. All very pretty—but what would happen when they tried that splendid game under the fire of well-entrenched infantry and cannon? That man Wolfe! Roger felt a grudging sympathy for stout old Lawrence with his harsh memories of warfare in the Nova Scotia woods.

Mid-May brought a touch of summer weather, stifling in the small stone jail, and the complaint of the prisoners brought the corporal and his men to take out the windows. In the hot nights they stood tiptoe on their stools, faces against the bars, sucking at the cool outside air until the strain of the position wearied them and made sleep possible.

On such a night, long after the other kennels rang with snores, Roger lay hot and awake. Some late wanderer whistled past the south side of the prison, tramping down the rough lane that climbed the slope to Spring Gardens. The sound came nearer as the fellow turned up Pleasant Street toward the town. It had a delusive quality, as if the man walked in the very shadow of the prison wall. Roger was vaguely irritated. Then, in a second, all his nerves leaped and tingled. That tune! He climbed on the stool. The roofs of the town were stark and silent on the lower slope. He could not see the foot of the wall, straight underneath. On Pleasant Street nothing moved. Silence everywhere.

Then the sauntering whistler again—below! The guard? The guard was asleep long before this, excepting the sentry in his little coffin facing the Spring Gardens lane and the palisade.

He put his mouth to the bars and took up a stave of that song of Sally Madigan, whistling softly like the other.

> *When the pie was opened the birds began to sing,*
> *Wasn't that a dainty dish . . .*

A hiss below. A rustling as of several feet in grass, a scrape, a silence; then a light touch of wood on stone.

Suddenly a head, enormous against the starlight. Old Hux and his beard!

"Roger?"

"Yes."

"All hands asleep in there?"

"I think so, but——"

"How's the mortar round them bars?"

"Pretty rotten. What are you——"

The head vanished. After a minute a pair of immense hands appeared in the starlit square and writhed about the end of the grating.

"Look here," Roger whispered hoarsely, "you can't——"

"Whist! I've got all my lads below, tailin' on the rope. One good heave and out comes the whole damned gratin' or they're no men o' mine. Listen, Roger! When it goes, climb out and let yourself drop— we'll catch ye. And be ready to cut an' run as soon as ye hit the ground."

"But the guard!"

A chuckle. "The guard'll have somethin' else to think about. Stand by!"

Hux disappeared. The whistle began again, but this time the tune was "Well Sold the Cow." At the end of the first bar it perished. From beyond the decrepit palisade about the south gate came a voice raised in the harsh, high war whoop of the Micmacs, tearing the peace of the night to shreds. It went on and on, in those yowling undulations which had been the very voice of terror for Halifax through the years. From the front of the prison the sentry fired his piece and tumbled out the guard, and from the direction of Horsman's Fort just up the slope came shouts, the rattle of a drum, a clatter of arms being snatched out of the racks. Finally a cannon sent a charge of grapeshot shrieking over the lane to fall among the starlit mounds of the burial ground.

"Heave!" hissed the voice of Old Hux below. A sharp creak of taut hemp, a momentary groan of iron under strain, and the grating vanished into the night.

Roger pulled himself up, squirmed through the hole, and—not without misgiving—dropped headfirst into the darkness.

It was not a long drop, and he was caught at once in a thicket of upreaching arms. "Now!" snapped Old Hux, and off they went, seven swift and furtive shapes flitting toward Citadel Hill through the upper pastures of the town.

Halifax came to life with a roar. A gun boomed from the Parade—the signal gun. At once others thudded from the three water-front batteries, from George's Island, from the Eastern Battery down-harbor on the Dartmouth side. From Horsman's Fort came a steady rattle of small arms as its guard shot industriously into the graveyard. In the barrack yard to the north the regiments of the garrison were turning out in a fine flurry of drums and commands.

From the dark shoulder of Citadel Hill the fugitives saw that even the fleet was alarmed, lanterns flitted about the decks, and all the gun ports seemed to open at once, like rows of wicked yellow eyes.

Old Hux led the way through a wide gap in the palisade and they passed across the south slope, leaping the low stone walls of the pastures, and came to the brook which flowed out of the common. This they followed down, blundering among the alders in the dark.

" 'Struth!" grunted Old Hux. "What a gripe I've got in the side! ... fit to split me ... no damned wonder ... hare and hounds at my age!"

"Where are we heading for?" Roger gasped.

"The jolly boat . ... at the waterin' place ... mouth o' this brook ... nigh to Black Rock ... *Fair Lady's* offshore ... ready to sail ... put ye in Louisbourg ... who's to know?"

"But how did all this come about, man?"

"Saw ye that night ... couldn't find out a thing ... then a woman came to the wharf in a closed chair ... Irish, by the brogue ... told me where ye were and what to do ... knowed more than common about jails and such ... dressed like a lady, too ..."

"But the war whoop—the Indians!"

"Just a bam to fool the sogers ... friend o' yourn ... Tom Fuller, captain of a ranger comp'ny ... asked him if he'd like to cut away to Louisbourg along o' you ... but he said no, he was payin' a debt ... an' somethin' about bein' an Englishman."

They trotted, breathless and drenched with sweat, into the open at last. Water gleamed under the stars and there was a rattle of beach cobbles. The boat lay waiting, drawn up among the raffle of last tide, with a fisherman standing guard—Killick, the late waterman of Tooley Stairs. Down-harbor, off Mauger's Beach, that smugglers' rendezvous, sat the dim shape of the snow.

"Phew! Fust we smuggle ye out o' Louisbourg, now we a-goin' to smuggle ye back, Roger." Old Hux chuckled. "What a lark!"

Roger put hand to breast and touched the little stone fish with reverence.

Behind them Halifax ruffled its drums and boomed defiance at the night.

PART FOUR

Invicta!

CHAPTER 36

Père Maillard

JOURNEYS which end in lovers meeting are seldom without difficulties, but Roger found the difficulties slight. Under cover of the eternal fog which in early summer clung to Cape Breton like a tight wig to a bony head, and with a fine smuggler's knowledge of the more chancy passages, Old Hux set him ashore on bleak Rochefort Point three days after leaving Halifax. He set off blithely over the springy moorland in the direction of the town and at once blundered into a stone breastwork manned by a detachment of Volontaires Etrangers.

He was questioned in bad French by their lieutenant, a surprised and indignant Teuton—the Etrangers were a German regiment sold into French service by an impecunious princeling—and marched off to Louisbourg between a pair of stiffly strutting privates in new white uniforms faced with green.

They entered the fortress by the Maurepas Gate, and Roger persuaded them to take him first to the establishment of M. Rodrigues. Rodrigues rescued him at once, cursed the soldiers for a pair of illegitimate blockheads, and dismissed them, kicking each stolidly departing rump with care and skill.

The merchant then embraced him with delight and launched into a long and detailed account of his investments, but Roger cut him short, demanding the whereabouts of Madame Foy.

"Caramba!" cried Rodrigues. "That sot Foy went off to France weeks ago . . . and this that was Madame is known in Louisbourg as Mademoiselle. For reasons," he added with a leer, "one can appreciate." And, seeing Roger's impatience, "On the south side of the Rue

d'Orleans, monsieur, between the Rue Dauphine and the Rue l'Hôpital . . . a small gray house with the sign of a seamstress."

Roger was off at once, running up the Rue Dauphine. He found the house by the sign of the scissors, a narrow and gloomy dwelling, half stone, half timber, on the chilly side of the Rue d'Orleans where the Cape Breton sun fell lightly in summer and in winter not at all. He hammered on the door.

It was answered by a tall woman with a red Norman face, but the sound of his voice brought a rush of petticoats down the stairs and Mary into his arms.

"Oh, Roger! I knew you'd come! I knew! I knew!"

He kissed her hungrily, and her mouth responded with the complete rapture of a woman who gives up her soul. The seamstress looked on, caught between pleasure and astonishment, and saw him slip a hand beneath Mademoiselle's chin and put her head back, like a boy with a stolen apple feasting his eyes between bites. Mary's cheeks were flushed, and when she opened her eyes he saw them full of tears.

"Oh, Roger, is it true? We're not dreaming?"

"It's true."

"And you've no regrets?"

"None."

"I'm . . . I'm alone, Roger. You understand?"

The seamstress departed, suddenly bored with this incomprehensible English.

Mary drew him into a small chamber at the front of the house, furnished with a squat Canadian stove, a pair of maplewood chairs, an escritoire, and an intimate little sofa covered with red velvet. They sat instinctively in the close confinement of the sofa, arms about each other, cheeks together, gazing with absorbed eyes like dreamers at the traffic in the Rue d'Orleans.

Beyond the little bull's-eye panes moved a colorful stream: fishermen and their women in homespun and great Breton sabots; merchants and clerks in broadcloth and brass buttons; seamen of Des Gouttes' fleet in untidy red shirts and nightcaps and short striped petticoat trousers; soldiers of the Compagnies de la Marine in white coats and blue breeches and gaiters; infantry of the line all in white, with a glimpse of scarlet waistcoat, artillerymen in red breeches and

blue coats; Volontaires Etrangers in white and green; twos and
threes of fine ladies in all the hues of the rainbow; hooded nuns;
brothers of the Frères de la Charité in dark soutanes; Indian men and
boys in clout and moccasins like images of bronze; squaws in caribou-hide smocks or rags and tatters of French petticoats; Negroes
from Haiti and Martinique clad in anything from sailcloth to castoff uniforms. Heavy-wheeled carts moved ponderously through the
mass, drawn by oxen or wiry Norman ponies. Officers ahorseback
and afoot. Now and then a cariole drawn by horses that would have
made a gypsy shudder.

"It's like Halifax," Mary said in a low voice.

"Oh? I was thinking how very different it was."

"The soldiers and sailors, I mean—so many to the townsfolk. Do
you know, Roger, I feel afraid. Not for myself but for all these people
who don't know what it means. It seemed a wonderful game once.
Now it's just something horrible, like a nightmare where a frightful
face approaches you and you can't turn your head away. Jamie would
despise me if he knew."

"I trust your brother's well?"

"Oh, Roger, he's changed. It's been so long. It was years before they
granted him a captaincy. He got a little extra money as an interpreter, but they've paid him wretchedly for all he's done. He's cold
and cynical, and he used to be so gay—quite sinful sometimes. Now
he'll have nothing to do with society—says the Louisbourg ladies are
an ugly lot who play cards from morn to night and the gentlemen
can talk nothing but fish. He keeps to himself and his books in a
little house on the Rue du Rempart. Some of the Regiment Artois
have made a garden for him. He goes off fishing for trout and salmon
sometimes to remind himself of Scotland."

"What does he think of this affair between Halifax and Louisbourg, now that it's come to push of pike?"

Her lips compressed. "He says the only hope is to beat the English
off the landing places. If they get their guns ashore, Louisbourg is
doomed."

Roger looked his surprise.

"Oh, it's just the bitter mood that's grown upon him, Roger, and
the jealousy of the French officers. He sees no good in anything now.

The ditch is dry, the walls are shaky, the gun carriages are rotten. The fortress was designed thirty years ago, when artillery wasn't so powerful and bombshells weren't so destructive as they are now. He estimates the garrison will be outnumbered three to one. The corps of officers is divided by jealousy—the Canadians, the veterans of Louisbourg, the officers of the new regiments from France—each faction poison to the other. As for the command, Des Gouttes is afraid to take his ships out and fight Boscawen and too full of his own importance to take orders from a soldier; Drucour's a dreamer, Prevost a robber and Franquet no engineer . . . and so on . . . and on. Poor Jamie!"

"And what do you think, Mary?"

She thought a little and put up her chin. "I think the English will do a lot of huffing and puffing at Halifax, as Loudoun did, and then go home. But if they should come . . . if they should come, Roger, they'll be slaughtered as they try to land. The French won't give up the beaches without a fight as they gave them up to the New Englanders years ago. They made great preparations for Loudoun's landing last summer—Loudoun who never came!—and Drucour's improved the beach defenses all this spring."

"And when the English are defeated?"

She said somberly, "Why do you ask me these things, Roger? Why make me talk like a musketeer?"

"I still think of you as a vestal. And surely the virgins talked about the flame sometimes?"

"I don't like the way you say that," she answered, flushing.

"Have you told Brother Jamie about me?"

"Only that I'm interested in a Halifax gentleman—a good Jacobite."

Roger's teeth grated. "Jacobite! Listen, my darling, I can understand your attachment to Prince Charlie's cause in the beginning—faith, I'd something of the sort myself—but a lot of romance has gone down the gutter since we left Europe, you and I. For one thing, the Chevalier's forsaken his own cause . . ."

"I don't believe it!"

"Believe this, then. He's a drunken vagabond, wandering about Europe in disguise with Tina Walkinshaw, a baggage he met at Stirling in the '45. He's had a child by her. And she's sister to a servant in the Prince of Wales's household in London—a pretty liaison! The Jacobites sent MacNamara to speak their mind about the woman, and Charlie consigned him and them to the deuce. No one believes in the cause now except fanatics like your brother—and there's a man I'd very much like to meet! I want to air my opinion of a man who'd throw his sister into the arms of a drunkard old enough to be her father, and then persuade 'em both to risk the hangman on some shabby enterprise that I've a notion was to benefit himself!"

Her eyes flashed. "Then you mustn't meet him, Roger! There are things I could say—things I've ached to tell you—but while James holds me to my promise I must hold my tongue. Please be patient just a little longer." She turned and put her hands on his shoulders, saying softly in the Gaelic, *"Luaidh mo chridhe,* My darling, don't tear my heart between my brother and you. Tell me you love me!"

"I love you."

"It's your mouth that says it, not your heart. And O my lover, there's so little time!"

The melting voice, the Gaelic made for love and sorrow, her haunted eyes, the pallid face made gaunt by the way she sat and the fall of the window light, all made her seem fey then. He was startled and yet charmed. Across his memory, like a whiff of peat across the nostrils, came an old wives' tale, heard in the long hiding after Culloden . . . of strange green-eyed maidens who danced in green gowns on the hills and sometimes wandered down the brae in search of mortal kisses. Woe betide the lad who granted them! Whimsically he hummed a stave of the song Calum Mor had sung there in the bothie in the mountains:

> *Her shoes were made of Spanish leather*
> *And her stockings were of silk,*
> *And her gown was green about her*
> *And her skin was white as milk.*

She asked him in an odd voice why he hummed that queer old tune.

He answered whimsically, "Because it came on me that I'd a Green Dancer in my arms and must pay the penalty. The lad loses her, and his soul as well, doesn't he?"

She laughed and wrinkled her nose. "You've no soul to lose, Roger. Besides, it's your heart I want."

"You have that now."

She put her lips to his for payment on account.

At Rodrigues' urging Roger took up lodging in the merchant's house. A drawing account furnished him with funds and a wardrobe which, if French, was none the worse for that. Mornings he spent in the countinghouse, going over those sprawling enterprises in which he now had such a substantial interest. In the afternoons he took his exercise, riding along the rough harbor road or strolling the ramparts, Louisbourg's favorite promenade, beginning at the Dauphin bastion by the main gate and sweeping in a great loop about the town, with views across the moorland and the sea. And every evening in the little chamber in the Rue d'Orleans he made love to Mary—discreetly, for she insisted on the niceties as if she were *jeune fille*, but with all the impatience of his blood. She said that he was "difficult." She was cold, he retorted. But no man who had her kisses could believe that.

One of these tiffs was interrupted when, hands against his breast, she felt the shape of the amulet.

"Roger! Whatever is this?"

"Nothing much—a talisman I got from the Indians."

"Do let me see it!"

Indifferently he unfastened his shirt, and she turned the thing in her fingers.

"It's very crude," she said, unimpressed. "What's it good for?"

"Luck—luck in all things."

"And has it never failed you?"

"In one thing only."

"And what's that?"

"It's supposed to provide good wooing, pleasure in love, and sure begetting——"

"Roger!" The wrinkled nose again. "Of all things—a superstitious Englishman!"

There was a stir at the door, the Norman woman welcoming someone, a quiet male voice advancing. The lovers sprang up and apart, self-consciously, Mary smoothing swiftly her rumpled sleeves and fichu, Roger gazing across the street at the imposing brick-and-stone hospital of the Frères de la Charité.

A wisp of a man came into the room, silent in moccasins, clad in a long and ragged cassock. An ivory crucifix hung from a silver chain about his neck. Baldness had given him a natural tonsure, from the round pink edge of which a straggle of short gray locks hung down. His face was the color of an Indian's and gone to skin and bone and long gray beard. In their deep sockets his eyes were intelligent and benign but a little vague, and he blinked as he looked about the chamber as if his eyesight had been dulled by books—or too much sun glare on too many journeys in the snow.

He exclaimed, "Ma'mselle, I have . . . eh! . . . Pardon! . . . You have a visitor."

He paused, embarrassed, in the middle of the floor.

"This is M. Sudden, Father. Roger, this is Père Maillard, missionary to the savages in Ile Royale."

"In all Acadie," the priest corrected gently, with a slow bob of head toward Roger. "I am what I was before the coming of M. Le Loutre."

"Le Loutre!" snapped Roger. "Where is he?"

"In an English prison, monsieur. The bishop sent him back to France after the unfortunate affair of the Acadians, but his ship was taken on the way. He has been three years a prisoner of the English in the Isle of Jersey."

This was news! Roger found it hard to restrain a grin. Cornwallis had always wanted to hang The Otter, but this was better than hemp. Durance in English hands, within sight of France, so near and yet so far, embittered with sour memories, what a purgatory for that man who had sent so many to hell!

"You speak French well, monsieur," the priest observed. "You are an Englishman, are you not?"

"M. Sudden," said Mary quickly, "is an associate of Rodrigues *et fils*. The war has driven him from Halifax."

"Ah!" The old man's wrinkles parted in a rather sweet smile. "But surely it is not altogether war which brings him to our Louisbourg?"

Mary looked down demurely. Roger's tongue could not hold back the cynicism Wolfe had flung at him.

"Where a man's treasure is, Father, there is his heart also."

The old man beamed. "My felicitations, monsieur! Ma'mselle is charming and of a generous heart. She has been an angel to my poor savages. You see, Ma'mselle, I have come to beg again!"

Mary turned pleasantly to the escritoire, and Roger gave a mental sniff. Priests! Always after money! As if this wheedling old man weren't supported by the King of France! That was the trouble with them all in Acadie—French agents first and missionaries afterward. He remembered tales of Père Maillard. Gossip in the Micmac lodges said that Le Loutre had come to despise Maillard as an old dotard, too feeble or too gentle for the warpath any more.

As Mary put two louis in the lean hand Roger suggested carelessly, "One thing you must be thankful for, monsieur—the movement of the savages toward the east during the past five years. Now that you are no longer young, *voilà!* your parish comes to you!"

The myopic eyes regarded Roger carefully. "Yes, one should be thankful for that, I suppose. The movement has been very slow. Many are still west of Canso, and of those in Ile Royale only one or two hundred have reached Louisbourg. It was a design of M. Le Loutre to gather the savages into this part of the country—for the better distribution of charity, of course."

"Of course! And how does it fare, this land of promise?"

The old man looked unhappy. "I regret to say that few in Louisbourg have the charity of Mademoiselle."

"But surely M. le Gouverneur . . . ?"

"The governor promises much. He expects to see a multitude of savages camped in the woods behind the town. But . . . even my frugal Micmacs cannot live very long on promises."

Roger was tempted to ask how long they could live in the face of English powder and shot. The missionary forestalled him, speaking slowly, cautiously, without once lifting that mild and candid gaze from Roger's face.

"Monsieur, I am a human being with a Frenchman's love for France. But I cannot disguise from myself the way in which our governor hopes to employ the savages in the war upon the English. Nor can I forget the desolation brought upon those unhappy Acadians by the misguided zeal of M. Le Loutre. That was like a warning from God, whose wrath is terrible. It seems to me that, like the Acadians, my poor savages have been too long a pawn in this game of nations. But the fault is not with priests and governors alone. The traders must share the guilt, Monsieur Beau Soleil!"

Roger started as if shot. He put an instinctive hand to his breast and found the shirt gaping and the little stone fish exposed.

"One has heard of you, monsieur," the old man went on calmly. "I regret that my weak eyes took so long to recognize the totem. What do you here in Louisbourg?"

"Mademoiselle has told you."

"But surely there is something else—something to do with the Indians?"

"Nothing, monsieur, absolutely."

"It is true," Mary broke in eagerly. "He came here for the love of me."

"*Eh bien!* If you came here simply for the love of Mademoiselle, monsieur, perhaps you will give me the little fish, for the love of God!"

Roger was taken aback. What, part with his luck? His unruly tongue rapped out:

"Is not the totem about your own neck good enough for them, *mon père?*"

"With the crucifix I save their souls. It is their bodies I am thinking of."

"I have my own body to consider, monsieur."

"Have you considered your soul?" the old man cried.

He bobbed his head to Mary in that funny old-fashioned way and departed in a shuffling whisper of worn moccasins.

CHAPTER 37

The Place of the Cormorants

THE TABLE of M. Rodrigues was renowned, and not merely for the excellence of its wines. In a soil and climate where vegetables grew poorly and grains not at all, where most of the populace lived off the sea, where even the officers' messes had a well-established reek of stockfish, the board of M. Rodrigues was unique. The wide reach of his busy trade enabled him to ply his guests with spiced dishes from India, the fruits of the West Indies, pastries of white flour smuggled from New England, Canadian butter, in addition to all the known delicacies of France. The savages kept him well supplied with such tasty matters as oysters from Ile St. Jean, maple sugar and syrup, choice cuts of moose and caribou meat, and an abundance of wild duck. Not even Governor Drucour, in his splendid quarters in the Bastion du Roi, could boast such fare.

Thus Roger fared, and in a fortnight came to know the gourmands of the garrison, not least among them Colonel St. Julhien of the Regiment Artois and Loppinot, the town major. Loppinot's favorite jest at table was a toast to M. Sudden, "Whom I bought from the savages, you comprehend, for two pounds of condemned powder, a dull knife, and a *velte* of the worst rum that ever came out of Martinique!" And he would add, amid the laughter and the clink of glasses, that *mordieu!* this gentleman had skipped his ransom and never repaid so much as a drop!

Roger found himself the object of much curiosity and not a little envy. It was known that he had in some way mulcted the English king of a fortune and escaped with it to Louisbourg. He parried questions with wit and clothed his past in mystery, partly because it suited his mood and partly for the sake of Rodrigues, who had something in common with Caesar's wife.

The younger officers accepted his reserve with good humor, but there was a certain hauteur in the older ones, especially those who had served long in Ile Royale. Old Franquet, the engineer, was heard to remark, with a glance at Roger's fine dress, *"La violette aime l'ombre,"* a quip which Louisbourg remembered and repeated.

This epicurean life lost nothing when on the third of June a great fleet of English transports anchored in Chapeau Rouge Bay, and Boscawen's warships filled with white canvas the seaward view from the ramparts. Rather there was a new zest in every wine and dish, a louder laughter round the board. The general note was one of confidence, but to Roger it sounded a little too high, a little too near the edge of hysteria. He became restless, and a few days after the appearance of the fleet he asked Rodrigues to procure him a permission to visit one of the posts toward Chapeau Rouge: "I should like to stay for a time, to watch events."

"Ah! That is excellent! I shall ask Prevost to grant you a commission in one of the Compagnies de la Marine."

"You misunderstand me. I am not a fighting man."

A sharp flick of the Basque's black eyes. "One has the impression that you are, my friend. But of course you know yourself best. You cannot go simply as an observer, however; the regulations will not permit. You must be prepared to serve in some capacity." He fished a horn snuffbox from his waistcoat and took a pinch of the coarse rappee he favored.

"If you merely want something to do, Roger, I could employ you very usefully on something else at the moment. I am instructed by M. Drucour to establish a great cache of provisions, blankets, clothing, and ammunition on the bank of the Miré River, fifteen miles through the forest from Louisbourg. For a secret purpose, you understand, in case the English should succeed in landing sufficient forces to cut off the town. The matter must be kept hidden from our savages especially, else they will steal everything. The place we have chosen—mark this carefully—is just north of the woodcutters' road which runs from Louisbourg to the long lake of the Miré. A small brook flows down to the lake through a ravine in a forest of firs. In that ravine. Every precaution must be taken——"

"But that is not what I want," Roger protested. "Besides, if the English succeed in landing while I am there I should find myself cut off from the town—and from Mademoiselle."

"Eh bien, then I suggest the post at Coromandière, an hour's ride from the town. You could go as an interpreter, shall we say, to the little band of savages employed as scouts by our forces there. It is a place of no importance—the English must land nearer Louisbourg, at Flat Point or White Point, where it is possible to put artillery ashore. Nevertheless Coromandière is well guarded lest the English attempt to land and turn our positions to the east. Yes," with a hint of sarcasm, "I think Coromandière is the very place for one who does not wish to fight, and yet—for the sake of his friends as well as himself—must give that appearance. There you will find old Colonel St. Julhien, whom you have met at my table. and his Regiment Artois. They are snugly entrenched at the head of the little cove and have a camp of tents in the woods behind. A charming spot, a pleasant time of year, and you may depend that St. Julhien maintains a very good table. You shall go tomorrow, my dear Roger. I shall make the arrangements at once!"

The Place of the Cormorants was picturesque if not quite the idyllic scene that M. Rodrigues had painted. In the craggy coast, just where it curved boldly west to form Chapeau Rouge Bay, the shallow cove made a gap perhaps six hundred yards across, with a strip of sand at its head. The beach had the color of rust, and so had the steep gravel face of the bluff behind it.

Along the bluff top ran the French entrenchment, with a parapet of logs. On platforms at intervals sat eleven cannon of various kinds —six of them swivel-mounted. Behind this position the land rose unevenly for about a mile, covered with scrub spruce woods. A small brook tumbled down the long slope and made a bright gleam on the beach at the east end. Among the raw tree stumps on either side of the brook ravine were clustered the tents of the Regiment Artois, and hundreds of men in soiled white breeches and red waistcoats dark with sweat were toiling between the woods and the sea, cutting down the tough, wind-blasted trees, dragging them to the bluff edge, and toppling them on to the beach. Already the sand was half hidden by this abatis, with the butts toward the bank and the wild branches pointing stiffly seaward. It looked like a thicket growing in the very edge of the sea.

Roger considered the approach. Boats entering the cove must come under the plunging fire of cannon as soon as they passed its broad mouth, and as they converged toward the tree-tangled beach they must face the blast of grapeshot from the swivel guns and the fusillade of St. Julhien's thousand men.

"What do you think of it?" demanded St. Julhien.

"Only a madman would attempt it," answered Roger with conviction.

"Nevertheless one wishes *ces fous anglais* would try," snapped St. Julhien ferociously. "The regiment has been posted here since the snows, standing in the water of these ditches, you comprehend, for the whole slope is a hanging morass covered with those witches'-

brooms of trees. Half my men have bad feet already. It is a *mot* amongst us that our enemy is not *les anglais* but *les engelures*. Yes! We are assassinated with chilblains! And those cursed flies and mosquitoes! And the fog, which freezes at night and stews in the daytime. What a climate! What a country! I ask you, is it worth all this?"

On the east side of the cove a spur of the main ridge came down to the sea. Upon it, just above the shore, stood a small earthwork and a platform of logs commanding a flank view of the beach. St. Julhien waved a hand.

"That magpie's nest was made for the Scottish officer Johnstone last year. He had a fantasy that Milor Loudoun might attempt to land on the other side of the butte—impossible, of course. The beach ends where you see. Around the point is nothing but a mass of rocks, broken and tumbled, where the sea breaks even in calm weather, and above it the steep face of the butte, and then the stunted forest itself, pressed by the winds into thickets where a goat could scarcely force its way. It is like that all the way to Flat Point, where Marin waits with his Regiment Bourgogne."

From seaward, beyond the rocky islet at the cove mouth where the cormorants nested, came the signal guns of the English fleet, a continual grumble in the fog.

"Aha!" St. Julhien cried. "He does not like his situation, M. Boscawen! To have his great fleet massed in this bay, with the wind east and a lee shore and a mist as thick as soup!"

"And the chance of Des Gouttes coming down upon him with the weather gauge," suggested Roger.

"Des Gouttes!" contemptuously. *"Cette vache n'a pas de cornes!"*

Almost as he spoke there was a sigh in the treetops from the west.

"Aha!" snapped the old soldier. "The wind blows now from Chapeau Rouge, which the English in their barbarous dialect call Gabarus. In an hour the fog will be gone. Des Gouttes has lost his opportunity! But at least we shall have a sight of our enemy!"

The white mass yielded reluctantly before the wind. In an hour the inner fringe of the anchored English fleet was visible and the nearest ships promptly put off boats to examine the shore defenses.

St. Julhien's gunners tried hopeful long shots with a 24-pounder. From Flat Point and White Point came the thunder of other guns wasting powder in the same attempt. The boats kept well out of range and finally withdrew.

"They have not seen much of your defenses," Roger commented.

"They have heard us growl, *en tout cas!*" chuckled a major near by.

"And they have seen the teeth of our coast," said St. Julhien, pointing to the heavy swell breaking on the rocks. He shook his fist at the ships, now fully revealed by the offshore breeze. "You will have to wait, my friends, perhaps for weeks! *Mon Dieu,* there are a lot of you!"

There were indeed. Four miles across the heaving swell lay Chapeau Rouge, blue now in the heat haze, and westward the bay ran a good six miles into the land, and all that dancing blue expanse was inhabited by ships ranging in size from broad-beamed Western Ocean merchantmen to small sloops and jiggers chartered in Halifax and the ports of New England. Seaward, against a wall of fog still rolling slowly back, gleamed the white topsails of Boscawen's men-of-war, cruising off the port and watching for Des Gouttes.

Roger felt a tingling in his bones. By the whim of Pitt, that gouty man, that Whig, this wild and lonely bay had become a busier water than the Thames at London. What a sight! He was impressed not so much by the ships as the magnificence of the gamble. Suppose Des Gouttes had ventured out and fallen upon that huddle of wooden sheep in the fog! Suppose they were caught by a hurricane as Holborn was last year, all embayed as they were. And all this hazard so far from home, with invasion and conquest only a channel width away!

He said to the French officers soberly, "One thing is clear—you are going to have a fight, my friends. Those men have come too far and run too many risks to turn back now."

"*Exactement!*" St. Julhien twisted hard at his gray mustaches. "They will gaze and gaze—and then one day they will chance all in one throw, they will fling themselves at these beaches, into the mouths of our guns, you comprehend, and that will be the end! It is magnificent! It is fate! And to think that it will fall to us—we ourselves—to cripple the power of England in a stroke! I have been a soldier of France nigh fifty years, and destiny has come upon me here, in this small fish-stinking corner of the world. Ah, young men,

it is something to serve long, to be faithful, to have patience after all!"
He was a little absurd, this gray commander with his wine-blossomed
nose, his loud voice and theatrical gestures; but there was nothing
absurd about his position at Coromandière. Death sat here in a thousand white coats, waiting.

At mess that evening Roger was listless and absorbed. Young De
Gannes set the long tables under the marquee in a roar with some
whimsical tale of dalliance in Louisbourg—"but ah, messieurs, I
would give them all for one kind look from a certain demoiselle in
the Rue d'Orleans . . . *cheveux blond ardent, yeux verts* . . . you
comprehend . . . but alas, she is of a cold blood like her brother, that
codfish Captain Johnstone." He capped this with a roll of eyes toward the canvas overhead and a doleful, *"Eh, l'amour, le doux
auteur de mes cruels supplices!"*

Captain Fagonde, seeing Roger silent in the midst of the laughter,
asked with some concern, "What is the matter, monsieur?"

"A little something—the heat, perhaps. It is nothing."

"Mordieu! When one cannot eat, that is a bore. When one cannot
drink, that is a misfortune. But when one cannot laugh at De Gannes,
monsieur, that is a calamity!"

CHAPTER 38

Calamity

THE NIGHT WAS HUMID and the tents hummed with mosquitoes. In
this clear weather the English ships had ceased their firing of minute
guns, but the surf beat and boomed along the shore like a cannonade
itself. Roger stirred and chafed in the campaign blanket, dozing uneasily and dreaming a fantastic procession of faces, most of them too
vague for recognition and all uttering remarks that had no connection and no meaning. A girl cried mayflowers in the Halifax market
square; a blank face with Cousin Penny's voice murmured plaintively
about the muddy road to Suddenholt; a sergeant in the colors of
Warburton's Regiment recited in a hoarse barrack-square voice the
ritual of the bayonet thrust: "The left hand under the swell below

the lowermost rammer pipe and the right hand acrawst the brass at the 'stremity o' the butt . . ." And so on, monotonously, until the next face and the next voice came along. Toward morning, as the air cooled in a dewfall, the faces and voices faded and he slept. But suddenly he seemed to hear the gay voice of Fagonde repeating that last word of his: *"Calamité! . . . Calamité! . . . Calamité!"*

He wakened then and found one of the savages shaking his foot gently.

"What goes?" he muttered in Micmac.

"The *Aglaseaou* move . . . many canoes . . ."

Outside in the starlight there was nothing to be seen from the darkened English ships except a single light at a masthead off Coromandière. Then he noticed two lights at a masthead somewhat to the east, and far beyond that a cluster of three. Signals? More likely an arrangement for marking the divisions of the fleet at moorings. But the French were stirring and the guard in the trenches was alert. Bayonets glinted in the starlight. Far to seaward the stars faded before a dawn which had yet to come over the horizon.

From the tents a subdued buzz of men turning out, the low, urgent voices of officers and sergeants, *"En éveil! En éveil!"* and St. Julhien hissing to the tambour major, "Not a tap! At your peril!"

The white coats of the Artois swarmed like ghosts into the trenches along the bluff. Everywhere sounded the slither of ramrods, the *snick* of gun cocks, the *snack* of pan guards coming down.

There was no sound from seaward, but as the first daylight smeared the eastern sky they saw a long shadow undulating over the water between the anchored ships and the shore. Boats! What a multitude! The Artois broke their unnatural silence with a shout.

The English fleet seemed gathered chiefly off Flat Point, where the New Englanders had landed in '45, and the great boat shadow moved slowly toward that beach. Marin was waiting there with his Regiment Bourgogne.

Only two ships lay opposite Coromandière, a frigate and a snow, and as the light increased they made sail and came in boldly to the Cormorant Rock and opened a smart cannonade on St. Julhien's position. The frigate looked like the *Kennington*. Roger was not sure. But he recognized the snow, a stout thing, much bigger than *Fair*

Lady. Her name was *Halifax*. Was that an omen? Birnam wood to Dunsinane?

Most of their shot fell short or thudded into the face of the bluff. The French replied with no better fortune except that a 24-pounder struck the frigate once and made the splinters fly. The shocked cormorants abandoned their nests and fled with dismal croaks into the west, and that was the chief result of all this powder-burning.

"So!" cried Colonel St. Julhien, mustaches aquiver. "A little *divertissement* while they land their forces at Flat Point. Hark, they do the same at White Point and beyond . . . those distant shots must be from Lorambec . . . but is it possible they think we are deceived? What animals!" He shook his fist at that vast flotilla moving in a great half-moon toward Flat Point. *"Mordieu!* How one wishes they would come here! Must those boasters of the Bourgogne have all the fun?"

The Artois were out of their entrenchment, sitting, squatting, standing on the log parapet, eager to see the debacle when Marin opened fire. The westerly horn of the half-moon was now quite close inshore, just out of cannon shot, and the first rays of sunshine awakened the bright scarlet of the English coats and made them like a vast and bloody wave, moving with a flicker of wet oar blades toward invisible Flat Point. In a few minutes they too would be hidden by the east shoulder of Coromandière.

But now, like an enormous lobster casting off a claw in some moment of crisis, the west wing of the floating red mass detached itself. For a moment its intention was obscure. The frigate and snow off Coromandière began to fire again with fury. St. Julhien's voice rose in a scream.

"Dieu! They come here! Down! Down, all of you!"

He and several other officers ran along the parados, striking at the men's shoulders with the flat of their swords. Into the trenches scrambled the Regiment Artois, yelling with excitement. Someone discharged a musket, and at once a ragged but tremendous fusillade spattered the surface of the empty cove like gravel flung into a puddle.

"Hold your fire!" screamed St. Julhien, dancing on the parados with rage.

But his regiment was past holding now. With enthusiasm, as fast as they could reload, they poured the fire of a thousand muskets into the blue water of Coromandière. A fog of gray powder smoke arose and drifted along the face of the trenches on the light morning air.

The English detachment came on at inhuman speed. Plainly the seamen had been saving their strength; now they toiled like demons, bare backs swaying all together, oars lifting and falling with a beautiful precision that must have set old Boscawen's eyes alight. Again Roger had that illusion of insects running over the sea, and they came on with the insensate purpose of insects driven by an instinct for self-destruction.

The foremost boats entered the cove, filled with men in red jackets and tall red caps—grenadiers. There were more behind, grenadiers in hundreds, the grenadier companies of the whole army apparently. Among them the figure of Wolfe was plain, his lean six-feet-three upright in a boat stern like a jack staff. They came straight on into that mortal storm. A cannon ball smote one of the leading boats; it stopped in a tangle of oars, wallowed, sank. A dozen heads bobbed, some dark and shining, some still in their white wigs, and one absurd head swam with the miter cap jammed firmly on the wig, like a small red boat buoy in an anchorage.

The boats came on. Now another suffered. And another. Now three together, holed and sinking fast. And now the musket balls were finding them. Men twitched, leaped up and dropped over the gunwales, toppled into the sea.

The noise was tremendous. Roger's ears pained and set up a high, ringing whine of their own, and through it, faint and far, sounded the voice of Fagonde at his elbow. *"Dieu!* This is not war! This is a massacre!"

Behind the grenadiers pressed other boats laden with men in red jackets and blue bonnets—Fraser's men. And on the east flank of the attack appeared the buckskin shirts and round caps of the rangers. The smoke was drifting that way, rolling in folds like dirty skeins of wool along the bluff; the spur and the "magpie's nest" were completely hidden.

Something he did not recognize, an instinct, a blind urge for action, turned Roger's feet toward the east butte. He began to run.

It was not far. He dashed through the stream and climbed the slope, groping in the acrid smoke for the log platform of the *nid-de-pie*. He bumped into it at last. The post was empty. St. Julhien had gathered every man into the trenches above the beach.

Roger ran down the steep west slope, floundering among rocks and stumps. He emerged into sunlight on the shore. To the west the French position was hidden by the smoke and the shoulder of the butte. Seaward swarmed the boats of the attackers, milling uncertainly now. Men in the leading boats were standing up, shouting over their shoulders, pointing to the beach, seeing at last the meaning of that strange forest where the swell broke. All about them the water jumped with flying lead. Roger's eye sought the tall person of Wolfe and found it close in to his right, staring toward the abatis. Suddenly the scarlet arm rose and waved back toward the sea. It repeated the gesture violently, and the leading boats began to turn away. There was sound of cheering beyond the smoke, the voice of Artois raised in a shout of victory. But there was no slackening in their fire. Rather it was increased. The Indians had run down from the woods and added their muskets to the fusillade.

Immediately before him, and just out of musket shot, Roger noticed a few boats—rangers, light infantry, Highlanders—creeping eastward to avoid the full blast of the French fire. They had not seen Wolfe's signal, or they ignored it. Roger looked at the shore below, a mass of ragged rocks, ice-bitten and sea-bitten, where the long swells broke and flung a wet white lace into the very grass at his feet. There was a nook, not large, enough perhaps to pass two boats abreast, and at the head of it a shelf of pebbles. The swell surged in there and rattled the pebbles as it withdrew . . . but it was possible . . . just possible . . . by a stretch of imagination, of course . . .

He looked again at the little knot of boats. The men were staring toward him, one indeed aiming a musket, but Roger's eye was drawn and held by a familiar figure in the nearest whaleboat. It was Tom Fuller.

Roger took off his hat and waved. Tom stared. They all stared. The man with the musket lowered it. Again a wide gesture with the hat, a sweep of arm toward the small gap in the rocks. They did not move.

Behind and above him came the voice of De Gannes, standing in the edge of the smoke drift, calling in a voice cracked with excitement, "M. Sudden! . . . What do you here? . . . M. le Colonel wishes you to gather the savages at once. . . . Monsieur! . . ."

Monsieur did not choose to hear. But Monsieur had no time to waste. He threw back his head and uttered the war cry of the rangers, that weird whoop first sounded by Gorham's half-Mohawks in the fighting about Fort Anne. Could they hear it in that hell's din from the trenches above the beach? He uttered the howl again. They turned their faces to each other. Perhaps they considered it a trap. Could they see De Gannes? That young rake was crying now in a bewildered voice, "Monsieur, the savages cannot possibly hear you there! Come up here . . . my colonel wishes . . ."

Roger leaped upon a great jagged boulder at the water's edge and threw his arms wide. "Tom! Tom! Come in, man! Here! Here!"

There was a decision out there. Tom's boatmen took up their oars and began to row in, cautiously, while Tom stood in the bow, staring . . . staring . . .

Suddenly his lips parted, his teeth flashed white. The rowers put their backs into the work. Another boat followed, with two light infantry officers standing upright among their men, staring under upraised palms. To their right a boat full of Highlanders moved in eagerly. Still farther to the right, on the edge of that maelstrom where the French shot flew and the retreating boats of the advance force were mingled and confused with those of the main body still pressing on, a number of other craft pointed their noses like questing hounds toward the venturers. By Jove, the thing was done!

But was it? There was De Gannes, an image of outraged astonishment, perched beside the *nid-de-pie* with a pistol in his hand; and behind him across the shallow ravine stood the left flank of the Artois, absorbed in the smoke and uproar of its own exertions. Roger turned and scrambled up the bank with eyes fixed on the white face of De Gannes. Slowly, as if fascinated, the lieutenant raised the pistol. Roger saw the priming flare. The spurt of fire from the muzzle and a violent blow on his chest came together. He staggered backward and nearly fell, the breath knocked out of him. Then he was going on again, on legs that did not seem to belong to him at all. De Gannes was tugging at his sword and crying wildly into the smoke, *"Adju-dant! Adjudant! Méfiez-vous! Les anglais!"*

Roger closed with him, grasped him by the sword belt. They fell together, struggling. They rolled once or twice. Then Roger's knuckles struck the empty pistol in the grass. He brought it up and smote the elegant white wig four times with the heavy barrel. De Gannes lay on his back, his thin nostrils fluttering.

To the west the cannon and fusils thundered as if St. Julhien de-signed to split the ears of the gods. Wrapped in his own powder smoke, that strutting gray cockerel was sure of himself, at any rate, already seeing, no doubt, the Cross of St. Louis, with its scarlet rib-bon, against his fine white coat. Roger looked back.

A handful of rangers, light infantry and Highlanders were ashore, swarming over the rocks, and in the surge behind them crowded boat after boat full of men. The boats were lifting and falling fright-fully in the surf, smashing to flinders one after another as they got among the rocks. The men were leaping out breast-deep and floundering toward the outstretched hands of Tom Fuller and the others. And there was Wolfe himself, poised on a bullet-splintered gunwale for the leap, pointing upward to the *nid-de-pie* with a tas-seled cane and shouting.

Most of the muskets were drenched. Already the Highlanders were throwing theirs away and drawing broadswords after their fatal habit. One volley, one rush of bayonets by a disciplined French pla-toon, might yet sweep them all back into the sea. Roger stumbled off along the spur. Every breath stabbed deep beneath his breastbone. He felt a small drip of blood inside his shirt. He turned toward the brook, carried down the long slope on those strange and desperate legs.

The dirty canvas of the camp loomed through the powder drift, and there was the red flicker of a cooking fire. Half a dozen officers' servants were grouped about it, staring at him openmouthed. Beyond squatted a little group of squaws and children oblivious of the battle, waiting stolidly for a chance at the scraping of the ration pots.

He ran straight down among them, gasping "Save yourselves! Run! Run! Pass the alarm! The English are between us and the town!"

For several moments they were silent, frozen in dismayed attitudes, a tableau of idiots. Then with the scream they raised the *sauve qui peut,* scattering toward the trenches, toward the woods, toward the rough track to the town.

Roger's legs surrendered then to his body's weariness and indifference. He sank on his knees beside the stream, his chest one great dull agony. As he crouched there, gasping like a stranded fish, two Indian women came to him swiftly. He heard a cry, "Bosoley!" and felt himself lifted, one at each arm, and dragged away up the ravine among the trees. He tried to speak, to beg them to leave him alone and at peace, but his tongue could not furnish the words nor his lungs the breath. After some distance the squaws left the stream and went on through the scrub spruce woods, following the slope toward the west.

Once they paused to give him rest, on a steep butte charred bare in a bygone forest fire. There was a clear view toward the sea. One of the squaws stretched out a brown sinewy hand, accusingly, as Lot's wife might have pointed to the Cities of the Plain.

"Ankaptaan!"

His blurred vision cleared, seeing the whole of Coromandière as from the gallery of a playhouse. A twist of the wind had blown away the smoke and cleared the stage, and the play had reached its climax. The knoll of the *nid-de-pie* was a red mass of British jackets spreading in ordered ranks along the spur.

A flutter of kilts passed rapidly down the slope—Fraser's men, eager to get at the French across the ravine or perhaps to storm the camp in the hollow. The broadswords glittered, and faint and far sounded their Gaelic yell. Still farther along the spur Tom Fuller's rangers moved swiftly toward the road, St. Julhien's only line of retreat, pausing to fire across the ravine. Their buckskins made them well-nigh invisible at this distance, but their progress was marked by the white powder jets springing from the thickets along the east lip of the hollow. Ranged unevenly along the west of the ravine stood the Regiment Artois, hastily drawn from its trenches to face this red apparition on the flank.

But the *sauve qui peut* was at work; the white-clad ranks were swaying in and out; the whole line writhed like an uneasy snake. From the front rank sprang irregular white puffs and a sound like the crackle of twigs came up to the watchers on the slope. The disciplined red files on the spur, drawn up precisely as Roger had seen them so many times on the shore of Halifax harbor, suddenly spat fire along the whole length, and the smoke rolled up and hid them for a moment.

In that moment Artois broke. St. Julhien's left flank disintegrated, became a scurry of white ants running toward the Louisbourg cart road. The rest followed, throwing to the wind their courage, discipline, even their common sense—for they still outnumbered the redcoats. One steady volley and an ordered advance with the bayonet across the dale would catch Wolfe between devil and deep sea even now—and for the British there was no retreat. The surface of Coromandière was littered with broken boats.

The squaw still held that lean, accusing gesture.

"Menadae!" she said contemptuously. "Cowards!"

Roger, swaying between the women, an arm over each, began to babble in English,

"Not fair, you know . . . seen good men run just like that . . . for no more reason . . . there comes a moment when one cry will do it . . . one cry, one white-faced man, one finger pointed at the flank . . . they'll be sorry in the morning . . . too late then . . . Wolfe . . . roll 'em all up now . . . St. Julhien . . . Marin . . . D'Anthonay . . ." And then in Micmac, realizing for a moment where he was, ". . . as the slit bark of the canoe birch yields before the peeling stick . . ."

"El-oo-wa-we," one of the women said. "He is mad."

The other dropped that pointing finger and turned to him a face seamed with weather, hunger, drudgery, and something else—a mass of bruises old and new.

He stared in horror. How could a woman age twenty years in four? It was Wapke.

She uttered the very words that hovered on his tongue. "O Bosoley, what have they done to thee?"

They eased him down on one of the boulders that shone like teeth in the old fire barren, and Wapke tore open his waistcoat and shirt. The women cried out together. Chin on breast, Roger saw a great contused patch over his heart, bleeding at the center and turning gradually purple. But the women were not looking at the bruise. Two fragments of stone hung from the ends of the thong about his neck. The little stone fish was shattered.

CHAPTER 39

The Warrior and the Priest

THE MICMACS' CAMP was beside a broad stream which they called Soolakade, with a range of wooded hills beyond. It was all remarkably like those days of his first captivity. He lay on a brushwood bed in a wigwam of skins and poles, attended by Wapke and one or two older squaws, peered upon by a succession of savage faces, some known but many strange. His wound was not so deadly as it first appeared, when he spat blood and his whole chest felt smashed. The amulet had taken the force of the ball. Nevertheless it was a month before he could breathe without a stab in his left lung. The great bruise healed slowly. Wapke kept it covered with a salve and made him drink an infusion of wild cherry bark, night and morning. For hours on end she squatted by the door blanket, with foreboding in her eyes. Conversation was difficult. Delicacy forbade any question about the four years past. The tale of her life with Koap was written in her ravaged face.

Once he asked her bluntly, "Where is San Badees?"

"He is hunting."

"Where?"

"In the hills. There is no food by the river; this country has been hunted bare."

"Then why do the people stay?"

She made no answer.

He had no notion how far they had taken him. Pain had brought delirium on the way, and he knew only that the two squaws had carried him for miles, slung on a pole like a haunch of venison. He supposed himself far from Louisbourg until one night a shift of the wind brought a sea mist over the low hills and a distant grumble of guns. The fortress was still holding out. That was astonishing in itself. Something had upset Wolfe's plans; he should have been thundering at Quebec by now.

The camp sprawled along both banks of the river for a considerable distance in both directions, and it was growing. There were parties of newcomers every day. He recognized the dialects of hunting grounds as widely separated as Cape Sable and the Restigouche. This, then, must be the culmination of that long migration begun by Abbé Le Loutre, the gathering of the Micmacs toward Ile Royale, where for the first time in their history they would comprise a single force. That was it. A weapon was being forged here by the waters of Soolakade. For what purpose? And whose hand?

The answer to these questions came with an almost forgotten figure that thrust past the door blanket one July afternoon and dismissed the sullen Wapke with a thumb. It was Gautier. The man was little changed. He wore clout and moccasins and stank of sweat and the rancid bear grease with which he had smeared his skin against the flies.

"*Kway!*" he grunted, regarding the healing bruise on Roger's chest.

"*Kway.*"

"So you have come back to the Meeg-a-maage, Beau Soleil! Have you seen Koap?"

"No."

"You were with the French at Coromandière, one hears."

"Yes . . . what goes? Louisbourg . . . ?"

"Louisbourg holds, after six weeks of siege. What goes? . . . Many things. In Louisbourg . . . we slip in and out by night across the anchorage, you comprehend . . . M. Drucour's mouth is so." He drew his mouth down at the corners comically. "He is too dreamy, that man, for the post he holds . . . and much too honest. The troops are this way, that way . . . the Artois lost their courage at Coromandière and the Bourgogne joined their flight *à pas de géant,* which is not good for one's breath or one's self-respect. But D'Anthonay's Germans are still full of war, and the Regiment Cambis is fresh from France and fierce for glory. The Compagnies de la Marine . . . neither good nor bad . . . they have the virtue of knowing the country. Madame Drucour encourages the artillerymen by appearing on the ramparts every day to fire one or two cannon with her own hands. The great scandal is the fleet. Des Gouttes . . . he is well named, that man . . . dribbles! dribbles! . . . he wished to leave the harbor when the siege began, but it was a sight of Brest he wanted, not a tussle with M. Boscawen! Drucour and the council forbade him to go. So he slipped two or three of his faster vessels out with dispatches, scuttled four to bar the channel and anchored the rest close under the guns of the town. He has taken the food and powder out of his great hulks and encamped his men in the town. But will he fight beside the garrison? Faith, no! He is at odds with Drucour, with fate, with the world! What an animal!"

"But . . . Louisbourg . . . the town . . . what goes there?" demanded Roger impatiently, thinking of that one house in the Rue d'Orleans.

A shrug. "What do you expect? The English were a long time getting up their cannons . . . it is difficult to land such heavy matters on an open beach in our Ile Royale weather. And they had not reckoned on the nature of the country . . . swamps, rocks, thickets, insects . . . a penance for their sins. They did not know how to make so simple a thing as a corduroy road across a marsh, and labored like slaves in their thousands to fill each morass with rocks and earth! *Dieu!* But now all that is done, and from every side they are pouring upon Louisbourg a fire of hell."

"But surely the walls——"

"Walls! Walls are nothing against mortars, which drop their missiles from the sky. *Zut!* I have seen bombs of a size like that"— he spread his grubby hands—"fizzing and bursting in the streets. What a *pétard!* What a *pétaudière!* Monsieur, do you wish the truth? The day of fortresses is past. The power of artillery has changed the face of warfare. It is frightful! Yet . . . Louisbourg holds, and that is sublime. If you doubt the ultimate victory of France in this new war, monsieur, remember always Louisbourg!"

"Nevertheless the town must fall, Gautier. What can save it? The English outnumber Drucour four to one, and they control the sea. No help can reach Louisbourg from France and I doubt if any comes from Canada. M. Montcalm has his hands full on the borders of New York."

A smile spread over the scout's swarthy features. He showed his stained teeth.

"Aha! That is what they think . . . M. Voolf and those others. At first, you understand, they were cautious; they surrounded themselves with skirmishers at every move, they made blockhouses and little stone forts on every eminence in the forest about their camps, their roads, their landing places . . . rooting among the rocks and stumps like pigs . . . what a business! We had only a handful of savages to trouble them, and those were withdrawn into the forest by that rabbit Père Maillard so soon as the English approached the walls. We have snatched a few wigs . . . a sentry here, a straggler there . . . fleabites, that is all. *Bien!* All this convinces M. Voolf that he has nothing to fear from outside. He has strung his army all about the fortress, the harbor—he has brought guns to the lighthouse point to bombard the island battery—even to Lorambec." He leaned forward in that habit of his when he wished to make a point. His black eyes shone.

"And well behind those lines of his, monsieur, lies the English camp strung three miles along a low ridge in the swamps, from Pointe Platte into the heart of the forest. What a fine worm for a hungry bird!"

"And who is the bird . . . San Badees Koap?"

Again the yellow teeth. "Who but our Boishebert?"

"Boishebert!"

"You are astonished, monsieur? The English shall be no less, I assure you. Boishebert is at Port Toulouse, twenty leagues to the west, gathering his *coureurs de bois,* hurrying these wandering Micmacs toward the rendezvous. Villejouin will join him here with a force of militia from Ile St. Jean, and other Acadians are on the way from the Miramichi shore—men who ran into the forest in '55 to escape the English expulsion, men with hate in their hearts like a flame that must devour or die. Yes! Along the coasts and through the forests they come, they gather, Indians, rangers, Acadians. And in a few days now he comes himself to the rendezvous—Boishebert, who has for three years defied the English to venture outside their forts in Acadie!"

"*Chansons! Chansons!*" Roger snapped to cover his uneasiness.

"What can he raise? A thousand . . . two thousand men at most. The English have twelve thousand and the fleet besides."

"Ships cannot·sail in the forest, Beau Soleil. As for their army, that is spread all the way from Cap Noir round to Lorambec—scattered through leagues of forest where a messenger must risk his scalp at every step. What can they do if Boishebert falls upon the camp? Who is to defend it? Several hundred camp followers—sutlers, wagoners, the women and children of the army, five hundred sick and wounded! A pretty crop of scalps, *non?*"

"You forget the English forces opposite the Dauphin Gate are only an hour's march from their camp."

"Good! That is all we ask—an hour! They dare not pursue us into the forest—these English soldiers who have never in their lives seen more than six trees together. If they do—*bien!*—Boishebert will have such an opportunity as Beaujeu found when that wild bull Braddock crossed the Monongahela three years ago."

"And the English rangers?"

"Braddock's rangers did not save him. Do you know where M. Voolf has posted his? In a stone fort in the forest behind the northeast harbor!"

"And where shall Boishebert get food and ammunition for this force of his?"

Gautier looked wise. "Somewhere, not far, is a great cache placed in the forest on orders of M. Drucour, weeks ago. Only Boishebert knows where, lest the savages gobble it up beforehand. You see, we understand these matters, we French!"

"I see! And this—this massacre of the English sick and wounded and their women and children—all this will save Louisbourg?"

"Why not? The destruction of their camp and stores will delay the siege for weeks—and it is now well past the middle of July. Next month begins the season of autumn storms when the English fleet must leave the coast, lest it be caught and shattered as the *Admiral Olborn* was last year. Time! Time fights for us, Beau Soleil!"

He left, grinning. The hairy little man was confident, and close to Boishebert's councils, that was plain. Now he was off to Port Toulouse with the latest word of the English dispositions.

Roger thought of the long straggle of huts and tents, shut in by

gloomy woods where Boishebert's savages, white and red, could move
at ease; and the chosen time, some chilly dawn with a sea mist thick
among the trees, dulling the sounds of attack and the cries of the
victims; and the English army thundering away at Louisbourg, oblivious of the slaughter until too late. A doleful fancy. He knew how
easily it could be fact.

He was still pondering these matters next day when an uproar
broke out in the camp—dogs, shouts, the yammer of women, the
slap and scurry of moccasins toward the waterside. It was all so like
the old bad days at Shubenacadie that he was not surprised to hear
the familiar scalp yell. It was taken up and screamed by the whole
savage throng, even to the naked children.

He leaped to the wigwam entrance and saw the people milling
about a tall and gorgeous figure. It was Koap—San Badees holding
high a pair of scalps still limp and bloody, and wearing, as usual, the
red coat of a British soldier. He was lean as a starved wolf from his
three years' foray with Boishebert on the trails of Acadia. Below the
coat skirt his long legs seemed all cords and bone. His war paint was
grotesque; a wide black stripe encircled mouth and nose, and the
rest of his face was a grid of red and orange bars. The deep eye
sockets were stained with red ocher, so that his black eyes glittered
in a pair of scarlet cups. His head was shaved to a narrow scalp lock
in imitation of Boishebert's mission Indians, and to that ocher-dyed
topknot, greased and stiffened with porcupine quills, he had pinned
with a bone skewer one of the flat, richly laced *chapeaux bras* with
which French officers minced about the streets of Louisbourg. Slung
to his shoulder were other trophies of his latest hunting—a British
musket, cartridge pouch, and bayonet. Ferocious, ridiculous, and yet
majestic in a barbaric way, he strode into the midst of the camp.

Behind him in the throng a cassock fluttered, and Roger had a
glimpse of Father Maillard, the haggard and gentle prophet of these
wastes. What was he doing here with Koap? The scalp yells echoed
across the water, where the Indians on the far side were running
down to their canoes. Already there was a scuffle and yelping
among the wigwams as the squaws and boys hunted down dogs
for a scalp feast. In the midst of the hubbub Roger heard his own
name uttered by several voices, with gestures toward the wigwam.

He saw the painted face of San Badees contorted in a fierce and incredulous smile.

"Bosoley!"

He went cold. All the peace and indolence of the camp were gone
in a trice, as if a north wind blew, and the air had a prickle of cruelty.

As if to forestall it Père Maillard cried, "Surely this man is a guest
in thy lodges, my children!"

Koap checked himself in full stride. "Dost thou say Bosoley is not
our enemy, *Paduleas?* If he has gone over to the French, as the
people say, still he is Bosoley and must answer for the blood of Peyal,
Malti, Gobleal, Glode . . ." Slowly, sonorously, he recited a long list
of warriors supposedly slain by Roger's men in the time gone by.

"We hear thee, San Badees," broke in an old chief of the Bras d'Or.
"But thy woman and that other who brought him told us that Bosoley bore the little fish and must not be harmed."

"Wah!" cried Koap with satisfaction. "It is time the little fish came
back to us. Is this true?"—turning to the people.

"*Weltaak!*" they shouted together.

CHAPTER 40

Kokwadega

ROGER CONSIDERED RAPIDLY. In a moment Koap would send a squaw to
call him forth—a gesture of contempt which would not be lost on
the attentive savages. Under the clothing his breast felt naked and
defenseless without the amulet. How long would he live once Koap
discovered its absence?

But there was no hesitation in the legs which had carried him to
the rocks of Coromandière. They carried him out of the wigwam
now with a steady and confident step, and the rest of him drew itself
erect. He was conscious of his sorry finery, the battered French shoes
and torn silk stockings, the wrinkled blue velvet breeches, the
rumpled ruffles of the shirt which Wapke had washed for him in her
slipshod fashion, the yellow silk waistcoat pierced by De Gannes'
ball and still showing the old bloodstain, the fine Mechlin lace at

wrist and throat gone black with filth. And he regretted his untended queue and the dense black beard, the growth of all these
weeks at Soolakade. He had a somber sense of destiny, of fulfillment
in some way.

The savages opened a way for him. A universal stare enfolded him
from head to foot like a swimmer in a sea. Even Père Maillard stood
aside in the edge of the crowd. Overhead the sky was blue, without
a wisp of cloud, a rare day for Cape Breton in July, and the still
waters of Soolakade reflected on their polished skin the green mass
of the Miré hills.

The paint concealed Koap's expression, but his eyes glittered with
a malevolent curiosity. He stood his ground with the air of an actor
confident in his own magnificence and aware of a large and interested
audience.

He, at least, is dressed for his part, thought Roger, walking straight
toward that bizarre figure. The silence was profound.

"O San Badees, I hear thy words," he declared clearly as he came.
"But to whom should Bosoley render up the little fish? What man
is worthy?"

"What warrior is greater than the others?" returned Koap
promptly. "I am that one, and I am now the chief sagamore of all
the Meeg-a-maage." He turned again to the crowd. "*Weltaak?*"

"*Weltaak!*" they answered.

There was no gainsaying his hold on them. He was one of those
remarkable creatures spawned from time to time by warrior tribes,
a man of great strength and ferocity, ambitious, treacherous in the
gaining of his ends, and gifted with a rousing tongue. He had a passion for bloodshed and The Otter's scheme for a confederacy of the
Micmacs had provided him in one stroke with a theme and a weapon.
Roger halted a few paces before him and folded his arms in the
proper attitude for Micmac oratory. Only wit could save him, that
was clear. But he was aware of an urgent something to be accomplished, something more than the mere saving of his own skin. What
was it? Like a traveler benighted in a Highland pass, he groped for
stones in the path while sensing mountains right and left.

"O San Badees, thy mouth is full of boasting, but where are thy
deeds? Lo, I traveled the forest many summers and winters and saw

no more of San Badees than that he was The Otter's footprint. Now The Otter is gone and so thou turn to Boishebert, because thou must have someone to say to thee, Do this, Do that. O Man, thou art a footprint still, and what is that but a mark in the dust? One day a rain shall wash thee out."

"I hear a rain of words," replied Koap mockingly.

What was he turning in that crafty mind?

"*Jiksutaan!* Hark!" Roger snapped. In the still heat of the afternoon there sounded a mutter from the east. "The English thunder, my brothers. There, O San Badees, is a storm that someday soon shall blow thee away and all who follow thee."

Koap grinned. "O Bosoley," he sneered, "the little fish has made thee bold. Thy tongue is sharp because it knows no man may shed the blood of him who wears it." Roger evaded that delicate subject. He addressed himself to the people.

"Brothers, how many winters more must ye hearken to the whistling of evil birds and take the hatchet in the quarrel of the French against the English? There be old men amongst ye who have never known the sunshine of peace. Scalps ye have taken, and heads; and ye have made prisoners and beaten them until they wept, sometimes until they died, and ye have burned them with brands, and with hot irons, and plucked out their nails and hair, and stripped the skin from off the living flesh; and oftentimes the French rewarded ye with blankets and guns and firewater according to thy deeds. But ye have paid in blood for all these pleasures, O people of the Meeg-a-maage. Where is Peyal? Where is Malti? Gobleal? Glode? Flanswa? . . ." He went on through the list that Koap had recited, name for name, as nearly as he could remember it, all in the deep, slow, nasal voice which Koap had used, with his head cocked at Koap's angle, and sweeping out his right arm in the gesture Koap loved.

A flicker of brown grins ran over the throng, their eyes full of a gleeful surprise. This was a form of humor they had never seen. And it was sharpened by Koap's own grotesquerie, the coat, the lean, protruding legs, the *chapeau bras* perched on his shaven skull, the painted face dripping dyed sweat in the sunshine. So far so good; but Roger saw in them no friendliness toward himself. They were amused; they hung on every word; they were eager for the outcome, seeing Koap's hate-distended eyes; but their faces had the expectancy of boys about a pair of snarling dogs; their eyes were lit with the careless cruelty of children.

"Bosoley," said San Badees softly through his teeth, "put by the totem and let us see if thee can say amusing things."

Again Roger ignored him, saying to the gathering soberly, "Brothers, what have the long wars brought but sorrow to the Meega-maage? The crows have picked the bones of thy bravest warriors. Their scalps hang in the lodges of the Long Knives. The Otter promised ye many things. Where is The Otter now? The Aglaseaou have taken him captive on the far side of the Big Water. Where are the Wenjoo folk of Acadie who gave ye food and shelter on the warpath? The Aglaseaou have burned their villages and carried them to Bostoon and beyond. Do ye remember how, twelve summers since, the whitecoats came to Chebucto with many ships and men as thick as leaves? Where are they now? Who sits at Chebucto? Do ye remember how the whitecoats beat their war drums every night at Beauséjour? Where are they now? Who sits at Beauséjour? Brothers, how have ye been so long deceived? What magic have the Wenjoo to match the war medicine of the Aglaseaou? *Jiksutaan!* Hear it! There speaks the thunder of the English and the doom of Louisbourg! They rain their lightnings on it—ye have seen these things— the walls crumble and the towers fall—and could ye stand before *that,* O fools?"

"*Weltaak!*" grunted a petty chief from the Musquodoboit, nodding.

"Brothers, what do ye here in this corner of the Foggy Country? Why have ye given up the hunting grounds of thy fathers, ye men of Piziquid, of Wejooik, of Piktook . . . M'tatamagouche . . . Chignecto . . . Miramichi . . . Lustigouche . . . Shubenacadie . . . Tawopskik . . . Kejumkujik? Are there more fish in these cold rivers? Are the caribou more fat in the barrens of Soolakade? What say ye, does the bull moose come swifter to the call here than in the hills of Cobequid?"

"We came here for the French king's bounty," said a man of the M'tatamagouche sullenly.

"Wah! I see the moccasins of my brothers worn with hunting in these hills. I see the squaws lean from their long traveling. I see their children famished as the dogs. I see my brothers with rusty guns and worn-out knives and tomahawks. I see their blankets gone to rags. Tell me, O Man, is this the French king's bounty?"

There was no answer from them. It was Koap who spoke, with a note of triumph in his anger, as if some twist of cunning had shown him at last the nice solution of a problem. "O Bosoley, thou talk in riddles and make laughter in the mouths of fools!" And then, with a surprising meekness, "I cannot fight thee for the totem of my people as my heart desires, lest blood be spilled and bring upon me the vengeance of the Sakawachkik. Yet there is a way to tell which is the better warrior, thou or I, without offending the law of the Ancient Ones."

"I find no fear in me," Roger said. "What is this thing?"

"*Kokwadega!*"

A delighted scream sprang from all the camp.

"Come, let us strive together as the young men do," pursued Koap cunningly, "and let the prize be possession of the little fish!"

Again the tumult of approval. Roger gritted his teeth. Caught! Caught, with his eyes wide open! In good hard health he might have been a match for Koap in the Micmac form of wrestling; there was a time when he might have exulted in the challenge; but that was before the months of ease in Halifax—and he had lain six weeks recovering from that unlucky shot at Coromandière.

He had seen *kokwadega,* a brutal sport, all strength and savagery with no rules, no ground marks, no time limit—and woe to the vanquished. He had seen arms and necks twisted and broken, and once, disgusted, he had witnessed the strangling of an opponent lying senseless on the ground, with all the people laughing round about.

Already Koap was throwing off the fantastic hat and the bloody English coat. He stood naked to clout and moccasins, showing broad and muscular shoulders and the narrow hips, the corded arms and legs of a hunter. His brown skin shone with grease. Slowly Roger shed the yellow waistcoat—and no more. To remove his shirt would reveal the absence of the totem. Grimly he meditated on the difference between a slit throat and a broken neck, so important to the Ancient Ones, such damned small comfort to the man who lost the bout.

Was this the end? He refused to believe it. Yet he knew that Koap could wear him down in twenty minutes by sheer strength alone—in less if he could get home one of the brutal tricks of the game. And once worn down, there would be no mercy. He cursed the loss of the amulet. What a strength it had been to him! Without it he felt sapless and lost.

The Indians were in high excitement, jostling for a better view, laughing in their husky, high-pitched Micmac voices. Most had never seen Bosoley until he appeared so strangely in their camp, but they had heard of the mysterious white man who possessed the totem, who traveled Acadie like the wind, whose word moved ships and companies of men, whose anger followed his enemies into the uttermost nooks of the forest. And here he was in the flesh, about to strive with San Badees to the death—San Badees who had slain with his own hand the English sagamore Howe, San Badees who had been forerunner to The Otter, San Badees the terror of every Englishman in Acadie, San Badees the greatest warrior between the Fog Land and the Great River of Canada!

They lifted their voices in a great *"Hé!"* as Koap rushed forward. Roger swerved to avoid a hurtling weight of muscle and bone and outstretched claws. He clutched at the naked waist without a clear notion of what to do. They went to earth with a crash and struggled on the ground. In a moment Koap had him about the ribs, crushing his sore chest painfully. His shirt was smeared with paint as the hard face dug itself into his shoulder. He half expected the grinning teeth to fasten on his ear in the manner of *kokwadega;* but that would have drawn blood, of course. Nevertheless he worked up a hand to the painted jaw and thrust it back violently, lest it yield to temptation, and was relieved to feel that rib-cracking embrace give way. He rolled clear and they scrambled to their feet. He was gasping already from the pain in his chest and simple breathlessness.

Again the warrior sprang, and again Roger sought to avoid that overpowering brown missile. There was a disapproving murmur from the crowd. Already the camp's sympathies were set. After all, Koap was one of their own—and they had the leaning of primitives toward the winning side. Some of the younger braves were crying out, urging San Badees to make an end of the white man now, to throw him down and wring his neck. The wrestlers went to earth again, and again there was a desperate struggle on the ground. Craftily, ruthlessly, Koap thrust elbows and knees where they would hurt most, struck hard blows with his bony fist, butted with his shaven head. A knee shoved into his groin made Roger writhe. He was still too strong to be throttled. But Koap seized the moment and leaped up, leaped into the air, aiming his whole weight and his hard heels at the undefended belly on the ground.

"*Hé!*" cried the braves again.

Roger rolled and took the shock on his flank. His side felt crushed. Nevertheless he seized the brown legs and with a wild heave flung Koap to earth and grappled with him swiftly, seeking to apply that neck lock the Lancashire man had taught him long ago. But he was baffled by his own weakness. Again and again he sought the hold, only to be turned aside by one of Koap's crude strong twists or to find his grip lost on the sweating brown skin.

Again the brutal pummeling. The strength oozed out of him by invisible wounds wherever those hard knees and fists and elbows struck home. He could only cling and hope for survival while his mind sought a way to save him. Surely there must be a way! His chest, his belly, his whole body ached intolerably; his mouth gaped in the effort to breathe. His head sang with that whistling roar which children hear in conch shells, and all about him the ring of savage faces seemed to waver like a seacoast seen far off in August weather. One face alone was clear, and that only for a passing moment, Wapke's, with an expression vehement and strange. Somehow he broke clear and staggered to his feet, holding body and wits together by a will to survive. Somewhere behind the conch roar in his skull the desperate mind still sought a way. Something! Something! And the struggle went on, the fury of arms and bodies and threshing legs, the breaking apart, the new leap of the great brown cat, the bruising shock, the fall, the gasping contortions on the hard-packed earth. And always the weakness growing, and triumph growing in the face of Koap.

They broke apart once more, and as Roger crouched, panting, bracing his unsteady legs for Koap's next rush, the Indian laughed and cried aloud, "O Bosoley, begin thy death song now. For soon now I shall take thy life from thee as I took Wapke—without the shedding of thy blood!"

It came to Roger then, out of nowhere, like a flash of powder in a darkened room . . . Manchester, Prince Charlie's camp in the melancholy Lancashire weather, the evening wrestlers defying rain and mud, the Cumberland men and their eternal talk of "chips," the Westmoreland men and theirs . . . cross-buttock, backheel, buttock, hank, click . . . words . . . incomprehensible words . . . the Highlandmen and their rude hugging and hurling . . . the Lancashire men and their swifter catch-and-throw which drew the better crowd . . . and then, suddenly, the slim dark man from Cornwall stepping into the circle with a challenge to Carlyle Jock. Jock and his terrible swinging hipe!

The memories came swiftly now and clearly . . . Jock refusing out of sheer good nature, and the Cornishman's insistence . . . then the grapple . . . the break . . . Jock stepping forward briskly for the hipe . . . the dark man putting out a hand and turning sharply away . . . and suddenly Jock, great Carlyle Jock, sailing over the slim man's shoulder and diving to earth headfirst. He remembered the open-mouthed amazement of them all, and how still Jock lay, and how some said it was a damned ill trick, and how the Cornishman explained the flying mare and swore it was a proper throw where he came from. How did it go? Ay, how?

Koap bounded forward, sweat-shining, paint-smeared, a nightmare figure, weird as the Micmac notion of Death itself. The thin lips sneered back from his strong teeth. His eyes widened a little when Roger made no attempt to avoid his rush.

The Englishman put out a hand, caught Koap's right wrist, and turned away swiftly, stooping, heaving, dragging the hard brown arm over his shoulder. What followed was amazing to them all. San Badees seemed to climb feet first into the air, head down, indeed head falling, right arm pinioned, left arm flailing wildly at nothing. For a flying moment he seemed poised with feet to the sky, and then he dived to earth headlong. There was a thud at the Englishman's feet, and a moment later the gleaming brown body bounced on the hard camp ground like a felled tree. There it lay very still, with arms and legs outflung. The mouth gaped, and from it came a hideous snoring sound. The eyes showed only their bloodshot whites. The stiff scalp lock was flattened and matted with bits of trodden brown grass. The eyes, the smudged paint, the trickle of blood from the flaring nostrils, the weird sounds in the yawning throat, all made a frightful object from which the Indians recoiled in awe.

The wizened Bras d'Or chief spoke respectfully: "This is magic, brothers. Mad indeed was San Badees to challenge him who wore the little fish. O Bosoley, show us the totem now, that our eyes may see fortune in the days to come when we go with Boishebert against the English camp."

Roger had fallen to his knees, too spent to care a whit. With cynical humor he drew from his pocket and flung on the ground the shattered bits of stone, the queerly carved back fin, the thong by which it had hung about his neck so long.

"Behold! It is finished, like the Sakawachkik, the Ancient Ones, who made it and whose bones were scattered long ago. So is thy fortune—and mine!"

CHAPTER 41

The Making of a Miracle

FOR A FULL MINUTE all was still. Then a hubbub sprang up on all sides at once, as if the camp had one voice—and that a shriek of anger and despair. Roger looked up and saw a knife in every hand, or so it seemed, and already the squaws were scuttling off to the wigwams for the hatchets of their lords. And it was odd to see how, even now, they retained some fear of him, for those who met his direct glance dropped a hand to their flanks, concealing the knife behind the thigh, and the voices yelling loudest for his blood were those from the back of the throng. But he had no illusions. They were working themselves up to killing pitch, and it would not take them long. The knives were itching in their hands. In a few moments now the charmed circle would be broken by the pressure from behind, and then would come a brown snarling rush, the short blades rising and falling, the bloody end. A pity, after coming so far and weathering so much, but per-

haps this way was best. The whole pattern of his destiny had been
changed at Coromandière, and for the worse as far as fortune went.
The future was a ruin, like Louisbourg itself. Mary? He could see the
scorn in Mary's eyes, hearing the tale of De Gannes.

The brown ring surged, and in that moment someone rushed from
behind and stood against him crying, "*Nenkoodum!* Stop!" He felt
the sweep of a skirted garment against his shoulder. Wapke? He
looked up and saw that it was Père Maillard, standing with arms upraised like the figure on his little crucifix. The old man's face was
alight with passion. His thin voice pierced the tumult like a sword.
The distorted faces gave back a little, muttering.

"Before ye slay this man, ye must slay me," Père Maillard said.

A young brave spoke. "This man who stole the totem of our people
now has broken it, and for that he must die. Stand aside, *Paduleas,*
for we do not wish thee harm."

"Nor do I wish thee harm!" the fluting voice cried. "Will ye never
learn? Ye have told me how in the olden time the great spirit Glooskap steered his canoe into the sunset and left six moons of winter
to the Meeg-a-maage forever. Why did he go? What did he tell the
Ancient Ones? 'O Quarrelers, the blood of men is always on thy
hands!'"

"True," a Bras d'Or warrior said. "Yet Glooskap left the little fish
to be a pledge that every winter should be followed by a spring, when
the Meeg-a-maage might journey down the rivers and live fat beside
the Big Water. What is our totem now?"

"Behold!" Père Maillard plucked the crucifix from his breast and held
it up dramatically. "Here is thy true and only totem now, O people
of the Meeg-a-maage, thy pledge from the great Munitoo who made
all things in earth and sea. What was the little fish to this?"

"Wah!" said a man of the Cobequid people. "The Otter gave me a
Jesus-totem to wear about my neck, that it might save me from harm,
and sprinkled water upon me and gave me a spirit name, Mahlee-
Sosep, even as he called Koap San Badees. What was the virtue of
these things? When we fought the redcoats by the waters of Chebucto one of their Mohawk soldiers smote me with a tomahawk and
cut my shoulder to the bone. When we fought with them at Beauséjour a ball went in my leg and I lay a whole winter with a great fire

in my flesh from hip to knee. And here is a strange thing. When we took the winter warpath with the French and slew the redcoat Noble in the snow, certain of the English lay dead under our hands with the Jesus-totem slung about their necks. What is the meaning of these things?"

"O Man," the priest said, "he lied who gave thee the Jesus-totem for war medicine. The Jesus-totem is peace medicine."

"Who says this thing?" asked the Kejumkujik chief doubtfully.

Roger staggered to his feet. "The *paduleas* says this thing! The Otter was a liar. The words of the *paduleas* are clear as the waters of a spring."

There was a stir in the edge of the crowd. Two squaws were picking up the snoring form of San Badees and dragging him away. One of them was Wapke, her face expressionless as wood.

"Brothers!" Père Maillard said. "Thy hunting grounds lie all the way from the Foggy Country to Chegoggin, and from Chebucto to the shore of the Great River. The English make their towns upon the coasts in places far from one another, for they are fishermen, not hunters, and their living lies upon the Big Water. So be it then. The land is wide, the Big Water is wide, and all we are very small. The great blue wigwam covers us alike, the stars look down upon us all, and all we are very small. When the virgin moon comes in the west does she not shine upon us all? When she has met her lord the sun beneath the world and come ripe into the sky again, does she not shine upon us all? Who does the sun warm in spring? Who does he burn in summer? The rain—does it fall upon one man and not another? Behold when the wild geese fly to the south their wings fan up the cold wind from the north, as all ye know—and does not the north wind blow upon us all? Is the snow deeper for the Meeg-a-maage than for the Aglaseaou? Does fire warm one skin better than another? The hunting is poor, and behold, ye hunger. The fishing on the Big Water is poor and behold, the Aglaseaou hunger. Is it not the same hunger?"

"*We-la-boog-wa*," murmured several. "These are good words."

"Brothers, San Badees talked to thee always of war. It is easy to talk of war. Squaws, children can talk of war. But when blood flows, what words can pour it back into the wound? The Meeg-a-maage are brave warriors. So are the French. So are the English. Have they not proved themselves all through the time of thy fathers and thine own? And is the hunting better? Are there more fish in the Big Water? Does the cold pinch less in winter for the blood that flowed in summer? The smoke in the wigwam—does it smart the eye less because a new scalp dries upon the pole? Brothers, there is a time for war and we have had much war. The death song of the warrior has silenced the birds in the forest. The wailing of the squaws is like the east wind in the reeds. Is there no time for peace?"

Silence. But it was a different silence now. The old man had caught them in the gust of his passion. Their eyes were brooding but the hate was gone. They looked at him in something close to awe and frequently stole glances at the crucifix glinting in the sunshine. But some of the young braves stirred.

One said, "These are the words of a coward. These are the words of the English, who have sought peace with us many times." He had a harelip.

"My brother is fresh from his mother's paps!" Roger snapped. "His mouth is split with much sucking. Who is he to talk before warriors?"

The young squaws giggled. The harelip scowled and showed a long white tooth.

"They fear who talk of peace," he insisted.

The Musquodoboit chief reproved him, saying gravely, "If the English wish to bury the hatchet, it is not from fear. At Chebucto, when the redcoats walk together to make spirit medicine on the seventh day, they seem as many as red maples in the forest when the frost is come; the earth shakes when their feet come down together, they make strong sounds with drums and reeds, and carry banners, and their sagamores wear shining things and the feathers of unearthly birds. Their eyes are proud, their faces have no fear. I have seen these things."

Again a silence. At last the withered old sagamore of the Kejumkujik stepped forward and addressed the people slowly.

"Brothers, in the olden time the great spirit Glooskap foretold that a race of pale men should come out of the sunrise and rule the Meega-maage, and when the Wenjoo came in their great canoes our fathers said, 'Ka-kei-ke-sed-wom-ke [It is fulfilled].' Then came the redcoats, and we have fought against them for the Wenjoo many years. But the redcoats had strong medicine and made great war; they have driven the Wenjoo from all the valley of Tawopskik, from Beauséjour as well, and now they and their thunder come to Louisbourg. Soon must the Wenjoo go from this the last of Acadie, and who are we to fight alone against the Aglaseaou and their medicine? Brothers, let us go with the *paduleas* then toward the west, to our old hunting grounds, and bury the hatchet with the English at Chebucto."

A Lahave chief spoke doubtfully. "Behold we have no food, and there is barren hunting in these hills. Our squaws, our children cry for meat even now. How can we leave toward the west without *moosok* in our baskets?"

"Wah!" cried He-whose-mouth-is-split, with his ferocious sneer. "Thou say the Jesus-totem can work miracles, O Paduleas—let us see it now provide us food and lead and powder, blankets and knives and hatchets for the long journey to the west!"

Father Maillard's lean right arm, bare to the shoulder where the loose cassock sleeve had fallen back, continued to hold the crucifix above his head. Beads of sweat stood on his brow and tonsure. A muscle in his brown cheek twitched. He was in agony, yet he would not lower his totem while the issue was in doubt. Whatever was in these dark minds, he had full faith in its power.

He spoke that faith now, passionately. "Brothers, the great Munitoo, who provided bread for His people in the wilderness long ago, will provide for thee also. It is written in the God-book, of which I have told ye many times."

The old Kejumkujik chief was nodding. All the chiefs were nodding. Père Maillard turned slowly, holding high the crucifix, surveying all those solemn brown faces one by one. What he saw there satisfied him, for he lowered the Jesus-totem at last and commanded, "Go then, and prepare to strike the wigwams in the morning. And rest well, for the way is far."

The crowd swayed, parted, scattered slowly to their wigwams, murmuring on these strange events like people in a trance. A handful of young braves lingered, staring at the fragments of the little fish upon the ground. Father Maïllard stepped forward, picked up the pieces and the thong, and, wordless, flung them into the river.

It was a wakeful night. The whole camp was restless. There was much prowling and talking. Distance lent beauty as well as bounty to the old hunting grounds; of peace with the English they were not so sure. The war had been going on so long that it was part of their lives, like the little fish itself. Must they part with every keepsake of the Ancient Ones?

Roger had invited Père Maillard to share the wigwam which had been his all these weeks. At first the old man talked excitedly about the work to be done once the Micmacs were back in their hunting grounds and at peace with the English.

"Among many things, monsieur, I have long cherished a notion to prepare an account of these people, so the world may know something of them; but first a grammar of their tongue, a system of symbols, translations of the Scriptures, so they may read the word of God for themselves when I am no longer here to read it for them."

After a time he seemed troubled and began to pray. Roger felt exhausted and sank on his couch thankfully, but sleep was fitful, and whenever he wakened there was the venerable figure still on its knees, praying aloud in the dark. The drone of its supplications carried beyond the skins and poles of the wigwam, and frequently a voice outside somewhere drove away the whining dogs, crying, *"Jegulaase!* Begone! The *paduleas* talks to his mother, the virgin Mahlee."

Toward morning Roger said to him softly, "You are troubled, Father?"

"I am aware of difficulties, monsieur."

"You mean Koap?"

"Koap is one, monsieur. In the morning he will have a sore head and a stiff neck—and an evil temper. That man is a devil. A human neck would have been broken by that fall. Tomorrow we start our long pilgrimage with this serpent in our midst. You know his influence. And if the miracle should not come to pass . . ."

"Be assured, there will be manna in the wilderness, Father."

"Ah, monsieur, you too . . . you too have faith!"

"I can even tell you where to look for it."

"Eh?" The old man's voice was startled in the darkness.

"Softly, softly! Soolakade is what the French call Miré River, is it not?"

"Yes, a little way below this camp the stream becomes very broad —some call that part of it *le lac* Miré—and it flows in a half circle through the hills behind Chapeau Rouge Bay and Louisbourg. That is why Boishebert wished the savages to gather here. These waters, which the English neither know nor care about, afford a route by which he can attack any part of their positions."

"That is what I suspected. Where is Boishebert now?"

"On the way up the coast from Port Toulouse. Somewhere about St. Esprit, or perhaps as far as Fourchu. Quite near, I am afraid, monsieur."

"Ah! Then you must first direct the people northward along the lake of Miré; I am told there is a portage over the hills to the waters of Bras d'Or. There you have a canoe route toward Acadie, is it not so?"

"Yes. It is long and hard, but we can go that way."

"Regard then, *mon père!* As you paddle north along the lake of Miré you pass the end of the woodcutters' road from Louisbourg."

"Well?"

"Past that place, a half mile perhaps, a small stream comes down from the east to join the waters of Soolakade. There is a ravine bordered by dense forest, well hidden from the lake. In its shadows, well covered with sail canvas and brushwood, you will find all that your people need for their migration—provisions, powder, lead, salt, clothing, blankets, tinderboxes, muskets, hatchets—everything. There is even some rum—but you had better stave the kegs before the young braves get wind of that."

"But how . . . I do not understand . . ."

"Must you understand? Where is your faith, *mon père?*"

"I have my faith!"

"No doubt M. Drucour could tell you why these goods were hidden in the forest, but it seems to me they were placed there so that God —or Father Maillard, let us say—could work a miracle."

The old man was torn between delight and doubt.

"But to steal . . ."

"Did the children of Israel steal the manna *they* found in the wilderness?"

"Ah, monsieur! . . . Monsieur!"

The morning was cool, with a low mist along the valley, and the
still air of the camp humid with scents of wet grass and fir forest.
Roger turned on his couch. Robins were whistling at the edge of the
trees and there was a music of song sparrows by the water. The
simple sounds and odors came to him with an astonishing freshness.
My God, he thought, I haven't noticed a flower at the wayside or
heard a bird sing in five years! What's been the matter with me?

The camp came to life with a murmur, with a yawning and stretch-
ing of humans and dogs, the crackle and snap of cooking fires, the
morning procession of squaws with pots toward the water. The
night's fast was broken with such scraps of food as could be gathered,
and after Père Maillard had performed a morning devotion the
squaws fell upon the wigwams and the men and boys prepared to
launch the canoes. It never took the women long to strike camp, but
now there was something feverish in the way they dismantled the
poles and carried the bundled skins down to the bank. Was it only
the prospect of a journey, of a change from this place of distant
thunders and too-adjacent famine? Or was it that they had for all
their savagery the hunger of all women for peace?

One wigwam stood when all the rest were down, conspicuous
in the trampled emptiness between the forest and the river. The door
blanket was drawn, and nothing moved. The people moved toward
it slowly, with curious faces and some awe. Roger and Père Maillard
pulled the ragged stroud aside.

In the shaft of light through the doorway they saw Wapke's face,
daubed with a mess of grease and charcoal that startled them both
and awakened in Roger a rush of memories. She was squatting on
the rush mat by the couch of her lord as if she waited for him to
rise. But San Badees would never rise this side the Good Hunting
Place. He lay on his side with knees drawn up a little, with the
English bayonet driven through his skull into the ground. A pool of
thick blood lay congealing with a stone beside it.

"My daughter," said Père Maillard gently, "what is this thing?"

Wapke's mouth parted the black mask. Hoarsely, but with pride, she said to him, "Bless me, *Paduleas,* for I have slain him as the woman slew the warrior in the God-book. He was evil. It was time for him to die."

CHAPTER 42

Into the Fire

A SMALL CLEARING on the east bank of *le lac* Miré marked the farthest venture of the Louisbourg woodcutters. The savages drew into the bank, gunwale to gunwale, a wild and picturesque mass on the shining water. They were no vast number, now that Roger saw them all together, no more than the lash on the human whip which Le Loutre had cracked at Beauséjour in '55. The rest of it was still coiling through eastern Nova Scotia and along the Bras d'Or toward the rendezvous. Father Maillard would turn it back as he journeyed westward.

"They have been three years on this migration," he observed. "They should return in two—for, after all, they are going home. Sometime during the winter of '60—yes, about then, I think—the sagamores will appear at Halifax to make their peace. All then will depend upon the English—I can answer for the savages. If your people are wise, there shall be a peace never broken. And when I have seen the hatchet buried at last, then I can go to my rest in God, through the mercy of Our Lady of Sorrows." He crossed himself devoutly. "My son, I have been twenty-three years in the wilderness."

How old and frail he looked! But there was a light in the weak blue eyes. Whatever happened on that long and arduous journey, the flame in Father Maillard would burn unto the promised land.

A few sagamores stepped ashore with him, grunting farewells to Roger with the indifference of their race, but one of them, the old Kejumkujik chief, said bluntly, pointing to the road, "Thou go to fight—and yet thou talk of peace!"

"I go to seek a woman, who alone can give me peace."

The chief nodded and turned away, saying in parting, "We shall meet again, Bosoley."

"I do not know," said Roger honestly.

"We know," the chief said calmly, and trod silently down to his canoe.

The people were eager to be off. Somewhere, not far now, the *paduleas* had promised them a miracle.

Beyond the low hills to the eastward came a steady mutter of guns.

"You know what that means, my son?"

"What, Father?"

"The end of Louisbourg. Once before I saw the English conquer Louisbourg—and give it back. This time they will not leave one stone upon another."

"I understand. My wealth is gone," answered Roger dully. "It is strange. For years I have believed in nothing but myself—and the little stone fish, which brought me fortune. The world was mine, for I owed allegiance to no one. I followed my destiny to Louisbourg . . . my treasure and my heart, you remember? . . . but at Coromandière all my life was changed in twenty minutes. I go now to witness my own ruin, and it may well be that Mademoiselle herself will turn a cold face to the man who would not fight for France. Yet I have no regret. What does it mean? Have I gone mad?"

The lean hand rested a moment on his shoulder.

Father Maillard smiled, the smile of a withered saint.

"When that pagan thing was broken . . . you lost everything, you say? . . . Yet you have something in return."

"But what?"

"Your soul."

With his soul then, and weaponless, Roger walked through the long July afternoon toward that sinister rumble of giants. The track was narrow and rough, a mere slot in the wilderness, cut by the French long ago in search of decent timber for the fortress. From Gautier he knew the distance to be something close on twenty miles, winding among bogs and rocky ridges. About halfway it passed within a mile or two of Chapeau Rouge Bay. It would have been easy there to turn off through the scrub woods to the shore, to hail one of the transport parties cutting fuel or filling water casks, and to see the issue safely from the deck of an English ship. They would not question him far; the woods were full of English wanderers, soldiers, sailors, camp followers. The chance of another encounter with Wolfe he could well risk.

But the sound of cannon drew him eastward like a deep chanting of siren voices, although he saw no siren faces, only Mary—Mary always, Mary in danger, Mary in pain, Mary dying or dead. The urge to reach her set him running sometimes like a madman, to pull up at last panting and sweat-sodden, to fling himself down like a parched beast at a wayside pool in a swarm of black flies, to stumble on again. As he drew toward the end of the long miles, where the road left its easterly course and turned south, the rumble had become a rapid succession of thunderclaps in front, each detonation clearly marked, gun by gun. He recalled Gautier saying how "M. Voolf" had thrust across the swamps from Flat Point to the west end of Louisbourg harbor and erected batteries on the high ground above the *barachois*—just as the "Bastonnais" had done in '45. So the British west attack was sitting astride the Miré road just where it joined the track around the harbor. He had not given these matters much thought. Confronted by the resounding fact, he rejected the southerly turn of the road and kept on eastward through the woods. Before long he stood on the shore of a small lake. A brook flowed out of it toward the southeast. The size of the trees had been dwindling steadily all the way from the Miré, and now he was among spindling stuff, cat spruce and juniper, the sure mark of the Louisbourg shore. He followed the little stream until he saw the northeast harbor shimmering in the last of the twilight, surrounded by shadowy woods.

From the edge of the thickets he peered forth. Before him lay the track to Lorambec and Lighthouse Point, well trodden by British patrols, and beyond it a narrow strip of stony pasture land stretched between the road and the harbor shore, fringed with the ruins of wrecked boat slips and burned huts. A number of Acadien fishermen had lived here, all gone now, the settlement destroyed apparently quite early in the siege. Southward from the mouth of the northeast harbor stretched the broad gleam of the anchorage. The light sea breeze had died. The still surface of the water caught a last pink flare of sunset from the western sky. From the direction of Light-house Point snapped Wolfe's east attack. Roger crept along the fringe of the open until he could see their red stabs in the dusk and the bombshells bursting over Battery Island in little showers of sparks. The island replied. A little red eye glowed for a moment here and there. It looked and sounded feeble.

Immediately to his right on the foreshore sat the Grand Battery, built to rake the harbor entrance—as if the cross fire from the Island Battery were not enough. It was gutted by fire but showed no mark of attack. The tall stone towers stood bold against the evening sky. Evidently the French had abandoned it and withdrawn into the fortress on Wolfe's approach through the woods.

To the south across the anchorage lay Rochefort Point, with Louis-bourg squatting black against the seaward sky. There was some firing from the ramparts, but it seemed dull and spiritless compared with the energetic beating of the British guns. Siege batteries were firing from hillocks in the swamps southwest of the town, from Green Hill and from the ridge north of the *barachois*, yes, and from the low knolls to the south of it. The British must have pushed their trenches almost to the morning shadow from the Dauphin Gate!

There were fires in the town. Roger could make out a smudged red glow in several quarters, and a long mass of black smoke hung over all like a tester over a bed. His skin crept with anxiety. It seemed an age before utter darkness permitted him to cross the harbor road and explore the shore. There on the little peeled-pole *cales* of the departed fishermen he found two or three shallops and felt over them carefully. They had been staved with axes, but there was one whose strakes were broken in two places only. It stank of fish. Be-side the nearest of the burned huts lay odds and ends of every sort known to the fishery, among them a prize—an oar of whittled spruce. He picked up some rags of canvas and stuffed the holes in the boat, and at some hour short of midnight pushed off boldly into the murk, sculling the shallop along.

A strange voyage. The water was thick with flotsam—spars, sails, cordage, planks, casks, fittings, the forlorn buoys of slipped anchors, raffle of a hundred sorts with an illusion of movement, creeping out of the gloom ahead. He had a queasy feeling that some of the mysterious objects nudging stupidly along the boat's sides were dead men, bloated and buoyant, and when from time to time his oar touched one of them he had an impulse to yell.

What did it mean, all this? It looked as if the French fleet had been destroyed, or a good part of it, at any rate. That ass Des Gouttes! He had refused to sail out and tackle Boscawen at Chapeau Rouge, with a windward gauge and all the advantage of a purely fighting force against an enemy cumbered with transports. He had sat in the roadstead, removed most of his men and stores ashore, and so left idle a floating battery of nearly five hundred guns while the British crept about the harbor shore and set up batteries to destroy it!

Roger estimated the distance at a mile and a half. It seemed much farther in the dark. The shallop crept despite his urgent efforts. For a long time he had a suspicion that the tide or some harbor current held it back or swept him slowly toward the Careening Cove and Wolfe's guns on the east. But gradually the hot red tongues of Lighthouse Point fell past his left shoulder, the flare and belch of the British mortars north of the *barachois* drew abreast on the right.

In mid-harbor he seemed to be in the vortex of the siege, with batteries spewing fire into the night on every side but the south. All his memories of war in the Highlands and about the shores of Fundy paled before this spectacle. It was stunning. And to think that the little island far across the sea, beset by foes at home, could yet put forth a power like this in the American wilderness! From east, north, west, and southwest the British guns were speaking with a tireless violence. Sometimes he thought he could trace the red dot of a bomb fuse sailing in a slow arc through the darkness and falling on the town. *God help my darling under that rain!*

As his shallop approached the big three-deckers anchored under the guns of La Grève a few lanterns glimmered from the ports. Des Gouttes was keeping anchor watches, then. This gave him some uneasiness, expecting a challenge and a blast of grapeshot at the sound of his lone oar, which groaned against the stern slot in a doleful way. But there was a spectacular diversion.

One of the shells falling into the great Bastion du Roi appeared to touch off some woodwork, and in a few minutes a great blaze appeared. It seemed to be the governor's residence, at the south end of the long barracks which formed the town side of the citadel. As the red light grew he saw that the barracks were gone already, burned out in some previous fire, and with them the tall clock spire, the garrison bakery, the officers' quarters and chapel.

All this glare threw into relief the hulls and rigging of two big ships anchored so close to La Grève that they must be almost aground. He recognized them—*Bienfaisant* and *Prudent*. Where were the other three ships of the line?

The light of the fire, reflected bloodily on the shoals outside the *barachois*, revealed to his startled gaze three burned-out skeletons of charred timber and seared ironwork and tumbled tiers of guns, still giving off a pale haze of steam. Undoubtedly *Célèbre*, *Entreprenant*, and *Capricieux*. Roger had seen them last looking potent and magnificent in the anchorage among the frigates . . . and what had become of *them* . . . *Arethuse* . . . *Chevre* . . . *Apollo* . . . *Fidele* . . . *Biche*? Escaped? Sunk to bar the channel? Or simply sunk? The littered harbor told a somber tale of some of them, that was sure.

The shallop nosed through other flotsam now, floating awash in dense masses like the soft mush of anchor ice in January weather. He put out a hand and scooped a sodden mess of tobacco leaves. He remembered then the hundreds of hogsheads of tobacco belonging to Rodrigues *et fils*, and the town major's half-humorous notion of stacking them along the Quai for a barricade against English assault from the waterside. Loppinot had won his way, and the British bombshells had found the hogsheads and scattered their contents into the harbor. What a waste! But how apt—so many pipe dreams perishing, all at once, under the beat of British guns. There was no challenge from the battery of La Grève, nor from the anchor watches in *Prudent* and *Bienfaisant;* all those eyes were on the burning Bastion du Roi. He sculled in to the shadowy beach of the smugglers through a Sargasso of tobacco leaves and thought; How easy after all! How simple it would have been for a British night assault, a golden opportunity for that wild man Wolfe unless the narrow squeak at Coromandière had sobered him.

Roger walked over the steeply shelving beach delicately to avoid a rattle of stones. The surface of the little lagoon gleamed in the light of the fire across the town, except where the Maurepas Bastion and the staked bridge cast long shadows on the water. The night seemed full of eyes and cocked muskets. He took off his shoes and tied them about his neck and waded out to swimming depth. The water was warm. He swam slowly, but for all his care the ripples seemed to rush away toward the waiting sentinels and the sounds of the bombardment were lost in the swish of water past his ears. But he felt the gunfire; whenever a bombshell fell in the cobbled streets the water seemed to strike his body a blow that tingled the whole skin.

Fortunately it was not far to the shadows of the bridge. Then he was groping along the slimy stakes for the smugglers' gap and shaking the water out of his ears for better hearing. No sign or sound of a sentinel on the bridge. He could hear an excited chatter from the Bastion Maurepas. The whole garrison seemed fascinated by that conflagration in the citadel.

The gap at last! He passed under the causeway and swam on as silent as a muskrat. Another hundred yards and his hands grasped the wet stone stairs of the boatmen's landing which led to the Rue du Quai. He paused in the shadow of a warehouse to strip and wring the water from his clothes. He was shivering in the warm air of the summer night. So near! *Ochone, Mairi, a ghraidh mo chridhe!*

He put on the clammy things, latched his broken shoes, and stole up the alley. The clamor of the siege filled all the world, but in the lulls there was a silence of death. The mean habitations along the alley were deserted. There were gaps, and the customary smell of fish had given place to a reek of charred wood and worse. At the Rue Dauphine he stared into the gloom toward the fish market and saw nothing. The stone walls of near-by warehouses made dim angular shapes a little darker than the night, that was all, and against the stars a pattern of rafters gnawed by fire. Everywhere that smell of burning. A few dogs prowled, and somewhere in a ruin a cat mewled piteously.

He turned up the Rue Dauphine, stumbling over fallen timbers and rubble and choking in gusts of smoke that seemed to come from a brisk fire toward the Rue du Rempart. Even in daylight it would have been awkward to find anything recognizable in these burned and tumbled streets; in the smoke and darkness it was a fantasy. Once he stood against a tottering wall while a squad of soldiers passed, coughing drearily and cursing in Low German. They carried their muskets slung and bayonets fixed; a street patrol of the Volontaires Etrangers. What a quaint affair it was, where Germans in French uniforms fought against the British soldiers of German George, and on the fringe of an American forest! The Jacobite in him smiled sourly.

Encouraged by the blaze in the citadel, the British gunners redoubled their efforts. Their aim seemed to converge upon the Bastion du Roi and the Bastion de la Reine, with some attention to the Dauphin defenses at the all-important west gate; but bombs from their mortars were less fixed of purpose, sailing high over the ramparts and falling in clusters on the town. The western quarter, between the Quai and the Place d'Armes, seemed to be getting the worst of it, but there were occasional sharp bursts to the south, in the Rue du Rempart or the Rue de Scatari, perhaps. The glare of at least a dozen fires besides the great one in the citadel flickered on the smoke pall overhead.

The French gunfire seemed to come entirely from the burning Bastion du Roi, as if in mortal defiance. Musketry sputtered in that direction also—sharpshooters posted along the covered way, he decided, trying to reach the British gunners in the advanced works.

He turned into the Rue d'Orleans and kept along the north side. He found the hospital without difficulty—the handsome façade was lit by near-by fires. The tall spire, so long a landmark to the fishermen, had made a good mark for the British gunners; yet it stood like a finger pointing into the smoke. The roof was stripped of its slates, and the brick walls had been pierced in several places. One wing had fallen in and burned. Through the gaping porch, in the light of the fires and of lanterns held in the hands of nuns, he saw that the floors were covered with bandaged and bloody men, all frightened and crying out. Several Brothers of Charity moved on their knees about the floor, giving extreme unction. Part of the rear wall had been blown out, and a mass of rubble and shattered wood had fallen into the little garden of the Brothers, where it flickered and smoked still. The small bakehouse and laundry at the garden corners had vanished. On the terrace, in the shadow play thrown by the burning debris, a platoon of cadavers lay side by side with toes and faces to the invisible sky. From a pallet near the main door a voice cried, *"Gare la bombe! Gare la bombe!"* monotonously.

Choking, Roger dived into the smoke that filled the street. But the little gray house of the seamstress was gone, all that huddle of wooden homes was gone, and there remained nothing but shallow cellars filled with hot ashes that glowed like molten metal and the gaunt chimneys tottering like drunken witnesses.

CHAPTER 43

Brother Jamie

ROGER TURNED AWAY shaking and sick. He shouted Mary's name insanely down the smoke-roofed tunnel of the Rue Dauphine. As if in answer, a bombshell fell thirty steps before him, the iron *carcasse* striking sparks from the cobbles; it lay in the middle of the street in the red play of a blazing shop, a black globe as big as a football with a short tow smoking in the fuse hole.

He walked straight toward it, as if it did not matter, as if nothing mattered any more. The thing exploded with an earsplitting clap. There was a whizzing past his head, a sharp *ting* of iron on stone about his feet, He was unhurt. The lower half of the *carcasse* lay smoking faintly, and as he stepped over it there was a reek of burnt powder and scorched iron.

"Hola!" said a voice from the earth. He looked to the left and saw a bearded blond face staring at him from a cellar hatch. He demanded of it, "Where is the Norman woman, the seamstress who lived in Rue d'Orleans?"

The beard addressed someone behind and below. *"Dieu!* The fellow walks amongst the bombs to get a button sewn!"

To Roger the beard cried, "How should I know? Dead, one supposes. But many hide themselves in the casemates under the bastions. Try the Bastion du Roi."

Rodrigues—Rodrigues would know!

"Where is the merchant, Rodrigues?"

"Ha!" said the beard, and spat into the street. "Rodrigues! That sou-pinching devil is dead, *mon vieux,* dead and burned in his own hell. The siege had sent him mad, like others—like you, one supposes. He saw his ships sunk at the Quai and his tobacco scattered to the codfish, and when that great warehouse burned, with everything he owned, the people could not hold him back. There was gold inside, he said, and rushed into the flames. All Basques are mad, of course. Are you a Basque?"

Behind the beard, in the pallid light of a candle stuck in a bottle, Roger could see the heads of half a dozen men, fishermen and soldiers, merrily looting a wine cellar.

He turned away and followed the Rue d'Orleans toward the Place d'Armes. At the corner of the Rue de l'Estang he looked up the slope and saw the big square of wooden barracks built by the New Englanders after the siege of '45 all blazing furiously at the rear of the Bastion de la Reine.

As he emerged into the Place d'Armes all hell seemed to spring up before him. The residency was burning, throwing a red glow over the wreck of the Bastion du Roi—the long stone foundations and tumbled brick and slate which represented the once fine barracks and chapel, the charred wooden barricades erected to protect the casemate doors from bomb blasts, the breached and crumbling ramparts where even now, like demons about the Pit, Drucour's gunners were struggling to reply to the British fire.

A company of the Cambis—he could see the red facings on their ragged white coats—had formed a bucket line from one of the garrison wells toward the flames. There was a good deal of running to and from the casemates, the stout fire-blackened doors opening and shutting, with glimpses of massed white faces inside. The air seemed alive with British roundshot, doing little harm—striking the ruins of the Rue St. Louis for the most part with sharp pings and thwacks. The bombs were another matter. Shells from the mortars across the *barachois* had blown the governor's garden into a tangle of shrubs and earth, and down the slope toward Rue le Fort, the garrison icehouse was blown to pieces, the sawdust heaps smoldering, the ice blocks glistening in the thrown heat from the ruins of the barracks.

The shells came in irregular bursts, as if a tree of explosive fruit were being shaken by an infuriated but fitful giant. Roger waited for such a shower, and while the battered houses facing the Place d'Armes still rang with concussions, and with the dust still flying, he darted across the square.

The small guardhouse before the inner moat was in a curious state: a bomb had fallen through the roof and blown the east wall clean out, leaving the others intact and scattering slates all over the walk. In this three-sided box, like a puppet show, crouched a corporal's guard with faces pale and haggard behind the fierce mustaches, all in the light of the flaming residency.

One cried at him, *"Hola!"* And, seeing that Roger's clothes were *gentil* if sadly bedraggled, he added with more respect, "M'sieu wishes . . . ?"

"Mademoiselle, the sister of Captain Johnstone. I must see her at once!"

The soldier hesitated. What ragamuffins they looked! And these were of the Cambis, the smartest regiment in Louisbourg, out from France just in time for the siege! The corporal spoke.

"She is in Casemate Four, m'sieu. Perhaps Five—but try Four first." He pointed.

Roger nodded and ran on. The dry moat which made a separate fortress of the Bastion du Roi was now choked with debris from the burnt-out barracks. The drawbridge was gone, burned and fallen, and in the little brick cave which housed the machinery he could see the forms of two soldiers, shattered and bloody, their dirty white uniforms smoking in the heat of the embers.

Roger swung along the front of the hot wreck of the *casernes* to a narrow passage between the moat end and the inner bastion wall. Here another sentry halted him, black-mustached like the others and with the same smudged waxen face.

"Mlle. Johnstone—Casemate Four!" Roger cried. The sentry stood aside.

Casemate Four opened its heavy door cautiously at his urgent knocking, and a gust of foul air, many times breathed and laden with unwashed human smells, flowed past him. As the door closed at his back, through the stout oak came the cry of *"Gare la bombe!"* and the rattle and scurry of the Cambis flinging down their buckets and running to cover. Roger was in a long, low chamber with floor and walls of native stone and a wooden ceiling which creaked and thumped with the movement of feet overhead. The place was lit by half a dozen guard lanterns in each of which a thick stub of tallow candle burned with a tremulous blue-yellow flame in the exhausted air. There were, at a guess, one hundred and fifty men, women and children standing, sitting, leaning against the walls. They had the faces of ghosts, with tight mouths and shadowed eyes that stared straight before them at nothing. A few heads turned at his entry and looked away again listlessly.

He hestitated to speak in this catacomb. His eyes roved from one to another, from side to side, all the way down the chamber. She was not there. Casemate Five, then! But as he turned he saw her almost at his feet, sitting against the wall with a ragged child in her lap and a fisherwoman asleep against her shoulder. She was dressed in something of a light gray, with a Barcelona handkerchief drooping a yellow fold across her breast. Her head was bare, and the chestnut hair made a red-gold aureole in the lantern light from above. She was asleep, or near it; her eyelids drooped; her cheeks, always a little gaunt in a healthy Highland fashion, seemed hollow now, and there were violet shadows beneath the eyes. Her lips had that mysterious suggestion of a smile which one sees on babies and sleeping girls and sometimes on the dead.

He was startled, seeing not Mary Foy but a Golden Woman made human by some alchemy that had to do with himself, as if he had looked upon her through a warped glass all this time and now in this gloomy place beheld her as she was. Fantastic! . . . and yet . . . and yet there she was. All his yearnings, all his journeys, had brought him infallibly to this place and to this moment. And there was nothing new or strange about it, for surely this was the revelation that must come to all young fools who seek the riches of the world—to find them in a living, breathing woman after all? Eternal quest, eternal answer . . . and eternal fools!

"Roger," she said in a drugged whisper. "It's really you?" She came awake, wide-eyed and alarmed. "But how? . . . Why? . . . *O mo chridhe,* why have you come back here?" She had the fey look.

"Is there a place where we can talk?" he asked in a low voice.

Her gaze went to a narrow flight of wooden steps against the farther wall. The fisherwoman lifted her head. "I will take the child now, ma'mselle."

He followed Mary up the stairs and passed into the second story of the casemate, a powder loft in other times, cleared out now for a number of wounded lying on the bare boards. The arched stone walls met overhead. Two nuns were busy among the prone figures. There was a stink of blood, of festered wounds, of sweat.

A shell exploded on the rampart overhead and jarred the whole cavern. A fog of white dust fell from the lime-washed stones and all the candles fluttered blue together. The wounded men cried out fearfully.

Mary picked her way toward a partition and a door. She knocked, and with Roger entered a tiny *cabinet* lit by a single candle on a table where an officer sat writing. He was an elegant man, nearing forty, and wearing the white coat and blue facings of the Regiment Royal de la Marine with the flaming ribbon of the Order of St. Louis. The coat was unbuttoned in the stuffy air, the wide skirts drooping to the floor, and it exposed the blue waistcoat of the regiment and a frilled shirt. There was a foam of fine Valenciennes at the throat and wrists. He wore a periwig, well powdered, and his long face and nervous hands made one hue with the wig. Plainly an officer whose duties had kept him from the rough-and-tumble of the siege.

He looked up and met Roger's eyes. Mary said, "Roger, this is my brother, Captain Johnstone."

"And a chevalier of St. Louis!" Roger said lightly, addressing him. "It used to be plain Jamie Johnstone of Moffat, didn't it?"

The chevalier stood up and said in French, "Name of a name! Is this he—the one you love?"

All the man's hatred of England was in that choice of tongues, and in his face.

"Yes, James."

"So! This—this *faquin* has returned to the scene of his crime! He must wish to hang! What are you doing here with this traitor—this coward?"

Roger regarded them. James was ten years older than his sister.

but the resemblance was distinct, except about the mouth. The mouth of this precious brother was weak—weak and self-satisfied, self-seeking, self-willed, a prejudiced and bitter mouth, where hers was strong and generous.

"James!" she begged.

"Why 'coward'?" Roger demanded coldly.

"You ask that!—you who raised the *sauve qui peut* at Coromandière—worse, perhaps! What was it De Gannes tried to tell us before he died?"

"Jamie!" Mary pleaded. "Pray don't quarrel. It's all so terrible, and O my God, how I wish I'd never seen either of you! To be torn like this!"

"What is it that you want?" James asked from his full height.

"I want you to take Roger with you—tonight!" She turned to the *faquin* impetuously. "Jamie's leaving for Quebec tonight, Roger—you must go and ask no questions. They would hang you in this place!"

Roger cocked an ironical brow at the chevalier. *"Sauve qui peut?"*

Johnstone snorted, *"Mordieu!* Why should I stay to be taken by the regiments of Lee and Warburton and Lascelles, who were all at Prestonpans in '45—what would they not give to lay their hands on me?"

"You flatter yourself, Chevalier! What could they remember? They never saw aught of Jamie Johnstone but his back."

The chevalier looked his hate for that and put a hand to his sword hilt.

Mary stepped between them. Her green gaze roved from one to the other.

"What does it mean, all this *jacasserie?"* she demanded imperiously.

Roger did not take his eyes from Johnstone's face. "Suppose you explain, my bonnie chevalier! I think your sister is entitled to know why she was sent to Halifax as the wife or mistress of that drunkard Foy."

"What the devil do you mean? John Foy is our uncle—Mary's guardian. What! It is possible you hadn't guessed that, monsieur—you who know so much?"

Roger turned to her, seeing light on many things, and with a singing in his heart. She flushed and put up a hand in an odd little gesture. He shrugged and said in English, with his hard gaze on her brother's face, "Then let me tell you why you came to Halifax, my dear. Jamie wanted advancement at Louisbourg; he was hungry for appointments. He wrote you of his austere life, his meager pay, the reasons why you couldn't come to Louisbourg. He didn't mention that he had a mistress here, the charming *patronne* of the True Cuckoo in the Rue du Quai, whose husband—conveniently absent—was the chief French spy at New York. Who was herself a very useful person to the secret service of France! Well, that service wished an agent in the new settlement the English were contemplating in America. *Voilà!* Mr. and Mrs. Foy! Later *la-patronne* sent a reinforcement, a prisoner ransomed from the Indians at Louisbourg, a man of known Jacobite sympathies. Jamie never knew the fellow's name—till now. A small world, isn't it?"

Mary cried, "Is this true? Why didn't you tell me, Jamie?"

Johnstone did not answer. He stood erect, all contempt and outraged dignity—all but the lower lip. The lip moved petulantly. Another bomb burst on the ramparts, and he seemed to shudder with the walls.

"Why don't you tell her now, Jamie? You couldn't lie to her, could you—*chevalier sans peur et sans reproche?* Tell her everything, Jamie, and I'll bear you witness. Tell her about Culloden. Or would you like to go back to the start, when you were aide to Lord George Murray . . . but found it too fatiguing . . . and how you were posted with a platoon of my Manchester lads to guard the artillery . . . but found the nights too cold and the rain too wet? Tell her about Carlisle, where Prince Charlie left us to guard his retreat . . . and how the Duke of Perth commanded you to stay with your company . . . and what you said to him . . . and how you decamped from Carlisle like a thief in the night! And Culloden, where you were posted on the left, and fled at the first English volley . . . remember? The only fighting you did that day was with another Highlander for possession of a horse to get away on . . . and you were getting the worst of that when Finlay Cameron saved you with his pistol. You didn't stop long at Ruthven, where the Highland army tried to regather, did you,

Jamie boy? . . . You kept on to Killihuntly, and thence to Edinburgh, and finally to London, where the English would never think
of looking for you. London was dull, so you took a mistress—what
was her name, Peggy?—and one morning as she lay in bed you
peeped from your lodging window and saw the Manchester officers
being taken to the scaffold on Kensington Common. Did your conscience trouble you for a moment then, my chevalier? I wonder! But
that alarmed you. You must get out of England. So you wrote to
Mary . . . sixteen, wasn't she? and full of a romantic zeal for the
cause, and for her gallant brother in peril . . . and she took passage
to Holland with Lady Jean Douglas and you . . . you went in livery
as her servant . . . *sans peur et sans reproche!*

"Ah, but Paris was gay, wasn't it, after all your trials and sacrifices?
You had a fine time there on Mary's money and your own . . . till
all was gone. The gallant and romantic *Capitaine Johnstone, écossais
et gentilhomme* . . . that was how you loved to describe yourself in
your expansive moments, I recall. All Paris heard of you in those
days . . . but one never heard of the little sister . . . I never guessed
until that poor young fool De Gannes said something in the camp at
Coromandière. Ah well, all that . . . past now . . ."

Mary had drawn herself away from them both. Her face was tragic.

"All this is true, Jamie? You don't deny it—any of it?"

He did not answer. She drew in a great breath and cried indignantly, "Then it's all a lie . . . all I've believed in, all this time? It's
been worthless . . . all the scheming and the lying . . . all for something false like you, yourself!"

"My dear girl," he said in the Parisian accent he liked to flaunt before colonial officers of the Marine, and in a tone of irascible virtue,
"am I to blame if you chose to be romantic? You pursued me with
letters, with entreaties. You professed your sisterly affection, your
faith in the Chevalier Charles, your hatred of all things English. You
wished to follow me to Acadie." He shrugged in a fashion exqui-
sitely Gallic. *"Bien!* The service demanded an agent with the English
expedition, and there you were, who spoke English so well, and
there was Uncle John to be your guide and your protector. You must
confess that things were well arranged. Your task was surely not unpleasant. You lived richly—when one recalls the lodging in Paris—

and you seem to have found time to fall in love. *Eh bien,*" he said sardonically, "I leave you to each other . . . till death do you part."

He turned to the rough pine-wood table, stuffing papers into a leather satchel with an odd air of washing his hands. They watched him in silence.

"My *folie,*" he observed, waving some of the papers. "The story of my life, someday to be published in Paris . . . if one reaches Paris, which God grant."

There was a respectful sound at the door, something between a scratch and a knock. It opened and there appeared one of the town militia, a small round man in homespun and a fisherman's striped nightcap and sabots, with a *bandoulière* in which a dozen paper cartridges were stuck, and carrying a rusty gun.

"The canoe waits at the Quai, *mon capitaine.*"

"*Allons!*" cried Johnstone gaily. He clapped a white-laced black tricorne on his wig, buttoned his coat, took up the satchel, bowed ironically to his sister and to Roger, and departed with the high-nosed haste of an actor making the best possible departure from a bad scene.

CHAPTER 44

Confessions

"JAMIE!" she whispered. The closed door mocked her. In the meager candlelight her eyes were glittering with unshed tears. Her mouth quivered; her air of ardent purpose was gone; she had the naïve look of a lost child.

"He didn't deny it, Roger. It was true, all of it?"

"He seems sure of a place in history, nevertheless, my dear."

Roger moved toward her eagerly, but she shrunk away.

"No! . . . No, Roger! Why did you come back?"

"Because I love you."

"That's not true, Roger. You never loved anyone but yourselves—you and Jamie. You're alike, and you've crushed me between you. But now it's over. I won't be hurt any more. I see you very clearly now. Do you think I don't know what De Gannes said? And now you've come back on some new deviltry that has to do with money, position, influence, the things you really want. And you'll get those things, Roger, without me. There are two things that wretched little stone thing can't give you—and I'm one."

"And the other?"

"Honor."

"I see," he said painfully. There was nothing more to say. Honor! All this passionate pilgrimage of hers had been made in the light of it—honor, loyalty, faith in the one cause. And she felt herself betrayed.

The door opened. Loppinot stalked in, his white uniform smudged and torn. His convivial face was putty-colored with fatigue; his eyes were pouched, his veteran mustaches wild. Behind him paused a corporal of the Bourgogne with bayonet fixed. The town major clicked his heels. "Ma'mselle!" And to Roger, harshly, "M. Sudden, I place you under arrest for espionage and treason, on information laid by Captain Johnstone."

"He is gone; how can he testify?"

"He left a deposition: and there are witnesses—from Coromandière, monsieur."

"The trial?"

"Summary."

"The punishment?"

"Death. What else?"

Mary uttered a small sound, of astonishment, of distress—it was hard to say.

The three men ignored her.

"In a summary case," Roger said quietly, "you will wish to save time, Loppinot. I am prepared to make a full confession."

The town major lifted his gray brows. "Here?"

"And now."

"*Dieu!* But . . . Ma'mselle?"

"I beg Mademoiselle to hear what I have to say. It will explain, perhaps, some things she does not understand."

"Ma'mselle?"

"I wish to stay," she said in a breaking voice.

"*Bien!* With the sister of M. Johnstone for witness . . . but we

should have another, should we not?" He called in the corporal.
There was a little silence in which all their breathing could be heard. Then the walls shook in another bomb blast.

"Begin!" said Loppinot through his teeth. A mist of lime dust filled the chamber and made a halo about the candle.

Roger wondered how to begin. "I, Roger Sudden, being of sound mind . . ." As one did in making a will? He cleared his throat and gazed at Mary as if she were the only person in the room.

"My name is Roger Sudden. I am an Englishman from Suddenholt in the county of Kent. When the chevalier Charles Stuart raised his standard in Scotland, I left the university to fight for him. In the campaign which followed I commanded a company of the Manchester Regiment. The result of that affair you know. I made my way to France and remained in exile until '49. In that year I returned secretly to Kent. There I found the Jacobite cause hopeless. I left for the colonies, a man without king or country, determined to make my fortune abroad. I came to Halifax and within a few months was carried off by Indians. I roamed the forest with them nearly five years, living like a beast of the forest. In the year 1754 the savages sold me to the French, as M. Loppinot remembers, and after a winter's imprisonment at Louisbourg I was given my release with certain instructions from M. Rodrigues.

"In Halifax I followed these instructions to the house of one M. Foy. He lent me money and I entered the Indian trade. I was enabled to go anywhere amongst the savages by reason of a small stone talisman which they—and I—held in great respect. It gave me the touch of Midas. In three years I had a fortune, gathered from French, Indians, and English alike. I knew M. Foy was an agent of France. I did not care. I remind you that I was a man without king or country. And I loved a lady in the household of M. Foy." Here Loppinot flicked a curious glance at Mary. "In the autumn of '57 M. Foy was discovered, and he and the lady fled to Louisbourg. I intended to follow—I had transferred the greater part of my fortune there in the belief that France must win this struggle in Nova Scotia and that Halifax was doomed. I lingered to wind up my affairs. When all was ready I was aware of a strong malaise. At the final moment I did not want to go. But matters were decided for me by an interview

with M. Wolfe, the English general, who placed me under arrest. I
escaped to Louisbourg and rejoined the lady and my fortune. I was
not used to idleness. I wished for something to do. M. Rodrigues
procured for me a post as interpreter with Colonel St. Julhien at
Coromandière."

Again the shock of explosions on the bastion; again the candle
flutter and the mist of lime. "All this"—Roger licked the dust from
his lips—"does not matter very much, I suppose. What follows is important. When the English approached Coromandière in their boats
I left the camp to watch events. Simply as an observer. I ask you
to believe that. Yet when I saw them plunge into the trap I was
deeply moved. Amongst their rangers were many old friends, men
who had fought and labored faithfully for me in Acadie. And there
were Scots, wearing the dress which I must always associate with my
own struggles in the cause of the chevalier Charles. Finally there
were the English grenadiers, some of them close inshore, perishing
under that rain of bullets." He paused. "Do you know the device
the English grenadiers wear in their caps?"

He had not taken his gaze from her. She answered in a bitter tone,
"Yes—the white horse of Hanover!"

"Ah! But the white horse is the ancient symbol of my home as
well—the land of Kent, which lies so terribly near the coast of France.
I make no excuse, you understand? I offer no defense. I tell you
simply there must come a time when the soil of his birthplace means
more to a man than all the world. I ask you to believe that my love,
my fortune, all my new hopes and old struggles were forgotten then. I
ask you to believe that Coromandière—Louisbourg—all new France
in that moment ceased to exist for me. It was Kent I saw, and the
men of Kent in arms to defend her—and I on the wrong side of the
Channel!"

"Fantastic!" Loppinot growled. Mary regarded them both with
haunted eyes.

"You understand," Roger went on, "that when one puts an impression into words the thing seems cold and clear. It was not like
that. It was like a dream. I found myself running down the butte at
the end of the beach. There were a few English boats offshore,
edging away from the fusillade. I beckoned them in. There was a

space among the rocks—enough for two boats abreast. They came. Then I heard young De Gannes'. He aimed a pistol at me as I ran at him. The ball struck me on the breast and shattered the little Indian amulet. Otherwise I should have perished at a stroke. I closed with him as he drew his sword, and beat his head in with his own pistol. It was his life or mine.

"My chest seemed broken. It was agony to breathe. I made my way to the camp and raised the cry of *sauve qui peut*. I make no excuse for that, either. I knew what would happen. I knew the poison of that cry to troops shaken by a surprise. I cannot remember all that followed. Two Indian women dragged me away into the forest. Once I looked back and saw the French break and run. After that was a darkness. I lay six weeks in a camp of savages beside the Miré waters, with a bruise on my chest as large as a spread hand. . . . Shall I go on, monsieur?"

"I think you have said enough," responded the town major grimly, but his black eyes had a sudden new interest. "These savages at Miré —what are they doing?"

"They have had enough of war. They have withdrawn with Père Maillard to make their peace with the English."

"Maillard . . . *paillard!* And Boishebert and his force?"

"Somewhere toward the Montagne du Diable—without food or ammunition."

"Ah, but supplies await him in the forest not far from here, my friend!"

"If you mean the cache at Miré, the savages have emptied it on their way toward the old hunting grounds. I told them where it was."

Roger watched the veteran's face as he broke this news, expecting an outburst of Gallic anger, a little dance of rage.

Loppinot's mouth sagged. He resembled an idiot. All the fatigues of the siege seemed to descend on him at once. He leaned against the doorpost with eyes closed. His lips writhed beneath the gray mustache.

He said in a flat voice, without opening his eyes, "My God, we have held out for weeks awaiting his attack. We have made sorties at great cost, hoping to strike a moment when he might be near." He opened his eyes very wide. "You lie! It is impossible! Boishebert has held the English penned up in their forts in Acadie for three years past. He is young, he is daring, he has the luck of the devil. A sword in the forest! All New France sings his praises—and M. Drucour has an Order of St. Louis ready to hang about his neck, sent by His Majesty himself! No, he would not let these matters come about, not he, not our Boishebert!"

Roger shrugged. "You smuggle the chevalier Johnstone out of the fortress tonight?"

Loppinot could not conceal the contempt in his voice. "He goes to Quebec—to seek an appointment with M. Montcalm, you comprehend."

"Bien! The woodsmen who go with him—tell them to examine the cache at Miré and send back word. It is not far; I came from there since noon today. I tell you they will find no Indians and no supplies. Neither will Boishebert."

"And the savage chief, Jean Baptiste Koap?"

"Dead."

The town major stared. He straightened himself abruptly. "You will remain here, monsieur, for the time. I shall place a guard. Mademoiselle!" He turned to her with a frosty politeness and gestured toward the door.

She came to Roger in a rush of skirts, her arms about his neck, her mouth to his, her slim body pressed against him as if to let her whole self speak an emotion for which she could find no words. Tears crept from her closed eyes and streaked her dusty cheeks. Roger put up a hand and stroked the bright hair.

Red gold. Golden Woman. What a pity, to find her and to lose himself. Suddenly she broke into an ungoverned weeping. He was calm, even detached, marveling at the fecklessness of life, which wasted so much passion, so much hope and struggle for no end.

All-powerful Munitoo stirred the soft heap of the world with an idle foot, and all the ants ran to and fro, and no one knew the meaning—not even Munitoo himself, who doubtless studied them with interest. Sometimes the scurryings approached a pattern and you thought you saw the purpose, but then the great moccasin swept across the heap again and all was changed in a moment. One thing was certain—that it would go on. Ants would perish in twos or threes or thousands as the great foot fell; the rest would drag the dead aside and take up their frantic pursuits again—and again.

"Mademoiselle!" said Loppinot again. She shuddered and drew herself a little apart from Roger, the green eyes searching his face as if they sought in every feature some memory for a lonely age to come. Her lips moved, and as always, when she was stirred, the words came in Gaelic: "Kiss me, dear of my heart. 'Tis an ill turn to the long road, but you I shall be loving to the end."

"*Gus a' chrioch*," he repeated gently, putting his lips to hers. "To the end!"

She straightened herself then and with a high chin walked past Loppinot and the sentry as an empress might sweep past a pair of gaping lackeys on the palace steps.

CHAPTER 45

Gus a' Chrioch

THE DOOR WAS CLOSED; the sentry stood outside. The candle guttered out and left Roger in darkness with a dismal feeling of suffocation. What hour was it? There could not be much left of the night. He felt hunger, faintly. He sat in the chair and put his head down on the table, on his folded arms, but for all his exhaustion he could not sleep, he could not even doze.

The bombardment slackened as if the British gunners had wearied at last. Out of ammunition, probably. He pictured the oxcarts with their Yankee drivers, the rigidly harnessed horse carts of the Royal Artillery, dragging barrels of powder, shot, and shell up the road from the British camp; and the infantry and engineers in the trenches, digging new saps, throwing up new parallels and gun platforms, inching closer, always closer.

The surviving French cannon continued to fire on those efforts in the dark, but they had a fitful sound—like minute guns at a funeral. Outside the *cabinet* he could hear the murmur of the wounded and the soft voices and movements of the nuns.

A military footstep came at last, and he stood up in the dark and braced himself for the thing it meant. A lantern dazzled him as the door opened. When his eyes recovered he saw an orderly with a plate and a carafe. Behind stood Captain Fagonde of the Artois.

"Monsieur!" Fagonde made a stiff little bow. "Here is something to break your fast. One regrets the biscuit and the poverty of the wine, but you comprehend our difficulties."

Roger murmured thanks. He did not move. The orderly placed the lantern on the table beside the provisions and withdrew.

"You wish a priest?"

"No."

"I have been sent, in the custom, to bear you company until the time."

"Again my thanks. Pray seat yourself." Roger pushed forward the one chair.

"One prefers to stand."

An awkward silence.

"It is to be hanging, one supposes?" Roger murmured.

"That is prescribed for spies," returned Fagonde in a chilly voice. "Unfortunately Gallows Hill is in the hands of the English, who use it for an observation post; and affairs within the town are not convenient. You are to be shot, in the moat outside the Bastion Maurepas —the only part of the defenses not under direct fire from the English batteries."

"I see. May one ask why you were chosen for this embarrassment?"

"The firing platoon is to be drawn from the Regiment Artois— for reasons you can guess, monsieur."

"Ah!" A pause. "May one ask . . . when?"

Fagonde shrugged. "Not today, certainly. Tomorrow morning, I think."

"In that case you had better take the chair for a time. I propose that we take turns sitting down. Come, relax yourself, Fagonde! After all, what is a little matter of death between friends?"

Distaste played over the officer's handsome face. "M. Sudden, we have made merry together at the house of Rodrigues and in the camp. You are a brave man—else you would have stayed in safety with your English friends. One respects these things—but do not call me friend, I beg of you."

It was Roger's turn to shrug.

They talked of other things, of Paris, of Italy, of summer in the Medoc where Fagonde came from, and its vineyards and its wines, of which he spoke with enthusiasm. Gradually the man unbent. After two hours he sent the sentry for a stool and a pack of battered cards, and they flicked away the minutes and hours with piquet. The delicacy which did not permit Fagonde to consult the watch that ticked in his pocket forbade Roger to ask the hour. In the candlelit *cabinet* there was no day or night. Roger had an odd feeling that already he was launched upon eternity.

The bombardment began again with more fury than ever. Under the whimsical teaching of Fagonde, Roger learned to distinguish between the four- and five-inch bombs, which said "Pah!", the eight- and ten-inch, which said "Ho!", and the earth-shaking thirteen-inch which said very distinctly, *"Mort!"*

The close of the long day was marked by the appearance of another orderly with the evening meal: cold boiled herrings, biscuit, and wine —this time in a flagon. The man also laid on the table some spare candles for the lantern.

They had run out of small talk by then. "Pardon," murmured Roger, and lay on the floor against the wall. He closed his eyes and summoned the image of Mary, going over that last brief interview, her looks, her movements, the somber passion in her face, the haunting music of the Gaelic on her tongue. All that beauty, all that flaming spirit given up to sadness—what a waste! His cynic's philosophy shielded him against self-pity, but his soul protested against the world for the waste of Mary Johnstone. After a time he slept, uneasily.

At intervals the casemate shook. Fagonde sat slumped on his stool, elbows on knees, regarding his prisoner gloomily. Once he took the watch from his fob and wound it carefully with a silver key. Later he placed the stool in a corner and sat back to doze, braced in the angle of the wall.

The bombardment died away again. From the ramparts not a gun spoke. The dead silence awakened them both. They looked at each other across the little chamber, but did not move or speak. Without warning the stillness was shattered in the direction of the harbor. An unusual uproar this, a cheering of several hundred voices and a

ragged but furious splutter of small arms. Fagonde sprang up, over-
setting the stool, staring at the door as if he could see through it and
the night beyond. Roger leaped to his feet also. A British assault by
water? Wolfe . . . Wolfe sick of delays and resolved to end the
siege in a stroke? By Jove! Captain Fagonde dashed outside, giving
Roger a glimpse of a startled guard and the strained attitudes of the
wounded, raised on their elbows and staring toward the north wall.
The sentry kicked the door shut.

The uproar died away as swiftly as it began. There was utter silence for perhaps ten minutes. Then gunfire, heavy and continuous,
from La Grève battery or perhaps the anchored three-deckers, or all
together. The attack had failed, then! La Grève and the ships could
sweep the whole water front with a storm of grape. With his memories of Coromandière, Roger was filled with ghastly fancies.

The cannonade went on for an hour. Then silence once more.

Fagonde returned, raging. "That pig Des Gouttes!"

"What has happened?"

Fagonde laughed hysterically. "You seem to have had a hand in
two of our disasters, monsieur. Is it possible you do not know of this?
M. Boscawen cannot bring his ships into the harbor to engage Des
Gouttes—not while the Island Battery holds—so tonight he sends in
five hundred armed seamen in boats, with oars muffled! One learns
from a straggler, who fell out of his boat and swam to the beach,
that the English had guidance from a smuggler, one Capitaine Uxley,
who seems to have known how to bring boats in to the anchorage
without awakening the island. *Dieu!* They might have stormed the
town, had they known all things . . . the gunners at La Grève were
some of those good-for-nothing seamen of Des Gouttes . . . asleep
. . . without even a linstock lit and ready! But the English came, it
seems, to capture our last ships of war—under the very guns of La
Grève! They were swarming aboard before the anchor watches could
lift a finger, and they cut the cables and hoisted the sails and set
their boats towing, to get the ships away. *Prudent* went aground as
soon as her moorings were cut, so they set fire to her . . . she is a
torch at this moment, close against the parapet of La Grève. *Bienfaisant* is taken, they sailed her away audaciously—and La Grève
could do nothing but shoot a few holes in her canvas!"

"But Boscawen cannot take her out past the island!"

"Why should he? His seamen have sailed her up into the north-east harbor. There they will put powder and shot aboard, and tomorrow we may expect a bombardment from her guns—our own guns, *pardieu!*"

He sank on the stool muttering something about *sacré comble de nos maux* and the extreme filth of that pig Des Gouttes.

As if the boats and their prize had signaled themselves clear, the British siege guns opened fire once more. Again they had a fine light on their target—every bastion thrown into relief by the flaring pyre of *Prudent* at the waterside. Roger thought of Boishebert at the Miré —that man must be standing, baffled, at the empty ravine by now, and watching the glare in the eastern sky. Tomorrow he would turn back with his *coureurs de bois* and Acadians toward Quebec—a fine escort for Jamie Johnstone in his flight!

Fagonde saw the smile on his lips and rasped, "You will laugh on the other side of your face in the morning, monsieur!"

"If the Artois shoot no better in the moat than they did at Coromandière, *mon capitaine,* one could laugh on both sides. But come! I have too good an opinion of the Regiment Artois to quarrel with their Captain Fagonde on my last night as his guest."

"You have reason," muttered Fagonde, nettled still. And with some of the sting in his pride, "The record of this siege will justify the Artois—all our forces—yes, even those droll *miliciens,* the townsmen. It is Des Gouttes and his seamen who shall reap the shame of history. This little garrison has held a ruin forty-eight days—and still holds!— against an army three or four times greater and a fleet whose seamen did not hesitate to labor and fight, afloat or ashore. We have lost our ships; our walls are breached, our bastions ruined, our town destroyed, our casemates crammed with women and children and eighteen hundred sick and wounded; we are alone; we have no hope of rescue now that the savages have failed us and Boishebert is left without supplies—and yet we hold, we hold!"

"And what does this accomplish?" Roger asked.

Fagonde drew in a breath. "We save Quebec—for another year, at any rate. The English cannot go up the St. Lawrence now; the season is too late."

"*Soit!*" Roger murmured.

A stir outside. The door opened and there appeared a young officer with a girlish face—Charnier, of the Artois, "La Pucelle" of the mess table. He looked unhappy, but his glance toward Roger was quick and cold.

"Daylight in an hour, *mon capitaine*. Here are the barber and the hairdresser."

In they came, a dark stout man in the white breeches and red waistcoat of the Artois, bearing razor, soap, bowl, and towel, and a dark thin man in black broadcloth rather the worse for wear, and carrying comb, brush, and scissors in one hand and a powder box in the other.

Roger bowed to the officers ironically, and Fagonde said seriously, "One wishes to look one's best at such a time, monsieur."

Shaving was a painful business. His beard was tough, the razor dull. From the hill by the *barachois* the British artillerymen threw over a succession of ranging shots in preparation for the dawn bombardment, and at every report the barber's hand shook alarmingly. The fellow was silent, impressed by the presence of the officers and no doubt the significance of his mission. The hairdresser was inclined to conversation, but Fagonde cut him short.

When all was done the barber advanced his bowl and washed the prisoner's face and hands, a curious rite that smacked somehow of the Old Testament, and the hairdresser produced a whisk and brushed and arranged Roger's clothes. ·

He thanked them gracefully, regretting the emptiness of his pockets, and they murmured politely and departed.

Charnier said in a strained voice, "One has a message for you, monsieur, to be given at the last moment." He passed a small billet which Roger opened slowly, lest his fingers shake. All it said was, "*Gus a' chrioch, Mairi.*"

The ink and pen of Captain Johnstone were still lying on the table. He stepped to it, smoothed the note carefully, and wrote on the back of it:

For value received I hereby sell and assign unto Mary Johnstone all my right and title in the snow Fair Lady, Job Huxley master, now

lying at the port of Halifax in His Majesty's province of Nova Scotia.
And I earnestly entreat the said Mary Johnstone to avail herself of
this opportunity to return to Scotland and there dispose of the said
snow unto the said Job Huxley at a price to be agreed between them,
their agents or assigns.

ROGER SUDDEN.

He folded it and passed the billet back to Charnier. "For Mademoiselle, after . . . You understand?"

Charnier took it, watching his face, and burst out, "How you are cold, you English! To be loved like that, by such a woman, and to receive it with a face of stone!"

"What the devil do you mean?" rapped out Fagonde.

La Pucelle glanced at him and back to Roger. "Is it possible you do not know how Mademoiselle has struggled for your life all these hours, without food or rest?"

Roger was silent.

Fagonde murmured, "Mademoiselle was tranquil when she left . . . the face high, the mouth firm . . . she seemed to accept what was inevitable."

"To deceive him!" Charnier cried, with a tragic twist on his girlish features. "How little you know of women, Fagonde! She went straight to the governor . . . I was there. She burst upon us with a superb anger. Men and their silly games! Their pompous rules! Their cruel penalties! M. Drucour was gentle—but firm. She fell on her knees and pleaded with him in a voice to melt a heart of ice. He was firm. She went away. She returned with Mme. Ducudrai—that slut! —and together they pleaded for his life. Drucour was firm. She went out into the bombardment and searched out the members of the Conseil Supérieur one by one, casemate by casemate, bastion by bastion, begging them to intercede. They would not stir. I went with her, you understand, because I have a heart that wept tears for her as she wept tears for M. Sudden.

"Tonight she returned to the governor like a tigress, demanding a formal trial. M. Drucour replied that the prisoner's confession had made a trial needless. Where were the depositions? she demanded. There were none except the charge of Captain Johnstone and his recommendation for execution. 'No written confession! No signature anywhere! No sworn witnesses!' she cried. The whole affair a crime in the eyes of justice, a dishonor to the name of France! Ah, but she was magnificent, magnificent! But M. Drucour"—the slender shoulders of La Pucelle lifted and drooped disconsolately—"is not to be moved, you understand."

"Where is she now?" Roger asked painfully.

"She has gone to the *commissaire-ordonnateur* to beg his influence in one last plea for your life. You know M. Prevost—a will of brass. Alas, how women never understand these things! They must always beat their wings against the bars." Fagonde pulled out his timepiece.

"Messieurs"—harshly—"it is the time. *En avant!*"

CHAPTER 46

Invicta!

THERE WAS LITTLE DIGNITY about the march. With Charnier and Fagonde he stumbled down the narrow stairs of the loft. The fetid ghosts in the lower casemate scarcely lifted a head. Outside, drawn up before a timber barricade all splintered with flying shell fragments, a platoon of the Artois shivered in the chill dark. In the east a gray smudge dimmed the stars and marked the approach of dawn. The ruins of the *casernes* still glowed and gave up pale wraiths of smoke. They set off at once, the prisoner walking between the two officers at the head of the platoon. In the middle of the Place d'Armes there was a salvo of British guns, and Fagonde yelled, "At the double pace!" They crossed the Place helter-skelter and gained the doubtful shelter of the shattered Rue d'Orleans all out of step, the sergeant swearing.

"*Peste!*" Fagonde cried. "The English have pushed up another five-gun battery under the noses of those dolts in the Dauphin!"

"I think they are all dead there," Charnier said. "That place is burst."

"We are all burst," Fagonde said. "*En avant, marche!*"

Along the smoking Rue d'Orleans it proved impossible to keep step, even to keep ranks, for the thoroughfare was heaped with debris, much of it hot, and in places the flames licked out from a building crackling and writhing close at hand and forced them to dash past in Indian file.

The British batteries broke into their morning eruption. There was no reply from the walls. The silent procession crossed the broken heart of the town, thankfully drawing away from the worst of the explosions. At the east end of the street the houses were poor things, but they stood, saved from the gnawing fires by their very isolation. Faces like pieces of blank paper stared from the dusty panes, lit faintly now by the rising light in the east.

The platoon debouched at last into the space before the eastern ramparts, where the Maurepas Gate reared its imposing pile of Caen stone, the back door of the town.

There was a slight delay at this point. A tumbril stood there awaiting the opening of the great oak gate and the lowering of the drawbridge. It was laden with corpses piled one upon another, the night's dead on their way to burial on Rochefort Point. Charnier was distressed and sought to engage Roger's attention elsewhere, pointing across the lagoon to the wreck of *Prudent* still burning on the harbor side of the beach. There was no sign of *Bienfaisant*. Roger felt obliged to show the sang-froid of an Englishman and remarked upon the sorry choice which had befallen the two ships—whether to be well disposed and yield oneself or to be prudent and burn.

The gibe hurt young Charnier, who cried out with a poet's passion that England had given such a choice to Jeanne d'Arc—and lost a war.

"Nevertheless," growled Fagonde, "one wishes that pig Des Gouttes had burned there with his sacred ship."

Seeing the gold lace at the platoon's head, the gate sentinels turned out the guard, a sleepy lot with bits of foul straw clinging to their uniforms.

The massive gate swung open with ponderous groans, and the guard, a beggar's dozen of the Bourgogne, presented arms and stared as the party went by. The tumbril rumbled across the draw and Fagonde turned aside, calling to the driver and his mate, a shaggy

pair in the red wool caps of fishermen. He lowered his voice delicately, but the order carried clearly in the morning air.

"Take this *fanage* beyond the glacis and wait. Out of sight, you
comprehend? There will be one more."

Charnier led the way, turning off to the left along the covered way
for a few steps and then down the counterscarp into the moat. It was
dry, or rather boggy, like most of the Louisbourg moat except where
the engineers had contrived to link one or two of the original swamp
pools in the scheme of defense. To discourage assault a row of sharp
stakes was planted down the middle. They were rotten now, in this
place anyhow, a sample of French indifference, or proof of confidence
perhaps, since Rochefort Point was nothing but a finger of moorland
thrust into the sea, commanded by the guns in Maurepas and Brouillant—the only bit of land outside the fortress where the French were
free to move.

Fagonde ordered the men to pull down a wide gap in the crazy
palisade. And in an apologetic voice, "It is necessary for the soldiers
to stand back to the counterscarp, monsieur, lest the sun get in their
eyes."

Roger nodded and walked across the moat through a mass of wild
flag in blossom, trampling these blue fleurs-de-lis underfoot as distant
Mr. Pitt intended to trample the white.

At the scarp he halted and faced about. The moat was lined with
black stone quarried at Cap Noir. He had worked with the prison
gang repairing this very place. The stones had tumbled again in several places with the action of frost and thaw, exposing the heart of
earth carted laboriously from pits in the forest by all those thousands,
all those years ago. What a poor sham after all, this Dunkirk of the
West, this fortified swamp whose walls collapsed of their own
accord!

He recalled whimsically his first impressions, the broad encircling
ramparts, the wooden town compact and gray with weather like
some old stone town in France, the bristle of cannon, the ships, the
tramp of battalions which filled the twenty-foot streets with a river
of steel, the clap of the dawn gun, the ruffle of drums beating
assembly along the ramparts at nine each morning, the sunset gun,
with the ports closed and bridges drawn up, and the final gun at

eight o'clock when the massed drums made the round again beating the tattoo. Strength! Strength!—all blown away now.

Along the whole face of the fortress exposed to the direct fire of the besiegers each round shot had brought down a rock slide into the moat. A shower of bombs had set the gray town flaring like a box of cartridges.

The superb regiments, experienced in all the arts of war, had broken and fled before a rush of ignorant redcoats under a madman. The gloomy forest which had been reckoned a barrier to all invaders now concealed an army of ten thousand who spat fire and death upon them.

Sic transit . . . Well, it was something to have had a hand in that. He could pretend that his life had held a purpose after all. Certainly no one else could have done it. And there was a fitting irony in the thought that few would know and none would remember what turned the scale at Coromandière or why Boishebert failed to strike his blow. History, which had so many puzzles to ponder, could well afford two more.

Why were they waiting? There was good light now. There had been a careful charging of fusils under the sergeant's eye, and the platoon had ported arms for Fagonde's inspection. He had criticized the priming of two or three, and one man was obliged to change his flint. Then, at a command, the party had grounded arms and stood at ease, leaning on their musket muzzles and staring across the moat at the figure against the scarp. From the embrasures of the Bastion Maurepas a number of curious faces peered. Fagonde rebuked them sharply, and the faces disappeared. He came to Roger slowly.

"You wish the eyes covered, monsieur?"

"No."

"We wait for Loppinot. The thing must be done in the presence of the town major, you understand."

"I understand."

Fagonde went on dropping words nervously into the silence. Roger gave him a polite attention, but his mind was far away. The air of morning had never seemed so full of the stuff of life. It came from the east, from the Big Water, from England perhaps, who could say? From Rochefort Point it carried a smell of wet wild grass, of moss and bog pools mingled with a smell of sea, like Romney Marsh in a wind off the Channel. Romney . . . did the luggermen still trundle ankers of Nantz up that dark and lonely beach? Romney and the Weald . . . and that handsome ruin in the beeches. Suddenholt! Did Charles and the Fiat Club still foregather to drink the king over the water? Assuredly, if Charles had any standing whatsoever with a wine merchant. Parson Balleter . . . Barcombe Tarver . . . Sir Miles Boyce . . . Cousin Penny, poor thing . . . All of them unreal now. Too far, too long ago. Illusions!

The emigrants of Tooley Street . . . a myth, a lost tribe camped in a desert of shadows like those green bones left by D'Anville on the Basin shore. Gautier . . . Luksi . . . Wapke . . . Foy . . . Mauger . . . Le Loutre . . . ghosts! Ghosts! An echo of voices in an emptiness. Good God, were they all phantoms . . . Fagonde? . . . Charnier? . . . The lounging soldiers in their draggled white coats? . . . Mary? . . . Ah, Mary was real; she had been real always, even when she seemed most mysterious and aloof. He knew that now and was sorry, thinking how simple *this* would have been if she had remained a shadow with the rest. The pattern of his life had made a cynical little comedy whose every act led on to some such end as this. The reality of Mary Johnstone marred the perfection of it, and his sense of fatality was disturbed.

The sun climbed and put down a hot tongue to lick the dew from the grass in the moat. The air shifted with it and brought a pungent smell of the forest. Lovely there now. Bunchberry flowering underfoot, and starflower, and the brown seed stems of the ferns flirting little clouds of dust about the tramping British legs. New seed cones on the junipers, each small and tight and scarlet like a rosebud among the fine green needles.

But the swamps were best: iris everywhere, and blue-eyed grass, and violets in the shady places—scentless, of course, not like the violets of home—and stunted sprigs of sheepkill in pink bloom, bake-apple ripening yellow in the sunshine, small black fruit like buckshot on the green bogberry tufts, the tall brown morocco-leather flowers of the pitcher plant, whole carpets of the charming Indian pinks, each small flushed face putting forth a yellow-furred tongue—like fever patients. Did the redcoats notice any of these things as they sweated about their guns and up the roads? Probably not. He had not noticed them in years until his mind was opened that morning at Soolakade.

Fagonde pulled forth his watch. *"Dieu!* Where is that man Loppinot! We have been hours here! What a misfortune! Monsieur, I ask God to witness that it is no fault of mine." He went over to Charnier, moodily stalking up and down amongst the green swords and blue banners of the iris.

A head grumbled over the glacis crest—the tumbril driver. Fagonde barked. The head vanished. A conference in undertones with La Pucelle. Charnier set off toward the town at a run.

The bombardment thundered on. The sounds were muffled in the hollow of the moat. Gulls cried overhead, part of the white cloud which hovered and squabbled about the fish slips in time of peace. Hungry now, poor devils; there had been no fishing in two months, instead this uproar and the fires and the hanging smoke. Strange how they stayed on.

So, too, with the plover, rising in swift ordered flocks out of the moorland, dipping, lifting, settling again, as if resolved that all these man-made nuisances soon must be gone forever and their ancient nesting ground at peace.

And how right you are, thought Roger. Had they known all along, with their marvelous instinct? Certain it was that with its drains choked and its wooden mass gone up in smoke, Louisbourg in a few years must revert to moorland as it was in the beginning, only the tumbled walls remaining, a monument to futility.

That old comparison of Halifax and Louisbourg disturbed him like a voice, a question demanding an answer. Somewhere in the story of the two towns was concealed the secret of French failure in America. What was it? The French built better ships, trained better soldiers; they understood the art of fortification as no other nation did. They had made alliances with the savages from Nova Scotia to the Great Lakes and all down the muddy reaches of the Mississippi. The continent was theirs, the English a scatter of interlopers clinging to the coast. And their American empire functioned with a brain at Quebec and a strong sword hand at Louisbourg, while the English had no unity and no strong arm anywhere. Yet what was Louisbourg now,

and what would Quebec be when another season passed? It was easy
to say that a mighty English fleet and army had come across the sea,
and charge it all to that. But was that all, a tussle of red coats against
white on the edge of a continent?

They were too small in that immensity. There was something else,
some other significance. What?

The sun stood at midmorning when young Charnier returned. The
guns had died away again, and in the quiet his running feet rang
loudly on the bridge. A sorry virgin now, hat in hand, powdered
hair all sooty from the burning streets, girlish face gone sallow and
outraged, a rash of perspiration on the fine curved upper lip. He
stumbled down to them, sobbing and out of breath.

"What the devil!" Fagonde snarled. "Where is Aide-Major Loppinot?"

"M. Loppinot . . . will not be here this morning . . . any morning
. . . any more . . . it is finished . . . lost . . . all lost!"

Fagonde's bold face was a study. "Idiot! Explain yourself!"

Charnier drew himself up stiffly. The Bastion Maurepas was alive
with heads again.

"M. Loppinot has gone out with D'Anthonay and Du Vivier to
surrender the fortress to the English!"

There was a sigh like an east wind from the firing party and from
the parapet above. "It is false!" shouted Fagonde.

"It is true, *mon capitaine*. At ten o'clock by the governor's order
a flag was hoisted on the ruins of the Dauphin . . . our drummers
beat a chamade . . . M. Loppinot went out with a letter asking for
terms . . ."

"And the terms?"

"Total surrender as prisoners of war!"

Fagonde gave back a pace, as if Charnier were unclean. "Without
honors? Name of a name! It's infamous! M. Drucour cannot accept——" He turned to Roger furiously. "After the battle we French
have fought, you English offer us the terms of dogs!"

Roger's voice was cold. "What terms did Montcalm grant our prisoners at Fort William Henry last year? He permitted his savages to
slaughter them—like dogs!"

Tears glittered in the blue eyes of La Pucelle. "At first M. Drucour decided to fight on . . . but you know the state of the walls, the bastions, the town . . . The people gathered about M. Drucour and his officers with tears and supplications . . . My God, it was terrible! . . . And so he gave in . . . I saw the Regiment Cambis weeping with rage in the Place d'Armes, burning their colors, striking their muskets against the stones to break the stocks . . . finished . . . all is finished!"

"All but one thing," said Fagonde harshly. His eyes were hot. "There must be one more whiff of powder, Charnier! . . . Monsieur, arrange yourself! . . . Platoon!"

It came to Roger then. This talk of walls. The French in America had surrounded themselves with walls and shut up their bodies and their minds. Only a handful of *coureurs de bois* and priests had ever penetrated the continent—and the *coureurs* had mated with savage women and spilled their seed in the wilderness, and the priests were wedded to God. They had not left a mark. He remembered a night at Beauséjour before its fall, when that queer broken fellow La Vérendrye had talked about an ocean of grass beyond the sunset, a range of rocky mountains that touched the sky, and somewhere on the other side the China Sea. Quebec had sniffed at his explorations and sent him to the little Acadian backwater where he could tell his tales and do no harm.

Walls! That was it! That was the difference and that was the secret. None of the English settlements had walls. Halifax had even let the first crude palisade go to rot. What seemed a weakness was in fact a strength, the spirit of men who would not be confined; ignorant, but willing to pay in blood for knowledge; ill fed, but seeing fields in the unbroken forest; grumbling, but driven out and beyond by that very itch in their English feet for new earth to tread, new rivers to cross, new mountains to behold.

By Jove, yes!—the restless English who would have no walls about them, who demanded to see and to move beyond, to march across a horizon that was always somewhere toward the west. The English who were not content to mate with savages but who took their women with them everywhere, resolved not merely to penetrate the wilderness but to people it!

How long would it take? Only Munitoo could say. But soon the march would mend its pace, with the French barrier thrown aside and the savages at peace. *Someday we English shall tread those prairies of La Vérendrye and cross those mountains and behold the great west sea.*

And it came to him in a rush of exaltation that this march of the English across the great north wilderness had begun at Halifax that day in '49.

Who could have foreseen it? That mob! Tooley Street! Men laughed at that old tale of the nine tailors of Tooley Street who inscribed themselves, "We, the people of England." By heaven, they *were* the people, the common people of England. And that was what made the Halifax settlement unique in all America, for its founders were not soldiers or sailors disbanded abroad to save the cost of transport home, no pious band of religious outcasts, no sorry throng of political exiles, no company of gentlemen adventurers, no trading post of some great merchant enterprise—simply the common people of England set down upon a wild shore in the West. The wilderness had purged them swiftly and terribly. The weak had died, the shiftless fled. In Halifax there remained only the unconquerable.

Unconquerable! The word rang in his mind as Fagonde shouted his last command.

He faced the muskets with a proud, unflinching gaze, and as the Artois pressed their triggers they were astonished to hear the Englishman cry out in a tongue unknown to them:

"*Invicta! Invicta!*"

December 1942–May 1944

The author

Thomas H. Raddall was born in 1903 at Hythe, near Folkestone, England, and the family moved to Halifax when he was ten years of age. Five years later his father, who was an instructor in the British Army, was killed in action at Amiens, and young Raddall enlisted as a wireless operator at the age of fifteen. For four years he served as radio officer on board transports and at radio stations along the Nova Scotia coast and Sable Island where he acquired the background for his writing. In 1923 he became an accountant for a pulp mill on the Mersey River in Nova Scotia and it was at this time he began writing his stories.

Raddall's published works, which embrace short stories, novels, and histories, include *The Pied Piper of Dipper Creek*, 1939; *His Majesty's Yankees*, 1942; *Roger Sudden*, 1945; *Tambour and Other Stories*, 1945; *Pride's Fancy*, 1946; *The Wedding Gift and Other Stories*, 1947; *Halifax: Warden of the North*, 1948; *The Nymph and the Lamp*, 1950; *Tidefall*, 1953; *The Wings of Night*, 1956; *The Path of Destiny*, 1957.

Three times winner of the Governor-General's Award, he has also received the Lorne Pierce Medal from the Royal Society of Canada.

A fully revised edition of *Halifax: Warden of the North* was published in 1971. Mr. Raddall is at present going through his correspondence and diaries, preparatory to writing his memoirs. (He has kept a diary ever since he went to sea as a boy of fifteen.)

THE NEW CANADIAN LIBRARY

A complete list of New Canadian Library titles is available from the publisher.